QUEEN OF CHAOS AND RUIN

EMBERVEIL EMPIRE

BOOK TWO

ZANDER WOLFE

COPYRIGHT

BOOKS BY ZANDER WOLFE

Emberveil Empire Book 1: Prince of Blaze and Embers

Emberveil Empire Book 2: Queen of Chaos and Ruin

Emberveil Empire Book 3: Knight in Secret Shadow

Prequel Short: PhoenixFire - Get for Free at ZanderWolfe.com

Allovan
The Shimmermere Sea
Calcaedus
Raven's Bane
Great Skymirror Lake
Emberveil
The Brakenstone Ridge Mountains
The Faewood
The Harrowhorn Mountains
Salazan River
Bramblebash
Sun Sea Isles
The Emerald Crest Isles
100 Miles
The South Cape Sea

THE PROPHECY

Passage from the Tomb of the Elements. Chapter 1, verse 1.

At the dawn of existence, the Great God Odiun blessed us with this world. He created the elements—scorching fire, life-giving water, the earth for safety and shelter, and the crisp air all around us. Odiun saw the beauty of our world and was inspired in its inception to create—us.

Perfect in our flaws, givers of hope and takers of life, we are—an image of our divine creator. Some are mighty and true, others are tempted by lust, and even some are tainted with evil.

Gigas of the Infernal Depths has equal pull at our hearts; a fallen angel, a fallen son.

When the Great God Odiun created us and the elements, he chose to combine those forces into the four most powerful of us. The Cinderyn command the unspeakable destruction of flame. The Aqualorians command the power of the restless seas. The Terradyne command the rocks, trees, and mountains. And finally, the Whisps control the ferocity of the rushing winds.

Of all the elemental-wielding forces, none compare to the Cinderyn. Competent in their lust for violence and power, none can compare in might to the strongest of all of Allovan. The

Aqualorians strive for peace above all else, going to war with the Cinderyn over the centuries. Great loss plagues all who go to war with the fire wielders.

But… the prophecy remains.

Spoken by the prophet Solemyn at the peak of Calcaedus, within the volcano, by the fires that brim within, Solemyn told, glaring into the wicked magma, that one day the Aqualorians would rouse the slumbering dragon within the volcano, and the great defeat of the Cinderyn would bring about peace unlike Allovan has ever known. Solemyn has the sight of divinity. He was the first Druidaan and spoke the word of Odiun.

When the slumbering dragon awakens, the Age of Cinderyn will end.

The dragon must awaken.

Vâllathór must awaken.

For if she is not awoken, and the Cinderyn capture her fire… the world will burn, then fade into eternal darkness.

Written by the Prophet Dantris Oireillus. 676 of the Ember Age.

CHAPTER 1

The battle had been won. The Blaze Queen had been driven back to Emberveil.

But it was just the beginning.

We were broken and battered, and she had an entire fucking fortress to recover behind.

And we were stuck in the middle of the Faewood, the ancient forest with so many mysteries I couldn't even begin to imagine them all...

"We take the fight to her." Courage and anger welled up in my clenching stomach and tingling chest like dragonfire as the words left my lips.

"Ash..." Bella muttered, the tear streaks down her face still wet from the mystic's inner words to her. "Whatever it takes... we're going with you to the end."

"To the end," Hunter, Cade's commander and best friend, said, clamping his fist onto his chest, over his heart on his copper-plated armor.

"We will see it through together." Those words from Cade sent my heartbeat into a mad race. The thought of him saying we'd be together to the end made me feel like the luckiest woman in all of Allovan.

Our kissing might cause us pain, our sex could nearly kill us, but he wanted to be with me. The Blaze Prince wanted to be with me!

It was a sobering thought. Of all the girls in all the cities and villages of Allovan, he'd picked a slave girl from Bramblebash of all places.

Up until very recently, I'd lived a life in chains; now—I'm a dragon rider.

Free to soar the skies, free to live my life the way I've always dreamed of. But I was also hunted, and hunted by the most ruthless of them all—Mortriana Vissex, queen of Emberveil and all of Allovan.

Krakos grumbled low, shaking the pain from his wings in the battle's aftermath with the Blaze Queen and her monstrous dragon Brigodon. I looked over my shoulder at the ebony dragon, terrifying in every right; if he wasn't on our side—we'd surely be dead. Sharp black scales, enormous wings as black as death, and its sleek muscular body rippled with power. His crimson blood-red eyes were like staring deep into madness. Krakos was the pure embodiment of power.

At his side was Talonor, Hunter's dragon, streaked with onyx black on the stone-gray scales that armored its back and wings. Its milky white eyes pierced me as if I were staring into a ghost— the most horrific ghost I could imagine... if he wasn't on our side...

And Errax, my magnificent dragon. Her hide sparkled in every shade of cascading blue I could imagine. Like glittering sapphires floating on a sunlit summer sea. She was spectacular. Emerald green eyes glistened in the sunlight as she growled, stretching her mighty, elegant, and fearsome blue wings out wide.

"The Stormscales... the Stormscales chased the queen off."

Bella eyed the injured Blaze Prince Cade Phoenixfire curiously, waiting for an expression.

I too was eager to see what Cade thought of his sworn enemies seemingly joining in on the fight against his stepmother. Cade stood stoically, like an enormous statue of shadow, looming over us like the fearsome predator he was. General of the armies of the Emberveil Empire, with more kills to his name than any man alive. He was dark, brooding, terrifying and... drop dead fucking gorgeous. Tan, perfect skin, wavy black hair like a midnight mare's, sapphire eyes that pulled me in like chains on my ankles, and a cock to die for.

The insides of my stomach churned, feeling like broken glass and acid boiling within. My heart ached knowing Cade had chosen me against his birthright; his name, and his entire world was flipped upside down... because of me.

"Let them chase her," Cade growled, suppressing a deep pain within. "She'll retreat back to Raven's Bane Castle. Once there, she and Brigodon will be protected, and she will recover from her wounds." He scowled, and his eyes darkened. "Those bastard rebels think chasing her back home will show a defeat? She's not defeated. But..." his dark eyes lightened as his enamoring gaze shot at me, softening and making my heart melt like fresh butter on a warm plate. "You did, Ash. You beat her. I've never seen anything like that. I've never even heard of an Aqualorian defeating a Cinderyn like that. That was... incredible."

I nodded, feeling my cheeks heat and flush. "I didn't do much. We did what we did together."

"Well," Bella laughed, wiping her tears away, "however you want to spin it. We did it. We at least live to fight another day." She stood tall and proud with her wavy sandy blond hair rustling at her chest. Her oceanic blue eyes deepened in color as she glared at me with a wide smile.

Hunter folded his muscular arms over his chest plate of his copper armor with black trim, as his long auburn hair danced behind his shoulders. "We won't live much longer if we stay here…"

I spun and looked back at the isolated, ancient structure behind us and the wise Mystic slumbering on the throne of thorns, not wanting to leave. The Druidaan Mystic made me feel safe, protected, and it saddened me to have to leave.

"We need a place to recover and plan our next move," Hunter said. "We need a place without the prying eyes of the queen's spies and a place where our dragons can rest in safety."

"The mountains," Cade said, shifting, clutching his ribs and groaning. "Harrowhorn Mountains. There's a place there we can go. It's deep in the range, far from spies and the queen's reach. But there are other things that live in the dark recesses of the mountains we will need to be vigilant of."

Things? He means monsters? There's always a catch with him. Why the fuck is there always a catch? Why isn't there ever anything easy in this world?

"We will make for the mountains at first light," Cade said. "We'll make camp here." The queen's army won't reach us this day. "Hunter, will you help me pitch the tents?"

"At once," Hunter replied, like the lieutenant he was.

Cade groaned, falling to a knee, causing me to fall with him, placing my hand on his massive, strong shoulder. He panted, as the breath from my lungs was sucked out at the sight of him. The most powerful man in all the realm had been nearly killed, beaten ragged within an inch of his life.

Even Krakos, the most fearsome dragon in all of Allovan, save for the queen's, had been embroiled and burned in the bitter battle in the sky.

I could still see the two engulfed in Brigodon's unworldly flames. And here he was, still alive, in my arms, and there's nothing I could do for him. The Mystic may have saved me from my injuries, but the Druidaan Mystic hadn't done the same for my prince.

"I'm alright, I'm alright," Cade grunted, getting back to his feet with my help. "I just need rest, and the dragons do too."

Cade stood before me, shining in his infamous, royal, normally shining black armor, covered in soot from dragonfire. His tan skin was completely covered in black smudges, his long black hair caked in smoke, and burned and frayed at its edges; he was still as ravishing as I'd ever seen him—even more so perhaps. His piercing glacier-blue eyes were mesmerizing, even when he was an asshole, forcing me away. He was my drug. I couldn't stop. I needed more. I craved more. Every second he was around, I wanted him. I wanted all of him.

Krakos groaned behind him, in the clearing before the sanctuary where the Mystic slumbered. The mighty ebony dragon stretched its wings as tendrils of flame lapped out of its maw like fiery serpent tongues. It then lay on the ground, laying its neck flat against the grass, closing its eyes.

"Aye," Hunter said wearily. "We all need a bit of rest."

Bella gave a scrunched face, with her nose and mouth twisted. "Are we really not going to talk about the Mystic back there? Myrathyn told us all secret answers to things we asked. Are we just gonna pretend that didn't happen?"

She looked to Hunter, whose gaze shied away behind him. Then, her inquisitive look darted to Cade.

"Mine's personal," he growled, not so much in a rude way to her, but speaking to himself, forcing himself to keep it buried deep down.

"I asked if I could defeat the queen," I said, blinking hard as I stared out foggily at Errax.

"And?" Bella asked with her arms out wide.

"He said… essentially no. But that it's possible. The odds of me succeeding, where all others before me have failed, isn't likely. He seemed sad when he told me. If I'm not able to, though, then the world will fall into chaos and ruin."

"You'll do it," Bella said, trying her best to hide any doubt that may reside within her. "You bested her this time, and you'll do it again."

I may have driven her off, but I had serious doubts about being able to defeat such a powerful woman. I'd never seen such raw power, even in Cade. It was as if she was more than human. Almost like she grew from the Infernal Depths, or her blood got mixed with dragon blood. Not even Cade matched her power.

Cade grimaced, angry with himself. "I should've done more up there. I'm sorry I wasn't able to help you more." But in an unexpected move, he turned and embraced me. "I'm so happy you're alive. I don't know what I'd do without you now, Ash."

He embraced me in his muscular arms, and I pressed my cheek to his chest, hearing the thudding of his heart. The smell of fire and sweat in his hair filled my nostrils, and it tickled my soft neck as he held me. He oozed raw power, and I lapped up every second of it.

"Thank Odiun that Myrathyn saved you from your wounds," Cade said. "Thank the Great God."

He released me. "C'mon, Hunter, let's get some tents up."

The two left in the direction of the dragons, getting packs down, muttering between themselves.

"What about you, Bella? What did you ask the Mystic?" I pulled my hair back and tied it.

"I'm not sure if I should say..." Bella folded her hands behind her back, swaying, staring longingly at the ground.

"You don't have to, but you asked everyone else. I feel like you want to say..."

Bella sighed deeply, her long sandy blond hair hanging at the sides of ash-covered face. I looked up at my friend, cupping her cheeks in my hands.

"It's okay," I told her. "You can tell me."

"I—I asked if we all survive this fight. And... and I asked if there was anything I could do to change the outcome so that we all do..."

I told myself then, I really didn't know if I wanted to know the answer to her question, but I asked anyway. "What did he say?"

Her head dropped like a sack of flour, her chin falling to her chest. "He said 'no.'"

"No?" I breathed.

"We don't all make it, Ash. And there's nothing I can do to change that. One of us is going to die, but he didn't say who!"

I wrapped her in my arms as she sobbed softly. "I don't want to lose anyone. I don't want any of us to die in this war. We all mean so much to each other. We've been through so much together in such a short time. And… there's nothing I can do to stop it…"

I pulled away, holding her by the arms, forcing her to look at me.

"Myrathyn said you may not be able to save us, but he didn't say I can't… I'll keep us alive, Bella. I promise. Somehow I'll make sure we all make it through this… together."

I brushed away her tears and forced a smile, causing one on her lips in return.

"You're the best, Ash. I couldn't ask for a better friend in this life."

"Ditto." I winked. "Now, let's get some food together while the boys set up camp. I'm sure we're all starved."

CHAPTER 2

The crackling fire cast dancing shadows across our weary faces as we sat in a circle, picking at the remains of the deer Krakos had hunted. The meat was perfectly charred—courtesy of Cade's fire magic—but even the savory feast couldn't lift our exhausted spirits.

I'd think surviving a battle with the Blaze Queen would call for celebration, but the weight of what we'd endured hung heavy in the air. My muscles ached from the intense fighting, and though Myrathyn had healed my worst wounds, phantom pains still lingered where the queen's magic had torn through me.

I watched the dragons resting at the edge of our camp, their massive forms outlined by moonlight. Errax's blue scales seemed to shimmer even in the darkness, while Krakos's black hide melded with the shadows. Talonor lay between them, his stone-gray form rising and falling with steady breaths.

Bella sat beside me, absently trailing her finger through the dirt. The mystic's prophecy about one of us dying clearly haunted her thoughts. Hunter maintained his stoic guard position, though exhaustion showed in the slight droop of his shoulders.

My gaze drifted to Cade across the fire. His head kept

nodding forward before he'd jerk awake, fighting against his body's desperate need for rest. Even half-asleep, he was breathtaking—his sharp features softened by the firelight, black hair falling across his face.

As if sensing my attention, his sapphire eyes met mine. A tired smile tugged at his lips as he pushed himself to his feet, wincing slightly. He crossed to my side and held out his hand.

"Come," he said softly. "We should rest while we can."

I took his hand, savoring the warmth of his touch—so different from the searing pain that came with deeper contact between our opposing elements. He led me to one of the tents Hunter had set up, ducking inside.

The small space felt intimate as we settled onto the bedrolls, close but careful not to press too tightly together. Cade propped himself up on one elbow, studying my face in the dim light filtering through the tent walls.

"I still can't believe what you did," he murmured. "That golden armor, the weapon you summoned—I've never seen anything like it."

I shook my head, remembering the surge of power that had coursed through me in that crucial moment. "I barely understand it myself. There was this voice in my head, telling me to be strong, to fight..." I trailed off, thinking of Eden, my magic, and wondering if Cornelius, my magical tortoise guide, might visit tonight to help me understand these new abilities.

"Whatever it was, you were magnificent." Cade's fingers ghosted along my arm, sending pleasant shivers through me. "You stood against my stepmother and lived to tell about it. Do you know how incredible that is?"

My body hummed with awareness of his proximity, desire warring with the knowledge that giving in to it could hurt us both. In his weakened state, the clash of our elements might even kill him. I am Aqualorian—he, Cinderyn. The recent revelation about my water elemental powers rocked me, especially since it made it nearly impossible to kiss him, a fire elemental, without pain. Still, I couldn't help imagining what it would be like to truly be with him, to express our feelings without the threat of pain. I wanted him. I wanted every part of him.

"I'm just glad we both survived," I said instead, reaching up to brush a lock of hair from his face. "When I saw Brigodon's flames engulf you and Krakos..."

"Shhh," he soothed. "We made it. We're here."

"But at what cost?" I whispered, tracing the scorched edges of his armor. "You're hurt, Cade. Badly."

He caught my hand, bringing it to his lips. Even that small contact sent sparks of both pleasure and pain through my fingers. "Worth it," he murmured against my skin. "Every burn, every wound—worth it to keep you safe."

My heart clenched at his words. How had I gone from being a slave in Bramblebash to having the most powerful man in Allovan willing to die for me? The thought both thrilled and terrified me.

"The Harrowhorn Mountains," I said, changing the subject before my emotions overwhelmed me. "What exactly are we facing there?"

Cade's expression darkened. "Ancient things. Creatures that have lived in those peaks since before the time of dragons. Some say they're fallen Terradyne who lost their humanity to the darkness of the deep caves."

A shiver ran down my spine. "Terradyne? The Earth elementals? I've only heard tales of them. I thought they were long extinct, or fled to the outer continents? And that's where we're going to hide?"

"It's the last place my stepmother would look for us. The mountains are too treacherous even for her Sythers to navigate. You'd need dragons to get deep into the mountains. Sythers are fast on foot, but even with their long arms, getting through those mountain passes is extremely difficult, and dangerous..." He grimaced as he shifted position.

I wanted to ask more, but exhaustion was clearly pulling at him. His eyes kept drifting shut, though he fought to keep them open. I gently pushed him down onto the bedroll.

"Sleep," I whispered. "We can talk more tomorrow."

He caught my wrist as I started to pull away. "Stay close? No wandering off in the night. I need to protect you. I can't let you get hurt again... My stepmother is back in Emberveil now, but she's not giving up on capturing you..."

How could I refuse? I settled beside him, careful to maintain just enough distance that our elements wouldn't clash. His breathing soon evened out into the rhythm of sleep. "I wouldn't *dream* of venturing out into the woods at night." We both laughed, knowing my past midnight adventures into the woods with Cornelius had caused headaches for both him and me.

His hand traced my arms, causing the hairs there to stiffen straight. He moved forward and kissed my lips. My eyelids dropped like weights and I leaned into it deeply. The feeling of his lips against mine sent a rush all the way from the top of my head to my toes. Tingling every inch of my skin. I wanted more. I wanted to tear the clothes off his muscular body and wrap him in my arms, seizing his body as mine. But I knew in his weakened state any kind of romantic escapade might kill him.

Our lips separated, and he pulled away. He smirked, and a deep weariness was heavy in his gaunt face. He laid his head on his pillow and was quickly snoring softly. My fingers ran through his wild hair, staring at his perfect features. I wanted more, but the damned curse that afflicted us was killing me! I needed him. I needed the deep connection to grow, but it seemed that even with the way I felt about him, we'd never be able to be together the way I wanted. The way I needed...

I lay awake longer, my mind racing. Would Cornelius appear

tonight? I had so many questions about the golden armor, about the voice that had guided me in battle. Eden, my magic, felt like a warm presence in my chest, but I still understood so little about it.

The Blaze Queen's overpowering, intense magic burned into my memory like a bitter tattoo. The memories of that battle were like a nightmare. How could I defeat such a monstrous force? Odiun protect me… and with Cade incapacitated like he is.. we need a miracle to survive the week.

I shuddered, remembering the dark red glow of her eyes, the way her silver hair had whipped around her dragon-helm like living shadows. She would never stop hunting me, never stop trying to steal my power.

But looking at Cade's sleeping face, hearing Hunter's quiet movements as he kept watch outside, knowing Bella slept nearby —I felt stronger. Together, we'd already accomplished the impossible. Together, maybe we could do it again.

Still, Bella's words about the mystic's prophecy haunted me. Someone would die in this fight. The thought of losing any of them made my chest ache.

I snuggled closer to Cade, careful not to touch, drawing comfort from his presence. Tomorrow we'd fly to the mountains. After that, we'd face the queen herself. But for now, in this moment, we were alive and together.

That would have to be enough.

My last thoughts before sleep took me were of golden armor shimmering in sunlight, of Errax's proud roar, and of the mysterious voice that had awakened something ancient and powerful within me. Whatever was coming, I would be ready.

I had to be. The fate of Allovan—and everyone I loved— depended on it.

CHAPTER 3

Dawn crept over the horizon like a shy maiden, painting the sky in gentle hues of pink and gold. The crisp morning air carried a heaviness that had nothing to do with the weather—we were all acutely aware of what lay ahead in the Harrowhorn Mountains.

I stretched, yawning as the brilliant sky and crisp air warmed my skin. In the gorgeous morning rays, I couldn't help but smile as my gaze fell on Errax. Her blue scales sparkled with morning dew, and she let out a soft rumble of greeting when she caught me looking. The thought of soaring through the skies again made my heart race with excitement.

Not long ago, I'd been nothing but a nobody in Bramblebash, owned by that monster Garris. Now I was a dragon rider. The transformation still felt surreal, like a dream I might wake from at any moment. Cade was already up and prepping the dragons for flight with Hunter. Bella stirred within a tent.

The burns on Cade's armor and the lingering smell of battle smoke reminded me this was all too real. My eyes drifted to where he was checking Krakos's wounds. The mighty black dragon's scales were scorched in places, testament to Brigodon's fury.

Even the most fearsome dragon in Allovan—save for the queen's beast—wasn't invulnerable.

"How is he?" I asked, approaching carefully. Krakos's crimson eyes tracked my movement, but he no longer seemed to view me as a threat.

Cade's face was drawn with exhaustion and pain he tried to hide. "He'll heal. Dragons are resilient." He pressed a hand to his own ribs, wincing. "We both will."

"You don't have to pretend it doesn't hurt," I said softly. "Not with me."

His sapphire eyes met mine, and for a moment, I saw past his walls—saw the vulnerability he kept hidden from everyone else. Then his mask slipped back into place.

"We need to move soon," he said. "The longer we stay here, the more likely my stepmother's spies will find us."

I nodded, but couldn't help glancing back at the sanctuary where Myrathyn still sat motionless on his throne of thorns. The ancient Druidaan had saved my life, had given each of us answers we sought—even if some of those answers were hard to bear.

While the others finished breaking camp, I walked to the sanctuary's entrance. The mystic hadn't moved, looked as if he hadn't drawn breath since yesterday. But I knew he lived—would continue his ageless vigil here in this sacred place.

"Thank you," I mouthed silently, meaning it with every fiber of my being. Without him, I'd be dead, and the queen would be that much closer to achieving her dark goals.

I helped Hunter and Cade pack up the tents, loading up the dragons ready for flight again. I daydreamed of the first time I was mounted upon Krakos' back with Cade sitting firmly behind me, his muscular arm wrapped around my waist.

Bella's voice called me back to the present. "Ash! We're ready!"

I turned to find her already mounted behind Hunter on Talonor, her arms wrapped securely around his waist. The stone-gray dragon seemed unbothered by the extra passenger, though its milky white eyes still unnerved me.

Getting used to dragons isn't as easy as I thought it would be... I'm just elated these are on my side!

Errax lowered her head as I approached, allowing me to climb onto her back with practiced ease. The familiar feel of her scales beneath my hands filled me with confidence. This was where I belonged now—not serving drinks to Garris and his drunken friends or warming some nobleman's bed, but astride a dragon, master of my own destiny.

"Stay close," Cade instructed as he mounted Krakos. "The mountains are treacherous enough in clear weather. In fog, one wrong turn could be fatal."

We took to the sky in formation, Krakos leading while Talonor and Errax flanked him. The morning air was crisp against my face, and I breathed deeply, savoring the mixture of wind and dragon smoke. Nothing in my old life could compare to this feeling of absolute freedom.

As we flew east, my mind wandered back to Bramblebash. How many times had I stared at the horizon, dreaming of escape? How many nights had I cried myself to sleep, believing I'd never be anything more than property to be bought and sold?

The memory of Garris's sweaty hands on my skin made me shudder. But that was behind me now. I wasn't that helpless girl anymore. I was Ashlyn Moonriver, daughter of an Aqualorian and a human woman, wielder of powers I was only beginning to understand.

Still, the queen's words echoed in my mind: "Your power will be mine." The memory of her blood-red eyes and cruel smile sent a shiver down my back, even in the warm morning sun. She wouldn't stop hunting us—hunting me—until she had what she wanted.

Hours passed as we flew, the landscape changing beneath us.

Forests gave way to rocky foothills, which gradually rose into steeper terrain. The air grew thinner, colder.

"There!" Hunter's shout carried over the wind. "The Harrowhorns!"

The mountain range rose before us like the spine of some ancient beast. The nearest peaks were a slate gray, their bulk solid and imposing. But as my eyes followed the range deeper into the distance, the mountains seemed to change. Their peaks grew sharper, darker, until they resembled massive spears of charcoal thrust up from the earth.

And there was something else—a fog that clung to the darker peaks, writhing like a living thing. It seemed to reach for us with ghostly tendrils as we drew closer.

"Stay together!" Cade called back. "The fog can disorient even experienced riders!"

We pressed on as daylight faded, the mountains growing more ominous with each passing minute. The fog closed around us until I could barely see Krakos ahead or Talonor to my right. Only the occasional burst of flame from one of the dragons illuminated our way.

Finally, Cade led us down toward what appeared to be a wide ledge. As we landed, I could make out the mouth of a cave in the mountain face, though the fog made it impossible to gauge its size.

"We'll make camp here," Cade announced, dismounting carefully. His movements were stiffer than usual, his injuries clearly hurting him. "Hunter, come with me. We need to secure the perimeter."

"Is it safe to split up?" Bella asked, voicing my own concerns.

"Safer than being caught unaware by what lives in these mountains," Hunter replied grimly. He helped her down from Talonor. He went and ran to the cave to inspect it, then minutes later, walked back out, remounting the dragon. He nodded to Cade.

"We won't go far," Cade assured us. "Stay alert, keep the fire small, and don't venture into the cave until we return."

I wanted to protest—wanted to insist on going with them—but I knew they were right. If there were threats nearby, they needed to find them before we settled in for the night.

The two men took off into the fog on their dragons, leaving Bella and me alone on the ledge. We gathered what wood we could find and built a small fire, though its warmth did little to dispel the chill that seemed to emanate from the mountain itself.

"So..." Bella said after a while, a familiar mischievous glint in her eye. "You and Cade seemed cozy in that tent last night."

I rolled my eyes. "Really? *That's* what you want to talk about?"

"Well?" She waggled her eyebrows. "Did you two...?"

"You know we can't," I said, unable to keep the frustration from my voice. "This curse is going to drive me insane. Every time we try... we get knocked out cold and are left totally weak. If I even tried anything last night, it could kill him."

"Might be worth it," she laughed. I cocked my elbow into her rib. "There has to be a way around that," she mused. "I mean, the way he looks at you... it's like you're his whole world."

I threw a stick into the fire, watching it spark. "Maybe. But for now, we have bigger problems than my sex life."

The fog swirled around us, and somewhere in the darkness, something screamed—a sound unlike anything I'd ever heard before. Bella and I pressed closer together, watching the shadows and praying Cade and Hunter would return soon.

The Harrowhorns had already begun to show their teeth, and I had a feeling we'd see much worse before our time here was done.

CHAPTER 4

As Cade and Hunter disappeared into the swirling mists, I could feel frustration building within me. Why were they the ones getting to investigate the perimeter, while Bella and I were left behind to twiddle our thumbs? Surely I was capable enough to handle whatever threats might lurk in these treacherous mountains.

But I knew deep down that my skills were still raw, my dragon-riding abilities not yet honed to the level of Cade and Hunter. Errax and I had only recently formed our bond, and I couldn't help but feel a twinge of inadequacy compared to the veteran dragon riders.

They don't trust me. After all we've been through together... they still don't fucking trust me...

Bella must have sensed my restlessness, for she placed a comforting hand on my arm. "Hey, chin up. I'm sure they're just being overly cautious, that's all. Besides, I need protecting too." Her smirk captured my frustration and the glint in her eyes cooled my anger.

I gave her a half-hearted smile. "I know, it's just..." I trailed off, unsure how to voice the insecurities that had been plaguing me since the battle with the Blaze Queen.

"You wish you were out there with them, proving your worth?" Bella finished for me, her perceptive eyes reading me like an open book. She looked down, spotting a shiny stone, far smoother than the rest, picking it up and placing it in her pocket.

I nodded, turning my gaze back to the swirling fog, willing the men to return safely. "I feel like I have so much to learn still. What if I'm not strong enough to face what's out there? Does Cade know that? Does he know something about me I don't?"

Bella squeezed my arm reassuringly. "Ash, you are one of the bravest people I know. You stood toe-to-toe with the Blaze Queen and lived to tell the tale. That's nothing to sneeze at."

"But—"

"But, nothing," Bella folded her arms. "Rest, train your magic while they're away. Cade knows what he's doing. You're going to have to learn to trust him more."

"Trust him? I can't stop thinking about him. I just wish he wasn't such a fucking rat sniffer."

"Rat sniffer?" Bella chuckled, covering her mouth. "Did you just make that up?"

I giggled and nodded. "Not my best, but you get the point."

Hours later, Cade and Hunter returned, their dragons emerging from the mist like dark, fearsome apparitions. I straightened, my heart pounding with a mix of relief and renewed anticipation.

"The area seems secure for now," Cade announced as he and Hunter dismounted, their faces grim. "But we shouldn't venture too far from this ledge. There are... things in these mountains that are best left undisturbed."

Bella's eyes widened. "Things? What kind of things?"

Hunter shook his head. "We didn't see anything, but the air carries an unsettling chill. Stay close to the fire and keep your weapons ready."

I nodded, my hand instinctively going to the pommel of the sword at my hip. Cade's gaze met mine, and I saw a flicker of something in his eyes—concern, perhaps, or a silent plea for me to heed his warning.

As Cade went to pitch one of the tents to rest, Bella and I set about making our little camp as comfortable as possible. Hunter remained vigilant, his eyes scanning the fog-shrouded darkness.

The silence was thick, punctuated only by the crackle of the fire and the occasional grumble from Errax or Talonor. I busied myself with brushing Errax's magnificent scales, taking comfort in the familiar ritual. But my mind kept wandering, wondering what unseen horrors lurked in the mountains beyond our little haven.

After a while, Bella broke the silence. "Hey, Hunter? What did you ask the mystic back there?"

Hunter's expression darkened, and he averted his gaze. "It's not important."

Bella frowned. "Well, it must have been important enough for you to ask. And whatever he told you..." She trailed off, her eyes filled with concern. "It's really bothering you, isn't it?"

For a long moment, Hunter said nothing. Then, with a heavy sigh, he spoke. "What Myrathyn told me is something I have to live with. I feel better keeping it buried. Telling you would do nothing for anyone, and there's nothing we can do to change it anyway. Some things are better left unsaid."

"Do you regret asking the question?" I asked, itching my thigh, curious of his response.

Hunter sighed, raising his chin and gazing up at the sky. He opened his mouth to speak, but then, Errax and Talonor both snapped to attention, their eyes scanning the fog warily. Cade burst from the tent, his staff glowing with arcane fire. "What was that?"

Hunter's hand flew to the hilt of his sword. "I don't know, but it didn't sound friendly."

We all fell silent, straining our ears for any sign of movement in the mist. The seconds ticked by, the only sound the crackle of the fire and the labored breathing of our mounts.

Then, out of the corner of my eye, I saw a dark shape emerge from the fog. At first, I thought it was Krakos returning from his hunt, but as it drew closer, I realized my mistake. This was no regular dragon I recognized.

The creature was massive, its leathery wings spanning at least thirty feet, blotting out the sky as it drew near. Its scales were a mottled, sickly green, like rotting flesh, each one glistening with a strange, oily sheen. Its long, serpentine neck was crowned with a horned head that resembled a demon's, horns like jagged daggers curving back towards its body. Beady, malevolent eyes, black as pitch, glared down at us with a hunger that made my skin crawl, and its jaws parted to reveal row after row of jagged, dagger-like teeth, dripping with viscous drool.

As if that monstrosity was not enough, more shapes began to materialize from the mist - a whole horde of these twisted, unnatural dragons. Some were smaller, their bodies contorted and their scales a sickly patchwork of colors. Others were larger, their hides thick and armored, their limbs ending in savage claws. Each one seemed to radiate an aura of pure, primal aggression, their glowing eyes fixed on us with unbridled ferocity.

The air filled with their guttural screeches, a cacophony of inhuman sounds that grated against my ears. They beat their massive wings, stirring up the fog until it obscured everything but their nightmarish forms, closing in around us like the jaws of some ancient, primordial beast.

"What in the name of Odiun is that?" Bella whispered, her voice trembling.

Cade raised his staff, the fire in its head blazing to life. "Get to your dragons! We're under attack!"

I didn't need to be told twice. Sprinting to Errax's side, I leaped onto her back, my heart thundering in my chest. The blue dragon responded instantly, her powerful wings unfurling as she roared a challenge at the monstrous beast.

Hunter was already mounted on Talonor, his sword drawn and gleaming in the firelight. "There's more than one!" he shouted.

Sure enough, as I glanced around, I could see the silhouettes of other dragons emerging from the fog, their numbers growing by the second. These creatures were unlike any dragon I had ever seen—their bodies twisted and warped, their eyes filled with a feral hunger.

Cade stood his ground, his staff raised high as he summoned a torrent of flames to engulf the approaching monsters. The dragons thrashed and screeched in pain, but they did not retreat.

"Ash, stay behind me!" Cade called out, his voice strained with the effort of his magic.

I wanted to argue, to demand that he let me fight alongside him, but the sheer number of these twisted beasts made my resolve falter. Errax was much smaller than Krakos, and I knew I was no match for these creatures with my mediocre riding skills. These were wild dragons!

I summoned Eden. I tugged at the strings inside me that connected her in my core. I readied her for when the moment would come.

So instead, I pushed Errax higher, maneuvering her into a defensive position behind Cade and Krakos. Hunter and Talonor flanked us, their combined strength and skill creating a formidable barrier against the encroaching horde.

The battle that followed was a blur of fire, claws, and teeth.

Cade's magic cut swaths through the ranks of the twisted dragons, but they kept coming, undeterred by the pain. Hunter and Talonor danced through the air, their swords flashing as they carved a path through the enemy.

And Errax and I... we stayed back, offering what support we could with her fiery breath and shots of golden flames from my Gilded Radiance. But I could feel the strain of the battle, the weight of my own limitations. How I wished I could be out there, fighting beside them, proving my worth.

Just as the twisted dragons seemed poised to overwhelm us, a sound unlike anything I had ever heard before echoed through the mountains. A deep, resounding horn blast that reverberated in my very bones.

The effect on the enemy was immediate and profound. The dragons thrashed and shrieked, their assault faltering as they turned and fled back into the mist. Krakos and Talonor remained unaffected, but Errax, too, seemed unperturbed by the strange sound. We all landed back at the campsite to regroup.

Cade and Hunter exchanged bewildered glances, their weapons still at the ready. "What in the name of Odiun was that?" Cade muttered.

Before anyone could respond, another shape emerged from the swirling fog. This one was familiar—the sleek, powerful silhouette of a Stormscale dragon. As it drew closer, I could make out the figure of a rider atop its back, clad in the distinctive armor of the rebel group.

Cade immediately raised his staff, the fire at its tip flaring to life. "Hunter, get ready!"

But before he could unleash his magic, I reached out and grasped the staff, forcing it down. "Wait!" I shouted. "It might not be hostile."

Cade looked like he wanted to argue, but the Stormscale dragon landed before us, its rider dismounting with fluid grace. The dragon itself let out a deep, guttural roar, and to my surprise,

Errax and Talonor responded in kind, their own cries mingling with the newcomer's.

The Stormscale rider approached us, his face obscured by the folds of his cloak and his stone-like helm with curling ram horns. "You are the ones they call the Gold-Marked," he said, his voice steady and measured.

Cade's grip on his staff tightened. "What of it?"

The rider raised his hands in a placating gesture. "Peace, Blaze Prince. We mean you no harm, this time…"

My eyes widened at the title, and I glanced at Cade, whose expression had darkened considerably.

"Then why are you here?" Cade demanded, his tone laced with suspicion.

The rider paused, as if considering his words carefully. "We have been… monitoring your progress. And when we heard the call of the Terradyne, we knew we had to intervene."

"The Terradyne?" Bella echoed, her brow furrowed in confusion.

"The ancient beings who dwell in these mountains," the rider explained. "Their horn is a warning to all who would trespass on their domain, and the wild dragons in these mountains hate it. Even a single blow of those magical horns cause them great pain." He turned his gaze to me, and I felt a shiver run down my spine. "You, Ashlyn Moonriver, have been marked by the power of the Gilded Radiance. The Terradyne are protecting you."

I opened my mouth to respond, but no words came. How could this stranger know my true name? And how do they know so much about the Terradyne and these mountains?

Before I could gather my thoughts, the rider continued. "We have come to offer our aid. The Blaze Queen's reach extends far, and you will need powerful allies if you are to defeat her."

Cade's eyes narrowed. "And what price do you expect in return?"

The rider chuckled, a low, rumbling sound. "Only that you

allow us to share in the glory of her downfall. The Stormscales have no love for the Emberveil Empire, but we have even less love for the Blaze Queen and her tyranny. You know this better than any, Blaze Prince." The man in the ram-horn helm glowered at Cade, a deep hatred brewing within.

Cade considered this, his gaze flickering between the Stormscale rider and the dragons behind him. "No way..." Cade returned a hateful gaze.

These two had probably murdered countless of each other's friends. I can't imagine them ever working together, but we may have to. I'm going to have to convince him to try.

The rider inclined his head. "We both want the same end. And now, Cade Phoenixfire, you've renounced your title, birthright, and all claim to your name by helping the Gold-Marked. She is the one destined to defeat the Blaze Queen and bring a new age of peace." He turned and whistled, and the Stormscale dragon let out a mighty roar, the sound echoing through the mountains. "Mortriana Vissex must die for our world to thrive and the Age of Cinderyn to finally end. As much as it pains me to say it... we must combine forces."

As if in response, more shapes emerged from the mist, dragons of all shapes and sizes bearing the familiar colors and insignia of the Stormscales—a circular red dragon cast across a pale full moon. I watched in awe as they landed around us, their riders dismounting and approaching with a mix of caution and curiosity.

"I will return tomorrow," the ram-horned helmed man with long silver hair and beard said. "Have your final answer ready. And if your answer is no, then we will resume our war with not only the queen, but you."

This was an unexpected turn of events, to be sure. But as I looked at the faces of my companions—Cade's fury and hatred, Bella's hopeful wonder, and Hunter's guarded resignation—I couldn't help but feel a glimmer of hope. Perhaps, with the

Stormscales at our side, we stood a chance against the Blaze Queen's monstrous forces.

Whatever challenges lay ahead, I knew one thing for certain: we were no longer alone in this fight. And that, in and of itself, was a powerful weapon against the darkness that threatened to consume us all.

CHAPTER 5

The silence after the Stormscales departed was deafening. The fog seemed to press in around us, thick with unspoken tensions and age-old hatred. I watched Cade carefully, noting how his jaw clenched and unclenched, his hands gripping his staff so tightly his knuckles had gone white.

I understood his struggle. The Stormscales had been his enemies for years, their bitter civil war claiming countless lives on both sides. Now here they were, offering an alliance against his stepmother, the Blaze Queen. It seemed almost too convenient, too neat a solution to our problems.

Yet I couldn't deny the strategic advantage such an alliance would bring. The Stormscales were formidable warriors, their mighty dragons and skilled riders were among the most feared in all of Allovan. With their help, we might actually stand a chance against the queen's forces.

"Cade," I began softly, taking a step toward him.

His sapphire eyes met mine, and I could see the turmoil raging within them. "Don't," he warned, his voice low and dangerous. "Just... don't."

"We need to at least consider it," I pressed, refusing to back down. "You know we can't attack all of Emberveil and defeat her alone."

Hunter cleared his throat. "She's right, my prince. As much as I hate to admit it… we are alone against your stepmother. The Stormscales numbers alone could prove invaluable."

"Knowledge gained by killing my men!" Cade exploded, whirling to face his friend. "Have you forgotten how many of our brothers and sisters died at their hands? How many raids we've suffered, how many villages they've burned?"

"And how many of their people have we killed?" I interjected, my voice sharper than intended. "This war has claimed lives on both sides, Cade. Maybe it's time to put an end to it."

He turned to me, his expression thunderous. "You don't understand. You haven't seen what I've seen. You haven't had to write letters to mothers and wives, telling them their loved ones aren't coming home because of Stormscale arrows."

The pain in his voice made my heart ache, but I stood my ground. "No, I haven't. But I've seen what your stepmother is capable of. I've felt her power firsthand. And if we don't find a way to stop her, there won't be any mothers or wives left to write to."

Bella, who had been unusually quiet, stepped forward. "What if we took some time to think about it? They said they'd return tomorrow for our answer. We don't have to decide right now."

Before anyone could respond, a familiar screech cut through the air. Krakos emerged from the fog, a strange creature dangling from his massive jaws. It looked like some bizarre hybrid of a deer and a goat, with curved horns and elongated limbs. The black dragon dropped his prey by the fire, then raised his head to stare in the direction the Stormscales had disappeared.

A low, rumbling growl emanated from his throat. Cade placed a hand on his dragon's neck, murmuring, "I know, old friend. I know."

The tension in the air gradually began to dissipate as we

busied ourselves with practical matters. Hunter and Bella worked on preparing the strange mountain creature for our dinner, while I tended to Errax, checking her for any injuries from our earlier encounter with the twisted dragons.

As I ran my hands over her gleaming blue scales, my mind wandered back to the Stormscale commander's words about the Terradyne. What were these earth elementals and why did they disappear into the Harrowhorn Mountains? And why had those corrupted dragons fled at the sound of that mysterious horn?

"You're troubled."

I was startled at Cade's voice behind me. He stood there, looking weary but less angry than before.

"Aren't we all?" I replied, keeping my tone light.

He moved closer, close enough that I could feel the heat radiating from his body. "I saw how you handled the situation with the Stormscales. You're becoming quite the diplomat."

I shrugged, trying to ignore how my heart raced at his proximity. "Someone had to be. You looked ready to start another war right there."

"Perhaps I was." He sighed, running a hand through his dark hair. "But you're right. We need to at least consider their offer."

I turned to face him fully, surprised by this admission. "Really?"

"Don't look so shocked," he said, a hint of his usual humor returning. "I can be reasonable when I need to be."

"Could have fooled me," I teased, then grew serious. "Cade, I know asking you to trust them is asking a lot. But maybe this is what we need - a chance to end not just one war, but two."

He studied me for a long moment, his sapphire eyes intense. "When did you become so wise, Ash Mist?"

"Moonriver," I corrected automatically, then blushed. "And I'm not wise. I just... I want this to end. All of it."

Something softened in his expression. He reached out as if to touch my face, then seemed to remember himself and pulled back. The familiar frustration of not being able to touch freely flashed across his features. I reached out and grabbed his hand, pressing it to my cheek. His muscular, calloused hand made my heart flutter. He felt so powerful, and he was... a heat rushed up from my core at his touch, and I involuntarily gasped.

"We'll discuss it more over dinner," he said finally. "For now, we should help Hunter and Bella before they destroy that poor creature completely."

I laughed. "Good idea. Though I'm not sure I want to eat something that looks like it came from a child's nightmare."

As we walked back to the fire, I couldn't help but wonder what tomorrow would bring. Would Cade ultimately agree to the alliance? Would the Stormscales prove trustworthy? And what other secrets did these mysterious mountains hold?

The fog continued to swirl around us, thick with possibilities and dangers yet unknown. But for now, we had food, fire, and each other. Sometimes, that had to be enough.

The mountain creature's meat proved surprisingly tender, though its taste was unlike anything I'd encountered before. As we sat around the fire, the fog pressing in around us like a living thing, I couldn't help but notice how the tensions from earlier still lingered in subtle ways - the careful distance Cade kept from the edge of our camp where the Stormscales had stood, the way Hunter's hand never strayed far from his sword hilt.

"What do you make of what they said about the Terradyne?" Bella asked, breaking the contemplative silence. She sat close to the fire, her oceanic blue eyes reflecting the dancing flames. "I've heard stories about them, but I always thought they were just that —stories."

Hunter shook his head, his copper armor gleaming in the firelight. "The Terradyne are real enough. Ancient beings of all the things that make the ground beneath our feet, older than dragons themselves. My father once encountered them in these mountains, though he rarely spoke of it."

"What did he say about them?" I asked, curious despite my exhaustion.

Hunter's expression grew distant. "Only that they were beautiful and terrible in equal measure. Like watching a storm at sea —magnificent, but deadly if you get too close. They look like people sometimes, and sometimes they are trees, rocks, they've even been rumored to be the mountains themselves!"

Cade stirred from his position against Krakos's massive form. "The Terradyne were allies to the first Phoenixfire kings," he said quietly. "Before the Great Betrayal, before the wars began. They helped my ancestors build Raven's Bane Castle."

"What happened?" I couldn't stop myself from asking, though I saw the pain flash across his face.

"The same thing that always happens," he replied bitterly. "Power corrupted, promises were broken, and those who were once allies became enemies." His crystal blue eyes met mine across the fire. "History has a way of repeating itself."

I understood his meaning all too well. The parallel to our current situation with the Stormscales was impossible to ignore.

"But it doesn't have to," I said firmly. "We can learn from the past without being bound by it."

Bella nodded enthusiastically. "Ash is right. Maybe this is our chance to break the cycle."

"Or maybe it's a trap," Hunter countered, though his tone was thoughtful rather than dismissive. "The Stormscales could be luring us in to kill us. It wouldn't be the first time they've used deception to achieve her goals."

"No," I said with certainty. "I don't think they're trying to trick us. I truly believe they need us."

"How could you possibly know that?" Cade pointed out, but his voice had lost some of its earlier edge.

"It's a feeling. I think it's our only chance. It's a chance we have to take..."

Errax chose that moment to raise her head, letting out a soft rumble that seemed to vibrate through the very mountain beneath us. The fog swirled around her blue scales, making them shimmer like sunlight on water. Sometimes I forgot how beautiful she was, how lucky I was to have her as my companion.

"What do you think, girl?" I murmured, reaching up to stroke her neck. "Should we trust them?"

She turned one emerald eye toward me, and I felt a warmth in my chest that had nothing to do with the fire. Ever since our bond had formed, I'd noticed my connection to her growing stronger. Sometimes I could almost sense her thoughts, her feelings.

"The dragons seem comfortable enough with the Stormscales' presence," Hunter observed. "They didn't attack them immediately when they came in. Dragons are usually better judges of character than we are. But, me personally, I don't trust them within an inch of my life, let alone all of ours..."

Cade grunted in acknowledgment, his hand absently stroking Krakos's scales. The great black dragon had remained unusually alert since the Stormscales' departure, his crimson eyes scanning the fog as if expecting them to return at any moment.

"There's something else to consider," I said carefully, knowing I was about to tread on dangerous ground. "If we refuse their offer, what's to stop them from attacking us? We're in their territory now."

The silence that followed was heavy with unspoken implications. We were all exhausted from our encounter with the wild, twisted dragons, and even with our combined strength, I wasn't sure we could fend off a determined Stormscale assault.

"I'd kill them. I'd kill them all," Cade growled, but I could hear the uncertainty beneath his bravado.

"By ourselves?" Hunter asked quietly. "We are vastly outnumbered now. We have no army. The queen has that now."

I saw Cade flinch at the thought of his men returning to the queen's service. I wanted to console him, to wrap him in my arms, but the distance between us—both physical and emotional—seemed to stretch like an endless chasm.

"If we're going to do this," Cade said finally, his voice tight with suppressed emotion, "we need guarantees. Assurances that they won't turn on us the moment the queen is defeated."

"What kind of guarantees?" Bella asked.

"A bloodcurse oath," Hunter suggested. "Binding both sides to the terms of our alliance."

I frowned. "Would that be enough?"

"Bloodcurse oaths are powerful magic," Cade explained. "Breaking one means death—I'm not sure the Stormscales would agree to that."

The implications of such an oath sent dread roaring through me. The stakes would be high for both sides, and the thought of losing Cade, was too much to bear.

"Then that's what we'll propose," I said firmly. "When they return tomorrow, we'll offer a bloodcurse oath alliance. Equal terms, equal risks."

Cade's eyes met mine across the fire, and for a moment, I saw a flicker of something that might have been pride. "You're really committed to this, aren't you?"

"I'm committed to surviving," I corrected him. "To all of us surviving. And if that means making allies of old enemies..." I shrugged. "Then that's what we'll do."

The fog seemed to thin slightly, revealing glimpses of stars overhead. Somewhere in the distance, that strange horn sounded again - fainter this time, more like an echo than a call. The twisted dragons were gone, driven back to whatever dark corners of the mountains they called home, but I couldn't shake the feeling that we were being watched.

"We should get some rest," Hunter suggested, rising to his feet. "Tomorrow will be... interesting, one way or another."

As we prepared for sleep, arranging watches and settling into our makeshift camp, I found myself drawn to the edge of the ledge. The fog parted momentarily, revealing the vast expanse of mountains stretching out before us. Somewhere out there, the Stormscales were waiting for our answer. Somewhere out there, the queen was plotting our destruction.

And somewhere, perhaps, the mysterious Terradyne were watching it all unfold, their ancient powers stirring in response to whatever destiny awaited us in these treacherous peaks.

"Ash?" Cade's voice was soft behind me. "You should get some sleep. I'll take first watch."

I turned to find him standing closer than usual, his face half-hidden in shadow. "Do you think we're doing the right thing?"

He was quiet for a long moment, considering. "I think," he said finally, "that you're showing more wisdom than I am in this situation. And that terrifies me almost as much as it impresses me."

A smile tugged at my lips. "The great Blaze Prince, terrified by a former slave girl from Bramblebash? What would your subjects say?"

"They'd say I was wise to listen to you." His expression grew serious. "Whatever happens tomorrow, Ash... thank you. For showing me another way."

The urge to touch him, to bridge the physical gap between us, was almost overwhelming. Instead, I simply nodded and turned back to the fog-shrouded mountains.

Tomorrow would bring what it would bring. For now, we had this moment of understanding, this fragile peace before the storm that was surely coming.

And somehow, that would have to be enough.

CHAPTER 6

 arkness enveloped me. Heat rose from the ground far below the dizzying battle below. Atop Errax, I swept through the swirling dark clouds as my heart pounded like war drums.

The clash of steel rang through the air, deafening and unrelenting. Sparks flew as my blade met the Blaze Queen's, the force of our strikes sending shockwaves through the battlefield. Cade was at my side, his staff wreathed in flames, his blue eyes burning with determination as he fought like a man possessed.

The queen laughed—a sound colder than the deepest reaches of the Infernal Depths. "You think you can stop me, child?" She sneered, her silver hair whipping around her helm like writhing serpents. "You think your love can save you?"

Cade let out a roar of defiance, driving forward. His sword cut through the air toward her throat—but before he could land the killing blow, shadows coiled around him like living chains. His body jerked back as if yanked by an unseen force, his sapphire eyes widening in shock.

"No!" I screamed, reaching for him, but my hands felt like lead, too slow, too late.

The queen's blackened blade drove straight into his chest.

Cade gasped, blood trickling from his lips as the life drained from his face. His body crumpled, collapsing into my arms. I cradled him. His warmth faded with every passing second, his breath coming in shallow, ragged gasps.

"Ash..." he whispered, his fingers weakly brushing against my cheek. "I'm sorry."

Then his hand fell limp, and his brilliant eyes dulled to lifeless glass.

I shook him, desperate, pleading. "Cade, please! Cade, wake up!"

The queen loomed above me, her laughter curdling in my ears, cruel and victorious. "Love makes you weak," she mocked. "And weakness will destroy you."

A storm roared in my chest—rage, grief, helplessness. My magic flared wildly, streaks of golden light crackling through my trembling hands, but it wasn't fast enough, wasn't enough at all—

The world unraveled around me.

Shadowy tendrils slithered across my vision, choking out the battlefield, swallowing Cade's body whole. I tried to hold on, to keep him in my grasp, but he disintegrated in my arms, turning to ash. My own screams echoed back at me, warping into a cacophony of sinister voices.

I felt broken. Like every part of my being had been ripped apart by the queen's wrath. I felt completely empty. A shell of myself. I was less than a slave then. I had lost the man that had broken my chains. The man that gave me my first breath of freedom. And there was nothing I could do to save him.

Then, nothing.

I gasped awake, my body drenched in sweat, the terror of the dream still pounding in my skull.

A dream... it was just a dream... a terrible nightmare.

The muggy air in the tent felt suffocating, thick with heat, as I struggled to steady my racing breath. My fingers dug into the blanket beneath me, desperate for something tangible, something real.

And staring at me in the dim flicker of firelight, massive and unmoving, was Cornelius.

The ancient tortoise barely fit inside my tent, his broad, ridged shell pressing against the canvas walls. His deep yellow eyes, streaked with fiery orange, watched me with quiet patience, unshaken by my violent awakening.

Leather creaked as I sat up too quickly, my pulse still hammering against my ribcage. The sensation of Cade's dying breath on my cheek, the queen's laughter—it all lingered, as though the dream had sunk its claws into me and refused to let go.

Cornelius blinked slowly. "A troubled dream?" His voice was rich and ancient, like the hush of waves over stones.

I wiped the back of my hand across my damp forehead, exhaling shakily. "You could say that."

"You dream of the queen?"

"And of Cade," I admitted, rubbing my arm to dispel the lingering chill. "I saw him die."

Cornelius's expression remained unreadable, his gaze shadowed with some distant sorrow. "A vision—perhaps of a possible future, or merely the fears that haunt you."

I frowned. "It felt too real. The mystic… he told Bella one of us was going to die."

The tortoise's voice lowered, grave and steady. "Magic flows through you stronger than before. It is possible your dreams are glimpses of what could be. But the future is never set in stone. We all die child. Even one day I will taste the final release of this world."

I let my head fall into my hands. That didn't reassure me. If I had the power to see such a fate, didn't that mean I had the power to stop it?

Cornelius regarded me for a long moment before speaking.

"Regardless, the path ahead remains the same. You must grow stronger."

I sat up straighter at that, clearing my throat. Cade wasn't dead. He was alive, back at the fire, brooding over something I lacked the energy to guess at. But the dream stayed with me, soaking into my bones like an unrelenting storm.

"Are you ready for more, Ash?" the magical tortoise asked. "We have little time, and I have much to teach you still."

"You think I'm ready for more training?" I asked, my voice firm despite my shaking hands.

Cornelius inclined his massive head. "It is not a matter of readiness, Ashlyn Moonriver. It is a matter of necessity."

I nodded once, resolute. The queen was still out there, healing, recovering. And the next time we met, she wouldn't underestimate me again. I wouldn't have the advantage of surprise.

So I had to make sure I was ready.

Together, Cornelius and I slipped out of the tent. Without a sound, we wove through the sleeping camp, the night air crisp against my overheated skin.

The dragons stirred as we passed.

Errax lifted her indigo wings slightly, watching us with quiet understanding. Krakos exhaled a low breath from his nostrils, embers flickering before he lowered his massive head again. Even Talonor remained still, his eerie white eyes tracking our departure.

None of them, however, made a sound.

And Cade, still hunched near the fire, did not turn. The dragons either knew not to alert Cade, or they somehow trusted Cornelius enough to keep me safe. Or perhaps they even understood that I *needed* to train.

Together, silent as shadows, we disappeared into the mountains.

～

THE JAGGED PEAKS of the Harrowhorns closed in around us like the ribs of a monstrous beast.

The darkness was absolute, swallowing everything beyond an arm's reach. The wind whispered through the cracks in the stone, carrying with it distant, eerie sounds I didn't want to try and explain. The ground itself was treacherous, uneven, as though it shifted beneath my boots just to spite me.

Cornelius led the way easily despite his massive size, his hulking form gliding as if the mountains rearranged themselves to accommodate him. His shell scraped against jagged rock, yet he remained unbothered—even regal.

"You are stronger than before," he said at last, his voice breaking the silence.

I exhaled through my nose. "Not strong enough."

Cornelius hummed. "Not yet. The queen will not be as reckless when you face her again. She will know your strengths. She will know your reach."

I swallowed hard. He was right.

Last time, I had fought through sheer desperation. The next time, the queen would be prepared for me. I wouldn't have the luxury of her underestimation.

"I won't let her take me," I vowed, my voice steady.

"Nor should you," Cornelius rumbled. "But survival is not enough. You must master both magic … and sky."

I blinked, tilting my head toward him. "Sky?"

"You are a dragon rider now, Ashlyn. And yet," he mused thoughtfully, "you do not fly as a true warrior."

I shifted uncomfortably, biting the inside of my cheek. I'd been trying, but… flying with Errax was still new, and I hesitated too much. Cade saw it. I knew he did.

"You hold back," Cornelius continued as if reading my thoughts.

I crossed my arms. "Cade's already training me."

The tortoise gave me a simply withering look. "Then train harder."

My mouth snapped shut.

Cornelius let the silence linger long enough that my shoulders began to tense before saying, "You must grow stronger. You must let him train you. You and your dragon need to become one as you tear through the clouds. Together you are stronger. When in flight, you must embrace the fear. Trust in Cade. He is brash, an absolute mess sometimes, but he's brave, and knowledgeable about this world... especially dragons."

My lips parted as if to argue, but I sighed instead. I hated it, but I knew he was right. No one was better at aerial combat than Cade. And despite my progress ... I still wasn't ready.

But I would be.

Cornelius stopped walking, his deep yellow eyes locking onto mine. "Then prove it."

His voice resonated like rolling thunder.

"Call upon Eden," he instructed. "Let her power flow through you."

I inhaled deeply, centering my focus, feeling the familiar presence of my magic surging to life deep within me—bright, burning, a voice whispering in my bones.

"Do not let it command you," Cornelius warned. "Command it."

I clenched my jaw and pulled Eden's power forth.

The night exploded in golden light.

My arms ignited in gilded flames, licking up my skin without harming me. Wild shadows danced along the cliffs behind me, the energy crackling, coursing through my veins like a living thing.

Power thrummed beneath my fingertips, raw and encompassing, the burn of it thrilling and freeing all at once.

Cornelius did not move, as solid and timeless as the mountain itself.

"Good," he murmured. "Again."

I did.

And this time, as the fire wrapped around me, I grinned.

I would be ready for her.

As DAWN SPILLED across the horizon, I returned to camp, my pulse still charged with the power I'd unleashed.

I wasn't the same girl the queen had fought last time.

She'd find something stronger.

Something dangerous.

She'd find me.

Ashlyn Moonriver.

CHAPTER 7

Sleep clung to me like a wet cloak. A mere hour—that's all I had managed after returning from my midnight training with Cornelius. My entire body ached, exhaustion creeping into my bones like an unwelcome guest. I'd burned through my reserves calling upon Eden, and now I was paying the price.

The scent of roasting meat and sizzling potatoes wafted toward me as I groggily pushed myself up from my bedroll. My stomach rumbled in appreciation, but my mind was still sluggish, thick with the memory of my dream—Cade bleeding out in my arms, the queen's laughter ringing in my ears. I shook my head, trying to shove the haunting images away.

Dragging myself outside, I was immediately met with Bella's sharp gaze. Her glacier-blue eyes gleamed in the morning light as she wrinkled her nose at me.

"Gods, you look like shit," she said, handing me a strip of dried meat from last night's kill.

I let out a groggy chuckle. "Feel like it, too."

Bella laughed, but my amusement faded when my gaze flickered past her—to Cade.

He was sitting at the edge of camp, near the fire, one arm slung over his bent knee. His long black waves hung loose, brushing his jaw, and the sapphire of his eyes blazed in the morning light. But his expression was hard, unreadable—except for the way his eyes cut through me. A glower. One that said, *I know.*

I swallowed down the panic that threatened to rise. Did he know I'd snuck off? Surely, he must have—Cade noticed *everything*. And if the brooding way he was glaring into the fire was any indication, he wasn't thrilled about it.

"Someone's grumpy," Bella murmured, leaning closer to whisper in my ear.

I sighed, rubbing the sleep from my eyes. "He's always grumpy."

Before she could respond, a sharp groan interrupted us. Cade stretched slightly, shifting in place, but the subtle hitch in his breath gave him away. He was still in agony from his wounds, moving carefully to mask the pain.

I clenched my jaw. *Of course* the stubborn ass refused to properly rest.

Hunter picked up on it, too. Straightening from where he was adjusting his belt, he glanced around at all of us and cleared his throat. "We need to talk about the Stormscales," he said, his voice steady. "We need to decide."

Silence stretched over camp like a second layer of mist.

One by one, we nodded. Bella nodded first, a wary but resolute look in her eyes. Then me. Then Hunter rested his hand over his heart and gave his own nod.

Only Cade remained motionless, his gaze fixed on the flames, expression unreadable.

But I knew what that darkness burning in his eyes meant.

He didn't want to do this.

He hated the Stormscales, still tangled in the memories of the war, in the blood-soaked past between them. And yet, after a long moment, he exhaled sharply. His fist clenched against his knee before he muttered, "If this is what you all think we should do, then we'll do it."

The words were bitter in his mouth, and it wasn't a decision made lightly.

And still... I knew it wasn't over.

~

HOURS LATER, the sky thinned, the mists rolling in as shadows moved among them. A distant roar rippled through the wind, low and guttural, as dark figures sliced through the fog.

The roar was more than just sound—it was a warning. A *presence.*

The Stormscales had arrived.

The dragons landed first, massive creatures of silver and black, their wings stirring the mist into spirals. The lead dragon, larger than the rest, bore an armored rider, and as he dismounted. Clad in the same storm-gray and ivory armor as the day prior, the man's sheer presence was enough to command attention. His massive frame, thick with years of battle-forged muscle, carried the weight of countless wars, and his every movement exuded the confidence of a man who had led warriors into hell and emerged victorious. His armor, etched with intricate swirling patterns resembling storm clouds, bore the wear of many battles, the silver inlays dulled and scratched but no less imposing.

A ram's head helm sat atop his head, its curved horns sweeping back in an almost regal yet savage display, the eye sockets hollow and menacing as they framed his face. Beneath its shadow, strands of silver hair tumbled past his broad shoulders, streaked with white like lightning through a storm. A thick scar carved its way from his temple down to his cheekbone—a brutal relic of a battle survived, proof of his resilience.

His sharp gray eyes were like polished steel, assessing and unreadable, flickering over us with the predatory calculation of a warrior accustomed to weighing strengths and weaknesses in an instant. His presence alone was enough to make even seasoned fighters hesitate, sensing the latent danger coiled beneath his disciplined stance.

When he finally spoke, his voice was deep, a rolling rumble of command and authority, like distant thunder before a tempest.

"Darren Iconnas," he introduced, nodding. "Leader of the Stormscales."

Not a title given lightly.

His gaze swept over us, before falling onto Cade. "Have you reached a decision?"

My gaze flickered to Cade instinctively.

For a beat, Cade didn't move.

Then, slowly, he rose to his full height, fitting seamlessly into his role as a warrior, as a prince—standing tall, dark, imposing.

"Despite our war, despite the history between us..." Cade's voice was firm, unwavering. "I'm willing to fight together to stop the true enemy of Allovan."

Darren studied him carefully. "And when she's dead?"

"When this is over," Cade continued, "I hope we can find peace between us. That we won't have to continue this war."

A tense silence.

Then, Darren exhaled sharply, nostrils flaring. A deep huff.

Cade extended his bare hand. "Since our past cuts deep, I propose we make an oath." He drew his dagger and sliced his palm, blood dripping down the blade and to the rocks between his boots.

For a long, agonizing moment, Darren didn't take it. "A bloodcurse oath, hmm? You mean to take this all the way then? If one betrays the other... death..." His gray eyes skimmed over us once more, suspicion lingering—then, finally, he reached out. "To kill that bitch of a queen, I'd do worse than a bloody handshake."

Darren Iconnas slid his greatsword from its sheath at his back, and cut deep into his leathery palm—then shook.

The moment Cade and Darren clasped hands, the ancient magic of the Bloodcurse oath ignited between them. From the points where their bloody palms met, swirling tendrils of red and black energy coiled around their wrists like living serpents. The crimson glow pulsed, veins of dark fire crawling up to their forearms, as if the very essence of war and vengeance had been woven into the spell. The air between them crackled with an unnatural heat, and for a heartbeat, it felt as if the mountains themselves trembled in response. Cade's jaw clenched, his sapphire eyes locked onto Darren's steel-gray gaze, both men unwavering as the oath carved itself into their very souls.

Then, a sudden surge—the red and black tendrils snapped tight, fusing into their veins like molten iron branding their flesh. A gust of wind howled through the camp, scattering embers from the fire as the magic sealed its will upon them. A shared pain flickered across Cade's face, mirrored in Darren's sharp features, but neither flinched. When the energy finally faded, dissolving back into the blood-streaked skin of their palms, the silence that followed was absolute. Their hands remained clasped, both warriors now bound by something far older than their hatred, far greater than their histories. A contract of death and loyalty signed in their very essence. And should either betray the bond—they would be the first to die.

"Then it's done," Darren said. "Come with us to our base. We have much to do. And we have little time. We'll plan from there."

But before I could respond, *before any of us* could respond, Cade spoke.

"No."

Every muscle in my body tensed at that single word.

Darren tilted his head. "No?"

Cade crossed his arms. "Not yet. We need to handle some things first."

Darren scrutinized him with a gaze sharp as forged steel. "And what would those things be?"

"A matter I need to figure out for myself," Cade responded coolly.

Still, Darren didn't argue. Instead, he reached into his belt and withdrew a horn. Simple, ancient, carved from a beast long forgotten. He tossed it to Cade.

"Blow it once when you're ready," Darren said. "We'll come and lead you to camp. Don't wait too long, Blaze Prince…"

And with that, he turned, mounted his dragon, and with a powerful beat of wings, the Stormscales took to the skies, disappearing into the mist once more.

The second they were gone, tension snapped through camp like a whip.

"What the *hell* was that?" I demanded, rounding on Cade.

He was already walking away, toward Krakos, his movements stiff with exhaustion and pain.

"You can't pull that kind of stunt after we just agreed to work with them!" I pushed, storming after him. "What the hell are we waiting for?"

He didn't respond at first, busy adjusting the straps on Krakos's saddle, but I saw his entire body tighten.

So, I pressed harder.

"Cade!"

Finally, he snapped. "Because the war is still going on, Ash!" His voice was sharp as flint, his eyes flashing as he turned on me. "Because we are still in the middle of it! And—because I need to figure some things out first!"

I opened my mouth to argue, but he was already mounting his dragon.

"Cade, you're injured—"

He didn't let me finish.

With a single command, Krakos flared his wings, and in a violent burst of wind and dust, they launched into the sky.

I cursed under my breath, glaring up as Cade vanished into the storm-gray sky, his dragon cutting through the clouds.

My fists clenched at my sides, nails biting into my palms.

"That. Absolute. *Asshole.*" It would be so much easier to hate him than to have these hard fucking feelings for that brat!

Beside me, Hunter sighed, rubbing the bridge of his nose before muttering, "Looks like you're getting to know him."

Bella snorted, biting down laughter. "Oh, *finally*, some perspective."

My glare swung to them both, but even I couldn't pretend I wasn't slightly amused underneath my fury. Still, frustration twisted in my gut like a knot.

Cade was gone.

And I had no idea what the hell he was doing.

But one thing was certain.

When he got back, I wasn't done with him.

"That arrogant, stubborn, infuriating..." I paced back and forth near the edge of camp, hands clenched into fists at my sides. The morning fog had burned away, leaving behind a crisp mountain air that did nothing to cool my temper. "Who does he think he is, just flying off like that?"

Bella watched me from her perch on a fallen log, her oceanic blue eyes following my agitated movements. "You know Cade," she said, trying to sound reasonable. "He probably has his reasons."

I whirled on her. "His reasons? We just made a blood oath with the Stormscales! And instead of moving forward with our plans, he just... leaves?" My voice cracked with frustration. "We don't have time for his mysterious disappearing acts!"

"Maybe that's exactly why he left," Bella suggested softly. "Whatever he's doing, it must be important."

I let out a harsh laugh. "Important enough to abandon us here? Important enough to risk everything we've worked for? And why the fuck is he so secretive about everything? Ugh!"

Hunter, who had been quietly tending to Talonor, spoke up.

"The prince wouldn't leave without good cause, Ash. You know that."

"Do I?" I challenged, my voice bitter. "Because from where I'm standing, it looks like he's running away from making actual progress with the Stormscales."

The words hung in the air, sharp and accusatory. Even as I said them, I knew I was being unfair. Cade had agreed to the alliance, had even proposed the blood oath himself. But his sudden departure stung like a betrayal.

"I need some air," I muttered, already striding toward the tree line.

"Ash, wait—" Bella called after me, but I was already gone, disappearing into the mountain forest with Errax's massive form gliding silently overhead.

The further I got from camp, the more my anger seemed to build. It wasn't just about Cade leaving—it was everything. The weight of prophecies and expectations, the constant threat of the queen, the frustration of powers I barely understood... it all crashed over me like a wave.

I stopped at a massive oak tree, its trunk wider than three men standing shoulder to shoulder. Without thinking, I slammed my fist into the rough bark.

Pain shot through my hand, but I welcomed it. Again and again, I struck the tree, each impact sending jolts of agony up my arm. Blood began to streak the bark, but I didn't care. I needed this—needed to feel something other than this helpless fury.

"Damn it!" I screamed, my voice echoing through the mountains. "Damn you, Cade! Damn all of this!"

"Violence against trees rarely solves anything," a familiar voice rumbled behind me.

I turned to find Cornelius watching me, his ancient eyes filled with something that might have been concern. The massive tortoise settled himself at the base of a nearby tree, his shell scraping against the bark.

"Do you know where he went?" I asked, hating how small my voice sounded.

Cornelius shook his head slowly. "I do not. But perhaps this time apart is what you both need."

I slumped against the bloodied tree, cradling my injured hand. "What I need is for him to trust me. To work with me, not... whatever this is."

"Then use this time to grow stronger," Cornelius suggested. "You have much yet to learn about yourself, Ashlyn Moonriver."

The name made my ears perk up, and a hard heartbeat to thump in my chest. "That name... the voice in my head called me that. What does it mean?"

Cornelius's eyes seemed to glow brighter. "It is a name of great power and ancient lineage. The Moonrivers were—are—royalty among the Aqualorians. One or perhaps both of your parents must have been of their bloodline. Your father or mother was a sea lord."

My heart skipped a beat. "My parents... were sea lords?"

"It would explain much about your power, would it not?"

I slid down to sit at the tree's base, my mind whirling. "I should have asked the Mystic about this instead of..."

"No," Cornelius cut me off firmly. "The question you asked was the right one. Knowing if you can defeat the queen is far more important than knowing your heritage. Your very survival depends on it. There will be time for researching your lineage later, after the war is over..."

I closed my eyes, remembering the voice that had guided me during the battle—strong, ancient, feminine. "The voice in my head... you know who it is, don't you?"

"I believe you already know the answer to that question."

And I did. I'd known for a while now, though I'd been afraid to admit it. "It's a dragon," I whispered. "The one sleeping in Calcaedus Mountain."

Cornelius nodded solemnly. "Vâllathór," he said, the name

carrying weight even in the mountain air. "The mightiest of all dragons. If the queen succeeds in drawing the last life from her, she will indeed achieve immortality."

My blood ran cold. "And that cannot happen."

"No," Cornelius agreed. "It cannot. You must awaken Vâllathór before the queen can reach her. You may be our last chance, Ashlyn Moonriver."

I absorbed this in silence, my mind racing with implications. Finally, I stood, brushing dirt from my clothes. "I need to think about all this. Thank you, Cornelius."

The ancient tortoise inclined his head. "Remember, young one—you are stronger than you know."

With that, he was gone, leaving me alone with my thoughts. Well, not entirely alone. Errax circled overhead, her presence a constant comfort. As I walked through the woods, her voice seemed to whisper in my mind—not words exactly, but feelings, impressions. Calm. Safety. Protection.

The sun was setting by the time I made my way back to camp. And there, silhouetted against the dying light, was Krakos landing with Cade on his back.

My earlier anger came rushing back as I stormed toward him. "Where the hell have you been?"

Cade dismounted gracefully, his expression guarded. "Not now, Ash."

"Yes, now!" I grabbed his arm as he tried to walk past me. "We need to be working together, not running off on secret missions!"

He yanked his arm free, his sapphire eyes flashing. "You don't understand. I'm fighting so many wars right now, I don't need you constantly—"

"Constantly what?" I challenged, stepping closer. "Questioning you? Caring about what happens to you?"

"Bickering with me!" he snapped, but there was something else in his voice now—frustration, yes, but also something deeper. "You need to learn to trust…"

"Trust?" I barked, unable to calm the growing, angry dragon inside me.

"Yes, Ash. I'm asking you to trust me. But instead you keep getting on my case. You don't know what it's like." His head slumped and his black hair framed his gorgeous face.

We were inches apart now, close enough that I could feel the heat radiating from his body. Without thinking, I grabbed his collar, ready to shake some sense into him.

But Cade's expression changed, softening as he looked down at me. "Gods," he muttered, "I can't stay mad at you when you look at me like that. You're beautiful when you're angry, Ash."

Before I could respond, his lips were on mine. The kiss was fierce, desperate, carrying all the passion and frustration we'd been holding back. I melted into it, my anger dissolving like morning mist in sunlight.

Somewhere behind us, I heard Bella giggle and Hunter clear his throat awkwardly, but I didn't care. All that mattered was this moment, this kiss, this man who drove me absolutely crazy in every possible way.

When we finally broke apart, I was breathless and light-headed. Cade's eyes were dark with desire, and I knew mine probably looked the same.

Gods, I hated him.

Gods, I wanted him.

And somehow, impossibly, both of those things could be true at once.

He knew exactly how to pull at all my strings. All of them.

"Don't think this means you're forgiven," I muttered against his lips.

He chuckled, the sound rumbling through his chest. "Wouldn't dream of it."

And sometimes, the most important battles weren't fought with swords or magic, but with hearts that refused to give up on each other.

Even if one of those hearts belonged to the most infuriating man in all of Allovan.

I barely had time to catch my breath before reality came crashing back in.

Cade and I pulled away from each other, just enough to breathe, just enough to register the sudden awkwardness that settled between us. His hands lingered at my waist, hesitant, and my fingers still clung to the collar of his tunic as if afraid to let go. My pulse was wild, erratic, and the warmth of his lips still burned on mine.

Gods, what had we just done?

A muffled giggle broke through the thick tension, and I snapped my head around to see Bella failing—miserably—to suppress her amusement. Hunter stood beside her, arms crossed, a smirk fighting its way onto his normally stoic face.

Even the dragons seemed intrigued by the spectacle. Errax had tilted her massive head, blinking at us with something I swore was smug satisfaction, while Krakos let out a deep huff that rumbled through the camp. Talonor flicked his tail, shifting his stance as if expecting something more.

Slowly, almost reluctantly, Cade took a step back, clearing his throat. "Well."

"Yeah," I echoed, my face burning. I crossed my arms over my chest, suddenly self-conscious.

Bella's amusement only grew. "You two sure know how to put on a show."

"Oh, shut up," I muttered, rubbing my temples.

Hunter, being the merciful one, stepped in to change the subject. "Right. Now that that's… settled, what's next?" His tone turned serious, glancing between Cade and me. "Are we heading to the Stormscales tonight? Or do we rest first?"

I hesitated. The adrenaline from the kiss was fading, leaving behind exhaustion from everything that had happened that day. The battle. The revelations. The argument. The storm inside me hadn't settled yet.

But I had something to say. Something we all needed to hear.

"Before we go anywhere," I said slowly, squaring my shoulders. "I need to tell you all something. Something important."

There was a shift in the air. The easy amusement from before dissipated. Cade's sapphire gaze snapped to mine, searching, analyzing, as if he could already tell something was different.

"Alright," he said, nodding once. "Let's talk."

We stood around it—Bella, Hunter, Cade, and me—while our dragons settled just beyond, their massive forms still and watchful. Even they seemed to understand the gravity of what I was about to say.

The mountains had gone eerily quiet, as if waiting. Listening.

I swallowed, glancing around the shadowed mist-capped peaks, an idea creeping into the back of my mind.

The Terradyne.

Cornelius had said they were real. That they had existed in these mountains long before men and dragons. The Harrowhorns were ancient, filled with secrets hidden in the winds and forests. Were they watching now? Hiding among the trees? Were they the reason the air itself seemed to hold its breath?

I exhaled slowly and began.

"Bella knows about Cornelius," I said, glancing at Bella, who nodded knowingly. She'd known of my secret meetings with the tortoise, though even she hadn't realized the full extent of our conversations. "I've been meeting with him. He's been training me, helping me understand my magic. And well… he's sort of this magical tortoise who appears from nowhere and teaches me magic. Well, about my magic and how to use it."

Bella didn't react, but Hunter and Cade exchanged looks. Their disbelief was subtle but present.

"You're saying a talking tortoise is your teacher?" Cade asked dryly. "And he just conveniently appeared when you needed him?"

I scowled. "Yes, and yes. He's real, I promise you, and—"

"And he knows more than any of us," Bella interrupted, arms crossed firmly. "I've seen him. I believe her."

Cade didn't argue, but I could see the gears turning in his head. He was analyzing. Calculating.

Hunter snickered, but got caught with a wicked pinch on his arm by Bella's fingernails. He covered his mouth quickly.

I pressed on. "That's not the important part anyway. What matters is what I've learned." I glanced at Cade. "What I know now."

His expression shifted, growing wary. "And what is that?"

I took a breath. "The voice in my head. The one that called me Ashlyn Moonriver. The one that's been guiding me this whole time—I know who it is."

The firelight flickered in Cade's eyes as he stared at me, waiting.

"It's a dragon," I continued. "Not just any dragon. The one

slumbering beneath the volcano behind Raven's Bane Castle. Vâllathór."

The name itself seemed to crack the air in half.

The flames wavered. The wind stirred through the trees. A distant rumble crawled through the mountains, low and deep, like a beast shifting in its sleep.

For a long moment, no one spoke.

Cade was the first to react. His brows knitted together, as if trying to piece together something that didn't quite fit. "Vâllathór," he said, tasting the name. His voice was quiet, almost reverent. "The First Dragon."

The mightiest of them all.

"She's been aiding me," I went on. "Guiding me. And she has to be awakened."

"Why?" Hunter asked, his voice level, but his grip on the pommel of his sword had tightened.

"Because if the queen is able to kill me and take my power," I hesitated, meeting Cade's eyes. "She'll drain the last of Vâllathór's power. And if that happens—"

"She'll be immortal." Cade finished the sentence for me. "Unkillable…"

Silence weighed heavy. The fire crackled, but no one said a word.

Then, Cade pressed a hand to his mouth, turning away, taking a few paces toward the edge of the mountain. His back was rigid, his shoulders tense.

I hesitated only a moment before moving to stand beside him.

The wind tugged at our hair, our clothes, carrying the cold breath of the mountains between us. We didn't speak immediately. I could almost hear his thoughts just from the way he stared out into the vast expanse of rocks and mist below.

"I know it's a lot," I said quietly.

He let out a sharp breath, shaking his head. "That's an understatement."

I studied his face, searching for... something. "Cade, this is bigger than us. The Stormscales, the mystic, Cornelius... it's all pointing to one thing. We have to stop her. You have to stop her."

He exhaled sharply through his nose. "You mean I have to take the throne."

I nodded. "You're the rightful heir. But beyond that... Allovan needs someone who can rule with strength, but also wisdom. Who can break the cycle. Who can bring peace."

A bitter laugh escaped him. "And you think I'm that person?"

"Yes," I said without hesitation.

That made him pause.

The moment stretched long, filled only with the whispers of the wind.

Then, finally, he turned back to face me, his expression unreadable. His sapphire eyes flickered over mine, searching, weighing.

"If what you've said is true..." He smirked slightly, but there was no humor in his tone. "Then you're destined to be more powerful than me."

His words felt like a shift in the world itself.

I stiffened. "Does that... does that bother you?"

For a moment, I thought it might. That the idea of me becoming something stronger, something greater, would unsettle him.

But then, to my complete surprise, his lips curled upward.

"It means I really need to teach you to ride your dragon properly," he said, crossing his arms. "If we're doing this together, you need to stop flying like a terrified squirrel."

My jaw dropped. "I do not—"

"Oh, you do," Bella chimed in from behind us. "I love you, but Cade's right."

Even Errax let out a snorting sound that was far too smug.

Cade smirked, the tension between us breaking slightly. "I'll teach you properly."

I clenched my teeth, but the challenge in his eyes had my pulse quickening. "Fine."

"Good."

The weight of everything still lingered in the air—the Stormscales, the war, the inevitable confrontation with the queen. But standing here, side by side, I realized something.

I wasn't alone in this. And neither was he.

Together, we would wake the greatest dragon in existence.

Together, we would end this war.

And gods help me—I wasn't sure what terrified me more.

THE NIGHT WAS QUIET, save for the crackling of the fire and the distant hum of the mountains. The silence in the camp was heavy with unspoken words and lingering emotions. As the others settled in for the night, Cade and I found ourselves standing awkwardly outside our shared tent.

We'd decided earlier to wait to join the Stormscales until the next day. And I admitted to myself I wouldn't mind one more night alone with the Blaze Prince…

"We should get some rest," Cade said, his voice low and slightly uncertain. Despite his attempts to hide it, I could see the exhaustion etched into his face, the pain that still lingered from his injuries.

I nodded, following him into the tent. The space was small, intimate, the air inside already warm from the nearby fire. I sat down on the bedroll, watching as Cade moved with careful deliberation, trying not to wince as he lowered himself beside me.

He looked at me, his deep blue eyes reflecting the flickering candlelight. "Ash," he began, his voice softening. "About earlier—"

"I know," I interrupted, my voice barely above a whisper. "We don't have to talk about it if you don't want to."

He reached out, his hand capturing mine, his thumb gently

tracing circles on my skin. "But I do," he said, his gaze intense. "I want to talk about it. About us."

I felt my heart flutter at the raw honesty in his voice. "Cade—"

Before I could finish, he leaned in, his lips brushing against mine softly. The kiss was tender, filled with a longing that seemed to resonate deep within me. I melted into it, my hands reaching up to tangle in his hair, pulling him closer.

His fingers trailed down my neck, sending shivers down my spine. I could feel the heat radiating from his body, the tension in every muscle as he tried to hold back his pain. He deepened the kiss, his tongue exploring mine, and I responded in kind, a soft moan escaping my lips.

He pulled away just enough to look into my eyes, his breath coming in short gasps. "Ash, I want this," he murmured, his voice hoarse with desire and pain. "I want you."

I nodded, my own breath coming in shallow pants. "Me too," I whispered, my voice barely audible.

He leaned back, his hands moving to the hem of his shirt. Slowly, carefully, he pulled it off, revealing the scars and bruises that marred his otherwise perfect torso. I reached out, my fingers lightly tracing the marks, feeling the heat of his skin beneath my touch.

He watched me, his eyes darkening with desire as I touched him. Then, he leaned in again, capturing my lips in a fierce kiss. He shifted, moving on top of me, his weight pressing me down into the bedroll. I could feel the strength in every line of his body, the need that coursed through him like a wildfire.

His hands roamed over my body, tracing the curves and valleys, each touch sending waves of sensation through me. I arched into him, my own hands exploring the planes of his back, feeling the muscles shift beneath my touch.

He broke away from my lips, trailing kisses down my neck, his breath hot against my skin. I shivered, my fingers digging into his shoulders as he moved lower, his lips trailing fire across my collarbone.

His hand moved down, sliding over my stomach, his fingers tracing the waistband of my pants. I gasped as he moved lower, his hand cupping me through the fabric, his fingers rubbing gently. Pleasure shot through me, intense and overwhelming, and I arched into his touch, a soft moan escaping my lips.

He looked up at me, his eyes dark with desire, his breath coming in ragged gasps. "Ash," he murmured, his voice thick with need.

The tent was filling with steam, the air growing thick and heavy with the heat of our bodies. I could feel the magic inside me stirring, responding to the intensity of our emotions. It was a wild, untamed force, and I struggled to keep it under control, to keep it from overwhelming me.

But it was too late.

As Cade's fingers continued to rub against me, and I felt my consciousness slipping away. The world around me blurred, the steam growing thicker, the heat more intense. I tried to hold on, to anchor myself in the moment, but it was like trying to grasp smoke.

Cade's breath hitched, and he pulled away suddenly, his body tensing as pain shot through him. He clutched his side, gasping for air as his injuries flared up, the agony etched into his features. I could see the struggle in his eyes, the battle between desire and the reality of his body's limitations.

"Cade—" I reached for him, concern flooding through me as I tried to help him sit up. But he waved me off, his face contorting in pain.

"It's okay," he rasped, trying to catch his breath. "Just... give me a moment."

I nodded, my heart pounding in my chest as I watched him struggle to regain control. The steam in the tent was dissipating, the air slowly cooling, but the intensity of the moment lingered. I could still feel the echo of his touch, the whisper of his lips on mine, but it was overshadowed by the stark reality of his pain.

As Cade sat there, his breath coming in ragged gasps, I couldn't shake the feeling of helplessness. I wanted to comfort him, to ease his pain, but I knew there was nothing I could do. The weight of our roles, our destinies, pressed down on me, making the air feel even heavier.

I couldn't stay. Not like this.

Without a word, I slipped out of the tent, leaving Cade to his battle against pain. The cool night air was a shock against my flushed skin, and I took a deep, steadying breath, trying to clear my head.

Walking a short distance from the camp, I found a small, secluded pool of water, its surface reflecting the glittering starlight. The mountains around me felt ancient and watchful, their silence almost comforting. I sat down by the pool's edge, drawing my knees to my chest.

The tears came unbidden, streaming down my cheeks as I stared at the water. The weight of everything—the war, the queen, the dragons, the imminent battle—it all crashed down on me at once. I felt so small, so insignificant in the face of it all. How could I possibly hope to stand against the Blaze Queen, to awaken Vâllathór, to change the fate of Allovan? All when I couldn't even be with the one I wanted?

I wiped at my tears, hating the weakness they represented. But I couldn't stop them. The emotions were too raw, too overwhelming. I needed this moment of vulnerability, this chance to let go of the facade of strength and bravery.

A soft rustling behind me made me turn. Errax stood at the edge of the clearing, her emerald eyes filled with concern. She lowered her massive head, nudging me gently with her snout. The gesture was so simple, so affectionate, that it brought fresh tears to my eyes.

"I'm okay," I whispered, my voice shaky. "Just... a lot to process."

Errax huffed softly, her breath warm against my skin. She lay down beside me, her body a comforting presence. I leaned against her, drawing strength from her silent support.

In the quiet of the night, with the mountains as my witness, I let the tears flow. I let the pain and the fear wash over me, knowing that I would face them again tomorrow. But for now, in this moment, I allowed myself to be weak, to be human.

Because tomorrow, I had to be more. I had to be Ashlyn Moonriver, the one destined to awaken the greatest dragon in existence, to stand against the Blaze Queen, and to bring peace to Allovan.

And I would.

For Cade, for Bella, for Hunter, for all the people who believed in me, I would face the challenges ahead. I would grow stronger, and together, we would change the fate of our world.

But for now, I cried.

CHAPTER 10

$\mathcal{W}$ater lapped gently against my skin. Cool, soothing, weightless.

Somewhere in the haze of waking, I could hear the distant rustle of leaves, the faint cawing of a bird in the canopy above. The scent of damp earth filled my nostrils, the freshness of morning dew clinging to the mountain air like a whisper.

Something nudged my shoulder.

I groaned and swatted at whatever it was, barely conscious, wanting nothing more than to drift back into the comfort of the water.

"Ash," came Bella's amused voice, a breath away from laughter. "You drowned yourself in your sleep."

I pried one eye open, peering up through strands of soaked chestnut hair to see my best friend crouched beside the pool, cross-legged with an expression torn between concern and utter exasperation.

"You good?" she asked. "Or should I start planning your burial in a puddle?"

I groaned again, sitting up slowly. "Did I seriously sleep here all night?"

"Yeah," she said with a smirk. "I was gonna yell at you for disappearing, but honestly, it checks out. You're an Aqualorian. Sleeping in water just feels right to you, I guess."

I stood from the pond-like puddle I had been lying in, shoulder deep. The realization barely registered as I wiped at my damp skin, squeezing excess water from my tunic and pants. It wasn't the first time I'd felt drawn to the water, the way its presence grounded me, soothed me. But I hadn't realized my body would just... give in to it. Being so far from the sea and Bramblebash had made me miss it. The crashing waves, the soothing seawater on my skin, the sunset above the forever stretching water.

"I needed to think," I murmured, rubbing a hand over my face. The night before came rushing back—Vâllathór, the Stormscales, the weight of what lay ahead. And Cade. I exhaled sharply. Gods, Cade.

Bella glanced at me sidelong, chewing her lip like she was debating something. "You wanna talk about it?"

I sighed, running my fingers through my tangled, damp hair. "Which part? The part where I'm supposed to wake up some ancient dragon god? Or the part where I was making out with Cade last night before we both got—?"

"Zapped?" Bella supplied with a half-smirk.

I narrowed my eyes at her. "More like... overwhelmed. And completely unable to take things any further. Again."

Bella tutted, shaking her head. "That man has got to be the single most frustrating person on this continent. Even when he's not trying to be."

"Tell me about it, *especially* when he's not trying to be," I muttered, accepting the comb she handed me as she went to work brushing out the ends of my knotted hair.

"It's—" I exhaled, frustrated. "I feel safe with him. I want him. But between the curse of our elements and the war and everything else—I don't know if we'll ever have that, Bella." I gestured vaguely. "That intimacy. That freedom."

"You will," Bella said firmly. "One way or another, you will."

I wished I could believe her.

"You two just need to figure out how to do it without igniting the sky or knocking each other unconscious." She smirked over my shoulder. "Well. Maybe Cade needs to figure that out more than you do. But your stubborn asses will find a way. I know it."

I huffed a laugh, even as my stomach twisted at the thought.

Pretty words wouldn't change the fact that every time we kissed too deeply, the magic between us threatened to break us apart.

Maybe it was a sign we were doomed.

Maybe it was a warning.

I clenched my jaw, unwilling to linger on the thought for too long. There were more pressing matters to deal with.

A sudden rustle of movement at the camp drew our attention.

Cade emerged from his tent, his steps slow, heavy.

I stiffened immediately—though for no good reason.

I wasn't expecting him to look at me, to acknowledge what had almost happened between us last night. But somehow, it cut deeper to see his usual controlled mask back in place, his regal, beautiful face, tired.

His raven-black hair was messier than usual, strands falling in wild waves around his strong jaw, his broad shoulders tense beneath the wrinkled fabric of his shirt. He looked exhausted. Weathered. Almost... angry.

At himself, maybe. Or at me.

I hated how much I wanted to smooth the tension from his brow, to run my fingers through his sleep-mussed hair and pretend we didn't have a war waiting for us just beyond these mountains.

Instead, I turned away, letting Bella detangle the last of my hair.

Hunter was already up, soaking the remains of the fire with the last of the evening's water, the rising steam murmuring through the hush of the morning. He said nothing when Cade walked over, merely nodded in greeting before muttering something I couldn't quite make out.

They spoke in low tones, their voices barely carrying over as Cade crouched beside him.

I watched them carefully, noting the way Cade's fingers curled over his injured ribs when he thought no one was looking. The way Hunter barely looked at him, as if giving him space. The quiet, unspoken understanding between them.

Bella clicked her tongue, crossing her arms. "So are you actually going to talk to him today, or are we just going to stomp around the camp pretending last night never happened?"

I shot her a glare. She grinned.

"For fuck's sake, Bella."

We got to our feet, brushing off, and made our way over before I could lose any nerve I had left.

Before I could say anything, though, Cade broke away from Hunter, straightening as we neared. His piercing eyes flickered to mine—brief, assessing, unreadable—before he spoke.

"Don't," he said simply.

I frowned. "Don't what?"

"Don't say anything." His jaw was tight, his expression unreadable. "Not right now."

I bristled. "Cade—"

He shook his head. "We have bigger things to deal with." He reached down to his belt, pulling something free.

The horn.

The ancient Stormscale horn Darren had given him.

Silence fell in the camp as the realization sank in.

Bella's breath hitched beside me. Hunter straightened, his usually relaxed stance sharpening to attention. The dragons, resting nearby, shifted their weight, wings tightening against their backs as if sensing the change in the air.

No one spoke as Cade lifted the horn to his lips.

The first note blasted through the mountains like a storm breaking the heavens.

The sound crashed down the valley, its deep, guttural cry reverberating across every stone and tree, stretching out for miles in every direction.

The dragons reacted instantly. Krakos lifted his monstrous, black-scaled head, his ember eyes narrowing before he unfurled his massive wings. Talonor rose onto his hind legs, an eerie screech escaping his throat as power coiled visibly in his limbs.

And Errax.

Beautiful, indigo-winged Errax let out a roar that sent my heart tripping over itself, her cry fierce, eager, full of purpose.

The war was coming.

The Stormscales would come for us.

And at long last… we would go to them.

THE FIRE HAD long since burned down to embers by the time Krakos stirred. And I had changed into a dry tunic, my sword fastened at my hip.

It started with a deep rumble in his chest, a low and bone-shaking sound like distant thunder. Then, without warning, the mighty black dragon rose from his place beside Cade and lifted his head sharply toward the horizon.

The other dragons followed suit. Talonor flexed his wings, shifting restlessly, his milky white eyes narrowing. Errax let out a soft growl, turning her head to the northeast. Instinctively, I stood, wiping dust from my pants, my pulse spiking. Something was coming.

Cade was already on his feet, his steely gaze cutting toward the sky. Hunter stood beside him, his usual calm demeanor tightening at the edges. Bella moved closer to me, her expression wary but not afraid.

The mists had begun to clear with the afternoon sun, burning away the morning's lingering shadows to reveal a vast stretch of sky beyond the peaks.

And on that horizon—dark dots.

Barely more than specks at first. Then larger. Closer.

Dragons.

Lots of them.

A ripple of anticipation ran through the camp. The Stormscales had answered the call.

They came in formation, silver-and-black shapes cutting through the open sky, the wind carrying the distant beat of their massive wings. Sunlight gleamed off the armor of the riders atop their backs, banners flowing behind them.

No turning back now.

The first dragon landed violently, kicking up dust and scattering loose pebbles as it touched down. Almost immediately, the others followed, creating a line of enormous, scaled beasts in the clearing.

Then, Darren dismounted.

The Stormscale commander was just as unnerving in broad daylight as he had been in the mist—towering, clad in his carved ram-horned helm, his silver-grey armor scored from countless battles. His scarred face remained half-hidden beneath his cloak, but his steel-gray eyes missed nothing.

He wasn't alone.

Beside him, a woman slid gracefully from her own dragon's back, shaking out her hair—a long cascade of blond streaked with silver. Her armor matched Darren's in color but lacked the heavy, bulky plating, clearly built for speed rather than sheer intimidation. Green emerald eyes, pale skin, rosy cheeks dotted with freckles. She looked no older than me, but war-hardened with a cold gaze sent my way.

Darren's voice was as solid as the stone beneath our feet. "Your call was heard."

Then he gestured to the woman beside him. "This is Carina. My daughter."

The contrast between the two was almost humorous.

Where Darren exuded cold calculation, Carina carried a lightness to her, a youth and wildness that reminded me of... Bella and me. Her bright mossy eyes flashing as she extended a hand.

"A pleasure," she said cheerfully.

The introduction barely finished before she went around shaking each of our hands, moving first to Hunter—whose grip remained tight but cautious—before moving onto Bella, then to me.

Her fingers were rough and calloused, the grip of a well-practiced warrior.

When she reached Cade, the easy amusement in her expression wavered slightly, replaced with something sharper, more scrutinizing. She met his gaze, waiting.

Cade didn't move to take her hand.

Instead, he simply said, "We have met."

Carina tilted her head, her smirk returning as she glanced back at him. "Yes. We have. You killed my friends."

"And you, mine," Cade growled.

She huffed a laugh. "Well, aren't you the perky sack of bones I expected you to be? I'll not be expecting any midnight banter while you're around, should I?"

Hells, I liked her already.

Cade remained stone-faced, though it was clear Hunter was watching him closely, his hands now resting on his belt near his sword.

Cade's jaw clenched, but he said nothing. Darren, to his credit, only nodded slightly, though he exchanged a meaningful glance with his daughter. "Let's be going. Get this over with. There's going to be a lot more mean glares and snide remarks where we're going."

Carina sighed. "Fine, fine. No punches thrown on day one, I guess. Besides," she added, stepping back toward her dragon, "you're coming with us, anyway. We needed to see that you meant to follow when called."

She turned her attention back to us. "You're about to get a rare invitation, you know."

Darren picked up where she left off, his expression unreadable. "The Stormscales have operated from a hidden sanctuary in the Harrowhorn Mountains for years. Very few outside our own ranks have ever seen it and lived to tell."

Cade's gaze darkened fractionally. "I'm sworn to our truce. As are you."

Darren gave a single, deliberate nod. "We want you to see where we prepare for war. Where we gather, where our dragons roost, where our people live." He met Cade's gaze evenly. "That kind of trust isn't given lightly, even now."

Cade didn't look at me, but I spoke up first. "Your secret's safe with us."

There was another pause. Then, after a long moment, Darren turned to his dragon, gripping the saddle. "Good."

And with that, he vaulted onto his beast's back.

Carina grinned and followed after, pulling herself easily up onto hers. The rest of the Stormscale riders did the same, their dragons shifting eagerly beneath them, itching for the skies.

Darren glanced over his shoulder. "Follow us."

I wasted no time.

I turned to Errax, feeling energy hum beneath my skin as I placed a hand against her shimmering scales. The wind swept through the clearing, sending the loose ends of my tunic snapping behind me as I hoisted myself into the saddle without hesitation.

Cade was only a moment behind me, securing his place on Krakos's back, his black-scaled war beast snorting smoke as he adjusted his stance.

Bella and Hunter shared a look before following suit, mounting Talonor together.

Then, the Stormscales took the lead, Darren's dragon beating its massive wings, lifting effortlessly into the air. One by one, the others followed.

Cade's voice cut through the wind. "Stay close."

"You think I wasn't going to?" I shot back.

Errax growled in excitement beneath me, her muscles tensed like drawn bowstrings.

And then—flight.

We took off after them, the world vanishing in a rush of wind and adrenaline as Errax propelled us upward. My stomach dropped, the air rushing past my face, my pulse thundering in sync with the beat of her powerful wings.

There was no feeling like this. No freedom like this.

The mountains stretched out below us, the valleys sinking into endless depths, the sky an open sea of possibility.

The Stormscales flew ahead, leading us into the unknown territory of the northeast peaks, their dragons gleaming like steel and shadow in the light.

Once again, the sky welcomed us.

And whatever lay ahead, I was ready.

CHAPTER 11

The wind roared past my ears, tugging at my hair, whipping against my cheeks. The cool rush of air filled my lungs, sharp and biting, but exhilarating all the same. My heart surged with the sheer thrill of it—of soaring on Errax's back, high above the jagged peaks of the Harrowhorns, chasing the sky.

This. This was freedom.

Below us, the mountains stretched endlessly in all directions —steep ridges, dark veins of stone carving through the mist, looming cliffs that jutted into the sky like the broken teeth of some ancient beast. The further we flew, the stranger the terrain became. The peaks here weren't like the ones I'd seen near Bramblebash. These mountains were untouched, wild—raw as something out of myth. Shadows curled across the valleys below, twisting through cliff side crevices, hiding secrets older than men.

To my right, Bella rode behind Hunter on Talonor, her blond hair whipping wildly behind her. The two of them kept a tight formation, Hunter's grip on the reins firm as the storm-gray dragon cut through the winds. Ahead of them, Cade and Krakos led the way, the Blaze Prince a dark, commanding figure against the bright sky. His black dragon sliced through the air effortlessly —his movements precise, calculated. And despite my irritation at him—at everything between us—I couldn't deny it.

Cade wasn't just a great rider.

He was the best.

And I wanted to learn. Gods, I wanted to learn.

A lesson from him on dragon riding was a dangerous promise —one filled with tension and unspoken things neither of us had figured out yet. But I had to push that aside. For now, I focused on the joy thrumming in my veins, keeping pace with the Stormscales as they led us deeper into unfamiliar lands.

I leaned forward, pressing my palm against Errax's back. "Faster, girl," I murmured. She responded instantly, her powerful muscles bunching as she surged forward, closing some of the distance between us and Cade.

Cade glanced back at me, eyes flickering with something unreadable before he turned his focus ahead.

Fine. He could ignore me all he wanted. But he would train me—whether he liked it or not.

The Harrowhorns grew steeper beneath us, the mountains sharpening, their sheer cliffs more treacherous than before. The mist thickened in some places, swirling through the rocks like a living thing. A strange quiet settled over the range now—no birds, no signs of life below. It was as if we had entered a forgotten land, one where nothing human had walked in centuries.

And then, ahead, nestled at the base of one of the highest peaks we had seen yet—a stronghold.

The Stormscale encampment spread across a massive clearing, halfway up the mountain's face, partially concealed by the natural rock formations. Over a hundred dwellings clustered together, their roofs camouflaged beneath massive tarps the same color as the surrounding stone. Dragons perched along ledges, their dark forms blending into the cliffs, while others prowled the clearing, their long tails shifting through the dirt. Warriors milled about, sharpening weapons, tending to mounts, moving with the quiet efficiency of seasoned fighters.

As we descended, the first thing I noticed was the silence.

The camp had been bustling a moment ago, but now—every single Stormscale had stopped, their attention locked on us.

No—on me.

A heavy lump formed in my throat, my excitement sputtering into nervous anticipation.

By Odiun—they were all watching me.

I swallowed hard, gripping the reins tighter as Errax's wings flared, preparing for landing.

The Stormscales weren't just curious about us—they were judging us. Judging me.

Cade stiffened in his saddle just ahead, his grip on Krakos ironclad as the black dragon landed first. His every muscle was strung tight, his back rigid. He knew this feeling all too well— years of being scrutinized, of walking into a room and having every set of eyes turn his way, not with admiration, but with suspicion.

For once, though, all those sharp stares shifted away from him.

Toward me.

I felt the weight of it settle on my shoulders as Errax touched down, her claws digging into the packed dirt. Around us, the gathering of Stormscales held their breath, waiting.

Darren dismounted first.

"Welcome," he said, his gravelly voice carrying across the clearing. His steel-gray eyes swept over us, lingering only a moment longer on Cade before turning to the crowd.

The tension was thick enough to slice with an ax.

Cade swung down from Krakos, landing with practiced ease, but his body was taut—coiled like a storm ready to break. I could see it in the way his hands twitched near his weapons, the set of his jaw, the barely-contained flickers of fire curling at the edges of his fingertips.

But even as some of the Stormscales tightened their grips on their own weapons at the sight of him, their gazes inevitably drifted back—to me.

I forced myself to breathe as I slid from Errax's back. Her warm scales hummed beneath my hands as she pressed her nose into my shoulder in reassurance.

Darren stepped forward, his gaze pinning me in place.

"This is Ashlyn Mist," he announced, loud enough for every gathered warrior to hear. "The Gold-Marked."

A ripple spread through the crowd at the words. Some expressions turned wary, others awed, a few skeptical.

I squared my shoulders, meeting Darren's gaze.

He gestured broadly. "And from this day forward," he continued, "she and her companions are counted among us. Storm-scales. Rebels fighting together to save this world."

A murmur swept through the warriors, brief but potent.

Carina grinned, utterly pleased with herself. "Well, that went better than expected," she muttered to me under her breath.

Cade folded his arms tightly across his chest, his expression unreadable as he surveyed the gathered warriors. I could feel something simmering beneath his skin, though, something unspoken.

He wasn't uneasy about the attention on him, and as he gazed at me with those perfect eyes, I felt the weight of all attention on me. And the mutterings that spread through the crowd, they were about *me*...

A shiver ran up from my toes to the tip top of my head, causing every hair on my skin to straighten.

I wasn't just an outsider here. I was something unknown. A risk.

Carina clapped her hands together. "Well then!" she declared, breaking the tension. "Now that the posturing is settled—shall we?"

Darren gave a slow nod. "Carina will show you the camp. You are free to roam. You are one of us now."

With that final decree, the warriors dispersed, but not without stealing one last look at me.

I exhaled quietly, pressing a steadying hand to Errax's warm scales.

I was used to being hunted. Feared, even.

But being expected to lead?

That, I wasn't sure how to handle.

Carina wasted no time once the crowd had dispersed, shaking out her silver-streaked blond hair, stretching her arms casually like she hadn't just walked us into a nest of warriors who may or may not want to see us dead.

"Well, I'd say that went better than expected," she repeated, grinning at me before glancing sideways at Cade. "And here I thought it was you they'd be most likely to kill on sight."

Cade glowered at her, but she either didn't notice or didn't care. Probably the latter. I liked her already.

"Come on, let's not linger here looking awkward," she said, gesturing for us to follow. "I'll show you the camp, let you get a feel for the place before tonight's feast."

I exhaled slowly, forcing the tension from my muscles, falling into step behind her alongside Bella. Cade and Hunter walked a half-step behind, and I could practically feel Cade's irritation simmering in the air. If he had his way, we'd be flying out in the middle of the night instead of settling in here. But he knew as well as I did—we needed them. The Stormscales, their defenses, their warriors.

We weren't winning this war alone.

The deeper into the camp we walked, the more natural it felt —despite the lingering glances from passing Stormscale soldiers who clearly weren't sure what to make of us yet. The mountain stronghold was built for endurance, for survival. No fancy castles or embellished ruins, just practical, sturdy dwellings reinforced with wooden beams, slabs of stone, and large tarps blended in with the environment. Clever—most of the camp could be mistaken for just another part of the mountain if seen from above.

Stormscale riders moved everywhere, tending to wounded dragons with steady hands, hammering out weapons at an open forge, reinforcing armor. Farmers worked small patches of land between the barracks on terraces of carefully cultivated soil, growing hardy mountain crops—root vegetables, medicinal herbs, hardy grains.

"It's self-sufficient," I noted aloud, impressed despite myself. "They flew up soil with the dragons. Smart..."

Carina nodded. "Has to be. Supplies don't come easy up here —we can't exactly ride down to the nearest seaside market. Everything we need, we grow, hunt, or forge ourselves."

"That means food is going to taste better here than it has on the road," Bella added brightly. "Actual meals. I could cry."

"You're in for a treat, then," Carina said, smirking. "Our cooks —make a mean spiced venison stew. If you're lucky, he might actually like you enough to give you a second helping."

"Normally I'd expect a dash of poison..." Hunter deadpanned.

Carina only grinned. "Definitely not. Our cooks are more of a stab-you-with-a-cooking-knife type."

A sharp whistle rang through the air, and we looked up to see a row of dragons perched on high stone ledges, great golden-yellow eyes tracking us from above. Not a single one of them looked pleased.

Krakos, Errax, and Talonor had parked themselves at the edge of the camp, clearly unwilling to mingle with the Stormscale dragons. Krakos had his wings partially flared, his red eyes searing into a particularly large silver-scaled brute eyeing him from atop the barracks.

"He doesn't like them," I said, nodding toward Cade's dragon.

Carina snorted. "Not surprising. Our kind have been at war with Emberveil for decades. You think the dragons don't know that?" She tapped her temple. "They're bonded deeper than we are. They remember things longer than we do—they inherit old grudges from those who came before them. Your dragon remembers ours. A testament to the bonds we carry with our dragons. They will respect our truce—despite their primal hatred."

Errax, though, was quieter in her displeasure. She'd known no war with the Stormscale dragons. She tucked her powerful blue wings tighter against herself, but I could feel her unease thrumming in my bones, our connection sparking with tension.

Carina shrugged. "They'll get used to it. Or they'll try to rip each other's throats out. Should be fun to watch either way."

I wasn't sure if she was joking.

"Welcome to Storm's End." She kept leading us deeper into the heart of the Stormscale stronghold, eventually stopping at the mouth of a cavern carved into the side of the mountain. "This," she declared, "is the escape route. Or, y'know, where we shove the dragons when things get nasty."

Storm's End? I like it.

The cavern stretched deep into the mountain, wide enough that even Krakos, largest of all the dragons here, could probably squeeze through if necessary. Damp, cold air seeped from within, the promise of dark tunnels stretching into unknown depths. Good to know they had a backup plan if the Blaze Queen ever decided to bring the fight here.

Carina led us further inside just long enough for us to glimpse sleeping chambers dug into the rock—narrow alcoves with straw mats and fire pits. Enough to house a few hundred Stormscale riders, at least.

"This is where our dragons den when they're not out hunting or training," she explained. "Safest spot in the whole camp. No prying eyes, no easy access for spies."

I shuddered at the word spies. Were they worried about the queen? Or about us?

Once the tour was over, Carina took us to a separate structure on the outskirts of the camp. "These are your quarters," she said, nodding toward the stone-and-wood building. "Figured keeping you lot separate from the barracks was probably wise. Less risk of someone sticking a dagger where it doesn't belong in the middle of the night."

Reassuring.

Inside the quarters, I was surprised to see beds—real beds— with thick wool blankets. Small chests sat at the foot of each, and hanging on the walls were weapons racks and armor stands.

Carina strode to the center, grabbing a bundle from one of the racks. "For you," she said, tossing something at me.

I caught it against my chest, unfolding the weight of it in my arms.

Armor.

Not Stormscale steel—no black-and-silver sigils. This was dark gold, polished yet sturdy, reinforced with fine leather straps, emblazoned with a crest of a golden dragon curling over the breastplate.

Bella received one too, her fingers running over the smooth plating. "Not exactly standard issue," she mused.

Carina smirked. "Symbolic," she corrected. "You're not Storm-scales, not officially. That doesn't mean you don't belong here."

Something shifted in my chest, something uncertain and warm.

"Tonight's feast is important," Carina continued, eyes flicking back to me and Cade. "They'll want to hear you both speak. To know why you're here. What you fight for."

Cade remained stone-faced. I, on the other hand, swallowed down immediate panic.

All I'd wanted was to fly. To earn my place through strength alone. Not through words, not through titles.

I was just some girl from Bramblebash. A former slave. Who was I to stand in front of them all and speak like I was someone that mattered?

But I had no choice.

Carina grinned. "You'll be fine. Just don't pick a fight before dinner."

She shot that last part directly at Cade.

He didn't dignify it with a response.

As the others settled into the quarters, Cade didn't speak to me until everyone had wandered off, giving us a rare moment alone.

I was still staring at the armor when he approached, voice low.

"After the feast," he said simply, "we start your flying lessons."

I looked up sharply, breath caught.

A quiet thrill rippled through me, all nerves about the feast immediately forgotten.

Finally.

CHAPTER 12

The Stormscale hideout, Storm's End, felt like a world apart from anything I'd ever known. It wasn't the way the air carried the rich scent of earth and fire, or how the houses —simple structures of timber, straw, and clay—stood resilient against the whipping mountain winds. No, what unsettled me the most was the hum of life here. Warriors sharpening blades, mending armor, tending to their wounded—yes, that I expected. But families? Children darting between the buildings, laughing and shrieking in play? That was something I hadn't anticipated.

It made this place feel… real. More than just another war camp. The Stormscales weren't just an army; they were people. Survivors.

The knowledge pressed against my ribs with a strange weight, making it harder to brace myself against my usual instinct to keep my guard up. These were supposed to be Cade's enemies. Yet here we were, walking amongst them freely, our dragons resting beside theirs, about to sit at their tables, drink their wine. This should've felt wrong. Instead, it felt unsettlingly normal.

Bella didn't seem to struggle with it nearly as much.

"Come on, Ash!" she called, already half out the door of our assigned bunkhouse. "I refuse to sit here and suffocate in the tension while there's an entire city to explore!"

Cade—of course—looked like he'd rather slit his own throat than go wandering through enemy territory, but one sharp look from Bella, and I was already rushing after her, leaving him to grumble and scowl as he trailed behind.

Hunter smirked as he followed us out, clearly entertained by the idea of watching Cade suffer through what he undoubtedly considered a pointless excursion.

Outside, the settlement stretched in a mess of winding paths and interconnected spaces, leading us straight into what could only be described as a market—though nothing like the lively, chaotic stalls of Bramblebash. Here, the air smelled of warm bread and dry herbs, of freshly tilled soil and roasting meat.

Stormscale farmers moved between stalls with quiet efficiency, their hands worn and calloused from labor. Tables displayed baskets of root vegetables—thick-skinned potatoes, sturdy carrots, bundles of strange leafy greens I didn't recognize. Jars of preserved fruits lined wooden planks, and further down, a woman baked flatbread over a stone fire, the scent making my stomach grumble.

But it was the sweets that caught my attention.

Bella gasped beside me, wide-eyed as she grabbed my arm and practically dragged me toward one of the tables. "Is that—? It is!"

Dark, rich blocks of chocolate, neatly stacked beside dried nuts and honeyed figs.

"Do you think they're for sale?" I whispered.

"Only one way to find out," Bella grinned, flashing her most charming smile at the vendor—a woman well past her elder years, with storm-gray eyes and hair as pale as ash tied back beneath a cloth. Her hands were steady as she wrapped pieces of chocolate in waxed paper, shifting her gaze toward us with a measured patience.

"We'd love to buy some," Bella said, glancing at me.

Cade—still hovering behind us like a miserable shadow—huffed impatiently, fishing out a few silver coins from his own pouch and placing them on the table.

The old woman glanced at them, then at Cade, then up at us both before shaking her head.

"We don't take coin here," she said simply, though her voice held no malice. "We are a community. Everyone gives what they can. Takes only what they need. Any coin we throw into a collection to buy things from the outside world."

That caught me off guard. I glanced back at Cade, whose expression remained carefully unreadable, though I could see the shift in his glare—the way he took in the woman's lined face, the quiet strength anchored in her weary eyes.

She had seen war. Lived it. And here, in this place, she had built something that did not need rulers or gold dictating who deserved to eat.

"Then what can we offer in exchange?" I asked.

The woman appraised me, gaze flickering to the sword strapped at my hip. "You fight for us," she said, as though it was already decided. "That is enough."

I wanted to tell her I fought for more than the Stormscales. That my war was with the queen, not her people. But now wasn't the time.

Instead, I nodded.

She handed each of us a small wrapped piece of chocolate. "Whatever happens," she murmured, meeting my gaze, "you'll be glad you tasted something sweet before the storm breaks."

A strange shiver traced my spine.

We moved on, winding further into the settlement, nodding at passing villagers. People watched us, some openly wary, others merely curious.

A group of children ran shrieking past us, caught in some wild chase of their own making. One—a girl no older than six, with chestnut curls and bright brown eyes—stumbled in her enthusiasm, tripping over her own legs and tumbling down to her knees.

She stared up at me, wide-eyed, and suddenly, the weight in my chest became unbearable.

She was me.

Too small. Too thin. Looking up at the world with a mixture of wonder and fear she probably didn't even understand yet.

I knelt down, reaching for her hands, helping her up as gently as I could. She barely even winced at the scraped knee, though her cheeks burned with embarrassment.

"You alright?" I asked softly.

She nodded quickly, swallowing hard.

"You're beautiful," I told her.

She blinked, startled.

I smiled, brushing off the dust clinging to her clothes before rising back to my feet, giving her space to run back to her friends.

Cade had gone silent behind me. So had Bella.

But I didn't turn back to them.

I just kept walking.

Because if I did look back, I might see that girl again.

And I might remember how long it had taken for someone to finally say those words to me.

By the time we reached the dragon caves, I was grateful for the distraction.

Unfortunately, the distraction turned out to be frustrating as hell.

"Sorry," one of the Stormscale guards said, crossing his arms over his broad chest. "No outsiders beyond this point."

Cade narrowed his eyes. "We are your allies."

"Aye," the guard answered, entirely unfazed. "And we're keeping you alive by following that rule."

I could feel the tension rising beside me—Cade's temper barely leashed, Hunter's irritation creeping into his stance.

But before the argument could escalate into a full-blown fight, Bella—ever the peacemaker—stepped between them, hands raised in surrender. "Fine! No cave-cruising today. Let's just check on our own dragons and be done with it."

That, at least, was allowed.

Though amusingly, none of the Stormscale attendants seemed keen on approaching Errax, Krakos, or Talonor.

"They're frightened of them," I whispered to Bella, barely suppressing a laugh as one particularly nervous-looking stable hand nearly dropped his entire bucket of water when Krakos so much as moved.

"Can't imagine why," Bella deadpanned. "It's not like they're enormous fire-breathing dragons that have been their cold-blooded enemies up until now."

Cade rolled his eyes but said nothing as we approached our mounts, murmuring soft reassurances to them as we checked their wings and claws. They'd survived plenty of battles already, but it still felt necessary—to remind them we were here, together.

By the time we finished, dusk had begun setting in, stretching golden light across the roofs of the Stormscale hideout.

"We should clean up," Hunter said, stretching his shoulders. "Try to look slightly less like we've been rolling through blood and ash before this feast."

I gave Cade a pointed glance. "You included."

He smirked. "Worried about me making a bad impression?"

"Always," I shot back.

But I was distracting myself. Because the feast wasn't what scared me.

It was everything that came after.

THE CANDLELIGHT FLICKERED around the room, casting warm golden hues against the rough stone walls. The small chamber smelled of fresh linen and the lingering scent of lavender soap—clean, soft, unfamiliar.

For the first time in weeks, I felt human again.

Bella sat on the edge of her bed, leaning forward as I carefully ran my fingers through her damp hair, working through the knots. She sighed in bliss, stretching like a contented cat beneath my touch. "If nothing else, this might make the entire miserable war worth it."

I laughed softly, shaking my head as I combed through another section. "All it took was a decent bath?"

"That and these beds," she groaned, flopping backward dramatically and inhaling deeply. "Gods, Ash, I forgot what soft sheets felt like."

I smiled, reaching for a ribbon to tie her hair back. My own locks were still damp, curling slightly from the wash. I'd changed into fresh clothes—simple, comfortable fabric worn soft with use—but I still felt out of place. Too clean. Too unburdened. It clashed with everything we'd endured to get here.

Hunter sat across the room, reclined against his bedroll with a book in hand—one we'd found in the bunkhouse when we arrived. I didn't know how he could focus on reading now, of all times, but his steady presence was comforting in its own way. When the world was chaos, Hunter remained immovable as stone.

Cade hadn't moved in hours.

He lay on one of the cots, his broad chest rising and falling in the slow, even rhythm of sleep. Rest was rare for him—I knew that better than anyone. His body was riddled with healing wounds, and exhaustion clung to him like a second skin. Even now, in sleep, his brow furrowed like whatever dreams had found him weren't particularly kind.

I studied him for a moment, my hands stilling against Bella's hair.

The way the candlelight carved sharp shadows across his

cheekbones, the way his dark lashes stood stark against the tanned skin beneath his tired eyes.

Warmth pooled in my stomach before I yanked my gaze away.

I didn't have time to entertain whatever this was.

A knock sounded at the door, making Bella jerk upright.

Carina stood in the doorway, arms crossed, her blonde-silver hair gleaming faintly in the candlelight. "It's time," she said.

Bella sighed in disappointment—a final moment of peace shattered. "And here I was hoping they'd forget about us."

Carina smirked, stepping fully into the bunkhouse. "You've got a few more minutes to get ready, but I'd suggest you," her green eyes flicked toward me, "think about wearing the armor."

I frowned, glancing at the neatly arranged gold-plated armor resting on the chair beside my cot. "For a feast?"

Carina nodded. "You're a symbol, Ash. Whether you like it or not."

That was the second time today someone had implied that.

I exhaled slowly, realizing it wasn't a request—it was an expectation. A test.

Behind me, Cade stirred, groaning slightly as he pushed himself upright. My breath caught as his sapphire eyes landed on me, taking in the fresh clothes, my damp hair, and—of course—Carina standing there waiting.

Without thinking, he reached out, wrapping an arm around my waist, pulling me toward him. The heat of his body seeped into mine, warm and grounding, resting his forehead lightly against my shoulder.

He didn't say anything. Neither did I.

But something settled between us at that moment—an understanding. A silent exchange of promises and regrets.

Then, just as quickly, he released me with a quiet sigh.

"Let's go," he muttered, standing stiffly as he rubbed the last remnants of sleep from his face.

I forced myself to move, to set aside whatever that moment had just been, and reached for the armor.

It fit snugly, secured at the waist with dark leather straps, the dragon insignia glinting faintly beneath the candlelight. It suited me in a way I wasn't prepared for.

I wasn't a soldier.

But I was something else.

THE HALL WAS the largest structure in the Stormscale hideout, built at the foot of the caves, its entrance marked by carved stone pillars bearing the sigils of old wars. It served many purposes—war room, gathering place, and, apparently, a temple to Odiun.

They were already seated when we entered, the low hum of conversation fading as eyes turned to us.

The silence pressed against my skull.

Hundreds of warriors, elders, families—all watching the outsiders walk in.

Carina led the way, bringing us up toward the head table where her father, Darren, sat waiting. The elders flanked his sides, hard-faced and sharp-eyed. Cade's shoulders tensed beside me, his expression unreadable, but I could feel it—the way his body went utterly still.

He recognized them.

Soldiers he'd fought against. Men who had tried to kill him.

And now, they were supposed to eat at the same table.

Tentative alliances never sat comfortably on Cade Phoenixfire.

We took our seats. I glanced down the long wooden table—roasted meats, fresh bread, bowls of root vegetables. Enough to feed an army.

The weight of everything—the expectation, the war staining this room like a lingering ghost—curled in my lungs.

Darren stood, the room drawing quiet in unison.

His gravelly voice filled the space with ease. "We are here tonight not as enemies, but as allies. As warriors standing on the precipice of the greatest battle Allovan has ever known. And before we march to war, we will share our tables with those willing to fight beside us."

Murmurs hummed through the gathering.

Darren's gaze settled on Cade.

Carina rose next, sweeping a hand toward where he sat. "Cade Phoenixfire." The name alone sent ripples through the hall. Tension, recognition. "A name every single one of you knows. A name many have cursed. Many have fought against."

Cade didn't flinch.

She smiled faintly, clasping her hands behind her back. "But he's here—in Bracken Burr Hall. And if anyone knows the queen's mind, it's him."

The hall shifted, waiting.

Cade pushed back his chair and stood.

He scanned the faces in the crowd with the quiet authority of someone born into their station.

"I know what you think of me," he said, voice calm, unwavering. "And you wouldn't be wrong. For years, we have been at war, and I have fought against you on the battlefield."

The words alone were enough to make some hands twitch toward weapons.

"But the time has come to put that aside."

The murmurs stilled.

He exhaled slowly, pressing his palms flat against the table before him. "My stepmother does not want an empire," he continued. "She wants eternity. A world where only she rules. Where there is no future—only her endless tyranny."

He stood taller, steel in every inch of his being. "This moment is our chance to stop her. Our best chance. Our last chance."

Silence wrapped tighter around the room.

"I have spent my entire life on the battlefield," he finished, his voice quieter, weightier. "And I am tired of war. I want peace. And I hope… that you do too. I took a vow. I, and your general, Darrin Iconnas, have agreed to work together, to fight together, and die together to make this world what it needs to become. Peace, unity, and love is what this world was meant for, and with that said, I make a vow to you, that I will push aside my hatred, my fury, and my vengeance, so that we may create this new world… together."

The words sat heavy in the hall before Darren gave a single nod.

Cade met his eye, then sat.

And then Carina turned to me.

I hadn't even realized I was gripping the edges of my armor, my knuckles white against the gold plating.

She smiled. "This is Ash Mist. You may not recognize her like you do the infamous Blaze Prince, but you have surely heard the tale of her short rise. She is the Gold-Marked. She is the one destined to help us defeat Queen Mortriana Vissex and end her bloody reign of death."

Still using my orphan slave name. I'd already almost forgotten, but was also quite sure I never truly would.

The shift in the hall was immediate.

This crowd—these warriors, these survivors—had been waiting for me to speak.

A cold knot coiled in my stomach. I had never spoken before an assembly like this. Never commanded a room.

But even as I swallowed down my nerves and stood, I caught sight of someone across the hall.

A flash of chestnut curls.

The girl from earlier.

And just like that, I knew what I had to say.

I took a breath.

"Weeks ago, I was a slave," I started, my voice steady. "I lived in chains. Owned nothing—not even my name."

The room stiffened.

I clenched my hands at my sides. "But here I stand now, before you, brimming with something I never thought I'd have—hope."

A beat of silence.

"The world is changing," I continued, my voice growing stronger. "And if we want to stand a chance at a better, brighter future, we have to change with it."

I found the girl's eye and smiled.

"I'm not your hero," I told them. "I don't feel like the one prophesied to stop the queen. But I am ready to fight. Because fighting is all I've ever known. I may not be what you expected. I can barely lift a hundred pounds, but what I lack in size and strength, I hope to make up for with spirit." Gathering Eden, I let the Gilded Radiance pour through me and unleashed a golden pillar of light fly to the center top of the hall, causing the spell to swirl around the glass chandelier then rested there. All eyes widened at the spectacle as the golden, sparkling, dazzling spell spun into a magnificent, radiant disc before fizzling off into the air. Only gasps were left as the spell died away.

I let the words settle, staring down at my wrists still marred with the scars of shackles, then exhaled, slowly lowering myself back into my seat.

The silence stretched. Many were left staring up at the ceiling where the spell had been, perhaps their first and only glimpse of magic… ever.

And then, like a great tide finally breaking against stone, they rose.

The entire hall erupted in applause.

It wasn't just clapping—it was the stomping of boots against the ground, the pounding of fists against the heavy wooden tables, the voices raised in a wordless roar of approval. The sound filled the space, rattling through me, shaking my very bones.

I hadn't realized I was holding my breath until I exhaled sharply, feeling the weight of a hundred gazes lifting in a single breath.

Relief washed over me in a slow, dizzying wave. I'd done it. I'd spoken. And they had listened.

Beside me, Bella beamed, her eyes alight with something fierce, something proud. Hunter nodded subtly, the flicker of a smirk at the corner of his mouth. Even Carina gave me an approving look, eyes twinkling with something like mirth.

But most of all, I felt Cade beside me—silent, still, watching. His oceanic blue eyes burned with something unreadable as he studied me, as if seeing me—truly seeing me—for the first time.

I forced myself to look forward again, to steady myself against the whirlwind of emotions threatening to swallow me whole.

Darren stood once more, waiting for the raging applause to settle before he lifted his hands.

"We dine with old enemies, and new allies," he declared, his gravelly tone carrying over the raucous crowd. "Tomorrow, we prepare for war. But tonight..." He gestured toward the feasts laid before us, the heavy platters of roasted game and spiced vegetables, the jugs of rich red wine glistening in the firelight. "Tonight, we drink. We eat. We remember what it is we fight for."

A deafening cheer answered him. And then, like a river breaking free, the feast truly began.

Food was passed down the tables in great baskets and iron pots, warm bread torn and shared, steaming meat piled onto wooden plates. The scent of spiced stews and seared venison filled the air, mixing with the smoky heat of burning torches along the walls. Wine splashed into tankards, laughter rang through the gathering hall, and for the first time since arriving at the Storm's End, I felt the edges of tension begin to ease.

Bella wasted no time piling her plate high, grinning like a

child on a festival day. I wasn't surprised. Food had been nothing more than dried meat and rationed bread for weeks—we hadn't had a proper meal in ages.

Even Cade took a sip from his cup, though he remained quiet, his movements more measured than before. I could tell he wasn't fully relaxed—not yet.

One dinner wasn't enough to undo years of bloodshed between the Stormscales and the Blaze Prince. But it was a start.

I reached for a piece of flatbread, still warm from the hearth, watching as Carina leaned forward on her elbows, surveying me over her own plate.

"You weren't lying," she said, a wry smile tugging at her lips.

I arched a brow. "About what?"

She tore off a piece of her bread, dipping it into the thick stew at the center of the table. "You don't want to be a hero."

I chewed slowly, thinking. "I don't."

Her gaze was shrewd. "That's good," she mused. "Heroes die first."

Cade, who had been silent until now, made a low, disapproving sound under his breath, but Carina only smirked at him before shifting her attention back to me.

"Still," she continued, "you've got them looking at you like you're the second coming of Odiun himself."

I saw what she meant.

Across the hall, from the clusters of soldiers and elders exchanging hushed words, to the hands raising glasses in our direction—there was a shift, subtle but undeniable. A weight to their glances. A quiet expectation.

It unsettled me.

I wasn't their savior. I wasn't a warrior born, a trained knight, a chosen one destined to fulfill some grand prophecy. I was just a girl still learning the edges of her own power. A girl trying to survive.

But survival had brought me here, and now... they were looking at me like I could be more than that.

I set my cup down carefully, feeling the thread of unease coil tight in my stomach.

Out of the corner of my eye, I caught a glimpse of movement —a small figure hurrying through the hall, weaving between tables, her steps hesitant, nervous.

The same little girl as before.

She lingered near the edges of the feasting crowd, her small fingers twisting in the hem of her tunic. The moment our eyes met, she froze.

For a second, I thought she might turn and flee.

But then, timidly, she stepped forward.

The hall carried on around us, unaware of the gravity of this singular moment, of the way my hands went still against the rim of my plate as the child reached me, close enough now that I could see the dust smeared across her knees from where she had fallen earlier.

My heart clenched.

"Here," she said softly, barely above a whisper.

Cade stiffened beside me as the girl reached up, pressing something into my palm.

A small, woven charm.

Handmade. Threaded finely with copper wire, the kind Stormscale children likely fashioned as festival trinkets.

A little dragon, carefully shaped, carefully given.

I swallowed thickly.

"For luck," she told me, shifting on tiny feet. "Before you fight the bad queen."

Gods.

I curled my fingers around the charm, forcing down the way my throat burned.

"Thank you," I murmured, meaning it with every part of me. "What's your name?"

"Haley," she said, like an angel had dropped from heaven and was smiling right before me.

"That's a pretty name." I smiled wide down at her.

She hesitated for only a moment before beaming, cheeks reddening, before turning and hurrying back into the crowd.

My pulse thundered as I watched her go.

This is real.

This is happening.

Whatever happened next, this war belonged to me now. To all of us.

I felt Cade's gaze on me—steady, unreadable.

I didn't look at him. I Couldn't. The weight of everything was pressing into my ribs.

The feast resumed around us with the ease of battle-worn soldiers who knew the importance of taking joy where they could. But I barely tasted the food after that.

The expectations in this room had shifted. I had known, stepping into this alliance, that I would fight the queen.

But now, I wasn't just a soldier in this war.

I was a symbol.

Odiun help me.

Cade barely made it three steps past the threshold of the great hall before I was grabbing onto the thick sleeve of his tunic, yanking on it like a child desperate for sweets.

"Come on, come on, come on," I whined, tugging harder when he didn't immediately answer.

He turned, raising one dark brow, the torchlight from the hall entrance casting sharp shadows across his perfectly brooding features. "Ash," he drawled, the hint of amusement in his voice betraying his otherwise irritated expression.

I grinned up at him, still clinging to his sleeve. "You promised."

"I don't recall promising anything."

"You did." Another sharp tug. "You said you'd train me."

"I said after the feast," he corrected. "That was the feast. Training comes later." A great snarky grin crept across his deathly handsome face.

"This is later," I argued, determined. "It's not my fault you move slower than an old horse and took your sweet time eating."

He exhaled through his nose, dragging a hand through his

raven-black hair before looking skyward, as if praying for patience. "Ash."

"Cade." I mimicked his tone perfectly, eyes wide, unrelenting. "Come on."

God, I wanted him. Even when he was being a cheeky brat bully. But right then all I wanted was something fire-breathing and scaly between my legs.

With a long-suffering sigh, he shook his head. "Fine."

Yes.

Bella, who had been trailing close behind with Hunter, sighed dramatically. "Must you antagonize him at every turn?"

"She must," Hunter answered for me, smirking. "It's become part of her charm."

"I don't antagonize him," I said primly, linking my arm through Cade's just to be a menace. "We are having a very normal, very productive training arrangement."

Cade shot me a look that clearly contradicted that statement. But he didn't shove me off.

As we made our way toward the dragons, I heard Bella mutter something about stretching her legs, glancing around the Storm-scale camp curiously. She had been watching the people all night, and while I'd been too preoccupied to think about why, it didn't surprise me when she finally blurted out, "I think I'd rather stay here. Walk around. Meet people."

She bit the inside of her cheek, shifting in place before glancing at Hunter. "You'll stay?"

Hunter nodded without hesitation. "Of course."

That was enough for her.

"Alright," I said, deciding not to pry—not yet. "We'll be back before dawn."

"Unless you fall off your dragon," Hunter added helpfully.

I narrowed my eyes.

But I didn't have time to argue, because Errax's high-pitched screech echoed over the clearing, scattering a few of the Stormscales who had been attempting—poorly—to strap a saddle onto her back.

One of them had barely dodged her snapping maw, staggering back on wobbling legs. "Gods, this beast is vicious," he swore, rubbing his forehead where sweat had gathered.

I had to bite back a laugh.

"She doesn't like strangers touching her," I said, brushing past them toward my dragon. "Especially not ones scared out of their minds."

Cade was already ahead of me, plucking the saddle from one of the unfortunate riders with an exasperated shake of his head. "Here," he said, handing it to me.

I grinned, taking the straps in my hands.

The saddle was well-crafted, lighter than it looked, designed to mold against the ridges of Errax's muscular frame without restricting her movements. I ran my fingers along the thick leather before giving my dragon a reassuring stroke down the length of her sleek neck.

"Easy, girl," I murmured. "I'll do it myself."

Errax rumbled, shifting her weight as I worked, her tail flicking in quick, impatient motions as I fastened the first set of straps. Her massive indigo wings twitched, lifting slightly with anticipation for what was to come.

Cade worked beside me in silence, securing the front fastenings without complaint. He was precise, steady—the way he did everything. In battle, in speech, in training. It was strange, seeing that same intensity applied to something as simple as fastening a saddle.

When he was done, he gave the straps a final check, then stepped back, surveying our work.

"You ready?" he asked, tilting his head.

I shot him a reckless grin. "Born ready."

And before he could say anything else, I grabbed onto the

saddle and pulled myself up, settling into the seat in one smooth motion.

The moment I was astride Errax's back, a rush of exhilaration went through me. She adjusted beneath me, spreading her wings ever so slightly, and from up here, everything felt... different. More alive.

I looked down at Cade. "Well?"

His expression was unreadable at first—until he smirked. "Not bad."

A spark of pride flickered in my chest.

He turned, checking Krakos's straps before swinging atop his own dragon with practiced ease. The ebony war beast shifted, nostrils flaring, eager for command.

Cade shot me a look through the dark. "Like you said," he murmured. "You don't always get to pick when you go to war."

And with that, Krakos launched into the sky.

I barely had time to react before Errax followed—her powerful muscles rippling beneath me as she kicked off the ground, her massive indigo wings slicing through the night air.

The sensation knocked the breath from my lungs.

I gripped the reins but barely held back a laugh as the wind rushed around me, cold and electric and endless. The camp below blurred into streaks of firelit gold, the mountains sprawling out like ink-black waves rolling toward an unseen horizon.

I was flying.

Not clinging onto Cade's back. Not just a passenger.

I was soaring.

And gods, if this wasn't the greatest feeling in the world.

Cade flew slightly ahead of me, his dark silhouette a commanding presence even against the vast stretch of open sky. The stars reflected in his glacier-blue eyes as he turned, watching me effortlessly steer Errax alongside him.

"Slow your pace," he called over the wind. "Let her lead, not your reins."

"Easy for you to say," I shot back. "You've had years of practice."

He smirked.

I adjusted my grip, loosening slightly, and immediately felt the shift—Errax moved smoother beneath me when I let her take more control, when I trusted her instincts to guide us through the air.

Cade watched with quiet approval before nodding.

"Not bad," he admitted. "For a beginner."

I rolled my eyes but couldn't hide my grin.

The night swallowed us whole as we climbed higher, past the jagged teeth of the Harrowhorns, breaking into a realm where only dragons and fools dared to tread.

I had never felt more alive.

And this was only the beginning.

The moment Errax's wings cut through the clouds, we were in another world.

The silver glow of the crescent moon bathed the sky in a haunting shimmer, casting pale light over the sprawling peaks of the Harrowhorns far below. The air was thinner up here, sharper, vibrating with some unseen energy. Stars wove themselves between wisps of drifting mist, stretching endlessly into the heavens, and for the first time in my life, I felt limitless.

Weightless.

Free.

The thrill of the sky consumed me. I tightened my grip on the reins as I adjusted in the saddle, shifting my weight instinctively. The armor felt strange at first, heavier than I was used to, but not restrictive. It compressed against my chest, molding to my body, solid and unyielding like a second skin. I wasn't just wearing it. It had become part of me.

Even the leather stirrups, the smooth horn of the saddle

beneath my grip, were an extension of something natural—something thrilling.

I belonged here.

Errax's muscles rippled like fluid beneath me, the powerful hum of her body burning with energy, guiding us forward through the endless night.

And gods, I loved the smell—thick and heady, a mix of burning embers and storm-laced air. The faint tendrils of dragonfire curled from the edges of her maw, leaving streaks of smoke in our wake. I breathed it in deep, my pulse thundering in time with the rhythm of her wings.

I cut a glance toward Cade, who hovered just ahead on Krakos, his dark silhouette aglow in the moonlight. He was watching me. Studying me.

"First lesson," he called over the rumble of the wind. "Evasion techniques."

I arched a brow. "Not offense?"

His smirk was sharp as a blade. "You can't deal damage if you're dead."

Fair point.

I steadied myself, anticipation curling hot in my gut as I met his gaze, waiting.

He dipped his head in approval. "You can feel her movements, right?" He gestured slightly toward Errax. "Lean in—anticipate what she's going to do before she does it. Give her your next move before you even think of making it."

I furrowed my brow, focusing hard, feeling the shift beneath me, the way Errax responded to every subtle shift in weight.

Then something clicked.

She wasn't just reacting to me. She was listening. Waiting.

I took a steady breath and pressed forward ever so slightly. I barely had time to register my own thought, and yet—Errax moved.

She dipped her head, rolling into a smooth, gentle curve around Krakos as if she already knew what I was about to do.

My heart lurched.

Cade watched, nodding slowly. "Now you're catching on."

I felt a grin twitch at my lips. "Do you have the same bond with Krakos?"

His smirk was infuriating. "Of course." His sapphire gaze locked onto mine. "It's not just about control, Ash. It's trust. A rider only reaches their full potential when they and their dragon move as one—not as separate beings, but as two halves of the same instinct."

I swallowed hard, the new understanding settling in me like an ember waiting to ignite.

Then, just as I processed those words, Cade's grin turned downright wicked.

"Are you ready to be chased?"

My pulse jumped.

My breathing hitched.

He was playing with me.

But two could play this game.

I tilted my head, letting a slow, teasing smile spread over my lips. "By you? Always."

Cade's brows lifted for the briefest moment, his amusement flaring before something darker flashed in his expression.

Then—*he moved*.

Krakos let out a piercing, guttural roar, his massive wings slamming down in one powerful burst of speed. The night air cracked around me as they shot forward, diving toward me with dangerous precision.

I panicked for the barest second before I remembered—*think ahead*.

Trust. Definitely not the easiest thing for me. I never had any reason for it. But I trusted her. I trusted Errax. After all, she led me higher than the tallest mountains. I better fucking trust her bringing me this high up into the sky.

I barely had to *think* before Errax responded.

She launched into motion.

The wind screamed past my ears as we twisted into a heart-clenching barrel roll, narrowly escaping Krakos's lunging assault. Air pressure crashed into my chest, the sheer force of the movement sending a wild thrill down my spine as we veered left.

Krakos stayed on us, Cade steering with expert precision, his every move anticipated, every shift of weight molding Krakos into a deadly shadow behind me.

My skin burned with exhilaration. Adrenaline coursed through my limbs with a terrifying sharpness, but by Odiun—I *loved* it.

This wasn't just training.

This was *him*.

This was *us*.

Errax carried me forward, soaring through the ever-darkening sky, my grip steady as Krakos surged closer again. I could *feel* Cade behind me, could *feel* his pursuit burning like fire on my skin. His energy, his heat—the very essence of his raw, untamed presence hunted me, suffocating me with delicious intensity.

And I knew he was feeling it too.

It was a game. A dangerous, exhilarating game that neither of us could ever truly win.

The chase was everything. I never wanted it to end. I wanted him to follow me to the ends of the world.

And it made me wet.

I clenched my thighs around the saddle, heart pounding, thighs shaking.

I could *feel* him.

Everywhere.

His breath was in the wind.

His touch burned in the way Krakos's every movement closed in on me, how his presence *devoured*. Images shot through my head like lightning strikes. Flashes of the hot passionate times we'd spent together. The way his hot skin rubbed against mine in just the right ways. My mind teetered at the brink of madness wanting him, and I wanted him to chase me. I wanted every part of him to want me.

Gods, he was chasing me, testing me, and some dark, wild part of me *wanted to be caught*.

I bit down a desperate sound clawing up my throat.

Focus.

Errax dove suddenly—too sudden—shit. She was reacting to my reckless thoughts.

I gritted my teeth, reigning in my senses as Cade caught the movement instantly, pressing forward again, keeping right on me.

"Don't fight it," he called over the wind, voice thick with amusement and something else—challenge. "You're thinking about the wrong things."

I hated how smug he sounded.

I twisted hard—hitting an angled turn that had my body twisting into Errax's reins. But even then, Cade followed. Every damn time, he followed.

Like he knew my every move minutes before I made them.

Like he *knew* me.

Gods, it was too much.

Heat burned across every inch of my skin, my fingers slick against the leather grips, my pulse hammering from more than just the chase.

I could feel my own sweat, the dampness growing between my legs, slick and hot and needing relief.

Fuck, fuck, fuck. Don't think about it. Ash, focus...

Cade surged ahead suddenly, cutting off my side route, leveraging his position to box me in—a movement so dominant, so suffocatingly precise, I nearly moaned.

"Careful," he taunted over the wind. "You're sloppy when you let yourself get distracted."

Gods, I knew what he was doing.

And that was the worst part.

He wasn't just training me.

He was *feeling this too.*

I knew it in the way he flew closer than strictly necessary. In the way laughter laced his words, despite the combat precision behind his every action.

In the way he didn't let me escape too easily.

I gasped for breath, sweat dampening my lower back as Krakos almost slammed into us—with perfect fucking control.

Then, he slowed just enough to let me breathe.

I inhaled shakily.

My body shook from the jarring jolt.

And I realized—this would never stop.

Not ever.

No matter how many battles we faced. No matter how many wars we won.

Cade and I would always be chasing each other.

And maybe... we would never stop.

His glacier-blue eyes burned when they met mine through the smoke-lit sky. The intensity nearly made me fall off the damn dragon.

"Better," Cade said. "But you're still too slow."

I bared my teeth. "Again."

The satisfied smirk stretching across his lips set my entire body on fire.

This wouldn't stop.

And gods, I didn't want it to.

CHAPTER 14

As Errax's wings beat rhythmically against the wind, I felt the adrenaline coursing through my veins like wildfire. The sensation of flying was intoxicating—a pure bliss that blanketed my fears and doubts in a warm embrace. We soared across Storm's End, the camp sprawling below us like a tapestry woven from stories of survival, battles fought, and lives lived amid the ideals of freedom and unity.

The thrill diminished slowly as I guided Errax down toward the clustered buildings, the cool breeze swirling through the air directly beneath my arms and spilling cool energy across my burning skin. A low rumble from the depths of the earth beneath me sent a thrill of excitement racing down my back to my heels.

"This isn't bad at all!" I called out to Cade, who was breathing harder on Krakos, keeping his distance behind my dragon. "I can't believe how much we did!"

"I'm glad that you're excited, but there are things to work on," he replied, his voice gruff yet edged with a hint of amusement. "You need to learn how to take control of your balance mid-air and stop trying to compensate with every move."

"Maybe I don't want your help," I retorted playfully, but the truth is—he'd helped me find my wings.

"If you want to keep up with me, you'll need it," he smirked back, the light glinting off his darkened armor as he kept pace with us.

The ground rushed up to meet us, and I felt the familiar tightening of adrenaline that surged through me as Errax landed gracefully in the open space of the Stormscale camp. The familiar thudding of her footfalls steadying me as I slid off her back with the practiced ease of someone accustomed to the motions.

The moment I did, I couldn't help the delighted laugh that escaped. I remained breathless, elated, and slightly dazed as I took in the sounds of the camp around me—the crackling of fires, the chatter of families breaking bread together, the low rumble of laughter echoing back and forth as we settled into the familiar rhythms of life. I looked back at Cade, seeking validation, but his expression was already focused on his dragon—Krakos, pawing eagerly at the ground, wings folding tightly at his sides.

"I think that went quite well," Hunter said, approaching as he apparently had watched much of our flight from the ground.

"It was great!" I beamed at him, still feeling the exhilarating buzz of the sky coursing through my veins. "I think I actually might be getting good at this."

Cade made a low sound of amusement as he slid off Krakos with ease. He didn't say anything right away, busying himself with the leather straps of the saddle, but his slow shake of the head told me everything I needed to know before he even opened his mouth.

"You're improving," he admitted finally, voice calm and measured. "But don't mistake excitement for skill. You're still reacting too slowly in sharp dives, and if I'd been a real enemy back there..." He gave me a pointed look. "You'd be dead."

The warmth in my chest flickered at his words, irritation

curling at the edges of my exhilaration. "But I wasn't," I shot back, shoving my hands on my hips. "You didn't catch me."

His sapphire gaze locked onto mine, and the weight of it sent heat spiraling deep in my stomach. "Because I chose not to."

Gods, he was insufferable. A complete ass of a man.

And I wanted to wipe that smug expression right off his face.

Before I could come up with a proper retort, Bella's voice broke through the moment.

"Well?" she said with crossed arms by Hunter's side. "How'd our fearless trainee do?"

"Great," I said promptly, flashing her a bright grin as I started toward her. "Absolutely flawless."

Cade, of course, had other ideas.

"She still has work to do," he said, just as promptly, handing Krakos's saddle to Hunter before following me toward the bunkhouse. "Evasion is still too slow. She hesitates when under pressure."

I spun on my heel to glare at him. "I didn't hesitate!"

He arched a brow. "You thought about hesitating."

I groaned loudly and threw my hands in the air. "I don't know why I even bother."

Bella stifled a laugh, exchanging an amused glance with Hunter as we reached the bunkhouse door.

"Regardless," she said, "I hate to ruin your little lovers' quarrel—"

"It's not a lovers' quarrel," Cade and I snapped in unison.

Bella ignored us, grinning. "But Darren wants us at the war council first thing in the morning. Which means we need sleep."

Hunter nodded, his serious demeanor returning as he brushed past Cade into the bunkhouse. "She's right. There's no telling what they're planning. We'd best be at full strength."

Cade gave a silent nod of agreement, but I caught the shift in his stance—the way his fingers twitched at his sides, as if suppressing some lingering frustration even I couldn't read.

Not that I had time to dwell on it.

Bella, already halfway across the space, made a show of brushing invisible dust from one of the cots before flashing me a wicked grin. "Looks like you and the Prince of Brooding will be sleeping very, very close to each other. Just don't forget that we have to sleep in here too. So keep your hands off each other, lovebirds..."

I groaned again and pinched the bridge of my nose. "By Odiun, just kill me now."

Hunter chuckled. Cade said nothing. He just walked to his cot —opposite mine, thank the gods—and started undoing the leather straps of his gauntlets like none of this was his problem.

Typical.

Sighing, I collapsed onto the bed, feeling the exhaustion begin to creep into my bones now that the exhilaration of flying had settled.

The night air seeped in around us, cool and quiet and thick with the scent of burnt wood and leather as the fires outside slowly died down. The sounds of the camp dimmed as the minutes passed, the murmurs of distant voices dwindling into deep silence.

Bella was snoring softly in her cot within minutes. Hunter wasn't far behind, breathing slow and even as he rested a hand against the hilt of his sword in sleep.

I should have been tired. I was tired.

But as I lay back against the thin mattress, staring up at the wooden beams of the bunkhouse, my mind spun.

I had flown tonight. Truly flown.

Not as a passenger, not as a burden. As a rider.

A dragon rider.

The thought sent a slow, warm thrill through me, soft and quiet and buried deep beneath the weight of doubts and memories.

For the first time since this journey began—since the first

time Cade had lifted me onto Krakos's back, since the first moment I felt fire licking at my skin—I felt as though I belonged.

I curled under the blankets, closing my eyes.

Sleep pulled at my limbs, dragging me under.

And the last thing I saw before dreams claimed me were indigo wings catching the wind, carrying me high above the world, where nothing could ever touch me again.

Where I was free.

Where I was home.

THE COUNCIL CHAMBER was colder than I'd expected.

Not from the rising chill of the morning, nor from the weak, struggling embers in the hearth. No, this cold seeped from the walls themselves, from the silence that stretched too long between the assembled warriors, from the stares that lingered heavy with memories of blood and burned cities.

From the weight of everything unsaid.

The war council had gathered just before dawn, the sky still streaked with the last vestiges of night, fading into the bruised purple and soft gold of approaching sunrise. The long table stretched between us, rough-hewn wood scattered with maps, empty goblets, and untouched plates of bread and salted meat. The scent of strong tea and bitter coffee clung to the air.

On one side sat the Stormscale warriors and their elders, heavy leather armor layered over warm wool, swords settled at their sides like natural extensions of their bodies. Darren loomed at the head of their table, his ram-horned helm resting within arm's reach as he spoke in measured, restrained words. His daughter, Carina, lounged beside him, casual but alert, sharp eyes flickering between her father and the rest of us.

The other side? Us.

Cade sat rigid in his chair beside me, arms crossed, jaw

clenched so tightly I could hear his teeth grind. Bella had positioned herself at the far end, near Hunter, ready to play mediator if things spiraled out of control.

"We cannot take the queen head-on," Darren declared, voice calm—too calm. It was the kind of tone that barely veiled the buried fury beneath. "She commands more than soldiers. She has beasts. Magic. Spies scattered through every stronghold in Allovan. We don't even know the full scope of her forces."

Cade didn't move. Didn't look up from the map. But the tension in his shoulders turned sharp as razor wire.

"I know these things," he said coolly. "We attack. Move faster than she expects."

One of the older warriors scowled, his thick gray beard twitching as he leaned forward. "And send our people to die in the process? You are reckless, Prince."

Cade's eyes flashed. "I am realistic."

"The Stormscales have fought her forces for years—" Carina started, but Cade cut her off with a dry, bitter laugh.

"You mean you've survived them." His sapphire gaze snapped up, drilling into hers with barely restrained fury. "There's a difference between surviving a war and winning it."

All at once, the council fragmented.

Stormscale warriors barked over each other, their voices rising, clashing, too many opinions spilling over into a cacophony of frustration.

"You expect us to trust your tactics?" one snarled.

"You expect to win this war by hiding behind your mountain?" Cade shot back.

"You would have us fight side by side with a man who has slaughtered our kin?"

"You speak as though you haven't done the same!"

A glass tipped over somewhere, the metallic clatter of a goblet echoing through the hall. Boots scuffed against stone as several warriors stood, their postures bristling with the sharp-edged fury of men who had fought too long, lost too much.

Bella muttered a curse under her breath, rubbing her temples.

Darren slammed his fist against the table with enough force to shake the wood. "Enough."

The room grudgingly fell into silence, though the tension burned hotter than dragon fire.

Cade exhaled sharply, shaking his head. "This is pointless."

"It's war," Darren corrected, his voice heavy with exhaustion. "Nothing about it is easy."

Cade pushed his chair back and stood. "Then find me when you're willing to actually fight it."

And just like that, he stormed out.

I felt the council's mood plummet instantly, shoulders sinking, hope bleeding out of the room like a gut wound.

Hunter spared me a single glance before rising to follow his prince.

The doors slammed shut behind them, their absence leaving a gaping void between the two clashing sides.

I swallowed hard.

The argument shouldn't have rattled me this much. I'd seen worse. Heard worse. I'd fought the queen myself, looked into her black abyss of a gaze and felt her hunger like circling vultures in my damned chest.

But this? This felt like watching cracks splinter through the last foundation holding us together.

Carina sighed loudly, running a hand through her hair. "Well. Total disaster. That's new."

Darren ignored her sarcasm, turning toward me. "He won't listen," he said bluntly. "Not if his pride blinds him to reason."

I bristled, barely resisting the urge to shove my plate across the table. "That's not true."

One of the elders scoffed. "He abandoned this conversation the moment it didn't serve his ego. His history speaks for itself."

A dozen pairs of eyes turned to me—waiting. Expectant.

And that was when I understood.

This wasn't just about Cade storming out.

This was about me.

I wasn't Cade Phoenixfire. I hadn't spent years fighting the Stormscales. Hadn't led armies against them. They didn't see me as an enemy.

They saw me as something more.

Something promising… and dangerous…

"We'd prefer to hear from you," Darren admitted, steepling his fingers. "You faced Mortriana. You survived her. If we are to act, we need to know everything."

My stomach twisted. Was this betrayal? No, not exactly. I wasn't going behind Cade's back. But I couldn't shake the feeling I was being used as leverage against him.

My gaze flickered toward Bella. She must have seen something in my eyes because her teasing grin had vanished, replaced by something more careful. More serious.

I should have answered.

I should have spoken, given them something—anything.

But the words tangled in my throat, a knot of guilt and uncertainty clogging my ability to breathe.

I couldn't do this without Cade.

I couldn't strategize about this war, talk about facing the queen again, without him. This is his war more than anyone's. He gave up *everything*… for me. His destiny, his future as king, fucking *everything*! It was more than just about the way we felt for each other. We were invested in each other until this war was over, or death do us part.

I pushed back from the table.

"Excuse me," I muttered, barely registering the confused murmur of voices as I turned on my heel and made for the doors.

"Ash?" Bella called after me, quick-footed as she jogged to my side, keeping pace as I shoved open the heavy wooden doors into the cool mountain air.

I didn't slow.

I needed to find him.

Cade's footprints were easy to follow, his scars on the dirt paths leading me toward the outer edges of camp, past tightened rows of tents and scattered dragon roosts. Many dragons' gazes followed me eerily. I scratched my arm as I walked past the frightful beasts.

Hunter was beside me as we neared the feeding grounds, his face unreadable, his expression quiet.

"Don't bother," he murmured as he passed. "Give him space."

I barely acknowledged him, my feet still moving, my heart pounding faster—not from anger. Not from worry.

But from something deeper.

Something I didn't yet have words for.

Bella exhaled loudly, dragging a hand through her hair. "Want me to go back?"

My jaw tightened.

No.

I needed this.

I nodded absently. "I'll be back soon."

She hesitated, but ultimately ducked away, heading back toward the council chamber.

I turned the last corner and finally saw him.

Cade stood at the edge of a high cliff, his back to me, his dark cloak whipping in the wind. Krakos lurked nearby, embers glowing faintly in his throat, restless.

I walked up and stood by his side, marveling at the breath-taking view of the sunrise that inched over the sharp-edged Harrowhorn peaks. For a long time, I didn't speak.

Just watched.

His shoulders had lost their rigid tension, but his hands still curled at his sides, as though containing something too dangerous to unleash.

"Cade," I said finally.

He didn't turn. "You shouldn't be here."

I ignored the warning in his voice. "Neither should you."

Silence hung between us, and I whispered, more to myself than him. "We can't do this without you."

"We?" His voice was sharp. Tired. "Or them?"

I swallowed hard. "Me."

That, at last, made him turn.

His icy blue gaze burned through me, across the distance, through the raging winds.

"You're the only reason I haven't burned this whole place to the ground," he admitted, voice barely audible.

I didn't know what to say to that. To him.

So I did the only thing I could.

I reached for him.

He hesitated. But only for a breath.

Then—he took my hand.

"Come," I mouthed, tugging at him. "Give it another try... for me."

"For you, Ash..."

CHAPTER 15

We entered back into the Bracken Burr Hall, an unease washed over the huge room like the tidal wave as Cade returned like a shadow. We both sat as Bella and Hunter nodded at us, eager for a hopefully peaceful talk.

"Shall we proceed?" Darren said in a strong voice that broke the unease like a war hammer battering splintering wood with a monstrous swipe.

"Yes." Cade's voice was just as commanding. "But I ask something from you first, General. I have a request, a favor. It's something I will ask in private though, as much as I expect that to displease those in this room. It's a request I need."

He was damned right that displeased me. What the fuck? It's as if he *still* doesn't trust me. My fingers curled to tight fists on the bench.

A hush rippled through the council chamber after Cade's declaration, his intense gaze pinning Darren in place. The table between them was strewn with worn maps and half-drunk goblets of wine, but at this moment, all anyone could focus on was the unspoken weight behind what he was asking.

A request. In private.

Darren's gray eyes narrowed slightly, his fingers flexing where they rested atop the aged parchment of Allovan's war-torn lands. Silence stretched thick and unrelenting.

Carina was the first to break it.

"You keep saying that word," she mused dryly, tapping her nails rhythmically against the table's surface. "Request. Pretty word for something that sounds a lot more serious than you're letting on."

Cade's expression remained unreadable, but I could feel the tension humming off of him like sparks ready to ignite.

"This war will not be won if we spend days bickering at war tables," Hunter said, leaning forward as he steeled his sharp gaze at the gathered Stormscales. "Every second we waste fighting amongst ourselves is time she is preparing for us. The queen may know we've allied. She's conniving and shrewd, with spies everywhere. We need to listen as much as we need to talk here."

A few of the older warriors exchanged long, unreadable glances—silent conversations passing between them like unspoken regrets.

Darren finally exhaled through his nose, his fingers tightening over the map's brittle edges. "I agree to your request. But as for the queens defenses and war plans—you agree to training my soldiers in what you know?"

Cade inclined his head. "Your men may be experienced, but they have never fought the kind of war I propose before. And training them to fight the queen's army is not a task to take lightly."

I shifted slightly at Cade's words, watching as Darren's gaze flickered downward, his brows furrowing in thought.

After a long moment, the Stormscale general spoke.

"You'll begin tomorrow," Darren decided at last. "Since you're so confident in your knowledge of the queen's defenses, I expect you to prepare my fighters for what's to come." He glanced briefly at me before adding, "And we will need both of your magic."

My heart gave a strange, uncertain beat.

I had fought the queen, yes—but had I truly gained control over my power? Eden was still not completely familiar to me, this strange entity that hummed beneath my skin, waiting to be unleashed. The way Cornelius spoke about it made it sound limitless, if I could just grasp it properly. But was that true? Could I actually wield it to its fullest?

I swore, for a moment, Carina was watching me more carefully than before.

Darren leaned back, shoulders stiff with authority. "I will grant your request, Phoenixfire. We will speak privately before the next council, if you speak true, and will pass on your insights to my men."

Carina jabbed his forearm with her elbow.

"And women, of course," he added.

I'm really starting to like this girl.

I should have felt satisfied by this agreement, but unease curled in my stomach.

Because what in Odiun's name was Cade planning?

Carina let out an exaggerated sigh, snapping the tension. "Well, that settles that. Maybe now we can actually start talking about the battle plan."

But before anyone could get another word out, a sharp gust of cold mountain air rushed in as the tent flap flew open.

A young boy stumbled inside, breathing heavily, his small hands clutching a rolled parchment tight against his chest. He couldn't have been any older than eight or nine, with wild black curls and clothes dampened from the night mist.

Every soldier in the room straightened at once.

Darren stood immediately. "What is it?"

The boy hesitated at the threshold, big brown eyes darting

across the collected faces, before finally stepping forward and thrusting the parchment toward Darren's outstretched hand.

"A raven, my lord," the boy said between sharp breaths. "It arrived moments ago, bearing a message from our spies near Emberveil."

A thrumming silence fell over the room.

Darren's jaw tightened as he took the scroll from the boy's hands, his fingers steady despite the unreadable look that passed over his weathered face. In one smooth motion, he broke the seal and unrolled the delicate parchment.

The war council hung on every second, waiting, breathing as a singular unit.

Darren's storm-gray eyes flicked back and forth over the writing, his brow tightening with every word. When he was finished, he passed the message silently to Carina.

She read it fast, her mouth pressing into a thin, unforgiving line.

A murmur rolled through the tent as the rest of us exchanged quick glances.

"What does it say?" one of the elders finally demanded.

Darren cleared his throat, his face unreadable as he relayed the message aloud.

"Our spies have reported that all of the queen's forces are pulling back to Emberveil," he said, his steady voice betraying the tension simmering beneath it. "Every regiment, every mounted cavalry. Everything is gathering there as we speak."

The weight of those words sent a ripple through the room.

Bella frowned slightly. "That's... good news then, right? It buys us time."

I nodded, though something about the report unsettled me. "It means she's staying in her fortress, fortifying her defenses."

Cade, however, didn't share our optimism.

He shifted beside me, his jaw stiff, eyes burning cold and

sharp. His fingers tapped once—just once—against the table before his voice cut through the murmurs like a blade.

"No," he muttered darkly, more to himself than anyone else. "You don't know her like I do."

That sent a creeping chill through my skin.

Cade's gaze locked onto Darren's, his expression like cut stone. "She doesn't pull her troops in to protect herself."

Darren regarded him carefully. "Then what does she do?"

Cade exhaled slowly, his fingers pressing firmly against the wood of the war table.

"She prepares to burn the world."

A silence louder than any explosion rippled through the tent.

No one dared speak.

No one dared move.

Carina muttered a quiet curse under her breath as she smoothed a hand along the back of her chair, eyes tracking Cade carefully.

Bella let out a slow, exhaled breath. "She's planning something."

Cade gave a single, sharp nod. "She's always two steps ahead."

Hunter folded his arms. "Then we figure out what she's planning before she has the chance to strike."

Easier said than done.

The queen was terrifying, ruthless, clever beyond reason. We had seen what she was capable of with Brigodon, with her Sythers, with every twisted thing that writhed in the shadows of her forces.

If she was pulling everything inward, it wasn't to huddle in defense.

It was to strike.

Hard enough to end all of this before it even began.

My heartbeat pumped in my ears.

Cade rubbed his temples, muttering again to himself, "What is she up to?"

No one had an answer.

But we needed to find one.

Fast.

Because if we waited too long, if we hesitated for even a moment—

She would be the last thing we ever saw.

The storm was coming.

And my body burned with the knowledge that I was right in the center of it.

CHAPTER 16

The air inside Storm's End war chamber snapped like a livewire. After the scroll arrived—after Cade's ominous warning that the queen wasn't retreating for safety but preparing for something worse—the Stormscales erupted.

"We need to strike now, strike fast!" one man bellowed, fists slamming against the war table. His leather armor creaked with the violent motion.

"She's pulling her troops inward because she's scared!" another shouted. "We should attack while her walls are vulnerable!"

"Fools," grumbled someone from further down the hall. "You think Mortriana Vissex would leave her flanks bare by accident?"

"That scroll said she's drawing everything in!" a younger soldier added. "She's gathering for protection."

"Or for war," snarled an older captain. "She's luring us. That's her game."

"And you'll just let her do it?" the first man snapped, turning on the room. "That's your plan? To wait until she's ready to burn Allovan itself?"

Darren watched the chaos with a carefully controlled stillness. His hands rested calmly on the table, but beneath them, the veins stood out sharply—stone under strain. He didn't speak. Not yet.

The roar of clashing voices, raised and impassioned. Commander against captain. Youth against elder. Anger eclipsing reason.

And I hated every second of it.

Because we didn't have time for this.

Cade remained immobile, arms crossed, his expression empty. Detached. He let them rage and spiral and tear into themselves like wolves turned on each other, his mouth a thin, flat line. He wasn't going to stop them. Not yet.

"What in Odiun's name are we doing?" I muttered under my breath.

Cade glanced at me sideways. "They're scared," he said quietly. "And fear makes leaders stupid."

"With all due respect"—I turned toward the table—"this is getting us nowhere."

No one heard me above the shouting.

"I said—!" I raised my voice louder, letting it cut through the din like a thrown dagger. "This isn't helping!"

Some heads turned. Some didn't.

But before anything else could be said, a sound cracked through the room like thunder.

A gnarled cane slammed heavy against the tabletop, a beat of finality that made the floor vibrate under our boots. Silence crashed over the room like an avalanche. No one was breathing. Not properly.

Every head turned.

At the far end of the hall, a woman stood.

Small. Bent-backed. Easily the oldest person in the room. Older than Darren, older than the wars and grudges that had hollowed the faces of every Stormscale elder around her.

Her silver hair was pulled into a long braid that coiled down one shoulder like faded strings of starlight. Her face was threaded with wrinkles like canyons across stone, and her eyes—gods, her eyes—were clear as ice and sharper than any sword I'd ever seen.

When she spoke again, her voice didn't waver.

It cut.

"Enough," she said. "All of you."

We all froze.

"You carry on about when to strike and when to wait. You speak of honor. Of strategy. Of fear. But not one of you asks what we are fighting for." Her gaze swept slowly across every warrior, every elder, every soldier clutching a blade at their side like it was the only thing anchoring them to this world.

"You forget yourselves in hatred. In pride. That will be our end."

No one dared contradict her.

Even Darren bowed his head slightly.

She pointed her cane—steady, purposeful—first at Cade.

"You," she said. "Have fought her and lived. You know her fortress, her armies, her monsters better than any man here."

Her cane swung to me.

"And you… you carry power the likes of which hasn't graced this land in an age. Gilded light and sea-magic in one breath. You are not just Gold-Marked. You carry the hopes of those who've never had a voice."

My throat tightened unexpectedly. How did she know I'm Aqualorian? How could she possibly…?

Then her eyes scanned the rest of the room, sweeping them all in with a gaze like winter wind.

"We will not win this war if we bargain in half-measures. We will not win if we let old grudges bleed over into new alliances. Our people—our dragons—deserve more than stubbornness and fear."

Someone shifted near the back, whispering something incomprehensible.

The old woman raised her chin slightly.

"You must listen to the Blaze Prince," she said. "You must follow what he says about her armies. And"—she paused, her gaze softer now as it landed on me—"you must trust in Ashlyn Moonriver."

My stomach fluttered like a stirred storm tide.

"She will be your shield in this. Just as she will be your sword. You all may be able to fight against men and beasts, but against the Queen of Chaos and Ruin, you will all die. Ash is the only one capable of even fighting against such evil. Listen to her, listen hard. For what's to come requires more than steel and wings."

Silence followed her words, deep and absolute.

No one moved. No one could.

Darren exhaled at last, rising slowly. His heavy boots scraped across stone as he stepped forward, placing both palms on the war table.

"The elder speaks true," he said. "We can no longer afford division. If we strike too soon, we risk annihilation. If we wait too long, we give her time to prepare."

He glanced at Cade and then at me, paused meaningfully. "I've waged war my whole life. Led dragons, watched cities fall. But this? This is different. This war is against something we do not understand."

He faced his commanders—his people.

"That is why we must listen to them. Trust our dragons. Trust her magic. And trust each other."

A long, grim pause followed.

Then, slowly, the other commanders nodded. A few uncertainly. A few with reluctance. But something in the room had shifted.

It wasn't consent.

It was commitment.

Cade stepped forward, and for the first time since this council had begun days ago, his voice carried like a commander, not a prince.

"Then we begin tomorrow," he said. "If the queen is preparing a final blow, we must ensure that it lands against steel, not soft backs. We train in dragon formations, aerial assault, breach maneuvers. My way."

He looked at Darren.

"And no one questions it."

Darren looked at him a moment longer.

Then nodded once.

"You'll get what you need."

Cade didn't smile, didn't even look pleased.

But tension left him like a slow release of breath.

He stepped back beside me.

"Ready to be their favorite instructor?" I whispered.

He smirked. "They won't like it."

"Good," I said. "They'll respect it instead."

Because if we were going to survive the queen—

We needed to be more than fighters.

We needed to become legends.

THE MOUNTAIN AIR hit us like a wall of ice as we left the war chamber, the sound of murmuring voices fading behind us. My heart was still thundering from everything that had happened— the scroll, the arguments, the elder's words about my power.

About who I needed to become.

Bella exhaled loudly beside me, running a hand through her sandy blonde hair. "Well," she said. "That was... interesting."

Hunter grunted. "That's one word for it."

We walked in silence for a moment, our boots crunching

against loose stone as we made our way back toward the main part of the camp. The sun had risen fully now, casting long shadows across the mountainside, warming the morning chill.

Cade hadn't spoken since we'd left the chamber. His expression was distant, thoughtful—the kind of look that meant he was turning something over in his mind, examining it from every angle.

Hunter noticed too.

"You're taking a risk," he said finally, voice low enough that only we could hear. "Teaching them our weaknesses."

Cade's jaw tightened. "I know."

"If they turn on us after the war—"

"If we survive the war," Cade cut in, "then Emberveil's defenses will need to change anyway." His eyes darkened slightly. "Everything will need to change."

The weight of those words settled over us like a physical thing.

If we won—if we actually succeeded in defeating the queen— Cade would be king. The thought made my stomach flutter strangely. Not because I doubted his ability to rule, but because of everything that meant for us. For whatever this thing was between us.

Bella, ever practical, cleared her throat. "So what's next? Before you start turning the Stormscales into your personal army?"

Cade glanced at me, his expression softening almost imperceptibly. "Ash needs to train. Both with her magic and with Errax."

I straightened slightly. "Both?"

He nodded. "The war is coming to a head faster than we thought. And you're—" He hesitated, as if choosing his words carefully. "You're the key to all of this."

My throat tightened. "No pressure."

"Your friend Cornelius," he continued, ignoring my attempt at humor. "He needs to keep training you. Your magic is growing stronger, but it needs to be ready."

I blinked in surprise. It was the first time he'd acknowledged Cornelius and how I needed him.

"And after that," he added, "we train in the air again. You're improving, but you need to be better."

"Charming as always," I muttered, but there was no real bite to it.

His lips twitched. "I mean it, Ash. What you can do with Eden... it's unlike anything I've seen. But you need control."

He was right, of course. The golden light that surged through me was powerful, but wild. Unpredictable. And if I was going to face the queen again...

"Fine," I said. "I'll find Cornelius first."

Bella perked up beside me. "Can I come?"

I turned to her, surprised. "You want to watch me train with a magical talking tortoise?"

She grinned. "Are you kidding? After everything that's happened, that might be the most normal part of our day."

I couldn't help but laugh. "Fair point." I glanced at her warmly. "Yeah, you can come."

Cade nodded once. "Good. Meet me back here before sunset. We'll work on your aerial maneuvers then."

The way he said it, sent through me the lovely feeling of harsh winds ripping through my hair—remembering our last training session, the chase through the clouds, the electricity that had sparked between us.

I swallowed hard and forced myself to focus.

"Ready?" I asked Bella, already turning toward the path that led away from camp.

She fell into step beside me, linking her arm through mine. "Lead the way to your mysterious mentor."

As we walked away, I heard Hunter say something low to

Cade, too quiet to make out. Whatever it was made Cade laugh—
a short, rough sound that carried on the wind.

The sound made my heart skip.

But I didn't look back.

I had magic to master, after all.

And a war to win.

CHAPTER 17

The mountain path wound through sparse trees, their branches reaching toward a sky that seemed impossibly close. Behind us, Storm's End bustled with the sounds of preparation—the clash of weapons, the beat of dragon wings, voices raised in command and response. But here, among the weathered trunks and wind-swept stones, everything felt distant. Ethereal.

Bella walked beside me, her boots crunching against loose gravel as we picked our way further from camp. The morning air was crisp though the sun fought valiantly to warm our faces.

"So," Bella said, breaking our comfortable silence. "What do you think he'll tell you?"

I exhaled slowly, watching my breath mist in the cold. "I don't know. With everything happening—the queen pulling back to Emberveil, the Stormscales preparing for war..." I shrugged, but anxiety coiled in my gut like a restless serpent. "I just hope he can give me some guidance. The fight might come sooner than any of us are ready for."

Bella smiled and her face softened with concern. "You're worried."

"Aren't you?"

She didn't answer immediately, her gaze distant as we walked. Finally, she said, "I'm terrified. But I also believe in you, Ash. In what you can do."

I squeezed her hand briefly, grateful for her unwavering support, even when I didn't deserve it.

We reached a small clearing where the trees thinned enough to let sunlight pool on the rocky ground. Perfect. I took a steadying breath, then called out:

"Cornelius?"

For a moment, nothing happened.

Then—a rustle of leaves overhead.

We both looked up to find the massive tortoise perched on a thick branch, his dark green shell catching glints of morning light. His ancient eyes, streaked with fire and wisdom, regarded us with familiar patience.

Bella's face split into a delighted grin. "Hello!"

"Greetings, young one," Cornelius rumbled, his voice carrying the weight of countless years. The branch beneath him creaked ominously, but held steady.

I stepped forward, squaring my shoulders. "I need more training."

Cornelius closed his eyes, as if deep in thought. When he opened them again, they seemed to glow with inner flame.

"The alliance you've forged with the Stormscales," he said slowly, "is crucial. Without their numbers, without their strength, you cannot hope to breach the queen's defenses."

Before I could respond, he vanished from the branch—only to reappear behind us with a soft whoosh of displaced air.

I spun to face him, my heart jumping despite having seen this trick before.

"Your magic requires more practice," he continued gravely. "But I fear time grows short. Much of what lies ahead will rest on your shoulders—on your instincts."

My throat tightened. "What does that mean?"

His massive head tilted slightly. "It means that your lineage—your connection to the Sea Lord—must be enough when the moment comes. The power flows in your blood, Ashlyn Moonriver. But awakening it fully..." He trailed off, something dark passing through his gaze.

"There has to be a way," Bella cut in, stepping forward. Her voice carried an edge of desperation I wasn't used to hearing. "Something you can do to make her strong enough to face the queen?"

Cornelius regarded her for a long moment, his ancient eyes full of sorrow. "I will continue training her, as I have trained all who came before." He turned back to me, his expression heavy with unspoken weight. "But when the final moment comes, may Odiun protect you where I cannot."

Ice slid down my flesh, erupting goose pimples all the way down my arms.

"What do you mean, 'all who came before'?" Bella asked softly, half not wanting to know the answer.

But Cornelius was already moving, his stumpy legs carrying him with surprising grace as he gestured for me to follow.

"I've trained many Gold-Marked, young one. The queen has defeated and consumed the magic of all that came before Ash. Come," he said. "We have much to do, and precious little time to do it."

I exchanged a quick glance with Bella, whose face had gone slightly pale, before hurrying after him.

"What do you mean?" Bella asked with arms wide.

"Queen Vissex has almost completed her journey to ascending to the role she wishes to hold in this world. Immortal ruler, unmatched magic and power, and none to threaten her eternal, Cinderyn reign."

"You mean... Ash is the last one?"

"She is our last hope to destroy the queen's dark plans,"

Cornelius said with a slightly somber tone. "If she can't accomplish what none before her have in the past decades, then none will."

"I'll do it," I said with as unbroken a voice as I could muster. "I'll do what I have to. But I know I need help."

"Help—you have," Bella said, wrapping her arm around my waist. "'Til the bitter end. You're just going to need to be as powerful as those Stormscales back there believe you are. You need to be as strong as *I* believe you can be. As powerful as you can be..."

"Your strength, young Bella Thornrose, will be needed. Keep that strength with you. Ash and the others will need it in the times ahead."

Bella nodded. Gods how I admired her. She wasn't only my best, and only friend, in Bramblebash. But she always exuded the kind of confidence and grit that I always wished I had.

The rest of the morning passed in a blur of golden light and power. Cornelius guided me through exercises that pushed Eden to her limits—summoning shields of pure energy, directing bursts of magic with increasing precision, learning to feel the flow of power before calling it forth.

But his earlier words echoed in my mind like a warning bell.

All who came before.

How many others had tried to stop the queen?

And how many had failed?

"THAT WAS INCREDIBLE!" Bella exclaimed as we made our way back toward Storm's End, her eyes bright with excitement. "The way you summoned that shield of pure light—and then that blast that nearly took down the entire tree!"

I couldn't help but grin, though exhaustion pulled at my limbs like lead weights. "It was something, wasn't it?"

The training had been intense. Cornelius had pushed me harder than ever before, forcing me to channel Eden in ways I hadn't thought possible. Golden light had poured from my hands in waves, each spell more powerful than the last. But gods, the drain of it left me feeling like I'd run halfway across Allovan.

"You're getting stronger," Bella said, linking her arm through mine as we walked. "I can see it. The way the golden light poured out of that golden rune on your neck, reminded me of the first time it appeared on the beach when Cade and the Stormscales fought above the beach in Bramblebash. The time you saved us from Krakos' fire."

"That seems like a lifetime ago, doesn't it?" I feigned a laugh, but a deep sigh followed.

"You've grown so much since that day. I'm proud of you, Ash!"

I nodded, though uncertainty gnawed at my gut. "I just hope it's enough."

The sun was already beginning to sink toward the mountain peaks, painting the sky in deep amber and blood-red streaks. My heart jumped when I realized how late it was getting.

"Shit," I muttered. "Cade's going to kill me if I'm late for training."

Bella snorted. "Pretty sure he'd find any excuse to be mad at you right now."

"Not helping!"

We quickened our pace, practically jogging back toward the camp. My muscles protested every step, but I pushed through it. The last thing I needed was Cade's disapproval on top of everything else. I needed him focused, not pissed.

When we finally reached our bunkhouse, however, we found someone we didn't expect waiting inside.

Carina lounged on one of the beds, her blonde-silver hair catching the dying sunlight from the window. Her lips quirked into an amused smile as we stumbled in, breathless and disheveled.

"Have fun playing in the woods?" she drawled.

I stiffened immediately. "What are you doing here?"

She sat up slowly, her green eyes sharp despite her casual posture. "Looking for the same thing as you, Ash. The truth."

Something in her tone made my skin prickle. "What's that supposed to mean?"

"It means," she said, standing fluid as water, "that while you were out there practicing your magic, my father and your prince had their little private meeting."

My breath caught. "Do you know… what it was about?"

Bella shifted beside me, her expression wary.

"No," Carina's smile dropped to a frown. "They locked themselves in Bracken Burr Hall. Just the two of them. Very hush-hush."

Anger flared in my chest, hot and sudden. "And?"

"And I don't like it." She crossed her arms. "Neither of them have been focused since. Distracted. Like whatever they discussed weighs heavier than the actual war we're preparing for."

I wanted to argue, to defend Cade, but… she wasn't wrong. Something had been off about him lately. More distant than usual. More brooding, if that was even possible.

"What do you think they're planning?" Bella asked quietly.

Carina's gaze flickered to her. "That's what I was hoping you might know."

"We don't. Cade's been going off on his own a lot. I think… I think he's searching for something. Something he won't tell us about," I snapped, perhaps too harshly. Through the window, I could see the sun sinking faster. "And I need to go. Cade's waiting to train me."

"Ah yes," Carina mused. "The famous dragon riding lessons from the Blaze Prince himself. I know by the way… I know you two are close. The others don't know it yet. But I can see it in the way he looks at you with those gorgeous eyes."

My body tensed straight. Not so much caring that she knew, but from the inflection in her voice. There was a hidden warning in her words, a darkness in her gaze, and danger in her posture.

I narrowed my eyes at her tone, but she was already moving toward the door. Just before she reached it, however, she paused. Turned.

Her next words came out barely above a whisper.

"We trust you, Ash." Her voice had lost its edge, replaced by something more earnest. More raw. "Everyone here—we trust you. You came from nothing, fought the queen herself, and lived. Not just lived—you nearly killed her."

My heart thundered against my ribs.

"The people don't look to Cade," she continued softly. "They look to you." Her green eyes burned with intensity. "You're their hope. Their hero. Whether you want to be or not."

I couldn't breathe.

"There may come a time," she said, "when you have to be the one to change the course of history. And when that moment comes..." She straightened, chin lifting slightly. "We're with you."

Then she was gone, leaving only the echo of her words behind.

Bella and I stood in stunned silence, staring at the space where she had been.

"Well," Bella said finally, her voice slightly shaky. "That was..."

"Unexpected?" I supplied weakly.

She nodded. "Are you okay?"

I wasn't sure how to answer that. My head spun with everything Carina had said—about the secret meeting, about the people's faith in me, about being their hero.

I wasn't a hero.

I was just... me.

A former slave who happened to have magic she barely understood. Who was falling for a prince she could never truly have. Who was terrified of failing everyone who believed in her.

"Ash?" Bella touched my arm gently.

I swallowed hard. "I need to go. Cade's waiting."

But as I turned to leave, Carina's words followed me like shadows.

We're with you.

And somehow, that scared me more than anything else.

CHAPTER 18

I left the bunkhouse before Bella or Hunter could stop me. Before I could talk myself down or convince myself that I wasn't mad.

I was mad.

Pissed, actually.

Cade had always been guarded—of course he was—but secret meetings with Darren? Retreating into silence and shadows like the brooding fucking prince he was while the rest of us spilled our guts and magic across the war table?

Yeah. I was pissed.

Don't be petty, I told myself as I stormed up the winding trail that clung to the side of Storm's End. Don't let something stupid ruin the one thing you've actually been looking forward to.

But the more I tried to push it down, the more it clawed its way right back up. I had laid myself bare to him, time and time again. From my magic, to my nightmares, to every vulnerable part of my past—and he still kept minefields walled off behind those glacier-blue eyes.

Maybe I should've held something back, too.

By the time I reached the high cliffside ledge where the

dragons roosted, the sun was melting into the peaks of the Harrowhorns like molten gold. Flames kissed the mountaintops, the sky bleeding with pinks, golds, and deep indigos that mingled with the ascending clouds like spilled watercolor.

And there he was.

Krakos stood like a sentry at the cliff's edge, wings tucked neatly to his hulking obsidian form, nostrils leaking tiny puffs of smoke that curled upward into the evening air. And leaning against the beast's shoulder—the very picture of infuriating stoic beauty—stood Cade.

The dying light caught the edges of his sharp jaw, shimmering in the raven-black strands of his hair as they swayed gently in the cool wind. He hadn't noticed me yet. His gaze was fixed on the horizon, as if waiting for an answer the mountains couldn't give him.

And gods help me, he looked—gorgeous.

No.

Nope. Not going there.

I stomped across the ground, making sure he could hear every angry step I took.

He turned his head at the sound, eyes finding mine like magnets, unreadable as always.

"You're late," he said coolly.

"Good evening to you too, Prince of Secrets," I said, shoving my hair behind my ears and striding past him toward Errax, who raised her head from her resting place and rumbled softly in greeting.

Cade narrowed his eyes, clearly deciding not to take the bait —yet. "You ready?"

I climbed into Errax's saddle without replying, my fingers moving automatically through the motions. Her scales were warm under my touch, humming faintly with energy that matched my own fury a little too well tonight. "Let's just go," I muttered, eyes fixed ahead.

The silence that followed was dagger-sharp.

Krakos shifted his wings, and with a bellowing roar that made the rocks tremble beneath our feet, he surged into the sky. Errax followed a heartbeat later, lifting us into the wind with a single mighty beat of her wings.

The camp vanished below us until it was nothing more than a toy village tucked into the curve of the mountain. Cold air rushed past my cheeks as we rocketed upward, cutting through clouds painted gold by the falling sun. The silence between Cade and me stretched all the way into the heavens, and despite the view—despite the sheer wonder of dragon flight—I could still feel the burn simmering in my chest.

He kept staring at me from across the sky like he knew.

Like he was waiting for me to say it.

I didn't.

"You want to do offensive drills tonight?" he finally called, his voice flat, like this was just another training session.

I snorted, glancing over my shoulder. "I don't know. Maybe I'll ask Darren if he wants to give me private lessons. You two seem to have a lot in common these days."

I saw his jaw clench even from thirty yards away.

"Drop it."

"No." I spun Errax sideways, holding her in a wide circle as I glared at him across the empty air. "You get to disappear without telling anyone. Walk into secret meetings. Decide what the rest of us do next while the rest of your little war council thinks I'm some fucking demigod from the heavens. You don't get to tell me to drop it."

His dragon surged forward suddenly until we were nearly parallel. "You don't understand—"

"Because you won't tell me!"

"I can't, Ash!"

I stared at him, incredulous. "Can't? Or won't?"

Lightning surged in my chest—a memory, a spark from Eden —my magic reacting to the chaos boiling in my veins.

"You think I haven't told you things?" I hissed, voice shaking with rage. "Every time you looked at me like I was just some unstable water witch from Bramblebash? You think it was easy telling you what Garris did to me back home? All the beatings, him giving my body to his friends like I was a piece of meat. I've been nothing but honest with you, and you—"

"I'm trying to protect you!" he yelled over the wind. "And... I don't want to..."

"Oh gods, don't you dare—"

But I didn't let him finish. I turned Errax sharply and kicked into her side, telling her to fly, to fly fast, to get me the hell away from him before I said something unforgivable.

She obeyed without hesitation. Wings snapped wide, and we sped off into the clouds, the air biting cold against my face as the world blurred below.

"ASH!" Cade's voice echoed behind me, distant and furious.

But I didn't stop.

I didn't look back.

Because I didn't know what I'd do if I did.

Errax cut through the sky like a streak of lightning, her indigo wings snapping behind us as we rocketed through the clouds. The wind hit harder the higher we climbed, biting into the sweat on my skin, trying to rip the anger straight from my chest.

But it clung there—hot and pulsing. Ache and fury rolled together like a wave I couldn't outrun.

Why in the hell couldn't Cade just trust me?

"Ash!"

His voice broke through the wind behind me, sharp with fury and... worry. But it only fueled my fire.

"Go back!" I screamed over my shoulder. "Just go back!"

"No!"

His shout echoed around us, a blaze of heat and steel behind it as Krakos surged forward, trying to get closer. "You're not flying out here alone!"

"I don't need you to save me!"

But even as the words tore from my throat, something inside me twisted.

Because maybe I didn't want him to save me.

I wanted him to want me enough to tell me the truth.

Errax pushed forward, sensing my turmoil, her body rippling with tension as she climbed into the massive cloud sea hanging over the range. Silver mist swirled around us until the camp below vanished entirely. Only the sky and air and my own thoughts surrounded me.

But the silence didn't last.

A low screech pierced the wind. Then another.

My heart paused.

Errax jerked mid-air, twisting as a massive shadow sped overhead.

"What—?" I yanked the reins, spinning us sideways just in time to see jagged wings slicing through the clouds above.

Dozens.

Long, gaunt bodies, mottled greenish-gray hides stretching over skeletal frames. Their snarling mouths bared rows of uneven teeth. And the sound—gods, the sound they made—like shrieking razors howling through a storm.

Wild dragons.

They were above us. Below us. Surrounding.

Errax let out a furious roar, and I knew—we weren't going to make it back.

"Cade—!" I barely got the word out before Krakos dropped like a meteor in front of us, fire already building in the monster's throat.

"I see them!" Cade shouted, yanking his staff from the strap across his back. Its phoenix-head tip flared with red runes as he pulled up beside me.

"No time!" I screamed. "They've already got our scent—"

Too late.

The first one dove, wings tucked to its back like a spike, eyes glowing like molten coins as it screeched straight for Errax.

I twisted in my saddle and screamed, "Eden!"

Golden light blazed across my hands, Eden spiraling through my veins like a furious river let loose. I thrust my palm outward, summoning the Gilded Radiance with enough force to tear the air.

The beam of pure, searing light exploded outward and struck the wild dragon mid-descent. Its scream cut short as it spiraled sideways, wings shuttering under the force of the spell before it dropped into the fog like a crumpling tower.

But the others didn't stop.

Seven more barreled toward us from the upper cloud line.

"Get behind me!" Cade barked—and I didn't argue.

Krakos roared like a storm let loose, inhaled—and exhaled a stream of fire so blindingly bright it was like staring into the heart of the sun. It tore through the nearest wild dragon, cleaving it in two before the blaze engulfed the next.

They shrieked. Fell.

But three more managed to dodge it, claws outstretched, wings slamming downward as they bolted toward me.

Errax screamed back, banking hard left as I summoned another spell, golden sparks drenching the air between us and our attackers.

But one slipped close—too close. Its massive claws raked down Errax's side, leaving gashes across her scales. She screamed and bucked, and my stomach flipped as we spiraled downward, wings flailing to catch wind again.

"Ash!" Cade roared, diving toward me.

"I've got it—!" I shouted, gripping the reins hard, "—I've got her!" I tried to soothe her with calming words in my head, but I gritted my teeth and yanked the reins hard. *Evade and attack, fight with all your strength,* I thought.

Errax rolled violently and caught air inches above the mountainside. I couldn't breathe—could barely think.

More wild dragons poured in from below like vultures scenting blood.

I summoned Eden again, her power flaring so bright my body convulsed with pain. I shaped the magic into twin pillars of light and hurled them forward.

Two wild dragons peeled away sharply, wings shuddering from the force. One caught a beam in the side of the neck and tumbled with a guttural shriek that made my blood chill.

But then—something cracked behind me.

An enormous impact.

Krakos had plowed full force into the heart of the swarm, his body a blur of flame and scale. Cade spun atop him, staff whirling and bursting with columns of flame that sent dragons shrieking as they scattered.

"We need backup!" Cade yelled, his staff glowing like a sun held in his hand.

I didn't respond.

Because I couldn't catch my breath.

Every beat, every flap of Errax's wings, was a cry of resistance. But they were everywhere—clawing, shrieking, diving past us with razored wings and jaws that snapped too close.

And then, deep in the storm clouds above—

The horn sounded.

The signal.

A long, low thunderous blast that trembled through the sky.

Stormscales.

Dragons burst from the clouds overhead in formation. Silver and black. Dozens of them, their sleek forms like shadows of retribution ripping into the enemy flank.

Talonor struck first, slicing into the chaos with long narrow jaws and a horrifying scream that cut straight through one of the wild dragons.

Behind him, Carina flew like death incarnate—her dragon spinning into the melee with precision-aimed breath. Wicked fire tore through the enemy sky.

The wild dragons, sensing the tide turning, banked and scattered.

Three more went down in lightning-fast spirals. Cade and I followed as the last trickle of them vanished back into the mountains, chased by Stormscales shouting war cries into the wind.

It was over. And we were alive.

I slumped forward over Errax's neck, my breath rasping in my ears, my heart trying to pound its way out of my chest.

And then, slowly, we descended.

The wind howled around us the whole way. Krakos landed first with a thundering slam. Errax hissed as her injured wing clipped too hard on descent, and I jumped down as soon as her claws hit the rocks of Storm's End.

The moment my boots touched the ground, Cade was off Krakos like a lightning strike.

"What the fuck were you thinking?" he shouted, storming toward me.

Oh no.

"No," I snapped, throwing my hand up, still trembling from the fight. "Don't do this—"

"You took off into the fucking clouds without a plan! Do you even understand how lucky we are to be alive?! How lucky they were to get here in time?!"

"Don't act like this is all on me!"

"It is on you!" he shouted. "You left! You ran! You flew wildly into a death trap because you were angry—because what, I didn't want to share every little secret with you?!"

"You kept a secret meeting from me!"

"And you nearly got killed!"

My voice rose with a scream. "I didn't ask you to save me!"

I didn't mean the words that poured out of my mouth like vomit.

Silence.

The camp stared. Dozens of soldiers, Darren, Carina, Bella, Hunter—all staring at us where we stood, breathing hard, broken, scorched and battered in the remains of battle.

And I'd never felt more humiliated in my life.

"I'm done," I said, spine rigid, throat burning.

Cade's eyes flashed. "Ash—"

"No." I stepped back, all warmth bleeding from my voice. "I needed you. And you shut me out."

He stared, frozen.

"I never want to see you again." Again, words I didn't mean, but I was too tired to fight them.

I turned on my heel and didn't wait for the echo, didn't wait for the whispers behind me or the looks of pity or the way Errax limped slowly after me, low and wounded.

I walked away. Through camp. Through shadows and firelight and the stunned gazes of war-hardened soldiers who probably didn't even know what had just fallen apart before them.

But I did.

I knew.

And gods help me—I didn't know if I'd be able to put it back together again.

CHAPTER 19

Rain began to fall in slow, misty sheets across the Stormscale field, the first droplets spattering across my shoulders as the sky above the Harrowhorns churned with gathering clouds. A dark storm was brewing in the mountains, like some vast beast rising from the stone.

Fitting, really.

Every warrior in Storm's End had gathered on the blackened grass stretching beneath the slate sky, arranged by rank and flight formation. Row upon row of polished leather and glinting steel. They didn't move. Didn't speak. The only sounds were the soft creak of armor, the flutter of dragon wings above us, and the quiet drip of rain falling onto the worn flagstones.

Cade stood beside me.

And we hadn't spoken a single word since our dragon flight, and our battle. In both senses of the word.

Not since last night—since the screaming, the blaming, the wild dragons, the public unraveling of every fragile, frayed thread holding us together.

Now, we stood shoulder to shoulder, silent. Strangers all over again.

His head was angled slightly forward, dark hair dripping steadily in the rain, his jaw hard and unmoving. A shadow wrapped in a royal tunic. He hadn't looked at me once. Not once.

And maybe I deserved that.

Darren stood at Cade's other side, his massive shoulders squared beneath a thick cloak lined with fur. The general was still despite the stirring wind, his scarred face unreadable as his daughter, Carina, leaned in close and whispered something through the hiss of wet air. Whatever she said, Darren didn't react. His focus was fixed ahead, on the audience of Stormscale soldiers that stretched across the field like a lake of silver-black fire waiting to be unleashed.

The rain kissed the hem of my sleeves and trickled down my fingers. Errax coiled behind me, low and watchful, her wide emerald eyes like cut stone, wings twitching at the thunder crawling distantly across the sky.

I shifted my weight. The ache from yesterday's wounds still lived along my ribs and thighs, but it wasn't pain that made it hard to stand still. It was tension. Memory. The wreckage Cade and I had left smoldering in front of half the camp just hours before.

He moved at last, stepping forward with his staff in hand—the one topped with the sculpted bird in rubies and flame.

The crowd straightened like they felt the shift before it happened.

And then Cade's voice rose.

It wasn't yelling. It didn't need to be.

His voice cracked like thunder.

"Stormscales."

Not a single soldier flinched.

Cade turned his whole body toward the crowd and raised his chin, letting the wind batter his long dark cloak. The rain had gone from a trickle to a steady patter now, water streaming off the scales of Krakos where he stood at the cliff's edge behind us.

"For years, you've known me as your enemy," Cade said, his words carrying across the wide field in perfect clarity. "You fought me across stone and sky. Our armies clashed over rivers and mountain passes. And for years, blood was our only language."

A few soldiers glanced at each other, but still no one spoke.

Cade's gloved hand tightened around his staff.

"But those days…" He paused, the wind pulling at his hair. "Those days are done."

Silence clung heavy to the skin, but it was the good kind—the kind that slides into the space before something extraordinary.

"We are not enemies," Cade said. "Not anymore. We are soldiers of the same war, drenched in the same grief, hounded by the same nightmare."

A low wind howled between the cliffs, the storm building behind him, as if the skies themselves bent to hear.

"I was raised in the fires of Emberveil. Trained by generals who studied nothing but conquest. Victory. Control. But what I found in that was not power—it was fear. Hers. Because Mortriana Vissex…" His voice twisted around the name like a weapon. "—rules through fear. She rules through false loyalty. Through poisoned magic and lies."

Now some expressions shifted. Soldiers no longer simply stared—they listened.

Cade took another step forward, shoulders broad and royal and immune to the wet.

"I will train you," he said. "I will show you how to fortify your fortress. I will map the weaknesses in her walls, show you where my old army bleeds behind their sermons. I will teach you how to fight them—" His voice grew sharp. "How to break them."

A sudden roar of stomping boots answered him, the Stormscale war cry echoing through the coming rain like the bellow of a beast awakened.

My heart jumped in my chest. I felt it in my bones, vibrating through the soles of my boots, shooting straight through my lower back to my scalp.

Cade didn't flinch. He let it pass over him, through him, and when it stilled again, he raised his voice one more time.

"This war has lasted too long," he said. "And yet the final stretch stands before us. The queen is amassing her forces. Her endgame is awakening beneath the mountain. You know what must be stopped. You know what is at stake. You are no longer just Stormscales."

His voice lowered, but somehow it struck twice as deep.

"You are the resistance. The reckoning. And you—" His head turned slowly, gaze colliding with mine like a punch to the ribs. "—will win this war. Because this—this one beside me... is Ashlyn Moonriver."

My chest tightened.

And then he said, without a hint of irony or hesitation:

"She is the key to our victory."

For a second, the world was still.

Then, all at once, the Stormscales shouted.

Every soldier. Every commander. Every beast and wing and voice raised with it.

The sound stopped my breath completely. A pounding roar that didn't fade.

They were cheering for me.

Me.

Ash Mist.

Ash Moonriver.

I stood there soaked and stunned, every scar from my past exposed beneath my armor, and yet somehow... I wasn't crumbling.

Because I wasn't just a former slave anymore.

I was standing in front of an army.

And they believed in me.

Darren stepped forward, his heavy boots squelching against

the wet earth, the hammering rain sliding off the metal of his pauldrons in long, glistening sheets. He glanced at Cade once, an unspoken understanding passing between them—a war shared in silence. Then he turned to face his army, his people, and raised a clenched fist into the air.

"The fight ahead will not be easy!" Darren's voice was like rolling thunder, deep and commanding. "It will not be swift. It will not be clean. Many of us… will not come back."

The breath caught in my throat. The Stormscales didn't flinch.

"But it must be fought!" Darren barked, pacing before the ranks now. "Because the woman that rules Emberveil is no queen —she is a demon. A venom in the veins of Allovan's heart. And the only cure for poison is fire."

That earned a few triumphant roars from the crowd, fists raised, blades pounded against breastplates.

Darren turned then, his voice dropping just low enough that the closeness suddenly made it feel like he wasn't speaking to soldiers anymore… but to family.

"Our alliance is stronger than her armies. We have dragons, we have skill, we have purpose." He raised his arm again, driving the next words through the mounting wind. "But above all that, we have her—"

He pointed right at me, water flying from the motion.

Ashlyn Moonriver. *Me…*

The crowd shifted immediately, every glance snapping toward me, blades of silver, brown, blue, and gold eyes sharpened under helms and hoods and rain.

"She has faced the monster Mortriana and lived," Darren growled. "She bested her. Wounded her. Survived her flames and refused to fall. You stand shoulder to shoulder with a survivor of the queen's hell—and more than that, perhaps… the one who will end her forever."

I stood frozen, rain cascading down my face and matting my hair to my neck.

What the abyss was I supposed to say to that?

Darren gestured toward me. "And now, she has something to say."

I snapped my head at him so fast my neck cracked.

"No I don't," I mouthed, utterly horrified.

Beside me, Carina gave me a bright, forceful nudge with her elbow and whispered, "Now's the time, Gold-Marked." Bella nudged me with a hardened expression and a slight, forceful nod.

Against every screaming nerve in my body, my feet moved.

Each step squelched against the sodden ground, and I could feel hundreds of eyes dragging across me like cold iron hooks, weighing me, measuring me.

Gods, I wasn't supposed to be here.

I wasn't a soldier.

I wasn't a leader.

I was a girl who used to cower behind cellar doors when Garris would drag screaming girls down the stairs. A girl who barely escaped Bramblebash with her skin intact.

And now here I stood. Facing the most feared warriors in Allovan. And they were waiting for me to offer them... hope.

I stopped just shy of the edge of the crowd, my hands clenched at my sides, nails digging into the soft leather of my gloves.

"I..." I cleared my throat. It came out raspy. I tried again, louder.

"I'm not like you."

A few brows rose.

"I wasn't trained with a blade. I didn't sleep on cold stone beside a fire. I wasn't raised by warriors or soldiers or nobles. I wasn't anyone."

A silence fell so deep it seemed to drain the wind from the field.

"Until her." My eyes narrowed as I stared past the crowd—past the mountains—toward the storm gathering over the queen's domain. "Until she hunted me. Until she tried to break me. All for a magical power I didn't know I had until very recently. My power, my curse, my destiny..."

I hesitated, exhaled. Closed my eyes.

"But I beat her once."

A chorus of murmurs rippled outward like a wave.

"And with your help..." I opened my eyes again, sharp and steady, even if my knees trembled. "...I'll kill her once and for all."

The field erupted.

Shouts thundered across the rocks like war drums.

Blades rose above heads, fists slammed into soaked chainmail, dragons behind us shrieked and pulled at the rains like they could tear the clouds from the sky. They cheered—not because I said something grand or heroic, but because I had tried. Because I'd stood there, truth and all, and made them believe I would fight with them.

For them.

The rain came down harder, thick now, drumming against our boots and shoulders like heavy hands. Bella grinned wide and winked my way.

Darren raised his palm, and even through the new wind, the clamor fell quiet again.

"From this moment forward," he said, voice low and sharp. "Your new training begins. Prince Phoenixfire will meet now with the flight captains. He has your drills and formations. He has your flight routes. You will do as he commands."

Cade stepped forward again, giving only the barest nod. "You'll learn how she thinks. And how to out-fly her dragons. Or die trying. We must fight past her dragon riders, her army, her legion of Sythers, and get Ash to face the queen, before the queen can get to her first."

No one questioned it.

The Stormscales began to disperse in long lines, captains motioning for units to split, dragons taking off to begin exercises in the rain as crews readied ropes, target dummies, high-altitude spears.

The war machine had begun its next rhythm.

And I—still wet, still cold, still raw—wanted nothing more than to flee right back to the bunks and drown myself in a fur blanket and a bottle of wine.

But Cade turned toward me.

It was subtle—just his body shifting slightly, his storm-dark eyes lifting from the newly rippling field to find mine.

His mouth opened.

And I spun around and walked away without a word.

Let the rain swallow my footsteps. Let the wind carry whatever apology he might've tried to give me to the gods.

Because I wasn't ready to hear it.

Not while secrets sat between us like blades in the dark.

Not when I still didn't know what he was hiding.

Not when I still didn't trust that he'd ever tell me.

So I walked.

Right down the slope. Past the dragons. Past the shouts and torchlight. Letting it all fall behind me.

Gods help me—I wasn't sure how this would end.

But I knew one thing.

I would not beg him for the truth. Not again.

Not even if it killed me.

CHAPTER 20

I stormed down the mountain path, boots slipping in the wet mud with each furious step. The rain was lighter here, just a mist that clung to my hair and soaked into my rolled-up sleeves, but it didn't cool the fire inside me.

Gods, I was still seething.

My fists clenched so tight my knuckles screamed from it. Every breath felt like another chokehold, dragging the night before back around my throat. Cade and his secrets. Cade and his brooding, silent, untouchable bullshit. He could stand in that field, giving rousing speeches like he was already king, but couldn't tell me what was really going on.

Not even after everything.

The trees welcomed me with dripping limbs and whispering leaves. The familiar bend of the trail led off the path into a grove, a patch of pine and moss deep in the woods where the air always felt older, quieter.

Good.

I needed something I could hurt. I needed to let out my rage. I needed to feel something else.

Before I even reached the center of the grove, I spun and slammed my fist against the nearest tree, the bark biting into my knuckles hard enough to make pain bloom up my arm.

"God damn him!" I screamed into the thicket. "Damn him and his stupid, perfect, gorgeous face!"

The tree didn't answer. It just stood there, bleeding sap from where I'd cracked the bark. I drew back and hit it again.

"He tells me I'm the key, says I'm the one who's going to end all this—and then he looks at me like he's carrying the whole world alone." My voice cracked. "Like I'm the one thing he has to keep in the dark!"

A twig snapped behind me.

I didn't turn.

"I swear, Bella, if you tell me this is all some Blaze Prince love language—"

"It's not," she said softly.

Her voice was calm, but her boots peeled across the wet moss like she was walking toward something fragile. I collapsed down into a crouch beside the same tree I'd just taken my anger out on, pressing my forehead to the bark as hot, angry tears prickled at the back of my eyes.

"I trusted him," I whispered, breath catching. "I told him things I've never said out loud. Ever."

"I know."

I didn't look at her. She didn't expect me to. She just stayed there, the way she always did, close enough to reach without making it a big thing.

The tears came fast then, burning hot down my cheeks. I sank down to my knees, dragging my palms through the slick grass as if the earth had somehow betrayed me too.

"All I've wanted," I choked out, "all I've wanted is to be free and safe and… and maybe cared for. Not pitied. Not protected. Just…."

"Loved?" Bella finished quietly.

I couldn't say it.

It felt too raw. Too exposed—like stepping off a cliff without a dragon waiting to catch me. But gods, she knew. She always knew.

"And when I think—I think we might actually be able to have that, that thing... those deep feelings, real ones... he just—walls off."

I slammed my fist into the dirt. "Every time. Every fucking time!"

A long pause.

"I'm so tired of having to chase people who say they care," I whispered, finally giving in as the tears slid down my face unchecked. "We fought the queen together. I almost died—for him. And he still won't..."

I pressed a shaking hand to my mouth to stop the rest. The sob broke through anyway, curling in my chest like a dying ember that wouldn't go out.

"I don't know what else I'm supposed to give."

The leaves above us rustled gently.

I glanced up—and there he was.

Cornelius.

The ancient tortoise sat quietly among the roots of a nearby tree, his deep golden eyes fixed on me in that unblinking, eternal way of his. He didn't say a word. Didn't move.

Maybe he couldn't fix this.

Gods knew I couldn't.

"I just..." I swiped at my cheeks furiously. "I wish there was some way to undo this curse. Some way we could really be together. Touch without burning. Kiss without losing the air in our lungs. Breathe each other in without falling to pieces."

My fingers curled in my lap, damp with tears and earth and regret.

"But there's nothing, is there?" I said aloud, shaking my head. "There's no fix. The Blaze Prince and the Aqualorian girl—just doomed to want each other from opposite sides of a battlefield we're both chained to."

Cornelius dipped his head slightly, but said nothing.

"Why can't he tell me?" I whispered. "After everything we've seen together, after everything I've shown him… why doesn't he trust me?"

Bella knelt in the moss beside me, wrapping her arms around my shoulders. She was warm and solid and kind in a way I didn't deserve right then.

"I don't know," she said. "But I know he cares."

I let my head fall against her shoulder, the weight of the past few days dragging me flat. "That's the worst part, isn't it?"

Bella sighed. "Yeah. It is."

The woods were quiet for a while, save for the light tapping of rain against the leaves and the far-off shriek of dragons in the distance. Somewhere over the peaks behind us, I could hear the barely-audible roar of drills—the Stormscales beginning their new training. Shouts echoed over the valley as riders launched into the sky.

"They don't need me," I muttered. "Not really. He's got the plans. The troops are ready. What if I just... went?"

Bella stiffened. "Went where?"

"I could fly north," I said. "Straight to Raven's Bane. Just me and Errax. End this now. Spare everyone the bloodshed. Catch her off guard."

"No," Bella said immediately, like she'd been expecting me to say something that ridiculous eventually.

"She wouldn't expect it," I mumbled, though half-heartedly now. "A single dragon, flying alone? I could—"

"You'd be dead before your boots touched her courtyard," Bella snapped. She pulled back to look me square in the eye. "Ash, you said it yourself—you beat her once. But barely. And even then you were surrounded by help, by Cade, by your dragon. Going in alone would be suicide."

I glanced toward the sound of the dragons training and felt something dark twist in my chest.

"I hate that he won't talk to me."

"I know."

"I hate that even after everything, he can't let me in."

Bella didn't speak, and neither did Cornelius. Sometimes there weren't words big enough to fix the weight of silence.

I just sat there in the dirt, sodden sleeves cold on my arms, my cheeks damp and raw from tears—and wondered how in all the countless battles we were about to face...

...the hardest one might be with someone who shared my heart.

And didn't know what to do with it.

The rain had relented by the time Bella and I made our way back to the training field, though clouds still loomed above the mountains like silent sentinels, watching and waiting. The scent of wet stone and scorched leather hung thick in the air, and the faint rumble of thunder still whispered through the peaks beyond.

Stormscales filled the field—hundreds of them. At least twice as many as I'd seen in the morning. Some practiced formation drills on the ground, shoulder to shoulder with spears balanced in perfect sync. Others mounted dragons and launched into the sky from the cliff ledge, their wings slicing the air with strategic rhythm. Cade's drills, no doubt.

I watched one group of four riders form a tight V and bolt upward into the low clouds, twisting in a spiral before breaking off like shrapnel. They recovered faster, cleaner than the drills from just yesterday. Already more coordinated. Stronger.

They were preparing.

I pretended not to see Cade standing at the other end of the field, not that it made a damn difference. I could feel him. In the set of my jaw. In the twist of my spine. In the way the center of my chest flared like there was still fire trapped somewhere inside it—and he was the only one who could burn it out.

His deep voice carried as he spoke to Darren and a half-dozen flight captains, gesturing across the chalked flight paths drawn in the dirt. Every time I moved, his gaze followed. I didn't have to look to know.

The problem was—I still wanted to.

Carina joined us partway through the walk, dressed not in her usual armor but in a loose tunic rolled at the sleeves, her hair braided back from her face in a series of intricate twists that exposed a fresh ring of bruises along one forearm.

"Training's brutal today," she said in greeting, nodding toward the far cliff where two dragons nearly collided mid-dive.

I quirked a brow. "What happened to you?" I nodded at the bruises.

"Too much faith in a rookie, not enough faith in my dragon," she said, waving it off. "I'll heal. You should see the recruit." She grinned—ruthlessly proud.

I glanced over again at the field, suddenly struck by just how many new faces I didn't recognize.

"Where'd they all come from?" I asked and heard the weariness in my voice. "The Stormscales… there are so many…"

"All over," Carina said. "Isles, southern coast, even some from beyond the sea."

I blinked. "Why? Do they just volunteer to fight for the good of our lands?"

Her face darkened. "Why do any of us come? Because they have nothing left."

I looked closer, and now, I could see it beneath the shinier bits—the cracks in the polish they wore.

The woman adjusting a saddle with a missing left hand and a deep burn that ran from chin to clavicle. The man helping strap down a launch point, his eyes milk-white from blindness yet moving with uncanny precision as his dragon listened to his whispered directions. Scars. Scorch marks. Dragged legs. Missing fingers.

"Many were burned in raids." Carina's voice was low now. "Some lost entire families to the queen's punishments—suspected rebel sympathisers, or just being in the wrong place at the wrong time. Like Rose Ridge."

I stilled. "Rose Ridge? The town?"

She nodded. "It used to be… She suspected someone in the village was smuggling a letter to the rebellion. They weren't." Her mouth twisted. "Didn't stop her from sweeping through with her Sythers and Brigodon. Women, children, livestock—nothing left standing by morning."

My gut turned cold.

"Now those who survived?" Carina glanced at the woman with one hand, then the blind man. "They train. Because the only thing they have left is revenge."

I didn't respond. I couldn't.

Because the sickest part of it all?

I understood that sentiment too well.

I looked down at my own hands.

The ones that had clawed through fire and claw marks and magic and grief, that had shaken while gripping a sword I barely knew I could wield.

Cade had fought in those wars. I had no doubt somewhere among these Stormscales were people who had bled because of him. Who had lost a brother, a sister, to a decision he'd made from a palace wall while wearing black and fire red.

But war took long, hungry bites out of everyone. And now, here we stood—different sides of the same wound.

I felt them—those soldiers—watch me. Eyes skimming over where the gold mark on my neck glowed when I casted. The rune that pulsed when my emotions flared, the sweat and agony and tears still clinging to me like another layer of skin.

And they still believed I could save them.

Gods.

I wasn't sure if that was hope or madness.

Then I felt him again.

I turned before I could stop myself—before I could talk myself out of it.

And Cade was there.

Walking toward me, head low against the wind, his steps purposeful.

I took a slow step back without thinking.

Not now.

I couldn't—gods, I couldn't do this right now.

He reached me anyway. Close enough that I could see the way the rain clung to his lashes. The way his eyes—blue, sharp, storm-cut and aching—never broke from mine.

I turned to walk away.

"Ash," he said, deep and soft and tired in a way I wasn't used to hearing from him. "Wait."

I didn't.

His hand caught mine.

I froze.

And curse me to the Infernal Depths, I let him hold it.

"Ash," he said again, gently now, like saying my name alone might keep me from spiraling off into the clouds again. "I know you don't trust me right now, but..."

Lightning crackled somewhere far across the sky.

"There's something you need to see."

I pulled at my hand weakly.

"Cade, I don't want—"

"Please." His fingers closed tighter. "Ash, you need to come with me."

He leaned forward, his voice a breath. A plea.

"I have to show you something."

I looked at him then. Really looked.

And gods, I hated what I saw.

Because despite everything, despite my anger, my pride, my pain—

I still wanted to follow him.

More than anything.

CHAPTER 21

I didn't want to get on my dragon.

Errax huffed quietly beside me, her indigo wings half-extended, dew misting her sleek blue scales as if even she wasn't sure what the hell we were doing.

Cade stood ten feet away, already mounted on Krakos, his black cloak whipping behind him in the sharp morning wind. And like everything he did, he wouldn't explain.

Not really.

Storm's End bustled at our backs—rows of Stormscale soldiers in tight formation, shouts echoing down the training field, the scrape of blades and clash of drills ringing out beneath the overcast sky. The camp was alive. Preparing for war.

And we were getting on dragons. Flying off. To gods knew where.

Hunter and Bella stood off to the side with matching frowns. Carina raised a suspicious brow but didn't stop us. Probably because she knew better than to try.

"What in Odiun's name is he doing?" Bella muttered as I adjusted the saddle straps on Errax for the second time, more out of frustration than necessity.

"I don't know," I said low under my breath, "but if he thinks flying me out into the clouds again is going to magically fix what he broke, he's got another thing coming."

Still, my boots hit the stirrups.

I swung a leg up.

And I hated how my heart fluttered—not with anger this time, but something smaller, something I wanted to crush before it grew feelings and started singing in my chest again.

Because he asked me to come. Me. Not Darren, not some flight captain, not even Hunter.

He asked me.

I settled into Errax's saddle with a sigh and caught Cade's eyes as he turned Krakos toward the ledge.

They were unreadable. Distant. But still locked on me.

"Where are we going?" I called, trying to keep the edge out of my voice. Mostly failing.

"I don't know exactly," he said, and his voice carried across the wind, low and even. "But there's no time to waste. This is important."

I rolled my eyes. "You know, if you ever start a religion, secrecy will definitely be one of your holy virtues."

He glanced back at me then, and for the first time, there was something on his face like hesitance. Like guilt. "I need you to trust me."

The words hit harder than I wanted them to.

Trust me.

I didn't answer. Just gave a sharp word to Errax, and with one mighty beat of her wings, we were airborne.

Below, Storm's End shrank quickly into a stack of slate buildings and silver glints of shifting scales. The clouds were low today, heavy and swollen over the sharp mountaintops, haze curling like smoke around the jagged peaks as we flew northward —deeper, further, beyond what the maps at the war council showed in detail.

The mountains changed around us.

They grew sharper. Darker. More hostile.

Trees thinned. Valleys deepened. Some cliffs dropped away so severely they looked like gods had carved the land apart with massive blades. It felt like old magic clung to the air here—an ancient, bone-deep chill that lived in the wind and tasted like forgotten storms.

Hours passed.

We flew through it all, silent.

Cade didn't turn to speak again, and I didn't ask.

But I watched him.

The muscles along his back were taut. His hand never strayed far from Krakos's reins, but even from a distance, I could see his fingers flexing, clenching. Like a man expecting something—needing something—and not finding it.

Eventually, he dipped low and signaled for us to land.

We touched down on the peak of a jagged stone bluff, higher than anything around us for miles. The sky felt thinner here, the air pulling hard with every breath. But the view?

Gods.

It was like staring into the crown of the world.

Canyons stretched far below like cracked porcelain, glittering rivers cutting through shadows. Mountain crags tore the horizon into bloody ribbons where the sun was setting faint and pale through the angry clouds.

Errax lowered her body, tucking her wings beside Krakos, both dragons unnaturally quiet.

I slid off her back and stepped onto the uneven rock.

Cade stood near the edge already, his cloak snapping in the high wind, his dark hair wild, untamed. He stared forward like if he kept searching hard enough, something would reveal itself.

"This your idea of a romantic getaway?" I asked, folding my arms.

He didn't answer.

He didn't even blink.

"What are we doing up here, Cade?" I asked, louder now.

He turned slightly, jaw clenched. "I'm looking."

I frowned. "For what?"

He didn't answer.

I walked forward, boots crunching against gravel. "Cade?"

His gaze narrowed toward the far cliff faces. Something taut and fractured coiled in his expression, his stance, the way his hand opened and closed into a fist at his side.

His armor gleamed faintly beneath his cloak, but it looked heavier today. Like he wore it out of habit instead of choice.

"What are we looking for?" I tried again.

His voice was quiet when it finally came.

"A waterfall."

I blinked.

"A… waterfall?"

He nodded once. Didn't look at me.

My stomach twisted.

"You dragged me into storm country to look for a waterfall?"

Silence.

"Is that it?" I asked. "That's the big secret?"

Still, he said nothing. Just moved to a rock nearby and sank down, shoulders bunched, fingers laced tightly together between his knees.

His eyes stayed distant.

Somewhere behind his glare was an old rage. Not at me.

At something else.

Something clawing.

I stood there, unmoving.

Until a glint of motion caught my eye.

Something shiny. Far off in the chasm.

I moved to the cliff's edge, boots scraping stone. From here, I could just barely trace the winding white ribbon descending from a shadowed ridge, cradled inside two jagged blades of stone.

A waterfall.

Barely visible... but there.

"There's one," I said, pointing.

Cade didn't move.

But I saw it then—the barest twitch in his jaw. The sliver of breath held too long.

Whatever this was... it mattered.

And by the look on his face—

We were nowhere near unraveling it yet.

Cade stood suddenly.

Rushed to me.

His boots scraped against the rock and his momentum almost startled me, but he stopped just short of colliding, his shoulder brushing mine, breath tight at the edge of his voice.

"Where?" he demanded, eyes locked on the horizon like a hound catching scent.

I lifted my hand again and pointed through the veil of mist swirling over the chasm far below. The waterfall I'd seen before shimmered between two jagged slices of stone, narrow and twisting like a silver thread cast between the rocks. Sunlight caught on it for the briefest moment—and there, coiled faintly in its stream, was something else.

A flicker.

Not sunlight.

Not water.

A glow—deep scarlet, flickering like candlelight behind a curtain.

My brows lowered. "Is that... red?"

Cade stiffened beside me.

I turned toward him. "Is that a red glow?"

His answer was immediate.

"Yes," he breathed, one word, entirely unguarded. "Ash, that's it."

Then, like something wild and caged had finally broken loose in his chest, he spun on his heel.

"We need to go," he said, fast. "Now."

Before I could blink, he was vaulting onto Krakos's back, already gripping the reins, yanking the saddle straps into place like he'd forgotten any world existed besides that waterfall.

"Cade," I called, but he wasn't listening.

Krakos launched skyward with a roar.

I cursed aloud, stumbling backward toward Errax. "He couldn't have even waited one godsdamned second."

Errax rumbled low, annoyed but ready. I mounted in two breaths and we took off, wings snapping wide and slicing through the air as we followed Cade down the ridge.

The wind howled as we dove toward the narrowing canyon, cliffs tightening like a noose of jagged teeth on either side. Cade kept pulling ahead, Krakos faster and leaner in the dive, his wings cutting the thin air like scythes. I felt the elevation drop in my bones, the wind lashing at my face harder the lower we went.

"Slow down!" I shouted. "You'll kill yourself if you hit something!"

Of course, he didn't. Cade Phoenixfire never slowed for anything—not fire, not war, not fucking common sense.

Still, I followed.

I always did.

By the time we reached the base of the chasm, the light had shifted. The narrowing cliffs blotted out most of the afternoon sun, casting everything in a strange shadow, cold and unreal. Moss clung to the high ridges. Water vapor filled the air.

And there—at the dead end of everything—was the pool.

It was flawless.

A perfect still sheet of glass, ringed by black stone and mist. The waterfall tumbled from between two massive cliff jaws, pouring out in slow, lapping streams—except not entirely.

Because threaded through the silver water like veins through marble were strands of red.

Light.

No—not light.

Flame.

Fire coiled through the waterfall like it was dancing. But not just any fire. This wasn't Cade's magic. Wasn't the wild blaze of Krakos or the horrific inferno of Brigodon. This was something older. Slower. More deliberate. As though the flames weren't just alive—but watching.

Beneath it all, the pool shimmered unnaturally. I stared down into it from Errax's saddle and saw no reflection, only a void that rippled gold at the edges. Like it didn't want to show me what was real. Like it needed to hide its secrets because if I saw them—

I'd never leave.

Errax landed beside Krakos who was already crouched, massive wings tucked close. Cade had dismounted before I touched down. I jumped off Errax's back without taking my eyes off the water.

He stood at the pool's edge. His broad shoulders were tense. His fists at his sides weren't clenched this time.

They were trembling.

"What is this place?" I asked softly, barely recognizing my own voice.

He didn't speak.

He couldn't.

He stared forward as though seeing something no one else could. Like his past was carved into the air before him. His mouth hung open. And for the first time, I realized how different this was from any battlefield, any camp, any war talk we'd had.

He wasn't a prince here.

Not even a soldier.

He was… searching.

"This is it," he said quietly, as if stunned the words were real. "This is what the mystic meant."

His words hit like a blow to the chest. I turned my eyes from the flames to him.

"Myrathyn," I breathed.

Cade nodded slowly, still staring at the water. "He told me it would be hidden. Beyond reach except by blood and desire. That only two bound by fire and water could find it."

Two bound—

Oh.

Oh, gods.

Everything snapped into place then—the secret meetings, the long absences, the frantic desperation in his training sessions, the nights he woke alone by the fire as if haunted by something unspoken.

This wasn't about the queen.

It had never been about the war.

This was about us.

"What is this, Cade?" I asked, my throat tightening. "What are we doing here?"

He didn't answer immediately.

But I saw it in his eyes.

This place... was personal.

Deeper than magic. Older than rage. Sacred in a way that made my skin shiver.

"I don't know what it is," he said at last, stepping toward the edge of the pool, his boots making no sound against the smooth stone. "But it's old. Ancient. Far beyond anything man or woman was ever meant to touch."

I joined him, side by side, close enough to feel the heat coming from the water's surface. It wasn't burning, not like his touch, not like our cursed kisses—but it was powerful. Wild.

"It's magical," I whispered, finally understanding. "Isn't it?"

His voice was distant but sure. "Yes."

I squinted up at the waterfall, watching the impossible curls of flame licking upward through silver streams.

"This… this shouldn't exist."

"It shouldn't," he agreed. "But it does."

"So why," I breathed, "why are we here?"

Cade was silent for a long moment.

Then he turned his head—finally, finally—his eyes locking with mine, dark blue and steady as the abyss.

"I'll show you."

And gods help me—

The way he said it?

It felt like he was about to split the world open.

"This is it." Cade's voice came like thunder whispered through glass—low but unbreakable. "This… is what I've been searching for."

He stood rigid beneath the flame-lit waterfall, his back damp with mist, his raven-black cloak clinging to the angles of his armor. Firelight crackled behind him as if the stones themselves bore heat beneath their hide.

"And what Darren helped me find," he added, glancing sideways at me—but not quite meeting my eyes.

I folded my arms across my chest, trying not to shake from the brisk wind snaking across the rock. "You and Darren have been out here… chasing waterfalls?"

He didn't flinch. Didn't even smirk at the joke like he normally would have. That scared me more than anything.

"This is the only one like it in the world," he said, stepping forward. "It glows like fire, but it flows like water. It doesn't feed into any known river system. No maps mark its location, not officially. But I knew it existed. I just didn't know where—until Darren helped me find it."

Something tilted sideways in my chest. "Myrathyn told you about it, and Darren helped you find it? Why didn't you tell me?"

Cade nodded once. "Myrathyn told me—'red water sings where fire sleeps. A deeply magical place where fire ripples through the secret falls.' I didn't understand it until recently. When we started working with the Stormscales, Darren remembered whispers of a place like this. Said it used to be sacred. Untouched except by those with the right to find it."

I took a slow step forward, jaw tight. "You think this is sacred?"

"I know it is."

"And... this is the thing you couldn't tell me? You've been searching all his time... for this?" I asked, voice sharper than I meant it, but I didn't pull it back.

He didn't answer right away—and that said enough on its own. But then his expression softened, just slightly, and he stepped toward me.

"I wanted to be sure," he said. "I didn't want to drag you into something half-formed, Ash. Not until I could bring you here. I—I didn't want to give you false hope, until... Until I was *certain*."

"Here," I echoed, scanning the silver-and-fire waterfall again before settling my gaze on the pool at its base. In the center of the water sat a pale, bone-like stone, half-submerged. It rose about four feet from the pond, narrow but jagged with a broad base like a round tabletop, tilting slightly like it had been thrown by some god-hand through the earth and left here to rot.

It did not belong.

Even from here, I could feel it humming.

Strange. Unnatural. Older than fire.

"We?" I said quietly.

Cade turned.

His hand was already outstretched. Flame-kissed water glinted across his wrist, and for once, I didn't hesitate when I reached back.

He caught my palm in one smooth movement.

"You..." I muttered as my heart pounded deep in my chest like a drum. "You asked the Mystic... about us?"

"Yes," he said simply. "We. Always—us."

I didn't have anything to say to that. Not yet. I was still reeling from the idea that this hidden pool—this fire-drenched waterfall—was the secret he held buried while we warred with one another through the sky and through our pain.

Of all the things going on in our crazy, fucked up world. The queen, the war, the deepest mysteries of Allovan... he chose to ask about... us.

I was certain I'd never felt that feeling before in my life. To feel... important. Like... seriously important to someone. And not just anyone. The prince of Emberveil. My legs felt as if they'd buckle and I'd crash hard into the pool, waking up from this incredible, unbelievable dream.

"Take off your shoes," he said suddenly.

I blinked. "What?"

"Your boots. Just... trust me. You don't want to step in half-frozen mountain water with leathers on."

I hesitated, eyeing him suspiciously—but he wasn't smirking.

He was serious. Reverent, even.

Still holding his gaze, I knelt on one of the smooth rocks. The laces stuck slightly with dried mud, but I peeled the boots off one by one, then rolled up the bottoms of my pants as best I could.

Cade did the same, armor groaning slightly as he crouched by the edge, then stood barefoot on the dark stone shelf beneath the water's line.

"You ready?" he asked, watching me with those terrible, beautiful sapphire eyes that saw too much.

Not for war. Not for death.

But for whatever this was.

No.

But I nodded anyway. "Yes."

Still hand in hand, he led me forward.

The cold hit first—sharp and biting as my toes sliced into the edge of the water—and then pain, not from the temperature but from something else. Something inside me responding like a blade pushing against the skin from the inside out.

My pulse surged. My skin buzzed with electricity that had nothing—and everything—to do with our touch.

We walked forward together.

The pool wasn't deep, just above my knees, but the pressure of the space was suffocating. Like the place didn't approve of visitors. Like it had been waiting for Cade alone... and didn't quite know how to process me.

The moment we passed the halfway point, the pain quieted.

The rune at my throat began to glow.

"Do you feel it?" Cade asked, his voice bare, raw.

"Yes." I didn't know what else to say. Magic coiled around my bones like a second skeleton, gold flickering at the edges of my vision.

He released my hand as we reached the center of the pond, and I stepped close to the stone.

It jutted up waist-high, completely unlike the smooth river rocks scattered around the pond's base. Its color was wrong— milky white with thin veins running down its sides like scars. It looked like a tooth pulled from something massive.

Or the tip of a coffin.

I frowned and reached out to touch it.

"What is this?" I whispered. "Cade... what is this place?"

He stared at the stone, dark hair dripping from the mist, his shoulders so tight they looked carved from shadow.

"This," he said, voice low and reverent. "This is everything."

The air around us thickened, heavy with anticipation and desire as Cade began to undress me slowly, his fingers dancing along the edges of my clothing, teasing me with each deliberate movement. He paused to kiss my neck, his warm lips leaving a trail of heat that spread through my body, igniting my senses. I shivered as he undid the laces of my shirt, baring my chest to his gaze. His breath caught in his throat, and I could feel the intensity of his desire for me.

As he removed my shirt, I reached out to touch him, to explore the chiseled muscles that lay beneath his own clothes. He stood before me, his shirt now discarded, revealing his broad, powerful chest, his muscular arms and abs, all dusted with a smattering of black hair that trailed down to the waistband of his pants. I couldn't help but stare, awed by his strength and beauty.

"What are you doing?" I asked, my voice barely above a whisper as he continued to undress me, his fingers working deftly to free my pants from their clasp.

"This," he replied, his voice low and filled with emotion. "This is all that matters to me in the world, Ash. It means more than winning the war, defeating my stepmother, and even peace. This is everything."

I looked up at him, confused. "What do you mean, Cade?"

He leaned in, his lips hovering just above mine as he whispered, "I need you, Ash. I need you more than I've needed anything in my whole life, and I wouldn't be able to live without you."

As he spoke, he began to fondle my breasts, his thumbs brushing gently against my nipples, sending waves of pleasure coursing through my body. I moaned softly, my head falling back as I relished the sensations he was creating.

Cade lifted me effortlessly into his arms, his hands firm and secure against my bare skin. The world around us seemed to blur into a haze of anticipation and desire as he carried me to the small stone island at the center of the pond. He laid me down gently, his body covering mine, his warm breath fanning across my neck, sending shivers down my spine.

"Gods, Ash," he murmured, his voice deep and resonant, "you are everything."

His lips found mine in a searing kiss, igniting a fire deep within me that threatened to consume us both. My heart pounded in my chest, matching the rhythm of our tangled breaths. The touch of his hands, rough yet tender, sent jolts of electricity coursing through my veins.

He trailed kisses down my neck, lingering on each tender spot as if it were a sacred ground. His mouth moved to my collarbone, then lower, igniting a trail of heat that left me gasping for more. When his lips closed around one of my nipples, a moan escaped me, raw and unbidden. I arched into him, my body yearning for his touch, needing more of this exquisite torture.

His hands roamed over my curves, exploring every inch as if it were a newfound territory. Each touch sent sparks of pleasure dancing across my skin, igniting a deep, relentless ache that only he could sate. When he finally slipped his hands between my thighs, I cried out, writhing beneath him as his fingers found the heart of my desire.

"Cade," I gasped, my voice barely a whisper against his heated skin. "Please. I need you. I don't care what happens. I'll take all the pain as long as we get... this."

He smiled against my shoulder, his breath scorching my skin. "Patience, love," he murmured, his voice an intoxicating mix of honey and thunder.

His fingers danced over my most sensitive spot, drawing out a gasp from deep within me. The world around us blurred, leaving only the feel of his touch, the weight of his body against mine, and the blazing fire that roared between us. Every stroke, every caress, brought me closer to the edge, and I found myself clutching at his shoulders, my nails digging into his flesh as I begged for release.

His lips found mine again, his kiss growing. And so was he...

Cade's impressive, erect cock pressed against my entrance, throbbing with anticipation. I couldn't help but stare, my heart racing at the sight of him, my body aching with a deep, primal need. He was gorgeous, every inch of him—from his chiseled chest to his firm, muscular thighs—was a testament to his strength and prowess. And his cock... gods, I couldn't tear my eyes away.

"I need you, Cade," I breathed, my voice barely above a whisper. "I want all of you."

He leaned down, kissing me deeply, his tongue dancing with mine, sending sparks of pleasure coursing through my body. I could feel his hard length pressing against me, teasing, promising everything I'd ever wanted and more.

"You're mine, Ash," he growled against my lips, his voice a deep, primal sound that sent shivers down my skin. "And I'm all yours."

As he pushed inside me, I gasped, the sensation overwhelming. He filled me completely, stretching me, making me feel whole in a way I'd never experienced before. The connection between us was intense, electrifying, as if every nerve in my body was firing at once.

We moved together, our bodies in perfect sync, every thrust deepening our connection. I could feel the magic between us, pulsing, growing with every movement. His cock was like a wildfire inside me, igniting every part of me, making me crave more, need more.

"Cade," I moaned, my voice a desperate plea. "You're so deep, so good. I... I can't..."

"Yes, you can," he urged, his lips brushing against my ear, his breath hot on my skin. "Let go, Ash. Let go and come with me. This is our everything."

"Our... everything?" I muttered, my words nearly drowned out by the moans that left my lips into his strong neck.

The world around us blurred as Cade and I reached the precipice, our bodies intertwined, our breaths mingling in a desperate, frenzied dance. The air around us thickened, heavy with the scent of magic and desire. Every thrust sent waves of pleasure cascading through me, consuming me.

Just as I felt myself reaching the edge, the world shifted. The energy around us surged, crackling like lightning. The heat inside me built until it was almost unbearable, and I could feel the magic coiling, ready to explode. But this time, there was no fear, only anticipation.

Cade's voice, low and urgent, whispered in my ear, "Let go, Ash."

And I did.

The world erupted around us as the heat and magic released in a torrential wave. The flame behind the waterfall roared to life, the water cascading down in a breathtaking display of fiery light. The intense heat and brilliant flames exploded with such force that the entire sky seemed to catch fire, illuminating the heavens in a dance of celestial flames.

The sensations coursing through my body were unlike anything I had ever experienced. Waves of intense pleasure and pain crashed over me, intertwining in a symphony of ecstasy that threatened to consume me entirely. I cried out, my voice echoing through the fiery sky, every nerve in my body igniting in unison.

As we reached the peak together, the magic between us surged, creating a bridge of luminosity that seemed to span the gap between life and death. The water in the pond turned a vivid blue, pulsing with an otherworldly light that enveloped us, our bodies transforming within the embrace of the magical fire and water.

The orgasm that ripped through me was more intense than anything I had ever known. It felt as if my entire being had been set ablaze, every inch of my skin tingling with a mixture of pain and overwhelming pleasure. I could feel myself breaking apart and being reborn all at once, the sensations so powerful that I could barely draw breath.

Cade's grip tightened around me, his own release shuddering

through him with a force that mirrored my own. His body convulsed, and his deep groans echoing as his powerful fingertips dug into my thighs, pulling me in as his seed spilled inside me. The heat swelled within me as he heaved, his muscular chest glistening in the fiery light of the waterfall.

His body collapsed onto mine with a deep groan, like the animal he'd become. My fingers ran through his hair, feeling his raw power, and the emotional, sensitive creature he'd revealed himself to be. By Odiun, I was completely obsessed with him, and there was never any going back. He was mine. He was all I ever wanted, and as he spilled his cum inside me, a sudden realization hit me like a frying pan to the jaw.

"We're... we're still awake..."

He lifted his head from my breasts and a wry smile caught his lips.

"Cade..." My mouth was fully agape and my mind whirled as if I were in a different, new world.

He laughed. "I—I think it... worked."

As we both caught our breath, I lay against the cool stone, the world spinning around us like the aftermath of a thunderstorm. Distant echoes of water and fire intertwined, melding into a symphony of pleasure that thrummed in my veins. The waterfall behind us was a roaring inferno now, its flames a brilliant dance of orange and crimson, reflecting the desires burning between us.

Cade's breath came in jagged bursts as he leaned over me, his blue eyes dark and filled with an intensity that made my heart race even faster. We had become something more than flesh and bone; we were magic, pure and unbidden. The connection between us pulsed with an energy I could barely comprehend.

"Did you feel that?" he breathed, his voice hoarse, filled with a raw urgency.

"I felt everything," I replied breathlessly, still grappling with the overwhelming sensations coursing through me. "I didn't know—it could be so good."

"I didn't either." There was a buoyant thrill in his gaze, a deep-seated wonder that made my chest ache. "This—what just happened—was more than I ever imagined."

I gazed up at him, the firelight casting flickering shadows across the sharp lines of his jaw. "You make it sound as if we've done this before."

"Everything about you feels familiar," he murmured, his voice a low growl as he leaned in closer. "As if the universe conspired to bring us to this moment."

The words resonated through me, each syllable wrapping around my heart like tendrils of gold. There was no denying the magic in our bond, the way it sparked and thundered as if it had a will of its own. My fingers found their way to his shoulders, gripping him tightly, anchoring myself to the sensation of being this close to him, of having him here with me.

His gaze faltered for just a moment, a flicker of uncertainty stirring behind his stormy eyes. "Ash…" he began, tension knotting in his voice.

"What?" I pressed, searching those depths, wanting him to reach out and take me deeper.

He hesitated, and my heart sank. "All that matters is this moment."

A rush of warmth flooded my cheeks. "I—I need you, Cade. For the love of the gods, don't ever stop what this is."

He caught my chin gently, glacier sparks glimmering in the depths of my vision, and kissed me deeply before pulling back, breathless, his eyes blazing with fierce intensity. "I need you, Ash. More than I've needed anything. This—us—means everything to me."

His words curled around my heart. "What do you mean?"

"The mystic was right. I asked Myrathyn and he told me how to lift our curse. Do you know what this means?" There was so much excitement in his gaze and on his breath I thought he may be about to erupt again.

My breath caught in my throat, and I reached up to trace the faint scar on his cheekbone. It was a reminder of all the demons we faced, the battles behind us that had almost broken him. "Cade, I—"

He silenced me with a finger on my lips. "Let me show you."

And with that, he leaned down, capturing my mouth with his again, igniting a fire that engulfed us whole. His kisses were deep and demanding, his body pressing against mine with enough heat to melt the stone beneath us. I moaned into his mouth, feeling the world slip away as desire coiled tightly in the pit of my stomach.

Every brush of his lips sent sparks dancing over my skin. I could feel the pulse of his heart, the drive of his need melding with my own as he explored the soft curves of my body, his hands trailing down my sides, each caress igniting a burning need deep within me. His hard cock still twitching deep inside me.

"Cade," I gasped softly between kisses, hunger taking control of my senses. "What if it didn't? What if we…"

"It's done." He pulled back just enough to gaze into my eyes, his darkness mirrored in mine. "This moment is ours, Ash. No one else exists. This, Ashlyn Moonriver, is the single best moment of my rotten life. You're my cure, my everything, my world…"

And that was all it took. The weight of his desire broke through every terrified thought, every worry clouding my mind.

"Gods, Ash," he murmured against my skin, his warm breath sending shivers down my spine. "You're beautiful. You're the most gorgeous thing I've ever seen in my whole life."

I gasped, feeling the heat from his kisses spreading through my body like a wildfire. Everything about him sent my senses reeling—his warmth, his scent, the way he held me, anchoring me to the moment as he continued to explore with his mouth.

I felt as if this was my second release into the world. As if I was being unshackled once again.

"Look at you," he said, almost reverently, his gaze flickering over my bare skin, drinking me in. "You're everything to me, Ash. This—what we have—it matters more than anything."

"What are you doing?" I whispered, surprised to hear my own breathless voice tremble beneath the weight of my desire.

Cade's gaze burned into mine, the intensity in his sapphire eyes sending shivers down my spine. He reached out, his fingers tracing the curve of my breast, teasing my nipple with a delicate touch that set my nerves ablaze. I moaned softly, arching into his touch, my body aching with need.

"I need you again," he said, his voice low and husky, filled with a raw desire that matched my own. His hands slid down to grip my hips, pulling me against him. The hardness of his arousal pressed against me, sending a jolt of pleasure through my core.

"Gods, yes," I whispered, my voice ragged with desire. He turned me around, bending me over until my stomach pressed against the cool stone. The contrast of the cold rock against my heated skin sent shivers through my body, heightening every sensation.

His strong hands gripped my hips firmly, pulling me back as he thrust into me, filling me completely. My walls stretched to accommodate his huge cock, the delicious friction sending waves of pleasure coursing through my body. I dug my fingernails into the stone, clinging to it as if it were the only thing anchoring me to reality.

"Oh, Ash," he groaned, his voice a low rumble that vibrated through my body. His fingers dug into my flesh, holding me in place as he began to move, each thrust driving him deeper, pushing me closer to the edge.

The world around us blurred into a haze of pleasure and sensation. Every thrust, every touch sent sparks of electric passion through my nerves. I gripped the stone tighter, my forehead pressing against it, my breath coming in short, desperate gasps.

"Cade," I moaned, his name a plea on my lips. His hands slid up my back, gripping my shoulders. Then he pulled me up, my back pressed against his chest. His arm wrapped around my waist, holding me close as he continued to drive into me, each thrust more intense than the last. I could feel the heat of his breath on my neck, his lips brushing against my ear.

"Do you feel that, Ash?" he murmured, his voice a low growl. "The pain is gone. Its just you and me sharing what we never could."

I nodded, unable to speak, my body trembling with the intensity of our connection. His hand moved up to cup my breast, his fingers teasing my nipple, sending waves of pleasure coursing through me. I arched back into him, my body moving in sync with his, our breaths coming in ragged gasps.

"Cade, I..." My words fizzled out as my mind raced, feeling him deep inside me, his hands exploring my most sensitive spots. I moaned deeply.

I took every thrust, every touch, every whispered word. I felt the pleasure building inside me, the heat between us growing until it was almost too much to bear.

His hand moved down, his fingers finding my clit. He began to rub, his touch firm and insistent, sending me spiraling toward the edge.

"Come for me, Ash," he groaned, his voice a low, desperate plea. "Let me feel you come undone in my arms."

And with one final, intense thrust, I did. I screamed his name as the pleasure exploded inside me, waves of ecstasy crashing over me until I was gasping for breath. He followed me over the edge, his body shuddering as he held me close, his breath coming in ragged gasps.

We remained like that for a moment, our bodies still joined, our hearts pounding in sync. The magic around us pulsed, the glow of the water intensifying as if it too had been swept up in the passion of our connection.

Slowly, he pulled out, turning me around to face him. His eyes were filled with a mix of desire and something deeper, something more profound. He cupped my face in his hands, his thumbs brushing gently against my cheeks.

His deep voice uttered words that melted every fiber of my being. "I love you. Now and forever."

Forever.

"Cade," I breathed, "I love you too."

His breath caught, and the world stilled once more.

"I know," he said, pure and honest, the words wrapping around us like a hushed promise beneath the moonlit sky.

I smiled through my tears, my heart swelling with gratitude, with love, with the knowledge that whatever lay ahead, we would face it together.

With that, all was right in the world. I had him, and he had me. Now, and forever.

CHAPTER 23

The water wrapped around us like silk spun from ancient dreams—warm, alive, and humming with a magic I could still feel tingling along every inch of my skin. My legs floated weightless beneath the surface, toes lazily brushing against Cade's under the water, and for once… nothing hurt. Not my body. Not my soul. Not even my heart.

The sky above was high and soft, a dark velvet painted in indigo and endless constellations, stars blinking like they too were stunned by what had just happened here. The waterfall still spilled flame over the rocks behind us, the fire ribbons thinner now, gentler, glowing like the remnants of a candle burned too low to flicker. Beneath it, the mist curled like incense smoke, wrapping around our temple of stone and secrets like a promise whispered between gods.

We lay together, naked in the stillness, the soft flicker of firelight catching gold off the surface of the magical pond.

Cade was stretched beside me, arms folded behind his head, the angles of his bare chest rising and falling in slow, steady rhythm. His skin looked kissed by moonlight, the water sheening across his abs like someone had painted touchable art across living marble. And gods, the man was gorgeous. It was annoying how stupidly perfect he looked, even after everything.

I curled closer, resting a cheek on his shoulder, letting my fingertips trace the fading water tracks across his clavicle. There was a peace in him now I'd never seen before. Not even once. Like some part of him, some tight, coiled, shadow-choked place, had finally let go.

And inside me was no different.

That ache, the electric burn between us that had once always come paired with pain—it was gone. Erased. For the first time, our connection hadn't left bruises. Hadn't drowned me in light-ning and fire and unconsciousness.

It had only left love.

And pleasure.

And quiet.

"So this is what it feels like," I murmured, mostly to myself.

Cade didn't move. "What?"

"This. Being happy." I closed my eyes against him. "I didn't think I'd ever get here."

His voice was low when he answered. "Me neither."

We stayed that way for what felt like hours. Days. A lifetime, maybe, where war didn't exist and queens didn't hunt girls with glowing runes and the man lying beside me wasn't a prince born into hell.

He was just Cade.

And he was mine.

The pond seemed made of warmth, of peace. It rippled when I breathed, and every movement sent soft whorls of golden light trailing through the water like some part of Eden had bled out and made her home here. Even the air smelled sweeter now—of pine and spice, of steam and embers and skin.

My mind drifted, relishing the afterglow of everything—the sex, the soul-deep release. I felt loose and content, softer than I thought I could be. My limbs had become syrup. My lips buzzed from being kissed so thoroughly. My thighs ached in the best possible way.

And Cade. That beautiful, maddening, devastating man, lay tangled beside me, silently running his fingers through the water near my hip like he didn't have a fucking war to win in a few days.

"Don't ask me to leave," I whispered, pressing my face into the curve of his bicep. "Not yet."

He turned his head, grin barely lit by the shimmer from the pool.

"I was just about to say we should probably go."

"No," I groaned. "Just a little longer."

A knowing hum rolled in his throat. "You're dangerous when you beg so sweetly."

I smirked, smacking his chest lightly. "I didn't beg."

"You did," he said, rolling lazily toward me on his side. "You just don't know it."

His eyes met mine.

And there it was—that stupid, gut-wrenching sincerity behind his gaze. Cade Phoenixfire, slayer of champions, terror of the skies, was looking at me like I was impossible. Like I was divine.

I reached up and touched the cheek of this gorgeous, ridiculous man who crawled through flame and ash just to show me something beautiful.

His eyes dropped to my mouth, and the moment stretched thick with slow, wicked heat.

Then, without a word, he leaned in and kissed me.

Not with the same desperate hunger from before.

This time, it was slower. More certain. The kind of kiss that starts soft and ends dangerous.

His lips traced mine with gentle hunger, pressing just enough to remind me how thoroughly they'd claimed me a few hours ago. My breath caught.

"Cade…" I murmured against his mouth, warning and invitation all at once.

But he didn't answer.

Not with words.

His hand drifted under the water, trailing across my waist until he reached the tender curve of my hip. He wrapped his palm around my thigh, pulling it up across his lap until I felt the hard press of him against me again.

"You sure?" I whispered, voice already dark with wanting.

Cade didn't answer.

Not to that.

Instead, he slid down between my legs in the water, hands gliding along my sides like I was music he already knew by heart.

"Ash," he said, voice low with reverence. "I never want this moment to end."

"Gods," I exhaled, lightheaded already.

Then his mouth was on me, and the pond exploded in stars. His lips found the inside of my thigh with reverence, a kiss so slow, so soft, it tore a sound from me I didn't even know I could make. The water lapped around us in a warm embrace, and I tipped my head back, eyes fluttering closed as the world narrowed to the space between his breath and my skin.

His hands gripped my thighs, anchoring me to him as he dragged his mouth higher, inhaling like my scent had become the only thing keeping him alive. Every inch he explored with his tongue was a prayer, each clever flick a whispered litany. My hips arched reflexively, offering, begging, trembling.

"Cade," I gasped, and it came out broken. "You're insatiable…"

But he just hummed low, like he was feasting on the sound, and returned to the heartbeat of my desire with a precision that shattered me. The heat of it bloomed outward—shockwaves rolling through my thighs, my stomach, catching fire beneath my skin. There was no pain now, no crackling edge from our powers clashing. Just the smooth glide of his mouth, the velvet press of lips, the swirl of his tongue on my clit that had me clawing at the stone beneath us before I even knew I'd moved.

Water rippled with every movement, as if the grove itself responded to our rhythm, to the soft cry I bit down as he sucked gently at the tenderest part of me. My fingers dug into the sleek rocks behind me, slick with mist and the dew of magic, and the cry that tore from my throat was pure, as if Eden herself had opened inside my chest.

He didn't stop.

He brought me to the edge with maddening finesse, teeth scraping lightly where he kissed next, his tongue drawing circles of liquid heat that had me trembling, gasping, unraveling.

And when release finally found me, my entire body went taut—every nerve taut with blinding light—and then burst, orgasm hitting like a wave against cliff rock. I cried out, breathless, thighs squeezing around his shoulders as the magic trembled visibly across the surface of the pond. A pulse of golden light spread from my chest, dancing over the water until it disappeared back beneath the depths.

I collapsed backward onto the stone, vision flickering red and white. "I—I..."

Cade rose slowly from between my thighs, licking his lips as if he hadn't finished worshipping yet. His eyes—gods, those eyes—were darker, hungrier, reverent.

"This," he said, breath ragged as he moved up to hover over me, "is all I need for the rest of my life."

I laughed then—an unguarded, shaky sound that dissolved into a sigh. "You're so full of it."

His grin was half-wild. "You didn't hear yourself."

I bit my lip, tugged him down into a kiss that still tasted like flame and water, and let myself feel light. Truly weightless.

For once.

We stayed there—just the two of us—bodies tangled, hearts slowing, the air humming with fulfillment. The fire in the waterfall had receded now, no longer blazing, but still warm, like a hundred glowing candles guarding our shared secret.

The curse was gone.

We'd survived it.

More than that—we'd obliterated it.

And it hadn't destroyed us.

That fact made me cry all over again.

Not the broken kind. The healing kind.

"It's lifted," I whispered as the tears slid down my cheeks, cooling instantly in the breeze. "Cade—it's lifted. I feel it. I… it's really over."

He held my face in both hands, his expression somewhere between agony and bliss. "I know."

"You're not hurting."

"Neither are you."

That was when the emotion overwhelmed him. His shoulders bowed forward, and he pressed his forehead to mine, exhaling like he'd been holding his breath for years.

"This is the happiest I've ever been in my entire miserable life," he whispered. "Ashlyn, I never thought—"

I kissed him, slow and sweet, letting our relief spill into the space between our mouths.

"And I never want this to end," he continued when we pulled apart, his voice wobbling around the edges. "I never want to live another breath without you in it."

My heart cracked open.

The last of the resistance inside me dissolved.

"Thank you," I said through new tears. "Thank you for not giving up on us."

"No." He shook his head, brushing a damp curl from my cheek, his hand trembling. "Thank you, Ash. You've changed my life in ways I never even dared to dream."

I touched his face. "I love you."

His breath hitched.

Then he nodded, voice choked. "I love you too. Gods, Ash—I love you so much it terrifies me."

We kissed again, sealing the words against our lips, binding them into something eternal.

Then, with a smirk that could have brought kingdoms to their knees, he shifted over me again. "I want you again," he said against my throat, voice velvet and flame.

I didn't reply in words.

Just wrapped my arms around his shoulders, pulled him tighter, and let the heat rise all over again.

The flames in the waterfall flickered higher, and the pond shimmered in anticipation.

And when he finally moved inside me again, the world didn't break—

It sang.

We dressed slowly, quietly, as if moving too quickly would break whatever fragile magic still hung in the mist around us.

The last warmth of the glowing water still clung to my skin, like embers refusing to fade. I could feel it under my clothes as I laced the ties of my tunic with shaking hands. Not from fear. Not this time. I was trembling with something else entirely. Fulfillment, maybe. Or peace. Or something dangerously close to hope.

Cade stood beside the pool, buckling the leather strap of his bracer, firelight flickering across the planes of his bare chest. His hair hung wet across his brow, and when he turned to me, my breath hitched a little.

Maybe it always would. I'd just made love to the most dangerous man in Allovan. I'd just witnessed what it looked like when fire and water didn't destroy each other—but balanced.

When we'd become something more than our elements.

Cade looked toward the pond once more. The flames within the waterfall burned lower now, softer. Not gone. Just… resting.

He stepped closer to the edge, his hands at his sides, expression unreadable.

I joined him, brushing stray curls from my cheeks where the wind had loosed them from behind my ears. The silence cradled us, unhurried and gentle.

"Thank you," we said together.

The words settled between us like a promise.

I blinked wide-eyed at him. He blinked too, almost surprised.

"That was…" I started, my voice lighter than I expected. "The best gift of my life."

There was something raw in his eyes. Something exquisitely bare.

I was afraid if I looked too long, I'd never want to look away again.

He reached for me—I didn't even hesitate anymore. I stepped into his arms, and our lips met in a kiss that was softer than all the ones before.

It wasn't hungry.

It was grateful.

"We should go," he murmured against my mouth. "Before Darren thinks we've flown off to make new heirs on another continent."

I laughed, and gods, it felt good—to laugh and mean it.

We pulled back slowly. He mouthed my name once more before letting me go.

And then he turned, striding toward Krakos at the pool's edge.

Errax waited nearby, her elegant form stretched and sun-warmed. When I grabbed her saddle and climbed up, she gave a low, pleased rumble. Like she'd known all along that this was coming.

I cast one last glance back over my shoulder.

The flaming waterfall burned against the stone like a heart exposed to open air, pulsing golden-red between the black cliffs where we'd left a piece of ourselves behind.

"Thank you," I whispered again, this time only for it. Thinking also of the Mystic and his guidance to Cade about this place. I didn't know if I'd ever return, I doubted it, but I knew I'd hold it in my heart for as long as I drew breath.

Then Errax leaped into the sky—and the world dropped away beneath us.

Krakos soared alongside, Cade barely a body's length away in the wide blue open nothing. The wind caught my hair, trailing it behind me like ribbons made of dusk. The air smelled like pine and smoke and clean mountaintop.

For a long time, we didn't speak.

We flew.

The kind of silence that accompanied peace, not absence.

I let myself drift, not in the sky, but inside the sound of my heartbeat—familiar now, not just mine, but somehow Cade's too.

Eden stirred deep within me, content and whole. Golden light didn't pulse outward in heated waves like before—it shimmered now, warm and steady in my chest. No burning. No backlash. Just fire and water. Balanced. Bound.

I pressed a hand to the rune on my neck.

The world had shifted.

Something long cursed had finally been undone.

And for the first time in so many days, I wasn't thinking about war.

I wasn't thinking about the queen or what came next.

I was thinking of the way Cade had looked at me when he first stepped into the pool with me. Of the way his voice had cracked when he told me he needed me. Of how, for the span of a few sacred breaths—we had been more than just rebels and royals.

We'd been human.

Together.

I glanced sideways at him as we dipped below the clouds, where the snow-capped peaks of the Harrowhorns stretched out like a dragon's spine weaving endless across the land.

He glanced back.

And he smiled.

And gods—as the wind curled around me, and my dragon carried me home beneath a sky full of light—I smiled too.

The queen would wait.

For now, we were flying.

And I was free.

STORM'S END came into view like a dream unraveling through the clouds—its stone towers framed in drifting mist, flickering torches aglow against the approaching dusk. The dirt paths winding through the stronghold pulsed with motion, soldiers lined in rows, dragons in formation, the entire camp alight with tension and restless movement.

Our dragons began to descend, Cade on Krakos folding in on the right, Errax and I easing down on the left. Her wings tucked close as the sharp wind tugged at the strands in my hair. I felt too light—like the world below couldn't tether me anymore.

Because how did you land after that?

How did you return to a world volleying toward war when your whole body was still humming from magic and love and a kiss that had lit every fiber of you on fire—then drowned you in something better?

Still, we landed.

The courtyard was crowded—more than usual. Word traveled like smoke in these parts. I could hear it already: whispers passing between soldiers like gusts of wind through broken gates.

"Where'd they go?"

"Has Prince Phoenixfire gone rogue again?"

"Why'd the Gold-Marked leave?"

"They were gone for hours—what's happening?"

Cade slid from Krakos with iron-steady calm, his cloak settling over his shoulders.

Errax landed with a soft thud beside him. My heart thudded with her.

Then—Bella.

She moved like a lightning strike across the field.

"Ash!" she cried, skirting two startled guards as I dismounted, her brows furrowed tight. "What—what the fuck, where were you?! You just flew off with Prince Grumpy without saying a word and then—"

She stopped.

For less than a blink.

As her eyes locked on mine.

Stared. Hard.

I tried to reply, but she gasped—and her whole face shifted.

"Oh my god."

She grabbed my wrist, sharp and sudden like I'd just admitted I'd kissed a god.

"You're glowing."

"I'm not—" But I was. I was glowing. Soul-deep, goddess-bathed, bliss-filled glowing. I could feel it radiating out of me like the fire in the waterfall hadn't stopped burning after all.

Bella leaned in, grinned wickedly. "What did you do?"

I bit my lip.

My eyes flicked—traitorous, ridiculous, telling—over to Cade where he was standing beside Krakos, giving orders to a young scout like he hadn't just worshipped my body like it was a temple only he'd ever been allowed to enter.

Bella gasped again. "You didn't."

"I—" I started.

"You did."

"But—"

"YOU DID."

She squealed, actually squealed, and yanked me by the wrist, dragging me toward the bunkhouse before even the dragons could react.

"You're going to tell me everything," she snapped as the latched wooden door slammed behind us. "Every detail. Every glowing, steamy drop of sin that just happened up in those thunder-haunted mountains."

"Bella—"

"Don't you dare start with the 'it's complicated' nonsense—your smile is already confessing everything!"

I laughed. I actually laughed. A choking, helpless, soul-lightening bubble of sound I couldn't even stop if I wanted to. The kind that burst like honey against my tongue and made my eyes sting for all the right reasons.

"I..." I placed a hand over my heart, suddenly breathless, "I think... I think he lifted the curse."

Bella's face went blank. "What?"

"We—he—" I blew out a slow breath. "We went to this hidden waterfall—the one the mystic told him about. It's fire and magic and something ancient... and it worked. Gods, Bella, it worked. For the first time ever... it didn't hurt."

Her eyes welled immediately.

"No burning?" she whispered.

"No unconsciousness, no bruises, no aftermath." I smiled, unable to stop the giddy pull in my chest. "Just... us."

Then she tackled me.

"Elven gods and saints of the sea, you had sex without consequence? Happy sex?! *Pure magical sex?*"

I was laughing so hard I couldn't breathe as she wrapped her arms around me, giggling like she was the one who'd just melted into bliss.

"I did," I whispered through a smile soft enough to fracture the world. "And it was the best sex of my entire life."

Bella let out a jubilant wail, bouncing in place like a tavern brawler who'd just won every bet. "I knew it! I knew you two had feral sexual tension built into your *bone marrow*—gods, Ash, the waterfall! That's so hot! Literally!"

We dissolved into laughter, leaning against each other on the edge of the bed until the sounds slurred into quiet sniffles and twinned tears trailing down our cheeks—not out of sadness, but out of joy we hadn't dared to believe for so long.

"I'm happy for you," Bella whispered, voice thick. "Like… actually, selfishly, truly happy."

"I love him, Bella."

She nodded, smiling wide through those tears. "And he—we all see it. You're his everything."

The knock at the door just before sundown.

The bonfire was already crackling in the training yard, sending shimmering sparks into the cooling evening air.

When we stepped outside, the entire camp had gathered, smoke curling skyward, torches lit, food spilling across rough-hewn tables. Music came from somewhere—pipes and drums, laughter and clinking mugs. Celebration pulsed through the soldier ranks like they'd caught a whiff of victory for the first time in months.

Word of the queen's vulnerabilities—everything Cade had taught them—had spread.

And they sang for it.

Stories around the fire. Songs of fallen cities and dragons rising from blackened earth. I caught Hunter leaning back against a barrel, tankard in hand, grin lazy and warm as he listed tactics to someone I didn't recognize. Across from him, Carina was reciting some harrowing tale of escape to a half-dozen wide-eyed recruits, grinning through sips of spiced wine.

And Cade?

He sat at the outer edge of the bonfire's glow, his legs outstretched, one arm resting across his bent knee, shadows drawn long across his features.

But his gaze?

Only on me.

I looked at him.

And heat spilled through every vein like wildfire.

He raised a brow, half a smirk tugging at his mouth.

I shook my head, biting a smile into my cup.

We didn't move across the firelight.

But we didn't look away either.

Not once.

By the time twilight gave way to full night and stars splashed across the sky like powdered sugar over ink, I was barely keeping my eyes open.

The music softened. Slowly, the crowd unraveled.

Soldiers made their way back to bunks, dragons settled down near kindled torches. Voices dimmed. The last ballad drifted into hush.

I wandered alone through the quiet to my cot.

The fire-glow of Cade's eyes stayed with me long after the stars winked into place.

And when my head found the pillow—

The last thing I felt was bliss.

My muscles sighed. My heartbeat slowed.

And as I slipped into dreams…

I knew peace for the first time.

Real peace.

Because now that we were whole—

There was no going back.

VÂLLATHÓR'S AWAKENING

Passage from the Tomb of the Elements. Chapter 20, verse 1.

Mother of all dragons.

The first of all that ruled the sky.

Vâllathór is the only remembered name of the great beast that slumbers from the old world.

As old as the gods, as powerful as the volcano it slumbers within, Vâllathór waits.

She waits for her second coming, she waits to draw in fresh breath of the new world. The first of all dragons awaits the day she will spread her wings, crack the foundations of the great volcano that rests at the tip of our world.

Prophecy foretells that she will awaken, and the Age of Embers will fade into a new world, a world that knows true peace. In this new age of peace, the Cynderin will fall. The elite race of near Demi-gods will crumble, leading to a new power that will shine upon our lands with prosperity and freedom unlike Allovan has known.

But prophecies are like oceans. Full of potential, vast and patient. The tide washes in and out, like generations of man, tempting to rise and wash away the filth of wickedness and corruption of the old cities.

The flood of retribution will come, and Vâllathór will awaken and spread her legendary wings, purging the world of the sickness that has consumed it. For if she doesn't wake, and the prophecy isn't fulfilled by the great Aqualorian hero, then our world will plunge into eternal flames.

Let the hero fulfill their destiny.

Let the great slumbering dragon rise!

And until that age, let the gods, old and new, watch over us, for the flames of the Cynderin do not burn without malice.

Our world is all we have, and if our destined hero falls and the great dragon falls into eternal slumber, then gods protect us all.

For the flames of oppression will spread. The corruption of the dark hearts will win. And those most pure of heart, most courageous in their virtue, and most valiant in their quest for hope, will fall.

Awaken ye hero!

Awaken the great dragon!

Praise the gods that light your path!

And gods help us all, should you fail...

Written by the Prophet Dantris Oireillus. 676 of the Ember Age.

CHAPTER 25

$\mathcal{S}$leep came easily that night, dragging me under like a warm tide after the events at the waterfall. My muscles ached pleasantly, memories of Cade's touch still ghosting across my skin. Even in dreams, I could feel the lingering warmth of our connection, the way our magic had finally found harmony instead of chaos.

But something pulled me from that peaceful darkness.

My eyes fluttered open to find the bunkhouse wrapped in midnight silence. Moonlight filtered through the narrow windows, casting pale stripes across the wooden floor. The others slept soundly—Bella's soft breathing, Hunter's occasional snore, and Cade's steady presence a few feet away.

Yet something felt... wrong.

I sat up slowly, pushing sweat-dampened hair from my face. My throat was dry, parched like I'd been calling out in my sleep. With careful movements, I slipped from beneath the blankets and padded across the cool floorboards toward the water pitcher.

The liquid was cool against my palm as I splashed some on my face, trying to shake off the strange unease that had settled in my bones. Outside, a low rumble echoed across the courtyard—probably just one of the dragons shifting in their sleep.

I took a long drink, letting the water soothe my throat.

Another rumble, deeper this time.

My skin prickled.

Something definitely wasn't right.

I moved to the window, pressing my palms against the rough wooden sill as I peered out into the darkness. Storm's End lay quiet beneath a blanket of stars, the usual guards posted at their stations, torches flickering in the cool mountain breeze.

Then—a shout.

Distant at first, barely more than an echo.

But it was followed by another. And another.

My heart began to pound.

The air changed—thick with something acrid, something burning.

"Cade," I called, my voice stronger than I expected. "Wake up."

He stirred immediately, years of battle-trained instincts kicking in before consciousness fully returned. "Ash? What—"

The explosion cut him off.

It ripped through the night like thunder given flesh, a burst of orange flame erupting from the eastern wall. The impact shook the entire bunkhouse, rattling the wooden beams and sending dust raining from the overhead rafters. My heart raced as I stumbled back, eyes wide, pulse pounding in my ears.

"No, no, no," I whispered, panic seizing my throat as I rushed back toward Cade and Hunter, who were already on their feet, weapons drawn. The others groaned awake, confusion and fear etched across their faces.

"What just happened?" Hunter demanded, scanning the room for answers.

"Something's out there!" I shouted, urgency fraying my composure. I could still hear the distant echoes of shouts, the rising panic thick in the air. "It came from the eastern wall!"

Cade's gaze met mine, his expression dark and determined, but there was a simmering edge of uncertainty beneath it. "We need to go," he ordered, pushing past Hunter and me as he dashed toward the entrance.

We followed, adrenaline surging through me, my feet pounding against the wooden floor. Outside, the world transformed into chaos.

The camp lay shattered in the aftermath of the explosion—torches flickering through thick clouds of smoke that twisted through the cool night air. I could see figures moving within the haze, soldiers rushing toward the source of the commotion.

"Dragons!" Cade shouted as several dark shapes took to the skies far above us. A shadowed horde rising from the eastern cliffs, silhouetted against the pale light of the moon.

My stomach twisted.

The wind bit at my face as we sprinted through the crumbling courtyard. Smoke snaked into the sky in thick columns, turning the stars to ash above us. The ground shook with the weight of landing dragons—massive, monstrous silhouettes breaking through the clouds, wings spread like sails of death.

Cade skidded to a halt on the stone stairs, his staff already blazing with fire magic. "Ash, get ready to summon Eden," he shouted, heat streaking off him in waves. "We're under attack..."

My fingers caressed the golden rune I felt glow on my neck, praying to Odiun it would answer without hesitation. "Eden," I breathed.

Golden light seared down my spine like a lightning rod had pierced me whole. The air around me shimmered as my power unfurled in golden threads, wrapping my arms, my chest, my legs in living tendrils of radiance. My eyes burned—vision sharpened like a blade. The chaos became clearer. The screams, louder. The disaster, undeniable.

"They're here," I said, horror blooming cold in my gut.

Cade nodded grimly. "She's starting her siege."

The queen had sent her army.

Dozens—no, hundreds—of scaled dragons filled the sky, their bodies cutting through the clouds like shark fins through waves. Hanging from their bellies or clutched in their claws were Sythers—those sickening, long-limbed nightmares with curved blades and snarling mouths filled with needle teeth. They dropped by the dozens into Storm's End like rain made of death, their screeches splitting the night open.

"Move!" Cade barked again. "To the dragons!"

Errax was already awake in the paddock, snarling, wings flaring with fury. Krakos was beside her, eyes glowing blood-red, pupils thin as splinters. Talonor sprinted into view next, skimming low across the training field as Hunter and Bella leapt onto his saddle without hesitation.

We tore through the camp, weapons drawn. Sythers hit the ground in waves, flailing as they landed on bent legs and began carving through the stone corridors with terrifying precision.

One lunged at me from out of the smoke.

Golden light erupted from my palm before I even thought about it—Eden working like instinct now.

The radiance struck the bastard point-blank, punching through his chest and sending him sprawling backward in pieces. My chest heaved, golden sparks spinning from my elbows like starlight.

Cade's fire answered immediately.

He spun his staff in a great arc, a blazing wall of heat roaring out in a circle that disintegrated two more Sythers in a single sweep.

"Show them no mercy! Hang on!" I shouted over my shoulder at Bella.

"This isn't my first dragon battle!" she called back, hair tangled and eyes wild as Hunter yanked on the reins, turned Talonor's head. The dragon snarled and bolted upward, launching into the sky with a beat of wings that sent Sythers tumbling across the ground.

I turned just in time to catch one leaping for my throat.

Errax's tail slammed into its back mid-air, snapping its spine. She stomped forward and roared deafeningly, daring another one to come close.

I jumped into the saddle in one smooth motion and screamed, "Fly, girl. Now!"

We launched skyward—straight into carnage.

The air was on fire.

Dragons battling dragons, firestorms detonating mid-air, bodies tumbling in flames through the clouds. Above us, Stormscale riders screamed commands, their dragons diving and clawing into the queen's forces with reckless fury.

It barely mattered.

We were outnumbered. Vastly.

Flames of dragonfire filled the sky—dragons spinning in intricate death spirals, talons slicing through wings, breath weapons igniting the air in every direction.

"Fly smart, trust your dragon!" Cade shouted, rising beside me on Krakos. "Push to altitude! We'll be pinned if we fight down here!"

"I see them!" I shouted as a trio of blood-scaled dragons descended, their Emberveil riders flinging dark javelins into the fray. One spear narrowly missed Errax, embedding with a metal shriek into a tower below me.

Cade turned Krakos with a shout—"Firas!"—and the black dragon opened his jaws wide, a cyclone of red-white fire tearing through two enemies in a single pass. The dragons screeched, one spiral-tailed beast rolling in agony as it dropped a Syther from its hind legs like a forgotten doll.

Sythers rained from the sky.

Some landed on rooftops, others dodged midair and leapt to latched onto passing dragons—Stormscales and enemies alike.

Watching them was like watching nightmare weavers orchestrate chaos.

"Above you!" Hunter shouted from behind as Talonor dove, cleaving through a winged beast with wide, blade-fringed sails.

My pulse drummed in my ears.

And down on the mountainside—the horror unfolded.

Stormscale warriors fought hand-to-hand in the flaming courtyards.

Sythers moved like spiders, their long limbs slicing through steel and bone.

I watched one drop an axe-wielding Stormscale woman with a single blow—saw her cry out once before smoke took her.

"Odiun," I breathed. "This is a slaughter."

"No!" Cade snapped, flying closer. "Don't look down. Focus. They're counting on us to win the sky!"

"But we're—" I shook my head. "There's too many!"

"Then make every second count!"

I whipped around and let Eden loose.

Light poured from my arms in twin arcs, forming whips of golden energy that crackled through the air. I snapped them forward as we dove through clustered dragons, Errax twirling like a blade unsheathed.

I caught one in the chest—twice. The third swing took off the rider's head entirely.

Cade soared past, Krakos spinning in a barrel roll as fire burst from the dragon's tail vents like twin engines of death. Two enemy dragons fell into a spiral of flame.

"I'm with you!" I breathed, golden sparks streaking from my fingertips again.

CHAPTER 26

The sky was on fire.

Flames arced across the clouds like gods hurling torchlight from the heavens. The air was thick with smoke and blood and the burning stench of scales blistering under spell-fire. It was chaos—total, unfathomable chaos.

And we were in the heart of it.

Errax dove through the fray, wings slicing the wind with thunderous force. Below her, the world was a tangle of silver, black, and crimson—the Stormscales rallying beneath the great torches of Storm's End, while Sythers poured over the mountain stones like a plague, their long arms slashing through walls and bodies with equal ease.

I couldn't think. I could barely breathe.

Cade flew ahead—Krakos a black comet streaking fire in every direction, his staff ablaze with red-gold death. Every flick of Cade's hand turned the sky into an inferno, burning two dragons out of the clouds above while a third spiraled after him in a savage dive.

My whole body trembled.

Not from fear.

From fury. From helplessness.

Golden power hummed along my limbs. Eden was alive beneath my ribs, her light begging to be unleashed. But no matter how many enemy riders we took down, for each one burned away, two more rose behind them. It was like hacking through a Hydra swarm in the sky—one head fell, and three more screamed from the smoke.

A Syther lunged from above, leaping from one of the queen's dragons and landing hard on Errax's wing—his curved spears slicing deep into one of the edge membranes.

Errax shrieked, fury cracking through her roar. I spun in my saddle, summoning the Gilded Radiance to my palms, and thrust it straight into its chest—knocking the creature clean off her back and into free fall.

Another took its place not twenty seconds later.

"We can't hold them off!" I screamed.

"I know!" Cade dodged left, Krakos banking under an enemy dragon as Sythers threw javelins like rain down onto the walls of Storm's End.

And below—

Gods.

Below…

Stormscale warriors bled in the ruins of their own home. I could see them from here—Carina fighting two Sythers with a broken spear, her left arm slick with blood. Behind her, Darren cut one open from shoulder to hip—but another climbed the wall behind him, claws rising as he turned.

The queen's monsters filled the courtyards like smoke-smothered nightmares, moving in grotesque, spiderlike bounds—ripping through armor as if it were wet bark, swiping with claws long as scythes.

And I was flying above them.

Safe.

I cursed.

"Should I go down there?" I shouted to Cade, breaking tight through the air beside him. "They won't last—"

"No!" he barked, eyes burning as Krakos's wings twisted through a tailspin. "I need you here!"

"But—we're losing—!"

"If you go down, you'll die!" he roared over the wind. "And then it's over!"

A jet of pure rage coiled in my chest. My eyes snapped back to the courtyard.

A Stormscale fell through the torchlight, blood gushing in a wide arc across a wall. Another turned, too late, his shoulder torn open by a Syther's blade.

They were dying.

They were dying.

And I couldn't...

I threw a shield of light toward a pair of diving enemy dragons. A sunburst of power caught them in the flank. One exploded in flame. The other careened sideways into a cliff side— screaming as it shattered into stone.

But my eyes still drifted back to the ground, torn.

"Fuck," I muttered, pulse hammering. "What do I do, what do I do..."

Errax screamed and twisted.

Two dragons cut toward us from opposite sides, flame streaking from their jaws as they dove.

"Move!" Cade shouted.

I pulled the reins hard—Errax flipped mid-air, plummeting downward as the fire shot by inches above her wings.

Below us, a Syther dug its blade into a younger Stormscale recruit—no more than sixteen—and tore him clean in half.

No.

No.

I couldn't just watch.

"We're not winning up here!" I yelled over my shoulder, voice shaking. "They need me!"

"And I need you alive!" Cade shouted back.

But it was too late.

I veered hard, Errax answering my cry before I could even form the command.

My magic surged—and I dove.

Eden screaming in my ribs.

I was going to save them—or die trying.

Errax screeched beneath me—an ear-shattering wave of rage and agony as we veered low over the courtyard. My fingers crushed into the reins, Eden burning through my body like a sun bursting in my bones, casting trails of golden flame across the sky behind me. The Gilded Radiance surged through my hands, filling the air around us with light that hissed and cracked and shattered on impact.

I struck the Syther that had been stalking the perimeter of the infirmary tent, scorching its elongated torso clean through. It screeched in its death-throes, then vanished in a hiss of wet flame.

Below, I saw Carina on one knee, a second spear clutched in both hands, her armor hanging off her in splinters. Blood streamed from the side of her head, but her eyes were locked—dead set—on a Syther climbing onto a building behind her.

"Carina!" I screamed, pointing.

Carina didn't flinch.

She hurled the spear.

It shot like a whip of silver through the dark, roaring wind, and struck the Syther between the eyes. The creature flailed—two jerking convulsions—then dropped off the roof like a broken marionette.

She looked up—found me in the air—and gave a half-snarl, half-smile beneath the blood pouring from her temple.

Pride, pain, and gratitude.

But she was exhausted.

They all were.

I flew lower—too low. I couldn't help it. My body demanded I see who was left, who was still fighting.

A shockwave snapped through the sky behind us.

"Shit," I hissed, turning Errax hard left.

The air cracked open.

Something massive collided with Krakos high above me.

My head whipped upwards—and I saw Cade.

Or—gods, I saw what was happening to him.

A rogue dragon rider—one of the queen's own—had slammed into Krakos from above, a steel-edged blade cutting deep across the top of Cade's shoulder in midair. Fire exploded in a wide radius around them from the impact site, Krakos whirling, tail swinging wildly to regain control.

But Cade—Cade went flying.

"No no no—"

He was tethered—barely. One of the last tethering straps from his saddle had gone taut, holding him like a ragdoll as he whipped violently beneath Krakos's belly, spinning in wide loops with rotating speed. His staff tumbled through the air and vanished into the gloom.

Krakos bellowed in pain and rage, spinning to try to shake the enemy dragon peeling away behind him. But Cade was out of control, dangling by one wrist—his entire body dragged violently through the sky like a broken pendulum.

"Cade!"

I kicked hard into Errax's side.

Go, go, gods damn you, go!

She didn't need the command.

Errax surged upward with a howl that split the clouds. I could feel her agony—the strain of injury, of exhaustion—but she obeyed my every movement as if she'd felt my fear, my rage, in the marrow of her own bones.

"Faster!" I howled.

Krakos was climbing again, trying to stabilize—but another enemy dragon rider shot in from the side.

"No no no—"

Too fast.

Too sharp.

I watched helplessly—frozen, horrified—as the rider drew a curved sabre, aimed for the reins Cade was dangling from…

…and sliced.

The strap severed clean.

Cade fell.

The world stopped.

He didn't scream.

He didn't even reach for anything.

He just fell—limbs slack, blood arcing behind him like ribbons —down through the fiery clouds, straight toward the jagged spires of the northern mountain cliffs.

"No!"

I was already moving, diving after him so fast Errax shrieked in protest. The air roared around us in violent swirls of heat and ember and rising regret. My heart beat so loud I thought it might rip straight from my chest.

My love—

He was falling.

And there was fire falling with him.

Too much smoke. Too little time. The world blurred, rocks rushing up from below like ancient teeth waiting to devour him.

"Cade!"

I shoved both hands forward, wrapping Eden around every part of me—not as light, but as force. A burst of raw momentum. I pumped it into Errax, into myself, with so much power I felt my skin flay open inside my armor. The air detonated beneath us, hurling us downward in a golden squall of radiant magic.

I could see him now. Arms flailing. Flashes of blood across leather. Spinning fast.

He would hit the rock in seconds.

Too fast.

Too close.

Too late.

But—

"Hold!" I screamed.

My voice cracked with magic, and Eden answered.

My light burst from my chest in a single, focused beam—a net of gold and light that shot forward like a lasso from the gods. It caught Cade mid-fall—wrapped tightly around his torso like a lifeline forged of desperation and love.

The magic clanged through my body with such force I nearly blacked out.

The recoil dragged us both.

Errax screamed at the strain as her wings fought to stay aloft under the weight of two bodies now—one dead weight still bleeding out, the other barely conscious.

But he was alive.

So madly focused on my magic, I didn't notice the encroaching attack until it was too late. Two dragons and their riders of Emberveil attacked Errax violently. They'd swooped down from above, tearing at her wings; savage teeth cutting deep.

Errax spewed hot dragonfire and twisted to break free. My hands shot to the saddle to cling to her back as the attack continued, and to my horror, my magic failed me. The golden light of my Gilded Radiance fizzled away to thin air. I screamed his name as the golden net faded to nothing, and my prince fell.

Faded magic and dragonfire stung my nostrils as we spiraled, and I watched through the maddening haze as Cade plummeted toward the war below in Storm's End. I screamed his name until my throat cracked. My chest felt as if it were caving in as he fell.

Errax, defending us from the dragons, tucked her wings in

tightly, and I felt the pull of gravity as we raced downward. I gripped the saddle for dear life. In her agile flight, we left the attacking dragons above, struggling to keep up with her speedy drop.

My mind raced as my eyes glanced feverishly for him. But even as we landed, I found no sign of him. Up, high in the sky, Krakos' huge black form still battled with the riders of Ember-veil, oblivious to his rider's plight.

Still atop Errax as she moaned from her crush injuries, I scanned all the area, especially where Cade should be. I shouted his name, waiting for a call back, but I heard nothing. Only the sounds of frantic battle, the chaos of war, and the shrieks of pain before the bitter silence of death.

CHAPTER 27

*S*moke rose like incense from the ruins of Storm's End, curling upward to marry the clouds, stretching toward Odiun's heaven like an unanswered prayer. Above me, the sky was still bleeding fire.

Errax screamed, a sound that cut sharper than any steel, and we ran to where Cade should be.

Cold mountain air, fire-drenched and bitter from death, filled my lungs as I clutched the reins tight as Errax ran through the battle. I couldn't breathe. I couldn't think.

Where Cade should be… there was… nothing…

"Ash, no—no no no!" Bella's voice chased after me from behind, Talonor's silhouette breaking through the black smoke as she shouted again. "You have to stay up! We need you in the sky!"

"I have to find him!" My voice ripped out in a cracked scream I barely recognized as my own.

"Damn it, Ash!" Carina's voice tore in like a lash from hell, distant but unmistakable. "If you die down there, it's over! He wouldn't want—!"

But I wasn't listening.

I couldn't.

I let Errax sniff where his body had tumbled through smoke and vanished. But there was… nothing.

My boots struck stone and I was off her back before her bloody wings had folded.

"Cade!" I bellowed, sprinting across the shattered paving stones, boots splashing through puddles soaked with more than rain.

He had been right here.

Right here.

But I didn't see him.

Just—gods—no.

My knees buckled.

My heart fractured.

He—he was—

"No, no, no…" My breath hitched and I fell to my knees among the wreckage.

Then—movement.

Shadowed forms cresting the southern wall.

Bodies, tall and contorted, blades curving across the red sky like scythes raised for harvest.

Sythers.

Three. No—five.

Gods help me, more than ten.

They raced across the cracked flagstones on those hideous, elongated limbs, shrieking half-laughs as they closed the distance. Their sword-spears gleamed, wicked and jagged like they were forged from shattered bone. Their pale bodies were already streaked with blood—Stormscale blood.

"No," I whispered, standing slowly.

Not like this.

Not when I still didn't know.

Eden hummed behind my breastbone like a heartbeat finally waking from shock.

I dragged it forward.

The golden light surged at my fingertips with the force of a tempest, crackling in a wide arc as I raised both hands.

Power exploded down my arms, her wrath unfurling like wings across the courtyard.

The Sythers didn't even flinch.

They never ran from a fight. Pity.

"Alright then," I snarled through clenched teeth.

They screamed as they charged.

I screamed louder.

And then I unleashed hell.

The Gilded Radiance erupted from me like a growing sun, twin beams of golden-white fury splitting from my palms and carving through the first ranks of Sythers with such force, the stone beneath them lit with fire.

Three were gone in a heartbeat—disintegrated beneath the blast.

The rest wavered—but only for a breath.

Then they were on me.

I ducked the sweep of a wicked scythe, twisted, and flung a disk of light into the creature's sternum—watching it arc backward twenty feet through the smoke, limbs flailing.

The others didn't stop.

Fangs gleamed. Blades slashed.

One blade sliced across my pant leg. Another embedded in the edge of my shoulder guard. I cried out, twisted again—ducked just fast enough not to lose an ear.

"Come on, then!" I bellowed.

And Eden answered…

Not with light.

But with rage.

The edges of my vision turned gold. Power coiled down my spine like coals tumbling through armor. My skin burned—not from Cade, not from pain. From fury.

The Sythers lunged again.

And this time, I tore them apart.

A wide circle of power exploded around me as I dropped to one knee and slammed both palms into the stone.

A shockwave of gold-pure magic rushed the courtyard like a tidal wave made of stars—tossing Sythers backward through the air like toys hurled by a vengeful god. They slammed into broken pillars, skidded through fire, shrieked unintelligibly as their twisted limbs contorted in ways bodies shouldn't move.

I stood, golden light haloing my body like armor.

I burned.

Not just with vengeance or terror.

But with purpose.

Because I couldn't find Cade.

I couldn't feel him.

And these creatures—whatever mockery of man and monster they'd become at the queen's twisted hand—would not take him from me.

"Come again," I whispered through clenched teeth, voice low. "Come again, and I will burn your queens's kingdom to the fucking ground."

The golden shield flickered again—just for a breath—but it was enough.

My body sagged forward, knees trembling, skin singing with overuse. Sweat dripped down my temples, past blood-smeared cheekbones and into my raw, burning eyes. Every pulse of Eden now cost me. She had given all she could—and I was still standing, but only barely.

And the Sythers knew it.

There were more now. Too many. Their long, pale forms cut through the wreckage in a blur of twisted limbs and scorch-mottled blades. They spilled over the ruined wall like insects, hunched and grinning, their jagged teeth soaked from throat to toe.

My fingers twitched. The magic pulsed again as I lifted my palm.

But it sputtered. Weak sparks danced at the tips of my fingers, dimmer than candlelight.

No. No, not now.

"Ash!" Bella's voice ripped through the courtyard. I twisted on instinct, eyes catching her atop Talonor as her dragon twisted through the flames. Hunter sat before her, his gaze dark as he scanned for his prince as well.

Darren chopped his way to me, cutting through a pair of Sythers like the war chief I knew he was. The general fought like a man already half in the grave and unbothered by it—blood slick across his arm, his silver helm riddled with dents—and still he cut down another Syther without faltering.

"You have to go!" Bella screamed again. "Get airborne—we can hold the ground!"

"I can't leave!" I shouted hoarsely.

"You're no good to us if you die!" Hunter roared over the clash of steel. "Ash, we've got to find him!"

But my legs... gods, they wouldn't move. My knees collapsed beneath me and I hit the stone on all fours. Blood soaked through the knees of my leggings, the dirty wet grit biting through fabric into skin.

"Get up..." I muttered, fingers clawing at the ground. "Come on, Ash. You've fought worse. Get the fuck up—"

"Moonriver..."

His voice was barely a whisper, curling through the heat and roar of battle like smoke.

My head snapped up.

"Cornelius?" But nothing was there.

Except...

A shimmer. Behind me. Barely visible. Like water catching starlight.

And then he was there.

The tortoise.

Half-invisible, half-solid, his heavy green shell shimmered like a mirage in the haze just beyond the flames.

"Your focus…" he said quietly, as if we were strolling a garden and not standing in the middle of hell. "…is in too many places. Find the truth. Look up."

"What truth?" I rasped.

He stepped beside me—silent, still vaguely transparent—and lowered his massive head so those golden-orange eyes aligned with mine.

"Look, little Moonriver," he whispered again, his voice a tide brushing over shore. "Look, and remember what matters most."

And then—he was gone.

Disappeared like mist in flame.

I stood faltering, lungs sputtering.

And I lifted my eyes.

Through fire. Through the rising smoke and descending ash. Past the burning towers and falling wings.

High above.

A dragon.

Dark red, massive.

Soaring alone. Away from the battlefield. Its rider whipping the reins feverishly.

Clutched beneath the huge beast, a man was being flown off far into the distance… toward Emberveil, and the queen.

"Cade."

It came out barely a sound. Like my lungs forgot how to speak.

I blinked hard, sweat and ash stinging my vision—and there, through the fractured lens of flame and fear, I saw him again.

Cade. His body limp, bound in thick claws of the crimson leviathan. Arms tight across his sides. Head hanging limply. His hair trailing like black silk in the wind.

"No…" My heart stopped. "No. No, no—"

He wasn't dead.

But he was being taken.

Away.

I screamed—raw, guttural, a sound born of agony too sacred for words.

"No!"

The Sythers didn't hear me.

But Errax did.

She roared behind me, and I spun, stumbling toward her as Eden surged back through my veins like a heart restarted by vengeance. Pain. Love.

Cade.

They were taking Cade.

She had him.

The queen.

She had taken him.

Back to Emberveil.

I pressed a hand to my heart where Cade's fire had once met mine—and swore that she would regret it.

She wanted the Gold-Marked?

Good.

Because I was coming.

Not to be captured.

Not to run.

But to set her world on fire.

And take back what was mine.

CHAPTER 28

Smoke clogged my throat like poison.

My boots slipped in the blood-soaked mud as I stumbled over the body of a Stormscale soldier—his silver cloak torn, one eye open to the sky, unblinking. His sword still wrapped in stiff fingers, as if he'd died gripping hope.

A Syther hissed behind me. I spun, both palms already lit with Eden's golden fire, and slammed it through the creature's snarling face. The blast sent its head snapping backward at an ugly angle before its whole body pitched into the mound of corpses cluttering the east end of the field.

There had to be thirty of them already. Maybe more. All cut down in the last hour by my hand.

And I didn't stop.

I couldn't.

Every swing, every spell, every fucking breath was wild and feral and so, so pointless—because they just kept coming. Crawling over their own dead sisters and brothers, curved blades raised like death's own grin carved from bone.

Around me, Storm's End was dying.

The courtyard had vanished into a haze of ash and firelight, parts of the keep already crumbling like brittle parchment under siege. A chunk of the north tower lay shattered across the northern training circle. The infirmary had been engulfed ten minutes ago—nobody even cried out anymore.

Cade was gone, my dragon was injured, Krakos was still battling madly above, and I felt as alone as I ever had… again…

Gods, who was even left?

"Come on then!" I screamed, voice ragged. "How many more of you can I burn?!"

Three Sythers snapped at one another nearby, picking through the corpses climbing up the mound toward me. Their elongated fingers slid over the dead like spiders across bone. They shrieked in that guttural, jagged way, as if even their language had been twisted by the queen's rage.

A fourth dropped from the low rooftop to my left, blades clicking against stone.

I didn't wait.

I flung forward another burst of my golden light, Eden crackling down my arms like lightning through a weapon already cracking with strain. The spell ripped through the air, arced hard, and smote two of the creatures where they stood.

Sparks burst from their jaws as they collapsed backward, choking on their own ichor.

But the power in my chest dimmed.

Not flickered.

Dimmed.

My heart hesitated.

I raised my hands to call another spell—but hesitation turned to horror.

Nothing came.

No golden trail. No heat. No radiance.

Just silence where Eden should've been.

A chill unfurled over the backs of my arms.

"No," I whispered. "No—no no no—"

I willed the power forward, curling my hand into a fist, drawing from every wound, scream, ache, everything I had left.

Still… nothing.

Gone.

"Eden?" I croaked.

And for the first time since my mark first glowed—

She didn't answer.

A scream tore from my throat—half rage, half panic—as I lifted my sword instead, the relic blade that had seen more fire than steel should've. The hilt burned hot against my palm.

Steel would have to do.

A Syther sprang from the heap. Its blade sliced for my gut.

I turned, parried, twisted low, and slammed my heel into the crook of its leg—the thing shrieked, convulsed, then dove at me again.

Our weapons clanged, jarring through my arms, and I drove the relic blade straight into its chest until the sound of wet tearing echoed like thunder across the pile of the dead.

It gurgled and crumpled.

I stood—panting, sobbing, trembling—alone atop a mountain of war.

And they were still coming.

Five more now, skimming between the gravestones of bodies like shadows sucking breath.

They would take me.

If I didn't move, they'd take me.

But… I couldn't feel Eden.

I was stripped bare.

They'd take me, and Cade wasn't here—and—

"Ash!"

Hunter's voice broke through the smoke wall behind me. His copper armor was battered, eyes wide and furious as he flew toward me. His bloodied sword behind him in one hand, and

Bella clung to his other—her golden braid undone, face covered in soot and tears.

"Get on Errax! Now!" he shouted.

"I—" I blinked through the fog. "I can't! I don't feel it—I can't feel it anymore!"

They landed beside me, quaking the cobblestones beneath them.

"Ash, Eden doesn't matter right now," Bella gasped as she reached me, her hands grabbing both sides of my arm. "Listen to me—we can't beat them all here. Not like this. You have to go."

"I can't leave you—"

"You can!" Hunter snarled. "Errax is still alive! She's still breathing—you follow her lead and you live!"

"But Cade—!" I cried, tears stinging. "She took Cade!"

"I know!" Bella screamed.

My legs wobbled as I grabbed the sides of the saddle on Errax's side, wings barely extended. Her eyes met mine—tired, furious, protective. Tears choked my vision.

Hunter shoved me forward. "Go! Before she can't carry you anymore!"

The Sythers shrieked behind us. I turned. The mound was shifting again. More climbing out of the ruins. Fifteen. Twenty.

Too many.

"What if she—what if I can't find him—"

"Ash!" Bella sobbed. "If you don't get back up into the sky now... then you won't live to find him."

My nails dug into her shoulder, not wanting her to be right. I wiped my tears away with my sleeve. This can't be happening, just when I thought everything had turned for us... he can't be gone... he just can't... and Storm's End... how did this all happen? What can I do? There has to be something...

And then—

A shimmer.

A shell-green glow at the edge of my vision.

Cornelius.

He stood among the burning wreckage.

Not a spot of ash on him.

Not a strand of fear in his eyes.

"Go," he said softly, and not to my ears—but deeper.

To something inside my chest I didn't know still listened.

"You've done more than they ever expected of you. Now let the gods finish the job they began. Flee now. Save yourself... and save him later."

I staggered forward, barely aware of getting into the saddle until I felt Errax grunt under me.

The moment I touched her, the dragon bolted upward into the black. Hunter and Bella took Talonor back to the sky as well, as a pack of Sythers rushed to fill the void beneath us, their weapons aching for our blood.

And as we cleared the burning wall of the courtyard, soaring into the storm sky, I looked once—just once—down at Storm's End.

And felt it.

Something was different.

The ground trembled.

The mountain's veins pulsed.

Something beneath it had... awakened.

The ground kept shaking.

I didn't know what it meant at first. Not until Errax's wings stuttered mid-beat, her long sinewed body glancing sideways beneath me like even she was... uncertain. Like the air had shifted somehow. The mountain range beneath us—a place I'd come to know, to fly over, to train above and bleed upon—was... humming?

A low vibration thrummed up through Errax's legs as her claws scraped a passing ledge, like something beneath her had exhaled.

Below, Storm's End writhed in its death spiral. Fire and blood.

Screams splitting wood. Sythers climbing over the last terraces of stone to claim what was left of the fortress. Dozens of soldiers still fought in the yard, battling through the bodies of their fallen kin. Some rose and fell within seconds, blades clashing only once before being cut down. Arrows still hissed through the fog.

But… something was wrong.

Or right.

I couldn't tell.

Something had changed.

The stones.

They were moving.

I squinted through the haze—and my next breath caught in my throat.

Eyes.

There were eyes in the earth.

One of the stones lining the ruined wall near the mess hall blinked. A ripple ran down its mossy face—and then it shifted. Rose. No, grew.

I watched as one of the courtyard boulders uncurled itself from a bed of ivy, rose as tall as five men, towering over the fires like a godborn beast. The surface of its torso cracked open with lichen-lined crevices that flexed and breathed, revealing bones of shining granite and arms thick as cliffside trees.

"What in Odiun's name?" I whispered.

Another tree moved. A cypress, gnarled and old, its base wound with ragged bark that had stood untouched for a hundred years—straightened. Its roots ripped free from the earth and punched into the ground beside a dying soldier being swarmed by Sythers.

Then it moved.

Fast.

Two great wooden arms pounded forward, and one of the Sythers exploded into pulp beneath a slam of limbs that shouldn't have even been animated.

"What the—" Bella screamed from below, still clinging to Talonor's reins as he dipped to avoid another swooping rider.

Hunter shouted something but his words were lost under the rising whine of stone grinding against stone—and then the earth ripped open down the center of the courtyard.

A massive fissure tore wide, splitting the square like a wound in the mountain's flesh.

And from the chasm…

They rose.

Creatures taller than towers. Formed of stone, root, vine, bark, and sediment. As if Storm's End had opened its ribs and offered up its children.

Giants stepped out of the torn land, glimmering with runic veins aglow in pale green and furious bronze. Their eyes blinked with awareness as their heads turned slowly toward the Sythers. Their movements were slow—but deadly. One struck the ground with its hand, and two Sythers were obliterated in a quake that knocked half the battlefield into a kneel.

"The gods have returned," Hunter shouted. "No…"

Cornelius appeared near the edge of the wall beside the command tower, unbothered by the wind or the stench or even the blood pouring from the eastern ramparts. He gazed upward —toward me—and smiled like a man who'd been waiting for this moment for centuries.

I landed Errax on instinct beside the battleground, leaping from the saddle and nearly collapsing to my knees as the earth bucked again beneath me.

The Sythers froze.

All of them.

They'd been swarming like flies over every corpse—tasted too much blood already. But now, their jagged snarling faltered. Their hunched frames stilled, long fingers twitching like animals smelling a bigger predator.

I turned toward Cornelius.

"What is happening?" I panted, barely on my feet. "Cornelius —what's going on?!"

He turned calmly, as if we weren't waist-deep in hell.

"You don't know?"

"Know what?"

Cornelius sat heavily at the edge of the crumpled stones.

"Then perhaps now is your time to learn."

Behind me, Bella clutched the edge of a broken ballista cart, eyes wide as moons, her voice a breathless prayer. "By Odiun…"

She looked up at me slowly. "Ash." Her face had drained of blood, her freckles standing in sharper relief under the soot.

"It's the Terradyne," she said reverently.

The name hit like a boulder.

"The Earth elementals," she breathed, barely able to say it. "They're alive."

The Terradyne moved through the battlefield like titans carved straight from the gods' own nightmares. The largest one —half the size of a Stormscale dragon—smashed a Syther with one swipe of its open palm, flattening it against the ramparts like fruit beneath a hammer.

Another bent down, ancient moss trailing from its arms like robes, and impaled two Sythers onto the horned roots that sprouted from its back. It moved with certainty, with ritual, stepping through flame and ruin without hesitating.

They were trees.

They were hills.

They were everything the queen thought she had poisoned— and now that toxin had turned into a cure.

One waved its massive hand over the infirmary ruins.

Ash spiraled—rising dust clung in the wind.

The Terradyne had come for war.

All across the courtyard, Sythers faltered.

Terrified.

Not of me. Not even of Cade's fire or the dragons shrieking above.

But of the legends that stood now at the gates of Storm's End.

They hissed.

Screeched.

And fled.

Dragon riders swooped like vultures, grabbing Sythers in their talons, snatching them bodily off the battlefield and rocketing skyward—retreating.

Their retreat horn blew before I understood what I was hearing.

High and long and shrill.

A blade carved of wind.

The queen's army was leaving.

They were escaping.

Dozens of dragons turned as one, circling the keep once— then vanishing into the storm clouds with the Sythers clutched in mangled claws, shrieking their foul curses all the way to the skies.

And with them…

Was Cade.

Still unconscious.

Still bound.

Tied like a prince in a coffin, carried away from me too far off to see

I screamed again, but the battle was already over, and my love was gone…

The dragons vanished into the clouds. All that remained was fire, ash, and the sound of the wounded.

Only this time… the wounded were surviving.

Storm's End was not burning.

Not fully.

Because the Terradyne had saved us.

Dozens of them.

They knelt across the broken halls, across the ruined spires, as if planting their bodies between us and the next wave of storm.

Stone and wind and earth bent to their shape.

I turned, trembling, toward Bella as she limped beside me.

"Did we win?" I asked.

She looked up at the Terradyne—and down across the dead.

And she didn't answer.

Because the answer was already written on the ground.

We were alive.

But Cade was gone.

Storm's End would survive.

But I had lost everything.

And I still hadn't saved him.

Cornelius waddled up beside me, serene and timeless even in the rubble.

"You did what you could."

I turned to him with empty eyes. "Was it enough?"

He tilted his massive head skyward as the clouds broke silver light down onto the tallest Terradyne's brow.

And softly, he said, "Not yet."

CHAPTER 29

The rain had washed away none of the blood.

It fell cold and quiet over the broken carcass of Storm's End, beading off twisted stone and shattered steel, off cracked shields and the splintered hafts of fallen spears. It ran in slow rivulets down the remains of the command tower and pooled in the ash-choked gullies where mortar used to hold this place together—but the blood stayed. Stained. Set in place like it belonged here now.

I walked through it numbly, boots sucking wet through mud that had once been our courtyard, now cratered, pocked with burns from dragonfire and craters where Sythers had carved trenches into our defenses with a hunger that hadn't slowed until the gods themselves stood between us.

What was left of the keep was no longer a fortress.

It wasn't even a camp.

The tents had burned or been trampled.

The dining hall was a smoldering memory, ribs of its former roof still curled sharp like giant fingers reaching upward in agony.

The stables, the dragon roost, our bunkhouse, even Bracken Burr Hall was gone.

Just... gone.

Behind me, I heard someone sob quietly. Maybe more than one.

I didn't stop to see who.

The grief moved through me like something half-dead, like a wound that had bled so long it had forgotten how to clot.

I should've been flying.

Should've been tracking Cade's captors.

But Errax was barely standing, and I'd used so much magic holding this ruin together I couldn't keep my hands from shaking. The energy had pulled free from my limbs like threads from torn silk, unraveling me with each breath.

My body wasn't broken.

But grief didn't care about bones.

My knees buckled once—just shy of the forge, now collapsed into rubble—and I caught myself on a half-burned beam, wood shrieking beneath my hand as I steadied.

I couldn't look up.

Not yet.

Couldn't face the mountain of dead that lived across this keep like roaches unwilling to leave the light.

I shouldn't have come this way.

I told myself not to go near the children's quarters. But my feet had turned here, anyway, dragging me to the place where I'd last heard laughter—where the young girl with chestnut curls and dusty fingers had handed me a copper-twined dragon charm woven in string not strong enough to survive storm-wind.

Please don't be here.

Please don't be here.

But the gods aren't merciful.

I saw her before I knew what I was seeing.

Just a little shape in rumpled gray cloth curled in the mud. Her bare legs streaked with soot. Her hand gripped around something—I couldn't tell what it was at first, not until I stepped closer.

A new copper dragon charm.

Still clenched in her tiny, lifeless fingers.

There wasn't enough breath in my lungs to scream.

I dropped to my knees beside her, mud exploding up around my shins as I tried—gods, I tried—to roll her over gently, to cradle her scuffed cheek in my hand like I'd shield her from the sky if I could.

Her face was cold.

Half-covered in soot. Half in rain.

And not moving.

"No," I whispered, my fingers desperate, unbraiding the wet strands of her hair from her forehead. "No, you're okay. You're okay—you gave me this. You—god dammit—"

My voice broke then.

It cracked open, raw and feral and not the kind of crying that makes you feel better afterward. The kind that just leaks pain without relief.

I choked on it.

My whole chest convulsed.

And then Bella was there—crashing beside me into the mud, arms around my shoulders before I could push her away, grounding me even as I fought to crawl closer to death.

I curled around the girl's form and sobbed like the world was ending all over again.

"I didn't save her," I gasped. "I saved no one—"

"Hush," Bella sobbed next to me, fierce and broken. "You saved the rest of us."

"No, I didn't!" I howled into the girl's hair. "The queen has Cade, and they're all dead, and I—I can't even feel my magic!"

She held me tighter. She didn't offer lies. She didn't say it's going to be okay.

Just let me break.

Let me fall, finally.

The trinket clattered against the stone as the girl's pale hand slackened, the copper threads unraveling in my fingers until it dropped into the mud. I stared at it.

This charm was perhaps made for someone, someone who would never receive this gift from this perfect child.

She'd given one to me.

Because she believed.

"Why would they believe in me?" I moaned.

"Because you're all they had," Bella murmured into my neck, her tears hot against my throat.

A voice split the mist.

"Damn you, Odiun—damn you!"

We turned.

Hunter stood near the broken outer wall, blood pouring from one shoulder, his sword planted halfway into the earth. His face was twisted in a raw expression I'd never seen—not from him.

From anyone, really.

He'd known loss.

But this—this was something else.

His voice cracked again, brimming with rage sagging under too much weight. "You allowed this! You watched this happen! You were supposed to protect them!"

He punched the stone beside him, and I heard bone break.

He didn't stop.

He just kept shouting at the sky. "You took my prince! You took them all!"

I stared.

Because I hadn't known until that moment how much Cade had meant to him.

Not like that.

Not like this.

The strongest man I'd ever known weeping and pounding the stone like pain couldn't leave fast enough.

I bowed my head and cradled the girl closer.

I didn't say a word.

The gods didn't answer.

Maybe they'd died here too.

The wind shifted.

Cold. Damp. Like something old and rotting moved beneath it.

Bella helped me to my feet slowly. Her fingers shook as they gripped my wrist. My knees wept with mud, the weight of the girl's body lingered on my skin like I was still holding her. I turned numbly to look for Errax, half-expecting her to have vanished into the storm—but she was there. Torn and winded, but there.

The world hadn't crumbled.

But it should have.

It damn well should have.

A shape moved through the haze behind the ruined command tower. A tall silhouette, one hand clenched tight around the hilt of a blade steeped in blood. The rain clung to him. The mountain didn't shake under his feet. It just... looked hollow now.

Darren Iconnas.

The Stormscale general wasn't yelling. Wasn't crying. Just standing where so many of his people had died, shoulders squared as if braced against the weight of a kingdom slipping down his spine.

Everything about him looked slower now. Or maybe I was seeing him differently.

Maybe war had finally crumpled the parts of him that weren't steel.

I walked to him—couldn't really stop myself. My feet barely felt the ground anymore, but the sound of water slapping against blood was sticky underfoot.

He didn't look at me when I came to stand beside him.

Not at first.

His sword was still in his hand, knuckles white with the grip. The hand of a man who wasn't ready to let go. Not of his battle. Not of his grief.

When he finally spoke, his voice scraped across his throat like it had rusted there.

"Storm's End was supposed to be unshakable."

His words hung heavy, like they remembered better days than we ever got the chance to live.

"And now it's just ash."

I didn't have the strength to tell him it wasn't his fault.

None of us did.

He blinked away rain that looked suspiciously like tears and gave me a long sidelong glance. "He loved you. Reckless as it was."

The words hit my chest harder than they should have.

But before the silence could settle too deep between us—Carina swept out of the sky like a dagger thrown by the wind.

Her silver-streaked blond braid whipped over her shoulder as her dragon thudded hard into a landing beside the remains of the armory. Smoke curled from the scorched wreckage like it still remembered fire. Tar fumes mixed with blood. Bones cracked under boots.

She jumped down with a grunt, armor flecked with Syther blood, one sleeve torn to ribbons. She stormed forward toward me and Darren, her mouth set in a line made more of exhaustion than anger.

But when she spoke—I saw fury buried in it.

"How the fuck," she growled low, "is this possible?"

Her voice trembled, not from fear. From betrayal.

"They were regrouping. That's what the report said! You—" she pointed at Darren—"you showed us the raven. We confirmed the handwriting. Gods, we all saw it. They pulled back to Emberveil."

Darren didn't speak.

Because none of us had an answer.

I opened my mouth. Nothing came.

And that's when we heard it.

A dry, rasping laugh.

From behind the half-fallen outer wall.

A wet, ripping sound followed it—like meat splitting from old bone.

Carina drew her dagger fast, eyes narrowing. "What the hell is—"

"Stay here," Hunter barked, stepping through the haze behind us, face streaked with ash and something much darker. His nose bled freely, and his right eye was swelling shut, but his sword was still sharp—and raised.

We followed him in silence.

To where the laugh was.

It was a Syther.

Barely.

What was left of one.

Half-buried beneath a pile of scorched timber and dragon bone, a massive spear driven through its chest. One of our weapons—storm-forged.

It should've died clean.

But the way it grinned at us—black teeth cracked down the middle, blood bubbling around its lips like ink—it looked like it was dying satisfied.

That made my stomach turn.

Hunter stepped forward, blade out, voice like a knife in the wind.

"What's so funny, freak?"

The Syther wheezed, chest rattling with each breath—a sound wet and obscene.

Beneath the blood, its small, beady red eyes lit up as they stared directly at me.

Then the laughter came again.

Worse this time.

Like a dying god choking on hubris.

"Don't give it air," Carina warned.

But the thing spoke anyway.

"Fell... for it," it gurgled.

My stomach dropped.

Hunter stepped closer. "What?"

The Syther chuckled again. More blood. "The queen... sends her love."

That sound—it wasn't language.

It was mockery.

Hunter bent low, pressed the point of his sword beneath the creature's jaw, forcing its head back. "What is your snake tongue going on about?"

The Syther coughed, voice shaking with glee even as life drained from its split chest. "Clever... little raven. You believed him, yes? Stormscale scout. Loyal. Brave."

Hunter pulled back.

"You're lying," he hissed.

The Syther's eyes gleamed.

"No. We pulled it from him. Through screams. Through burning toes. Through threats to his children."

Bella gasped behind me.

I covered my mouth with one hand and staggered backward.

"We... made him write the Raven's scroll, after a full day of torture and threats." The Syther coughed again, blood pouring freely now. "One lie... one perfect lie... and you laid down your shields..."

My legs buckled.

My knees hit the ash.

All the weight of a broken war came slamming into my chest with those words.

The queen hadn't pulled back to Emberveil.

She'd never pulled back.

She'd baited us.

Retreated in name only to lure us into false security.

To make us vulnerable.

To make Cade vulnerable.

So she could strike fast.

So she could take him.

"I'll kill you," Hunter muttered, his voice utterly empty.

He drove the sword forward.

The Syther choked, once—

And died still laughing.

Silence fell heavy afterward.

Bella stepped up beside me, one hand gripping my shoulder so tightly my bones hurt.

"She tricked us," I said aloud, numb.

Darren bent slightly on one knee, gripping the ground as if it might run from him. His eyes were hollow. Ghost-lit.

"She tricked all of us. Always two steps ahead, just like Cade said she was..."

The rain kept coming.

The fire kept smoldering.

And the queen's triumph echoed all the louder in the silence she left behind.

So quiet.

So absolute.

Hunter stood motionless beside the corpse, rain streaming down his face in long red lines. I watched him strip the blade from the dead thing's jaw as if expecting it to twitch one more time, to spit another final insult.

But there was nothing left.

Just grief.

Just the cold.

And the sound of the Earth itself... breathing.

Behind the wall, the Terradyne loomed tall like haunted towers.

Yet none of us felt victorious.

"She has Cade," I whispered, more to myself than anyone. "She knew exactly what to do. Saw my weakness. Pulled the world apart down the seam she found in my chest."

"Not your fault," Carina murmured, though it sounded more like prayer than reassurances. Her voice was trembling. "She was recovering. She needed him. She waited for the right time."

Darren lifted his face to the sky, red-streaked with blood, then down toward the muddy trinket still tangled in my braid.

"She took the Prince of Emberveil," he said at last. "There will be no hiding now. No war table. No more waiting."

I looked up through the smoke toward the mountains.

Through the haze, I saw one last dragon shape heading north, toward the sunless ridge where Emberveil crouched.

And I swore then, standing among the bodies of the innocent and the damned alike—

I would follow.

Me.

Ash Moonriver.

Born with a slave's name, raised in fear, scarred in silence.

The queen wanted to break me?

Good.

Let her try.

Because war was coming.

And I had her name on the end of my sword.

CHAPTER 30

The rain trickled down like the gods were too tired to mourn, so they let the sky do it for them.

What was left of Storm's End smoldered at our backs—torches drowned by ash, flags clinging ragged to splintered stones. Smoke curled from the broken bones of the fortress, black fingers reaching up through silver mist like even the walls were clawing at the sky, searching for something lost.

Ash-coated wind dragged through the courtyard in slow, wheezing breaths. The kind of silence people mistake for peace.

It wasn't.

It was the kind that comes after screaming stops. After fire eats the last roofbeam and leaves nothing else left to burn.

Bodies were everywhere.

Slumped against shattered parapets. Curled in corners where spears had punched through heart and armor alike. Wrapped in the arms of the ones who still lived—as if holding them tighter might warm their bones, might slow the bleeding.

I stood at the edge of it, shaking, my hands stained with ash and golden light dried into dark streaks. Eden had gone quiet after the battle. Muted. It wasn't that she was afraid.

I was.

Of what had happened.

Of what I had done.

And most of all—of what would happen next.

"He's out there," I said through my teeth, the words a rasp half-swallowed by threat. "She's got him."

Beside me, Bella stood like a ghost in the rain, droplets streaking her cheeks—but I wasn't sure if they were part of the clouds or just what was left of her grief. Her braid had come undone in the fighting. Long pieces of it clung to her jaw.

Carina held a cloth against a gash on her upper arm, her gaze distant as she watched Stormscale soldiers dragging bodies from the wreckage and laying them in quiet rows by the eastern wall. She didn't cry. But her fists trembled.

Hunter paced beside his dragon Talonor, muttering in low tones. Krakos was gone—still wheeling above us somewhere in the clouded heavens, the sound of his furious cries raking down the mountainsides like thunder.

He was looking for Cade.

Still.

"What now?" Carina asked softly, voice hoarse.

Darren stood like a statue amid the stillness, blade hanging from one hand like it had long since become too heavy to carry. His armor was cracked across the chest. His left pauldron missing. Blood and soot streaked his face, collected beneath his eyes like he hadn't slept in days.

None of us had.

I turned to them.

To my makeshift family: two warriors, a dragon prince's best friend, and the girl who'd saved me more times than I could count.

I didn't even feel the tears until they overflowed. They slipped past my lashes hot and sick and silent, dropping to the mud without splash.

"We have to go after him," I said.

Darren blinked slowly. Hunter stopped pacing.

Carina didn't even look up.

"He's gone," Bella said, almost a whisper. Like she thought if she said it too loud, it would shatter me into pieces too small to be picked up.

"I don't care," I said.

The breath caught in my throat as I turned, my voice rising, cracking like the thunder that didn't come. "I don't care if Brigodon himself stands at her side. If she throws every damn Syther from the northern cliffs to the Southern Sea—I'm going."

"Ash…" Hunter's walk slowed, his eyes wary. "We understand. You loved him—"

"That's not enough," I spat, my voice sharp with the edge I had left. "He gave everything. Every piece of who he was. For me. For this war. And now she has him, and I'm not sitting here pretending that's acceptable."

Bella stepped closer, arms wrapping tight around me, and for a second I let it hold me up.

But I couldn't stay small beneath her forever.

"I am going to kill the queen." My voice cracked again, but it didn't break. "She took him. I'll take her head."

They stood with me in that silence—my people. The last ones standing.

None of them said it.

But I could feel it behind their eyes.

If you go now… you'll die.

If you run into the dark to save a burning star, you won't come back.

And maybe that was true.

But death wasn't frightening anymore.

Watching Cade fall had already killed too many pieces of me.

And then—

A sound ripped upward through the clouds.

Krakos.

He howled.

A devastating sound.

High and broken, not rage as much as grief. He wheeled low over the field, his massive black wings trembling in the air as if they couldn't bear the weight of his sorrow.

He circled once. Then again.

Then a third time.

Until the whole battlefield stilled—every movement stopped, every death scream smothered by the dragon's agony.

The winged shadow beat hard against the sky. Black smoke trailed his edges like the remnants of a dream burning fast.

Hunter held his arms wide, even as his blood soaked the ash-kissed ground, even as the dragon descended like calamity made flesh.

"Krakos," he said, more quietly as the great beast landed near the foundation that had once been Bracken Burr Hall.

Krakos touched down gently, pawing at the earth like he thought he might find Cade buried underneath it.

The dragon that had screamed death over corpses fell quiet, his shoulders slumped.

His eyes—those blood-gem eyes—scoured the battlefield frantically.

We didn't have to tell the obsidian dragon. Not that we spoke dragon. Errax had seen what had happened to Cade. All of it. She screeched to the black dragon, and a fury took Krakos.

He reared back and screamed—an unholy, breaking sound that cracked the stones beneath his claws, that echoed through the mountain valleys like a war horn sounding for a soul now claimed.

He called for his rider.

Again.

And again.

And there, on the ruined ground of Storm's End, I finally dropped to my knees and sobbed for the man who held my heart.

"I'm coming for you, Cade," I whispered through helpless, burning tears.

"Hold on, gods damn you."

"Hold on."

Because I was not done.

Not yet.

Not even close.

The rain did not stop as the morning broke across the ruined battlements of Storm's End—it only changed. From thin streaks of mist to long weeping curtains that clung to skin, wrapped around your bones, and made it feel like the whole mountain was mourning with us.

They buried the dead in silence.

No songs. No rites. Just the weight of grief and soaked leather, and the sound of picks through the earth.

The earth gave easily. As if even it was too heartbroken to resist.

Stormscale soldiers moved like phantoms through the wreckage, dragging broken swords behind them, laying cloaks gently over cold limbs. Darren stood at the center of the field, watching his people dig graves in neat rows across the ridgeline behind what remained of the east watch. The rain ran over the stone, carving lines through the blood that hadn't yet faded.

He hadn't spoken since Krakos landed.

Not until now.

"We bury them," Darren said, his voice low, like the thunder that rolls in after the flash. "Then we talk. Then we plan."

His words hung there, heavy.

But Carina wasn't silent.

She couldn't be.

She stood near one of the makeshift pyres, a sword she wasn't holding anymore hanging loose in her hand, her golden braid uncoiling in the wind like a rope frayed near snapping.

"She made one of us lie." Her voice rasped through the downpour, sharp and bitter. "She made one of our own betray us—with a scroll and a seal, and a lie soaked in his blood."

She didn't blink. Didn't move.

"He was loyal," she said, and the pain behind her eyes cracked her voice like ice splitting under weight. "Ferran was the most loyal of any of us. He trained my damned dragon, and she made him fold like parchment."

I turned toward her then, slowly.

Carina's eyes swam with tears unshed—maybe not for Ferran alone, but for whatever it cost her to admit she couldn't blame him.

"She made him," she whispered. "You know that, right? With blades, and knives to throats, and threats to the only damn family he had left."

No one dared speak.

Because there was nothing you could say to that kind of loss.

Carina just stared at the fire as it hissed over rain-soaked logs and took its slow, devouring hold.

Hunter gritted his teeth beside me. "We should've seen it," he muttered. "The sudden quiet. The timing. Stars be damned, we should've known it was bait."

"We were tired," Bella said softly, curling her arms around herself. "A collective breath. We needed to believe it was true."

She was right.

The queen knew that.

She gave us hope.

Then set fire to it.

Hunter glanced up, eyes bloodshot. "What about them?"

It took me a moment to understand.

Then I followed his gaze—and the hairs rose all along the back of my neck.

The Terradyne.

Earth elementals, still towering like ancient sculptures along the ridge. They hadn't moved since the last of the fighting. Not even to flinch when stormlight cracked the hills behind them. They just… stood. Tall. Stoic. Watching.

They made no sound. No gesture. Nothing human.

But they watched.

"You think they're waiting for something?" Bella asked.

Hunter shrugged stiffly. "Or mourning in their own way."

Talonor sat nearby, licking at a wound on his wing as slowly as a wolf tending its haunch. Krakos still hadn't moved from where he curled near the crater in the command wing. His huge head rested on the scorched stones, his body wrapped in tight circles like a dog protecting its last scrap of hope.

My pulse thudded quietly in my ears as I found my way forward, toward the center of the hill where the largest Terradyne rested—stalwart among ash. It had the shape of a man, mostly—broad shoulders, thick arms ending in hand-like stubs made of bark and shale. Its torso pulsed with dull green light, like phosphorescence deep in the sea. Moss trailed from where a beard might've been. Roots curled down from its knees and into the soil, like it was both statue and garden.

It turned its head as I approached.

Only a fraction.

But it moved.

I stopped, boots sinking an inch into soggy soil.

"Thank you," I said. Voice no louder than wind across a leaf.

No answer.

Of course not.

But something shifted.

In the air. In the soil. Maybe in the dead weight of magic that still lingered around the bones of the fortress.

"Cornelius said…" I swallowed, blinking mist from my lashes.

"He said you were... alive. I didn't believe him until I saw you rise from the fissures. Until I saw you save them."

The Terradyne blinked—I think it blinked—and then its massive torso tilted gently, like a tree nodding in slow wind.

"I don't know if you can hear me," I whispered, my nails digging into the palm of my grimy hand. "I don't know what you want. I don't know what brought you here. But you saved us."

A gust of air passed between us, stronger than the rest.

And I wasn't sure, but I thought—just for a moment—I felt... warmth.

Low and deep from beneath the surface, not in heat, but foundation.

"You knew the queen was coming," I murmured. "You rose for us. For Storm's End."

The Terradyne didn't move.

Maybe it didn't need to.

Behind me, the camp shifted with the weight of the fallen.

Ash continued to swirl softly in the melting rain.

Stormscale flags fluttered half-mast from the pauldron of a soldier's makeshift spear.

And the queen still breathed beyond the mountains.

With Cade in her claws.

"I need help," I said.

I felt something beneath my feet—earth grinding slightly.

A tremor.

A heartbeat.

"I'm going to kill her," I said aloud.

My voice didn't shake this time.

"I'm going to Emberveil," I whispered. "And if you remember what she did to your forests—your mountains—if you feel the sting of magic twisted into poison..."

I lifted my chin to the Terradyne's face.

"Then come with me."

And for a long heartbeat, I thought the silence was all I'd get in return.

But on the wind—I swear I heard it:

The crack of bark bending.

The grind of roots shifting.

And the slow quake of stone as something ancient stirred in the deep earth.

Their heads tilted as one.

And I knew.

They were listening.

And that might be the beginning of everything.

CHAPTER 31

The field where we'd buried the honored dead had turned quiet again, but not empty.

Not with them standing there.

We approached slowly. Me, Bella, Hunter, Darren, Carina, and dozens of the last Stormscale soldiers still steady on their feet. Our breath curled visibly in the morning chill, clinging to the fog that rolled low along the ridgeline. The soil was soaked, not just from rain, but from the blood of good men. Good women.

But the Terradyne—if Cornelius had named them right—did not move.

Not one of them.

They stood like cathedral statues, unmoving, unblinking, taller than dragons, limbs of bark and living stone, torsos wide as fortress doors. Some had shoulders woven with live moss, their roots curled around loose boulders the way my hair curled after a storm. One of them had a hollow in its chest where a small tree had grown, bent sideways in the wind.

Gods preserve us. They were beautiful. And terrifying.

I tried not to flinch when one of them shifted—just its head, tilting with the creak of a thousand-year oak bowing its limbs—and regarded me like it was still deciding if I was beast or kin.

They were old. I could feel it in my teeth. Not just old in years.

Old like riverbeds. Like forgotten dreams.

And still they watched us.

Like curious gods.

So we stopped. Ten paces from the closest one.

They loomed over us like cliffs had come alive and grown faces.

Not human faces. Nothing so familiar. There were shallow indentations where eyes might go, a ridge of stone where a brow might rest like a shelf beneath the clouds. One had arms thick with overlapping plates of granite, swirled with runes I couldn't read—lines that glowed faintly with green-blue mosslight whenever it exhaled.

I squinted at one.

Then stepped forward.

"Okay," I said, softly. "Let's try this."

They didn't blink.

"My name is Ashlyn Moonriver."

Still nothing.

I cleared my throat. "Former slave. Dragon-rider. Current enemy of your worst ruler."

Still nothing.

I tried not to glance at the others behind me. I could feel Bella chewing a fingernail with nerves and Carina shifting her weight like she was about to grab her spear.

I swallowed.

"I... I want your help."

One of the Terradyne—taller than the rest, its shoulders sloped with moss and bark etched like seal lines across its chest—tilted its head again.

A sound escaped it.

Like the cracking of a glacier.

Then another noise followed… and another.

I wish I could say it was a voice.

But it was more like listening to mountains speak through an avalanche.

The closest one opened its mouth—if mouth was even the right word—and I didn't hear words.

I felt them.

A rumble through the ground, through the bones in my feet and up the back of my skull. The sound of stone snapping, of boulders tumbling, as if rock itself had a dialect street bards never sang about for fear of splitting their tongues.

And then—impossibly—came something like speech.

Not like ours.

Rough, layered. Rolling like an earthquake through the soil.

The syllables were slow. Deep. Carved from earth.

"What are they saying?" Bella whispered in awe.

I shook my head, squinting at the creature's mouth. "I don't know. It's more... felt. Not heard."

Another sound, lower this time.

Another mountain, another voice.

They were answering me.

I could feel it in my chest.

They were telling me their names.

Each one had a different tone, a different thrum. One was jagged, sharp—a shale crack. Another softer, like rain pattering on slate roofs.

And even though I couldn't understand the shape of their language…

I thought I understood this:

They were introducing themselves.

But before I could ask anything more, before I could dare try to parse the impossible—

A ripple of power tickled the edges of my senses.

And then—

"There you are, child."

Cornelius—the tortoise, the creature, the impossible—appeared.

Right beside me.

Literally.

Just… there. Where before had been air.

Everyone shouted.

Darren drew his sword immediately, feet shifting to a wide stance as his hand went instinctively to the dagger on his belt. His blade gleamed in the broken sunrise.

Bella let out a panicked half-scream. "Gods, Cornelius!"

Hunter raised an arm in front of her.

But Carina—

She stared at him wide-eyed a moment, blinked once… then barked out a laugh.

"By Odiun's mangled beard…" she said, eyebrows shooting into her filthy hairline. "There's a fucking talking turtle there."

Cornelius looked completely unbothered.

"I prefer tortoise, thank you," he said plainly, blinking those golden, lava-streaked eyes. "Though I suppose accuracy is the first thing to die in battle."

Silence.

Everyone gaped.

Except me.

I was smiling.

Because suddenly… not all was lost.

Not yet.

I stared at Cornelius, fingers slack at my sides, mouth stuck partway open as my brain tried to catch up with the new chaos of the moment. The Terradyne were real. Sentient. Speaking. And now—so was a giant, lava-eyed tortoise with sass and wisdom in equal parts standing at my side openly… in front of everyone!

"Can you…" I asked softly. "Can you understand them?"

Cornelius gave a patient blink. "Yes."

Relief spread warm across my ribs like sunshine through mist. "Can you speak their language?"

Cornelius tilted his wide, weathered head slightly. "To a degree. It is not a language so much as it is... resonance. Feeling. The deep tones of the stoneborne are not meant to be translated —not fully. But I can grasp their intent."

I nodded, uncertain but grateful. "They... introduced themselves?"

"They did," he replied. "Each one. Their names are layered in geologic echoes—tones that stretch backward through the ages. I could not say them if I tried. Not with this voice."

"Well... then can you tell them this for me?" I swallowed hard, glancing again at the silent giants who watched us with unmoving grace. "Can you say... thank you?" My voice cracked. "Tell them—thank you. For helping us. I don't know why they did. I don't know how to repay them. But... we wouldn't have survived without them."

Cornelius said nothing at first. Then, he lowered his gaze with reverence, and the light in his eyes flickered brighter. The air thickened as he turned back to the Terradyne and let his voice deepen—not his tone, not his charm, something older inside him, as if the earth beneath him borrowed his lungs just long enough to speak.

The Terradyne listened.

The stoneborne truly listened.

And then, one moved.

Not the largest, nor the closest.

A tree-shaped Terradyne stepped forward.

He loomed like myth—his entire form towered at the edge of the courtyard where he'd first stepped from the broken earth.

Unlike the rest, this one bore a full canopy of copper-toned leaves that fluttered gently, even where no wind stirred. His bark glistened along wide shoulders like burnished ironwood streaked with vein-like cracks of glowing emerald sap. Vines wound through his torso like armor, braided down his barrel-wide legs to knotted feet sprouting moss that left luminescent prints behind as he walked. Butterflies—tiny ones the color of moonstone—clung to his upper branches, as if they'd nested there for generations.

He moved with all the grace of an elder who remembered stillness as the only path worth walking.

When he stopped just paces from me, towering so high his head was haloed by the very clouds, the ground beneath us trembled like it was bowing in respect.

Bella sucked in a breath. Carina muttered something that may have been an expletive.

The tree being looked down at me, and spoke.

It was stone striking stone, bark cracking beneath weight.

And deep—a sound that skittered through my ribcage like grinding roots through cave walls.

All of them turned to Cornelius. His eyes closed, lips still. Listening.

When he opened them again, the gold in his gaze shimmered as it settled back on me.

"This one," Cornelius said reverently. "The old one. He knows you."

I blinked. "What?"

"He recognizes your power," Cornelius continued. "He says he has felt it in the wind for years. Beneath the rivers. He has seen images of you in dreams passed down through his root-line. You... smell of her magic."

I reeled. "Whose magic?"

"The one who split the earth to create the oceans. The first Aqualorian."

My breath caught.

"He says..." Cornelius's voice softened, almost reverent now. "He is sure you're the one."

The words fell like stones dropped into a still pond.

Carina swore again.

Bella's hand came to rest on my arm, grounding me.

I didn't move.

Didn't speak.

Because suddenly, I was standing in front of creature ancient as the mountains—who believed I was the answer to a prophecy so old even Cornelius only whispered of it in fragments.

And I couldn't deny him.

I didn't know if he was right.

But I knew I wasn't ready to tell him he was wrong.

Because gods help me, we needed them.

If the Terradyne believed I was the key to destroying the Cinderyn—the queen—then I wouldn't give them reason to think otherwise.

Let them believe I was a goddess.

If it meant I might get Cade back.

The tree Terradyne spoke again, his voice shaking droplets from every nearby roof.

Cornelius nodded slowly as he listened. "He says they have waited centuries for this moment. For fire to meet water once more. For vengeance to awaken in stone. They helped build Emberveil long ago—the Cinderyn tricked them, and betrayed them to a great, terrible demise. Seduced their strength with promises of harmony... only to betray them."

I shivered.

"The Cinderyn used them," Cornelius said softly. "Used their roots and veins to raise Emberveil from the bones of the mountain. And when the fire elementals no longer needed them... they slaughtered, burned and buried them."

My throat was so tight I couldn't speak.

They didn't move like men shaped for war.

But I could see it now.

They didn't fight because they hungered.

They fought because vengeance was buried in their marrow.

I stepped forward, just half a pace.

And bowed.

Low.

Hands curled into fists at my sides, breath trembling.

"If you will help me," I said through the silence, jaw set. "If you will fight again... help me destroy the queen. Help me free the slumbering dragon buried beneath Emberveil. I swear—all of Allovan will know what you've done."

The forest giant said nothing.

Neither did any of the others.

They remained still. Towering. Watching. Listening with ancient ears carved by wind.

Time passed.

Long enough that I looked to Cornelius for help.

His voice was like winter breaking gently across still water.

"They do not decide quickly," he said. "They are a reclusive people. Cautious. Thoughtful. A decision of this magnitude may take days."

My heart clenched.

"I don't have time," I snapped, then shook my head, breath catching. "I don't even know if I have days. Cade, he's suffering— she'll kill him, or worse—she'll use him." I pressed a shaky hand to my chest. "We need to go now."

Cornelius met my eyes calmly. "And would you burn what balance remains to do it?"

I didn't answer.

Because I wanted to scream until the stones cracked.

Until they flew with me.

Until we stormed the gates of hell itself.

But I didn't.

I swallowed the rage.

Held in the tremor crawling up my spine.

Anger wouldn't win them.

Anger wouldn't save him.

So I nodded.

And stepped back.

Carina stepped in beside me, muddy blood at her knees. She let out a shaky breath like she hadn't realized she'd been holding it.

"Then we wait," she said simply.

Darren echoed it. "We bury our dead."

"And plan what's next," Hunter added.

"If anything," Bella murmured.

And so… we waited.

Among the giants.

Among the dead.

Among the ruins of prayers not yet answered.

And far, far away, across mountain and storm…

The queen waited too.

CHAPTER 32

*E*mberveil was not a city—it was a wound in the world.

From the black mountains of Calcaedus, it bled upward, carved directly into the heart of stone and ash like some unknowable claw had hollowed it out and built a kingdom from its carcass. Where Storm's End had been forged from resilience and grit, all winds and sharpened cliff edge, Emberveil was malice made manifest—pyramids of shadow sloping up into poisoned sky. The sun rarely touched this place. It didn't dare. Smoke belched in spirals from the city's veins, and the clouds above choked black and orange like a dragon's dying breath. Lightning lived here. Always low. Always hungry.

The city's outer walls stretched in waves across the face of the mountain—three, maybe four, fortress rings of obsidian stone, each layered tighter, sloped like a rising spiral eye. Beyond them sat the towers—too tall, too sharp, like jagged teeth jutting out of the cliff face. Raven's Bane Castle, they called it. At the center of it all, half-consumed into the bleeding slope of Calcaedus itself, was where the queen ruled—a heart that pumped hatred as lifeblood to all of Allovan.

The gate towers bore the faces of kings—carved in shadowed relief, mouths gaping like they were being devoured still.

And from within that tangled labyrinth of shadow and sharpened spires, inside the scorched black keep where even the breeze dared not wander, lay me.

I came to slowly.

Pain came first, blooming across my ribs like a fire that wouldn't catch. My throat was raw. Each breath cut like ice. My back ached, scraped and battered from how they'd dropped me.

My mouth was iron-clamped. Gagged with thick leather. Damp. Blood-tinged. My wrists were pulled behind me, coarse rope biting into skin rubbed raw from struggling. My ankles were just as tightly bound. And every muscle in my body ached with the memory of how much they had enjoyed making me bleed.

Blinking slowly, my vision swam.

Where—

The world swam into shape.

The throne hall.

I knew it, even through the haze. Even with blood crusting my lashes and sweat stinging my swollen cuts.

Great towering pillars stretched around me like prison bars. Black marble streaked with veins of crimson. The high ceiling vanished in shadow overhead, smoke curling in thin, dancing strands from braziers that burned with colors not found in nature—blue flame, deep violet edge. The throne room ran long —a vast canyon of onyx tile leading up to the dais at the end.

And there it sat.

The queen's throne.

The Ember Throne, they called it.

Sheared from some ancient ebony stone twisted with volcanic glass, forged with jagged lines and ridged plating. It looked like a claw emerging from Calcaedus itself—the upper arms of the chair curved like fangs around a crown of daggers. The back of it loomed ten feet up at least, flanked by bone-like spikes gilded in blood-gold. The arms were carved to resemble broken wings, each inlaid with red jewels that flickered like dying fires.

It wasn't just a throne.

It was a fucking altar.

And before it… I burned with fury. My magic… my magic… it was gone.

I tried to move.

Couldn't.

I've… never not felt my magic in me… What has she done? What has my terrible stepmother done now?

I felt as if a part of me had been severed. Like a leg had been torn off by a great ogre and cast into a bottomless pool. My heart thumped thick in my chest, and a blank hole where my magic should be was an empty void.

Sythers flanked me in a wide semicircle—four on each side, long-limbed and twitching, eyes beady. Curved bladed spears gripped in pale, clawed hands. Their long arms hung unnaturally low, swinging with a twitchy rhythm like predator insects waiting to pounce. Their yellow fangs gleamed wet with hunger even now, some of their faces split with twisted grins as they watched me breathe.

I tasted blood on my tongue.

My staff… gods.

Across the room.

My staff—my blade.

There. Resting on a polished obsidian altar thirty feet away near the entrance. Like a trophy. My sun-gilt weapon cast in scarlet light, its elegant phoenix crest now a symbol of impotence, untouched.

I clenched my jaw beneath the gag.

I reached inward—searched for fire.

Nothing answered.

Only… silence.

I knew the moment I first tried to summon my power and felt only cold—that she'd done something. The queen. She'd severed me from it. My magic. My spirit. I had felt it—watched it spiral through me at Storm's End like molten fury. And now it was dead.

Blocked.

Or worse.

A shadow fell across the far entrance.

The Sythers stirred, twitching with glee.

My chest locked up.

Because I knew. No horn trumpet. No fanfare. No hellish declaration needed.

You knew when Mortriana Vissex entered a room.

Her presence smothered the very air. It wrapped around your neck like an invisible chain and squeezed.

She didn't walk.

She arrived.

Bare feet glided softly over blood-polished tile, the hem of her black-and-red gown gliding behind her like a serpent made of silk. The dress clung in sharp lines to her figure—more skin than shield, long red streaks drawn in whorled patterns down the front like veins converging beneath her navel.

Layered bangles clinked softly on her wrists—gold, black, silver, blood-red enamel. A twisting crown wrapped around her sculpted white-blonde hair, styled high above her head in cruel spirals that gleamed like silver flames.

Her jewelry shimmered with gold trim and firestones… rubies mounted in her earrings, glittering from rings shaped like tiny talons, dancing from chains that dripped down between the curve of her breasts.

But it was her eyes that chilled.

Ink-black. Limitless.

Eyes that had looked on oceans and let them boil.

Eyes that had turned kings into corpses.

She paused only once.

To smile.

At me.

But it wasn't mockery.

It wasn't even disdain.

It was… ownership.

She sat on the throne like it had been built for her loneliness. Her limbs draped with grace sculpted by centuries. One finger curled beneath her chin. Another trailed the armrest.

And still, she said nothing.

I didn't move, glaring up at her from the floor on my side, the gag already soaked with spit and iron. My hair clung to the side of my face, damp and wild. My mouth bled from the corner. My ribs barely rose.

But the rage in me…

Gods.

The rage in me carved through every inch of the pain.

I would kill her.

Or she would kill me.

One of us wouldn't leave this room.

Good.

The queen leaned forward slightly, her long fingers folding beneath her sharp chin as she regarded the crumpled figure at the foot of her throne—me.

A smile touched her blood-slick lips. Slow. Savoring.

"Welcome home, Prince Phoenixfire. You've been a bad boy… haven't you? Playing where you shouldn't be playing, eh?"

My whole body tensed at the sound of her voice. Cold and clear as frost splitting stone, but laced underneath with something acidic—amusement wrapped in poison. I bared my teeth behind the gag, a useless snarl, all iron and fury with nowhere to breathe.

She tilted her head the way a cat might when pawing its prey to the edge of twitching death.

"I must thank you," she cooed. "Storm's End was beautifully open. Almost like you wanted me to find it. And you did help me, didn't you?" She tapped her lower lip with a claw-tipped finger. "So generous. Finally leading me to the Stormscales' little hole in the mountains. Who knew treason could be so... delicious?"

I lashed against my bonds, dragging in a stifled breath that sounded like fire meeting wet coal. My eyes burned holes through her. If I had flame left in me, she'd have been ash.

She only laughed.

Help? She doesn't mean me... She couldn't mean that I... helped. No. She's lying. She's just trying to hurt me.

"Shhh, I know. I know this comes as a surprise. But surely, deep down, you sensed it. Why else would such betrayal taste so bitter?"

Her hands unfurled with grace as she stood, descending from her throne as easily as a shadow uncoiling. She glided across the marble, each step silent, slow steel brushing velvet.

"I've kept you alive longer than most expected," she said as she drew closer, voice quieting to something nearly soft. "When your father died—do you remember? His lifeless body spilled across the obsidian steps of Emberveil, blood steaming, his crown still warm from battle. I looked at you and I wondered..."

She crouched beside me, her long black gown pooling like silk ink around my ruined body.

"Could I kill him? Could I kill the little boy who watched his father taste my wrath and beg to follow him into death?"

Taste your wrath? You don't mean you... you killed him? I knew it! Somehow I knew it! I'll kill you for this, stepmother. If I wasn't bound and had my magic... I'd...

Her voice dropped even lower, almost gentle now. "And I almost did. Gods know I was tempted. But I made a decision."

She reached out, brushing her perfect fingertip—adorned with a serpent-styled ring—against the edge of my temple.

"I decided not to waste you."

A growl tore through my throat beneath the gag.

"And you rewarded me," she went on smoothly. "You grew sharp. Obedient. Passionate. Reckless in the right ways. A fire I couldn't snuff—so I guided it instead."

My anger transformed to a deep sickness in my gut, my stomach twisting like hot iron spikes being poked through soft flesh.

I jerked violently against the ropes. My eyes were wide now, half-covered in sweat and blood, but still burning with the last of my fury. My body wanted to fight, but I could feel something wrong. Magic absent. Hollowed. Like the fire inside had been replaced with embers that no longer knew how to feed.

It wasn't just because of injury.

It was her.

How? Was she using me all this time? It's impossible. I fought her wars, but I never belonged to her...

"That staff," she whispered, rising to her full height. "You cherished it. Beautiful thing, wasn't it? Golden, etched with pain and promise. Nothing Emberveil wouldn't bestow upon her favorite prince."

She turned, glancing toward the polished black pedestal at the far end. My staff gleamed there—as silent and false as a grave marker.

No... it's impossible. She couldn't have... of course she did. I swallowed my pride and knew she'd beaten me... again...

"A pity your gifted relic carried a little more than dreams." Her smile split wider. "A thread of me, sewn in beneath the core. A simple spell. A fragment, really. How could you have known?

Woven inside so tight that even you—" she clucked her tongue, "didn't feel it."

I froze.

I understood now.

I should've known. I should've been strong enough to feel it. Now... the war is lost... and it's all because of me. Ash... I'm sorry Ash... I'm so sorry I let you down. I let them all down. You never should've trusted me...

The queen nodded as if watching the realization settle like wet rot behind my wounded eyes.

"Yes," she said, circling slowly toward the grand window that overlooked the east cliffs. "It's how I found you. How I followed you from fortress to fortress. From campfires to crowns. When you first found her—Ashlyn Moonriver—and turned your back... oh, I was so very cross."

A Syther snickered beside me.

"But then I saw the potential," she went on. "Oh, how I learned to adore your little betrayal. Because now that she's revealed herself... well..."

She turned to face me again, grinning like the fever of death.

"It's time to end the war, darling. And once the Gold-Marked dies... peace begins anew."

I roared against the gag. Spit lashed behind the leather as I writhed like a chained beast.

"I could sense you were deep in those nasty Harrowhorns, but getting that weasel to spill their secrets... now that was... truly delicious..."

The queen giggled.

Giggled.

"Well now," she said, eyes playful. "Someone's feisty. I suppose I should unbind the tongue if I'm to properly enjoy your final tantrum."

She turned slowly and nodded at one of the Sythers.

It slithered forward.

The creature moved with clicking joints and sweeping limbs like it belonged more in water than stone. Gleaming teeth flashed wetly as it bent and untied the gag.

The leather dropped.

I coughed.

I spat.

And when I lifted my blood-slicked head, my voice was steel licked in flame.

"Ash is coming for you. You may be stronger than me, but you're an ant beneath Ash's boot. She'll take your miserable, selfish, greedy life."

The room chilled.

It didn't matter that my voice was still gravelly from smoke and blood.

It didn't matter that I looked half-dead and broken beneath the queen's towering shadow.

The fury in my words...

It silenced the entire throne hall.

The queen's expression did not shift at once.

But the air did.

Her smile didn't reach those pits she called eyes now. Not anymore.

They narrowed.

Then—she laughed. A peal of velvet cruelty sweetly stretched across a blade.

"Coming?" she echoed. "Oh, blessed is the flame—the girl does not cower?" Her grin turned. Twisted. "Excellent. Saves me the hunt. Let her come. If she thinks there's any saving you, she's got another think coming. She doesn't know you like... I do..."

My jaw tightened, throat shaking with effort as I forced the weakness from my lungs.

"She'll kill you," I rasped. "She's more powerful than you can ever imagine."

The queen's smile faltered.

Just a flicker.

Then returned sharper.

"No," she said. "No, I don't think she will."

"She already beat you once," I hissed. "She's stronger now."

"As am I," the queen replied calmly. "And you misunderstand something, dear Cade…"

She leaned close again—until her gown brushed the ropes binding my hands.

"I hope she comes. By Odiun, I want her to come. Let her bring her light. Let her summon her Gilded Radiance in all her blinding arrogance. Let her walk right up to my gates with fire in her chest and brimstone in her heart."

She rose.

And something wicked bled into her grin.

"Because her death is going to be so, so sweet. Her death will be most exquisite to watch."

I blinked.

Watch?

"What do you mean?"

She turned her back to me, already walking away.

I shouted again, voice hoarse. "Say it!"

"My Sythers? My dragon riders?" she called over her shoulder. "They are many. But no—I believe she's ready for them."

I glared. "What do you speak of?"

There's something twisted in her. She's planning something.

She turned slowly, her eyes once more twin pools of shadow carved from absence.

"When she arrives," the queen hissed, "she will find a surprise."

And when she said it—I felt something cold crawl down the inside of my ribs, nest behind my spine like a new kind of fear.

Because her smile wasn't just cruel anymore.

It was personal.

And very, very patient.

"I've saved someone special," the queen whispered down to me. "Especially for her."

She crouched once more, hand feathering the blood in my hair.

"Because before she dies," she murmured against my temple, "I want her to suffer."

I said nothing.

I couldn't.

The queen stood.

"You're too immature to see it, Cade, but you don't love her. You think you do. But it's a deep flaw in you. Your pride betrays you. You don't love that miserable orphan. You've just always wanted what you can't have. You fuck her to betray me further. To embarrass me, your father, and your blood." Her face twisted tightly and her thin nose scrunched as if she wanted to spit right between my eyes. "You disgust me."

Then she turned again.

No. You're wrong. I love her. I love Ash more than anything. I know it. I feel it with every fiber of my being.

And as she walked back to her altar-throne, her crown glinting in light stolen from old sun gods, I collapsed fully onto the stone.

Alone. Bone-deep afraid.

Because for the first time in a long while… I wasn't sure if Ash was going to be enough.

Not this time.

Not alone.

And as I closed my eyes and heard her laughter echo through those damned gracious halls—

I prayed.

That someone would stop her.

That someone would save Ash.

That justice might burn the throne from underneath this cursed mountain.

And that I—

That I'd live long enough to see it.

"Ash is going to kill you, stepmother. And when she does, the world is going to celebrate like never before. She's too powerful for you to kill now. You'll see. When the time comes, you'll know even with all your planning and plotting and scheming, you weren't enough to kill the slave from Bramblebash."

A conniving light flickered in her dark, demonic eyes.

"Who said I was the one who was going to kill her, Cade?"

CHAPTER 33

I stood before the fresh grave, half the size of an adult's. Mud heaped over where the girl's body rested, and I felt as full of fury and helplessness as when I'd been a slave.

The stone I'd tied the dragon charm to was barely the size of a footstep, but in a field full of tall spears and carved shields etched with Stormscale crests, it had more weight than any of them.

I knelt before it.

My knees pressed into the cold, wet dirt, and the rain slid in thin threads over my back, tracing the seams of my armor. I barely noticed. My fingers lingered on the copper dragon charm, the one she gave me. The one tied to her gravestone was meant for someone else. Now warped from flame and rain. It swayed slightly in the wind, the frayed braid knotted tight around the pebble's edge.

I tied it myself.

Because there'd been no family left to do it.

No mother. No father. No one to grieve her.

Just me and the Stormscales.

Ashlyn Moonriver, Gold-Marked, dragon rider.

Silent, powerless mourner.

I couldn't bring myself to pray. Not to Odiun. Not to anyone.

What could I say?

What do you say to a girl who gave you a gift like you were the sun, only for her to die while it was still warm in your hand?

I let the tears fall freely.

No one was nearby. No one was watching.

Except maybe the gods, and they could look away if they didn't like what they saw.

"I'm sorry," I whispered. My voice cracked. "I'm so—so sorry."

I bowed low over the stone. My forehead touched the dirt beside it.

My shoulders shook with the effort of holding back the storm inside me.

It shouldn't have been like this.

We should've been ready.

We were supposed to be ready.

But the queen had known. She had planned for our hope. Played it like a fiddle and let us bow the strings until they snapped in our hands.

And now...

Storm's End was broken.

The little girl whose name I never even asked for was dead.

And Cade...

Cade was in chains. Or worse.

And I couldn't feel Eden.

The one thing that made me more than what I was—the thing that turned me into something the queen should fear— was quiet now. Silent inside me like a dead hearth, cold and hollow.

I pressed a hand against the stone again, fingers splaying over wet copper braid.

I didn't feel powerful anymore.

I didn't feel brave.

I just felt empty.

"Hey." Bella's voice came soft behind me, careful, like she knew one wrong word would crack me open like a dropped vase.

I didn't look up.

"I just wanted to—" she stopped. The silence breathed between us before settling down like her cloak over my shoulders. "I saw what you did. For her."

"She was just a child," I said. My voice scraped low, like gravel caught in my throat. "She gave me this and then died with her fists curled around another one." I slowly lifted the other copper dragon from my pocket—bent, half-melted. I'd pulled it from her hand myself when we buried her.

Bella slowly crouched beside me, knees in the damp earth. "Ash…"

"She believed in me."

"You gave her hope."

"I gave her nothing," I snapped. The words lashed out before I could stop them.

Bella didn't flinch. She just sighed, brushing brassy hair damp from her forehead, eyes trained on the stone as if it could offer answers.

"You gave her something better than any sword could," she said after a long moment. "You gave her a reason to believe the world could change. That she mattered. That you'd protect it for her."

More tears welled up in my eyes. I was so fuming with rage I wasn't sure which would win—my grief, or the hatred that lived right behind it. Curling like a storm inside my ribcage. My whole body shook as if the world itself were trying to spill out of my skin.

"I want vengeance," I breathed. "I want it so bad it hurts, Bella."

She glanced sideways at me.

"I want to rip the queen's heart out of her chest and drown

her in all the innocent blood she spilled—and I know that makes me just as cruel."

"No," Bella said firmly, her voice low but sure. "It makes you human."

I laughed, but it came out broken. "No—I think it makes me something worse."

"Good." Her eyes flicked to mine, fierce now. "Because to stop her, you're going to need every ounce of the fire inside you."

A soft scraping behind us made both of us stiffen—

And then, calmly, like he'd known exactly where we'd be, Cornelius padded into view.

The rain kissed his shell and turned darker across his wizened head, but he moved through it like it was nothing more than time passing.

He said nothing at first.

Just looked at the stone-shaped grave.

Then he looked at me.

And said, simply, "They have reached their decision."

I stared up at him, frozen.

My heart forgot how to beat for a moment.

And in the silence that followed, thunder rolled across the peaks.

We walked—quietly, all of us—to where they waited.

The Terradyne stood like mountain-cast gods along the upper ridge, a coliseum of colossal beings whose bodies spanned trees, moss-blanketed boulders, and root systems that ran so deep the mountain seemed grown from them instead of the other way around. Their silhouettes rippled across the jagged skyline, their stone faces half-swallowed in mist and encroaching dusk.

They weren't arranged like an army. They didn't posture with weapons. They lingered like sentinels forged from regret—silent, still, timeless in their patience.

Errax padded beside me, limping but resolute, her breath still ragged, wounds scabbed. Around me, Bella and Hunter walked in silence, their shoulders squared. Carina was a storm barely contained. Her fists clenched white around the haft of her spear. Darren followed behind, slower than usual, one arm bandaged, the other hanging loose, like the weight of Storm's End had carved every motion from stone.

But it wasn't just us anymore.

The survivors had followed.

Dozens of them, limping or leaning on makeshift splints, armor still charred, cloaks still damp, all of them bearing the raw ash-and-iron stink of war. The children who could stand were cradled on shoulders or clung to hips, and I saw fear in their eyes, yes—but also flickers of something else.

Hope, maybe.

Or something fragile enough to need hope like soil needs the first drop of rain after famine.

Cornelius led the way up the slope, his short legs finding footing none of us could see. He carried no banner. Wore no colors.

But when he stopped at the base of the Terradyne's gathering, even the wounded held their breath.

The ancient tree—their leader, or so we'd come to believe— stepped forward.

Not with haste.

Not with hostility.

But with a thunderous creak that rippled downward through the ground like he was shifting tectonic plates beneath his feet. Moss-wrapped bark shifted along its spine, and its roots pulled free from the stones deep as rivers, dripping with soil and the scent of earth never kissed by sun.

The others behind it did not move.

They only watched.

Cornelius turned slowly to me.

And the tree spoke.

The sound rolled across the ridge like the sky itself had cracked wide open.

Boulders locking and unlocking. Water spiraling into limestone caverns. The groan of glacial weight pressing down on the bones of the world.

But no words I could understand.

And when it finished, the leader stood still once more. Immovable. Eternal.

Cornelius closed his eyes. He nodded.

And my heart sank.

"No…" I murmured.

The word barely left my lips before I spoke louder.

"What did he say?"

The tortoise opened his eyes, ancient and tired.

He wouldn't meet my gaze. Not at first.

"They have made their… judgment."

My throat tightened. Darren shifted beside me. Hunter looked down and away, fists curling. Carina cursed softly beneath her breath.

Cornelius exhaled.

"The Terradyne will not join the assault on Emberveil."

Silence.

Heavy. Crushing.

I stared at him as if he'd struck me.

"They refuse?" My voice was sharp. Bitter. "But… they saw what happened. They fought alongside us. They—"

"They defended Storm's End," Cornelius said gently. "But to march on the queen's fortress, to awaken the ancient one beneath Calcaedus… they say it is not time."

"Not… time?" My hand trembled as I shoved my wet hair from my eyes. "Are you kidding?"

Cornelius's head dipped again. "The Terradyne believe the Stormscales require years to rebuild. They say the army we have is not enough to invade Raven's Bane Castle. It is a battle we cannot win."

The words swept like a blade across the crowd.

Gasps. Cries. The murmur of grief waking again like a wound already stitched once, slashed back open.

"We don't have years!" I shouted, taking a step forward. "Storm's End is burning! Half the Stormscales are dead—the rest bleeding or crippled. We might not even survive the godsdamned week!"

"We know," Cornelius said softly. "They do not—"

"I don't care what they know."

My voice broke then.

I shook all over.

I stepped further toward the Terradyne.

Toward that massive, moss-covered being who'd once looked at me like prophecy.

"Cade is still inside that mountain! The queen has him! He's the most powerful man in the world, and he turned to help fight against everything he's every known! And now you're turning away from the fight because it's hard?"

The Terradyne said nothing.

Its ancient eyes remained still.

Watching.

And behind it came movement.

A grand and terrible motion.

One by one, the Terradyne turned.

Not like men in rank.

Like forests in retreat.

Like mountains remembering how to crumble.

"No!" I shouted, stepping into their path. "You can't! You can't leave now—we need you!"

They did not pause.

The rustling of their limbs was like familiar wind threading through hollowed trees.

They were going.

"Stop!" My voice cracked louder. "I'm going to Emberveil with or without you! I'm going to kill the queen and awaken the slumbering dragon! I am going now! You can't just rest after this —you don't get to walk away now! This war isn't over, not by a thousand fucking miles!"

They moved silently, disappearing into the cracks and crevices of the mountain. Into the soil. Into the stone.

Vanishing.

One by one.

Until only the breeze remained.

And I was alone again.

I fell to my knees.

I felt empty.

"You can't leave," I whispered.

"You can't," I said again. Louder.

"You can't."

Bella caught me before I fully crumpled.

"I'm sorry," Cornelius said.

I didn't answer.

I couldn't.

Because the moment their backs became the skyline—

I realized.

We were alone.

Again.

The queen had my heart.

The earth had closed its hands.

And all we had left… was each other.

That would have to be enough.

Even if it wasn't.

CHAPTER 34

Night cloaked Storm's End in brittle silence. The kind of still that settles over graveyards after the last eulogy's been whispered, when even the ghosts have run out of strength to haunt.

The stronghold was a corpse held together by splintered beams and the will of grieving soldiers.

Our fire crackled low in a blackened ditch at the shoulder of the outer courtyard, where loose stones still held the heat of the day's sun, and the shattered remains of the walls cast long, quiet shadows. Bella, Hunter, and I sat huddled close beside it—cold, blinking at embers like they might explain something we'd missed.

The other Stormscales kept to themselves across the field. Scattered fires flickered like dying stars, each small circle of survivors clinging to warmth with hunched shoulders and silent eyes. No songs. No toasts. No gods-damned celebration for our survival.

Because we hadn't really survived.

Not all of us.

And until I had Cade back… none of it mattered.

I cradled a tin cup of wine in my palms, palms still stiff from magic I couldn't feel anymore. Eden stayed quiet. Still curled into some quiet corner of my soul, like she knew I needed rest—but even more, like she was too tired to rise. The threads of my power felt like frayed silk floating in water, glittering but unanchored.

For the first time, Bella looked more defeated than I. She already looked like the ache behind her bones was trying to crawl free.

"We need to move soon," I said softly, watching the flames eat through the last half of the blackened log beside us.

Bella blinked slowly, dark circles under her eyes. "You want to march into Emberveil... tomorrow?"

"No," I muttered. "Not march. Fly. Burn. Rip through the sky on Errax's back and rain hell down on her walls until every Syther in that cursed fortress screams."

I drained the rest of the wine and set the cup down hard.

"And get him back," I whispered.

Bella slid closer, shoulder brushing mine.

The silence was thick between us, heavy with everything we didn't say. The slow unraveling of an army, the quiet realization that no one from the outside world was coming to help. The loss crowding nearer every day.

We were all we had now.

Except—someone wasn't moving.

Hunter sat across the fire, his gauntlets off, eyes fixed on the flames like they were trying to tell him the secret to unbreakable stone.

I studied him in silence, waiting for him to break the stillness, say something snide, or comfort me the way he always had when things felt too big to face.

But he didn't.

He hadn't said a word since we sat down.

Bella noticed too.

Her gaze slid to him, sharp eyes narrowing beneath ash-matted lashes. She leaned in, elbows pressed against her knees, posture tense like she was waiting for a fight.

"Hunt?" she asked, soft but insistent. "You've barely said a word."

Hunter closed his eyes.

Let out a long, slow breath.

Like someone who was trying very, very hard to keep the world from snapping in half.

"I'm fine," he said.

But it was the worst lie I'd ever heard.

Bella arched a brow. "Bullshit."

"I said I'm—"

"No, you're not," I interrupted, gentling my voice as I studied him. "You've sat through raids, dragons, Sythers, and three too many war councils without blinking. But now? You look like you're ready to break something."

His hands curled slowly over his knees.

Then up into his hair.

He clutched at his temple like his thoughts were made of razors.

"I thought I could stop it," his voice cracked, just a breath, barely above the wind winding through the crumbled bones of the keep. "I thought I could change fate."

My spine stiffened.

Bella frowned deeply. "Stop what?"

Hunter didn't look up. "The prophecy."

The fire popped.

Bella and I froze.

My voice was barely a whisper. "From the Mystic."

Hunter nodded.

Slow.

Like every movement hurt now.

"I kept it from you," he said. "I—that day, when we visited

Myrathyn—I asked something I thought I'd never speak aloud again." He exhaled, voice tight. "I asked… if there was anything I could do—anything—to help my Prince survive this war."

I didn't breathe.

Bella leaned forward. "Hunter—what did he say?"

His knuckles turned white in his hair.

Then, very quietly, like the remnants of a confession soaked in salt, he whispered:

"No."

Bella's mouth fell open.

But I couldn't speak at all.

"He said," Hunter choked, fingers sliding down over his face, "that Cade Phoenixfire would not make it to the end of this journey. That he would fall into a place worse than death."

Worse than death.

I'd never heard prophecy twist the knife so cruelly.

Bella's voice was shaking now. "Why—why didn't you say anything?"

"Because I didn't believe him! I couldn't!" Hunter growled, fists balling. "Because fate doesn't touch Cade. He's always outrun it. Always defied it. We've stood in dragonfire—faced warlords, rebels, assassins—and he survived it all like the gods carved him from fire and left him here to prove a fucking point."

He swore and stood, pacing like the flames at his feet suddenly scorched his skin.

"I thought if I could shield him just enough, fight beside him just right… the gods would be wrong."

He stopped. Looked down at us.

Looked destroyed.

"But I was too fucking weak."

"No—" Bella stepped to her feet too. "You are not weak."

"Hunt," I stood slowly, meeting his eyes across the smoke. "You would've followed him into hell. You still would."

"He is in hell!" Hunter roared. "And I let it happen. I couldn't stop her. I couldn't even stop him from falling—and I knew. I knew."

He dropped to his knees beside the fire, breath ragged with grief.

Bella looked at me.

I looked past her—

North.

Toward Emberveil.

And the prophecy we hadn't rewritten yet.

Not yet.

But we would.

We had to.

Hunter's sorrow hovered over the fire like smoke refusing to leave. The weight of prophecy sat on his shoulders, coiled deep and cruel like a serpent that had been waiting its whole life to sneak under his armor and bite.

I sank back down beside him, knees weak, fingers locked tight in my lap.

Worse than death.

The words wouldn't leave me.

They echoed again and again, each whirl louder than the last. What did that mean? What was worse than death to a man like Cade?

Torment?

Torture?

Being caged like a beast in the place he'd once called home, by the woman who made his life a living hell?

Or maybe… Maybe it was something crueler.

Maybe it was the look in the eyes of a woman he loved, arriving too late.

"Worse than death," I repeated under my breath, voice trembling like my ribs were starting to crack. "What the hell does that mean, Hunter?"

He blinked at me slowly, like he'd just remembered I was still here. His jaw flexed, firelight dancing shadows across the side of his face.

"I don't know," he said. "I've been thinking about it every damned night. I can't sleep without hearing it. Can't close my eyes without thinking the queen's already broken him. Already—"

He stopped himself.

Bella stepped closer to him, her voice small but steady. "You said the Mystic told you Cade would fall. Did he say when?"

Hunter shook his head once, sharply. "Just that it would be 'near the end.'"

My stomach twisted around itself like a snake devouring its own tail.

I could see it. The queen—Mortriana Vissex—slithering around Cade's broken form with that cruel smile of hers, reinforcing chains every time he spit defiance. I could hear her whispering in his ear in that voice of silk-twined blades.

"Her plans aren't just about war," I said quietly, the words falling from my mouth before I even thought them through. "Or power. They're about control. She's always hated Cade. Not just for rebelling. But because he looks too much like him."

Bella frowned. "Like who?"

"His father," I said. "The Blaze King."

"She sees Cade as a failed version of the man she could never break," Hunter added, his voice dark again. "She's always said he was too soft. Too human. So she makes him pay for daring to be better than her."

The fire snapped between us, sparks leaping like it was choking on smoke. Somewhere in the distance, Krakos let out a low, mournful cry—deep and ancient, rising across the valley like grief that couldn't find legs to walk, only wings to wail.

I froze.

So did Bella.

Hunter blinked hard and turned toward the sound.

That dragon… he was screaming for his rider again.

For his prince.

His heart.

"What are we doing sitting here?" I stood up suddenly, too fast, the blood rushing to my head. "Why the hell are we still waiting around inside the skeleton of what used to be our home?"

They didn't answer.

"We need to go," I said, my voice louder now. Sharper. "We need to fly to Emberveil. Tonight."

Bella's eyes widened. "Ash—"

"We take Errax, Krakos, and Talonor," I continued, pacing now, fury tightening through my limbs. "Just us three. We fly under moonlight. Slip past whatever's left of her outer defenses. And when we land—I find the queen. I kill her."

Hunter rose slowly, expression trapped between pain and disbelief. "Ash, listen to yourself—"

"No!" I pointed toward the northern cliffs, the way the wind whistled through shattered windows and tugged at the tattered banners still clinging to the battlements like they hadn't given up yet. "She has Cade. There is no war strategy. No alliance-building. No waiting for backup. It's just her. And me."

"There is no just her," Hunter snapped. "You forget where she is. Emberveil isn't just a throne room." He raised a hand as if ticking off a death list. "You want to reach her, you have to pass tiers of stone gates, each fortified in obsidian and locked by spell runes that take arcane blood to undo."

"I'll burn them down."

"You can't," he said flatly. "Your magic needs to rest and recover. And even with Eden—one of those gates took the Stormscale architects fifteen years to design. There are dragon-pearl nets strung over the lower tiers—those will drop your mount straight out of the sky the second they sparkle. There are Syther nests in their towers—like an infestation has taken root. And she guards all of it with her soldiers and dragon riders."

"I'll find her," I growled. "I can kill her. I know it."

"C'mon Ash… You're gonna… what? Kill her alone? You don't even know what's waiting for you inside her chambers. I don't mean traps or assassins—I mean her power. Mortriana's been feeding off captured magic for years. Decades. She has Cade now, and only Odiun knows what she's planning for him—"

"Don't," I snapped, voice breaking.

"I'm saying you're worth more than a suicide mission," he said, his tone hard but his eyes anything but.

I turned on him fully.

Bella stood between us now, shaking her head softly. "Hunter's right."

But I didn't want to hear it.

I couldn't.

Hope felt like a noose tonight, and every word only pulled it tighter.

"So, what—what, then?" I choked. "We do nothing? Wait for her to break him? Watch her wrap her throne in his bones before we make a move?"

"No," Hunter said after a long pause. "But we can't go tonight. Not like this. She wants you desperate. That's her trap. She's always ten steps ahead, remember?"

I sat back down slowly, my whole body shaking, arms wrapped around myself as if I could hold the anger in.

But it didn't work.

Because he was gone.

And I didn't know if I'd ever get him back.

And waiting—

Waiting would kill me.

CHAPTER 35

The stars didn't look the same anymore.

Maybe because my eyes wouldn't let them. Maybe because every constellation reminded me of a place I failed to protect. A person I failed to save.

Storm's End lay in fragile hush behind me, the broken bones of its stronghold still exhaling heat from where the queen's dragon riders' fire had tried to gut it clean. Even buried, the halls moaned. Wood cracked, stone split in slow groans, shifting under its own weight like it was tired of pretending to be shelter.

I lay in the shale above the ridge, wrapped only in a blanket someone—Bella, probably—had tucked around me while I slept. If I'd slept.

I hadn't.

My eyes hadn't closed since the fires had. Not since Cade's silhouette vanished beneath dragon claws.

So I just lay there, elbows propped beneath the back of my head, staring up at a sky that shouldn't be smiling.

Stars blinked like smug little gods too far away to help. Too far away to care.

As if nothing had happened.

I hated them for it.

Above me, constellation after constellation burned cold.

My fingers tightened around the edge of the blanket, knuckles aching faintly. I breathed. But it didn't feel like breathing. Just a tired motion because my chest hadn't given up yet.

What was even the point now?

The prophecy?

She was a lie written in starlight, wasn't she?

The Terradyne wanted me to wait years for the Stormscales to rebuild. I didn't have years. Cade was there now! He was suffering unknown cruelty at his stepmother's hand. I needed to leave now! He needed me, now!

They were like old men who hadn't known a damn thing about being chained beneath wood floors and sold like cattle.

They'd never known what it felt like to hold a little girl's body in their arms and cry because they'd failed—not in magic, or prophecy, or battle—but in kindness.

And Cade...

Stars. Cade.

I felt my throat catch.

"Fuck," I muttered, eyes squeezing shut. "What even was all of this for?"

The stars didn't answer. Neither did Eden, whose golden hum stayed buried somewhere in the back of my chest like a sleeping fox refusing to wake.

I rolled onto my side and wiped angrily at my cheeks.

"Cornelius?" I called, voice barely cracking the night air. "You out there?"

The mist didn't part.

But a moment later, he was there.

No sound. No shimmer. Just a gentle pressure on the old stones behind me and the quiet crunch of crusted moss as his tree-stump legs waddled carefully to my side.

I didn't look right away.

I felt him first.

That odd hum he always brought with him—a peace that settled behind the ribs like a lullaby written in stone and salt.

But tonight, even that wasn't enough.

"Didn't mean to wake you," I murmured.

He blinked.

"You didn't," he said softly. "I was watching the stars as well. Contemplating."

I scoffed. Glanced up beside me. "They look the same. But they're liars, aren't they?"

Cornelius didn't answer.

I clenched the blanket tighter around me.

"So is this it?" My voice dropped lower. "Is this how it ends?"

Still nothing.

I turned my head, locking my eyes on his slow, patient face.

"You can tell me," I insisted. "You know how this works. You've known since the beginning. If I die, if Cade dies, if she wins... is that just it? Is the world just... hers?"

He breathed gently, steam curling from the sides of his neck like low fire banked beneath bark.

Then—I saw his head tilt.

And sink slightly.

Like something slipped loose behind those golden eyes.

"If you have failed, Ashlyn," he said, "then I have failed as well."

The words hit like a punch.

He kept speaking, and I wanted him to stop—gods, I wanted him to stop—but the words were already unraveling everything inside me.

"I have spent many lifetimes of man listening to the same music," he said. "Waiting for the next Gold-Marked. Praying it would be you. Praying you would make it where the others never could."

Something cracked in my chest.

"I thought you might be different," he whispered.

I sat up.

Fire licked hot behind my breastbone, something feral biting at the back of my throat again.

"I'm sorry," I whispered as I knelt beside him.

Rain matted my hair to my cheeks.

"I'm sorry, Cornelius," I choked. "I—I can't do it."

His eyes didn't blink.

But I saw them dull, just slightly.

"I don't know what to do," I whispered hoarsely, hands trembling as I pressed my palms against the curve of his shell. "I can't hear Eden. I can't fly without Cade. I can't even scream loud enough to make the gods give a damn. I just keep losing. Every battle. Every person. I'm so tired."

Tears fell, hot against my hands.

"I'm still that girl," I whispered. "The one from Bramblebash—starving, afraid, too small to carry anything but scars. I thought I'd changed. I thought I'd become someone. But I haven't. I've just... lost slower than I used to."

One hand went up to my face, wiping wet hair away. The other stayed on Cornelius's side, holding him like he was the last solid thing left in my spinning world.

"I feel like I'm back there. Shackled. Used. Forgotten."

My chest cracked open.

"I feel helpless again."

A low rumble passed through the stones underfoot.

Not sharp. Not threatening.

Just steady. Like thunder purring. Like the mountain itself exhaling, reminding me that the world hadn't stopped turning just because I had.

I felt it before I saw her.

Errax.

I sniffed and rubbed the back of my wrist along my cheek, dragging away the tear trails. My heart was still cracked wide open, but something behind my ribs shifted, just enough to breathe through the pain.

I turned.

And there she was, descending from the black treeline above the shale overlook.

Moonlight caught the edges of her scales—the brilliant shimmer of indigo and cobalt blue gleaming like starlight painted over armor. Her wings moved slowly, folding down with care as she stepped toward me. The great arches of muscle beneath her shoulders flexed once, like she hadn't had full command of her own limbs until tonight and now she finally did.

She looked—whole.

Healed.

How?

My dragon padded through the clearing without a sound, each step as graceful as morning wind across still water.

I sat back on my knees and wiped my face as she approached, half-hoping she couldn't smell the fear still clinging to my skin. But of course, she could. She'd always known my moods before I even let myself feel them.

Errax lowered her head gently beside me, her warm breath brushing damp strands from my cheek. I pressed my palm to her snout, and the contact grounded me instantly in the way only she could.

"You're... okay," I breathed. "You... you're better..."

A soft growl pulsed low in her throat, and I swore stars danced in her eyes—a fierce kind of knowing, deeper than language.

Then, suddenly—

A voice rippled across the edge of my mind. A whisper. A flicker. Not words exactly.

More... intent.

Don't give up.

I froze.

My hand curled tighter around Errax's scales.

Hope lives.

Another breath.

Even in cinders.

My eyes widened. "No," I whispered aloud, shaking my head. "No, no, no—was that… was that—?"

I turned toward Cornelius so fast that I startled the old tortoise right off the mossy rock he'd settled on.

He blinked, blinking again like he wasn't entirely sure if he was dreaming.

"Was that Errax?" I said, heart hammering in my chest. "Was she just inside my head?"

Cornelius tilted his head, and oh my gods—the smirk that slowly ticked up the side of his turtle beak nearly knocked me on my ass.

"Well, what took her so long?" he muttered.

I stared between him and Errax, jaw somewhere between the stars and the dirt.

"You— You knew?"

"Not exactly," Cornelius said. "I suspected. You were bound too deeply not to break that wall eventually. The bond between you and your dragon is… old. Sacred. Most riders never feel it go beyond shared instinct. But you"—his brow furrowed with something like reverence—"you have something ancient in you, Ash. And not just Eden. Your blood remembers. Her blood remembers."

I turned toward Errax again, still breathless.

I put both hands on her snout.

"You can speak to me," I said, more to myself than her. "You've always been able to. I knew you could hear my thoughts, but… I didn't know…"

She blinked slowly.

Then I felt it again.

Stronger this time.

Inside my chest. Across the space between us.

My voice inside my own mind whispered softly—What do I do?

Her answer rolled like a distant river finding its path.

You are not alone. There are... others... wild others... out there...

My breath caught. I swallowed hard. "Cornelius," I said hoarsely, eyes fixed on Errax's glowing gaze, "she… she says there are others."

Cornelius perked immediately, his whole shell angling slightly toward her. "What others?"

"She didn't say yet," I murmured, trembling now, heart lifting higher than it had in days. "But she says they're still out there."

Cornelius stood straighter, water streaks slipping down the curves of his shell like glinting veins. "Ash," he said, "ask her. Ask her now."

I closed my eyes.

Cleared the panic. The pain. The grief strangling my throat.

Then I reached deep.

Errax?

A breath.

A pulse.

I felt her dragon language like mist at the edge of my conscious mind.

The golden warmth of her voice filled my head like sunlight baking through cracked temple stone.

What others are you speaking of?

There was silence for a moment—but not absence. Just... anticipation.

Then a slow, smooth thrum filled the back of my skull, almost like birdsong weaving through low thunder.

I felt her power surge.

And then the words came.

There are those that are as fierce as the winds and seas and fires of Calcaedus itself. They are unbound and unallied. But you... You, Ashlyn, you may be able to call them to your side.

I couldn't breathe.

I opened my eyes and turned to Cornelius.

"We were wrong," I said, voice shaking.

He blinked. "Wrong how?"

I stood.

"Stormscales weren't the last. The Terradyne weren't the last."

I turned toward the east, toward the horizon lit faint with the promise of sunrise.

"There are others who might join our fight... We have to find and rally them. That's... that's at least a chance for the help we need."

Cornelius's eyes narrowed with shocked awe. "She told you this?"

"She did," I said.

He gave the slowest, widest smile I'd ever seen on his weathered old face.

"Then the fight is not over," he said. "The world is still listening."

I faced Errax again.

She was watching me.

Waiting.

Her eyes soft.

Resolute.

I took a step forward.

In my mind, her voice came again.

Ashlyn Moonriver—

If you would save him... if you would burn down the last gate, shatter the last lie, break the throne itself...

What would you be willing to do?

I didn't even blink.
In my mind—and in my heart—
I said one word:
Anything.
And I meant it.

CHAPTER 36

The stars were still pinned in the sky when I kicked Hunter in the shin.

He groaned, sat up impossibly slow, rubbed sleep from one eye. "By Odiun's scorched balls, Ash, if this isn't a Syther stabbing me through the gut, I swear—"

"Get up." I crouched beside his blanket, already lacing my boots. "We're leaving. Now."

He blinked at me, bleary and bare-chested, wrapped in a rough wool cloak like a drunken saint. "It's still black out."

"I know." I yanked at the blanket under Bella next, who responded with a long string of mumbled curses and the kind of tired groan that suggested murder.

"Stop," she hissed, fingers clawing back for the warmth I was stealing. "Unless the queen herself is personally lighting my hair on fire, I'm not getting out of this blanket."

"Errax is ready," I said, unbothered and vibrating with nerves. "She's already waiting."

"Hells, who?" Bella sat up fast, curls splayed like seaweed across her face. "Waiting for what?"

"To fly. Tonight. Right now! Get up you two or I'll tie you to Talonor's wings!"

That got Hunter's full attention.

He sat up straighter, arms flexing as he propped himself upright. "This had better be good, Ash."

"Hurry," I said, already standing, brushing dust from my pants as I turned to the slope beyond camp. "Clarity. Finally found it."

"Ash." Bella stood now too, squinting at me beneath the tangle of her braid. "Are you talking about going to Emberveil?"

"No."

Her relief was immediate, exhaling it like air too long held in the lungs.

"Because that's—good," she breathed. "Because going in now? Just us three? That'd be suicide wrapped in vengeance."

I turned to her with something sharp in my smile.

"We're not going to Emberveil."

Hunter narrowed his eyes. "Then where?"

I jerked my head toward the eastern sky, just barely pinking at the edges with approaching dawn. "We're going to find allies."

Bella blinked. "What?"

"On dragons," I said, fully grinning now. "With as much speed and secrecy as we can. Now get your lazy asses moving!"

Hunter blew air through his teeth in pure disbelief.

Bella stared. Hard. "You rolled out of your blanket in the middle of the night, spouting nonsense about flying to find allies? Did you have a dream? Can't this wait 'til morning?"

"We need to move while we still can," I said, bouncing to my feet with renewed energy.

Hunter rubbed his face with both hands, battling sleep's grip. "Please tell me you're joking. Allies? What allies?"

"Errax knows where to lead us," I said, a rush of excitement bubbling beneath my ribs despite the weight of our reality still hanging heavily over us. "She'll guide us to those who will fight with us. We can't wait around to die in this backward little camp-site. If we have a chance, we need to take it now."

"No offense, but this isn't exactly the best time to be taking sudden jaunts into the dark," Hunter groaned, still half-buried in his blanket. "Not with the queen's guards prowling around looking for any sign of weakness, not to mention the dragons and who knows what else out there. We can wait until daylight."

Bella finally sat up, brushing the sleep from her curls, and squinted into the dim light breaking through the trees. "And you think flying off in the middle of the night is a solid plan?"

I felt my frustration bubble. "I didn't want to wake you with my big ideas. But we're sitting here while the queen has Cade. We need to gather allies now. If we wait, she'll pull her forces together and close those gates tightly."

"Excuse me for being a little concerned," Hunter muttered, shifting his weight as he pushed himself off the ground. "You do certainly love impulsivity. Don't you? No offense. Especially into enemy territory at night?"

"I've done it before," I countered, defiance surging through my veins.

"You got lucky before," Hunter said, pacing across the ground as if he could somehow will sense into his tired brain. "You're telling me you want to surprise some unsuspecting group of rebels and hope they rally behind your tiny, stubborn ass after everything we've been through?"

"I can't sit and wait!" I exclaimed. "We're tired and bloodied. The queen won't wait for that! She's already shown her hand!"

"Great," Hunter replied in a deadpan tone. "And we're going to fly into the night to what? Gather our friends over stolen drinks and hope they all take us into their arms for safety?"

"Maybe!" I snapped, spinning around to face both of them again. "Maybe I'm done being afraid. Are you coming or not?"

～

THE WIND WAS sharp and cold along the ridge as we saddled our dragons.

Above us, the stars watched in tense silence.

Below—Storm's End slept. Or tried to. Smoke still curled from the remains of broken towers, lazy and gray, like even the fire had lost the will to reach. Most tents had flattened in the storm; the few that remained sagged with the weight of despair.

Errax waited near the edge of the drop, wings folding and unfolding in slow, measured rhythm. It's remarkable how quickly the dragons can heal. They truly are deserving of their legends. Her eyes glowed gold-green in the dark like twin torches buried in the fog, and every time she exhaled, the grass beneath her curled inward, like the earth couldn't decide whether to grow or flee.

I pulled tight the final buckle on her saddle with trembling hands.

Not from fear.

From something more dangerous: purpose.

Hunter stumbled up beside me, barely keeping his bedhead from unraveling in the breeze. His armor hung open at the shoulder, and his sword was sheathed wrong—slumped on his hip like it didn't want to come.

"You realize this makes no sense," he muttered, squinting up at the dark sky. "We're three half-dead messes on tired dragons flying straight into whatever mysterious threat Errax thinks counts as an opportunity."

"She's leading us," I said, patting the blue shimmer of my dragon's flank. "That's enough. I trust her."

Bella arrived next, hair braided tighter now, face cleaner—mouth set like someone who didn't want to be convinced, only needed to believe.

She looked at me, hands on hips, and finally said, "If we're going to do this, at least say goodbye to someone."

"We don't have time for drawn-out speeches."

"It's a suicide flight, Ash," she shot back. "Spare me ten seconds and spare Darren an ulcer."

I huffed. Rolled my eyes.

But she wasn't wrong.

So I turned back toward the ruined camp—and found them waiting.

Darren. Carina.

Standing in the shadows beyond the half-crumpled arch of what had once been the Commander's Hall. Armor loosely buckled. Weapons still slung low at their hips. Their faces were unreadable in the dark—stormworn, dirt-streaked—but their eyes found me. Both of them.

They hadn't tried to stop us.

And they weren't trying now.

I gave them a single nod across the distance.

Darren crossed his arms and nodded once in return, slow and quiet like he understood.

Carina didn't nod.

She looked at me like I'd lit the end of the world on fire again.

Then, just under her breath, she said, "Don't die."

I huffed. "Wasn't in the plan." Then louder, across the night: "We will return."

Carina's jaw flexed, her shoulders straightening.

"You better be right, Ash," she said. "Because if you're wrong…"

"I'm never wrong," I called back, knowing the words were a complete lie. But it seemed like the right thing to say. Something inside of me was telling me, no, *screaming* at me to listen to Errax.

Errax grumbled under me. Her scales were already warm beneath me. I barely needed the reins—our bond was better tonight than it had ever been. We were alone in so many ways, but not in this one.

She crouched low as Bella and Hunter mounted behind me,

Talonor snorting beside us, impatient. Krakos prowled beyond the black ash line like a shadow forgotten by the moon.

I reached into my chest—just for a breath—and tried to feel Eden.

Nothing answered. She either was recovering from the battle or knew she wasn't truly needed. Or perhaps both.

But Errax did.

Her wings stretched wide, shimmering in the faintest kiss of starlight.

I looked down once more.

Storm's End was just a wound now. Smoldering. Stubborn. Alive.

Like me.

I didn't speak another word.

Just leaned forward, and Errax launched.

The mountain tore away beneath us in a heartbeat, the air slamming into my lungs so fiercely it stole every thought I hadn't let scream loose already.

Talonor took to the sky beside us with a deep-throated roar, his gray wings cutting long arcs through clouded starlight.

I glanced back.

Bella flashed me a look that said: if we die tonight, I hope you're haunted for eternity.

Hunter just gave me a single, solid nod—one warrior to another.

Then Krakos rose behind us, a shape of shadow and red fire, impossibly large. He didn't shriek. Didn't roar. Just followed.

And gods help me, there was something comforting in it.

I don't know how high we climbed before I stopped feeling the cold.

The air was sharp, burned through my lungs like it hated being shared. But we kept going, soaring farther into the sky until Storm's End was only fireflies scattered across the black mouth of the valley.

Above us, the stars splintered across the sky—silent and watching. Always watching.

I leaned low into Errax, letting her instincts pull us forward, toward a path only she knew. Her wings beat steady and strong now, each motion driven by some ancient compass buried in her blood. The wind whipped past my cheeks, tugging tears from my eyes—not fear, not cold. Just the weight of moving forward. Of not knowing where forward led.

But her voice rang in the back of my mind—not words exactly, more like intent forged in fire and purpose.

I will find them. You just fly.

Bella came up alongside me, crouched against Talonor's neck, her braid snapping behind her like a war banner unwilling to yield. Hunter flew ahead, a dark silhouette tilted against the moonlight, his hands tight on the reins, watchful eyes casting outward.

The world below us faded into jagged peaks and winding valleys, black rivers glistening in mooncolor, and I thought—not for the first time—that the land beneath us looked like an old god's scar map. The kind someone might file away under "things better left buried."

But I didn't care.

We weren't flying over this world anymore, not like we occasionally had for war's sake or to deliver warnings. No, this time...

We were carving new lines into it.

"Anything yet?" Hunter's voice reached through the wind, crisp and cutting.

"Not yet," I called back, trying to listen past the rush of blood in my ears. "But she's hunting."

"She better be," Bella muttered from behind us. "Or I swear, Ash, if this turns into a cosmic sightseeing tour I'll throw you off your own god damn dragon."

I smirked. "You'd never."

"I'm not above it," she said, but her grin betrayed her.

That was when the air shifted.

Not drastically.

Just… different. Like we passed through a layer of sky where something old had breathed once and left its scent behind.

Errax let out a low sound, more pulse than growl, her wings tilting slightly. Her head canted to the left. The others felt it too—Talonor adjusted mid-glide, and even Krakos slowed, massive wings spreading wider to bank in tandem.

I inhaled.

Something shimmered far ahead.

Not light exactly.

Movement.

Large.

Low.

Gliding faster than wind.

"Hunter!" I pointed forward. "There. Look."

He turned and his mouth dropped before he clenched his jaw and his hand gripped his sword.

Through the mists we saw them filling the air like a swarm of wasps buzzing around the hive.

Dragons… Wild dragons…

The Harrowhorns weren't a mountain range—you didn't climb them or fly through them, you bled for the right to survive them. And tonight, high above valleys that had never known sunlight, blanketed in a mist so thick it tasted like smoke and salt, I could feel the mountains licking at our wings like they wanted to drag us down with the dead.

"Errax," I breathed, pressing low into her silver-blue scales, my fingers clutching tight the neck ridge just ahead of the saddle. "You still sure about this?"

She didn't answer with words.

No thoughts slinked into my mind.

Just a sense.

Steady.

Like a great stone hand pressed against my spine and shoved me forward.

She flew harder.

Her wings sliced clean through the mist, narrowing with each thunderous beat as we dipped lower into the unseen. Behind us, I heard the other two dragons breathing ragged and close. Bella and Hunter had tucked low into their saddles, nearly silhouettes against the swirl of fog, bolts of shadow painted against a canvas of stormclouds.

"We're not circling!" Bella shouted hoarsely through the wind. "Why are we still descending?"

"She's following something," I called back, even as my heart slammed against my ribs. "Just stay tight!"

We dove deeper, cloaked in the sound of dragon fire pulsing faint and fast. The winds screamed at us now, dragging icy claws down my cheeks and teeth into my sleeves. The air thinned too quickly for comfort.

Errax screeched once—loud enough to shake the wind—and the mist beneath us parted like breath against a mirror.

And that's when I saw it.

Or didn't see it.

Rather—I felt it.

Heard it.

A trembling chorus.

Echoes.

Dozens. No—

Hundreds.

Screeches. Roars. Shrieks warped by age and wildness. Sounds layered like a storm had swallowed every dragon's scream across centuries and was now vomiting them back through this cursed pass.

The wild dragons.

Errax didn't pause.

Not even a wing hitch.

She flew us straight toward the nightmare.

Through the fog, shadows began to move.

One by one—shapes larger than warhorses slid through the white.

Massive wings webbed in torn membranes.

Jaws rimmed with yellowed, sharp teeth.

They didn't move like Krakos or Talonor or Errax—no grace

of the sky, no calculated rhythm. They hovered jaggedly, descended in lurches, circled like vultures with fire in their veins. Wild, barely contained muscle bending through the air like something the Gods regretted making.

"Oh, gods," Bella gasped from Talonor's back just beside me. "There's too many."

She wasn't wrong.

They were everywhere.

One blink, and the mist behind Errax lit with glowing claws.

Another, and an obsidian-scaled shape swept overhead, screeching like bones fractured midflight.

Hunter tightened his grip on Talonor's reins, the copper-shaded dragon's frost-edged wings carved wide as if to shield Bella. Behind them, Krakos snarled low—a deep, controlled rumble, fire leaking from the sides of his maw like he dared these creatures to come close.

But even he wasn't making the first move.

"What is this place?" Hunter asked, voice gritted behind his teeth.

I didn't know.

But Errax did.

She tucked her wings tightly and dove again—wings slicing faster now, sharper—her instincts unbothered by the war flapping around us. She dropped us lower through a narrow canyon layered beneath the cloud cover where the mist began to fade.

And then we saw it.

The nest.

A chilling, sprawling peak high above the rest of the Harrowhorns—its summit cleaved flat, like the gods had snapped the tip off a mountain and left it bare to the stars. A massive crater sat at its heart, ringed by jagged spires of stone so sharp they looked like dragon teeth buried too shallow in the ground. Ridges of glowing moss clung to the cliff-face, pulsing faint emerald. And draped over every ledge, every crevasse, every crumbling stone—and across the wide basin itself—were dragons.

Hundreds of them.

Layered like smoke.

All of them still.

All watching.

"Oh," I breathed. "Oh no."

Not one blinked.

Not one so much as twitched a tail.

The wind howled once—sharp—and the entire nest exhaled a warning. A breath shared between gods.

They knew we were here.

They'd known for some time.

Errax leveled her wings and slowed to a hover just beyond the ledge, her long body stretching above the basin like a banner pulled taut in the storm. Krakos and Talonor flared wide beside her, but none of the wild dragons moved. Not yet.

We passed through the final veil of mist into the nest.

And the sky cut silent.

"Careful," Hunter said under his breath, voice taut across the distance between us. "They're not diving. That means they're deciding if we're prey."

From this height I could see the whole of it—the mountain peak curved in a sheer bowl carved by ancient rage or older fire, and dragons layered every surface of it. Some roosted with claws hooked into stone, their long necks curved and still as hunting serpents. Others clung upside down along the shadowed ledges above us, glowing eyes peering down with unnatural stillness. Like they were waiting for the signal.

"They're not attacking..." Bella whispered. "Why aren't they attacking?"

Because they're waiting to see if we deserve to be eaten. I didn't say it. I didn't need to.

I felt it in the air. In the beatless pause before breath.

Errax moved forward.

Bold.

With purpose.

As if nothing in this crater could scare her.

As if she'd done this before.

"Trust her," I breathed, not only for myself.

Krakos exhaled hard, a stream of heat washing over our flanks. Talonor stayed tight to the right, his long gray tail snapping slowly in warning. I knew if the wild dragons made a single wrong move toward Bella, he'd gut them all before dying.

But this wasn't a death spiral.

Something else stirred.

Something older than the frenzy of fang and flame.

Errax flared her wings once more and dropped lower.

Five yards. Ten.

Down until she hovered just above the center of the crater—and then folded inward.

A landing.

A challenge.

Or a bow.

Please, gods, let it be the right one.

The wild dragons shifted as one.

All heads turning. All eyes narrow-slitted in silence. I felt panic leaping up my throat fast, beastly, raw. My fingers trembled where they gripped the rigging of the saddle—and then froze altogether.

Because from the heart of the nest… she moved.

I tasted it before I saw her. The magic. Old. Weighty. Greyer than shadows and heavier than stone. A sacred magic that tasted like storms clinging to bone.

And then she emerged.

A dragon unlike anything I'd ever seen.

She rose from a cave mouth tucked into the northern arc of the summit wall, a chasm that gaped like the open jaws of some long-forgotten god. At first, she didn't simply move—no, the stone parted, and she unfolded from it.

A mountain at first glance. A ridge in the rock.

Until her wings stretched.

Enormous.

Four times the size of Krakos. Her body a gnarled, ancient gray that faded into stony violet at the joints where skin met scale, the hide thick and cracked like old tree bark slaked in silver blood. Her wings creaked as they extended, vast and weathered, like sails woven from ruin and flame. Torn in places, veined with glowing lavender light in others. They unfurled with the grace of royalty and the sound of world-fallen dust.

And her eyes—

Gods.

Her eyes were pale. Not white. Not silver. Not dead.

But faded.

As if she had cried so many lives and burned through so much sky that her soul had been too large to be contained behind irises for long.

She was terrible.

Beautiful.

Impossible.

"What…" I whispered, breath arrested. "What is that?"

"Her," Hunter croaked, voice dry as old bone. "That's… their elder. It's a Great Mother Dragon."

Krakos bowed his long neck and expelled a great puff from his nostrils.

"Yes," Bella added, barely audible. She clutched Talonor's reins tighter. "I've heard about them in songs. I never, *ever*, thought I'd live to see the day to see one with my own eyes…"

"We'll see if we live long enough to tell about it," Hunter muttered. "This one… she's one of the last ones. Look at her… she must be thousands of years old. Amazing… Absolutely amazing…" His voice trailed off as he covered his mouth in awe.

A myth wrapped in teeth and time.

I too had heard the songs.

Dragons nearly as old as magic, queen to the sky before the gods carved language into it. One of the first. Hidden in the mountains by choice, silent counsel to no one and enemy to all who dared forget that dragons did not come from man's command but from storms and fire and blood writ in scale.

And she was watching us now.

She stepped into the circle of the nest like winter steel, each clawed foot echoing through the crater like a war drum beat at half-speed.

The wild dragons parted for her—moved aside without sound, many bowing their heads, others simply crawling backward into the walls. Not fleeing. Just opening the way.

For her.

Errax held still.

So did we.

Not even Krakos made a sound as he watched her with a sort of… reverence…

The wild dragons barely breathed.

They were coiled in silence, death disguised in scale and fang, wings folded like blades not yet drawn. Every glowing eye shifted, focused, narrowed on us—on Errax, on Krakos, on Talonor.

On me.

Because of course, I was the one stupid enough to come.

I swallowed hard and pressed my fingers tighter around Errax's neck ridge, her scales warm beneath my touch despite the chill licking across the summit.

"You better know what you're doing," I whispered in my mind, hoping she could hear it.

She gave no answer. Just kept walking forward, slow and smooth, claws tapping lightly on stone as we approached the Great Mother Dragon.

For all her presence, standing before her was like staring at the end of time. She didn't move like something alive. She moved like stone melting. Like night descending. The sound of her massive limbs shifting through the crater echoed with a weight that felt older than language.

Her eyes didn't blink. They just… looked.

Through me.

Into me.

Hunter and Bella landed beside us, nearly trembling from the sheer pressure thickening the air around us like syrup. Krakos landed last, his massive wings folding as he let out a low, warning growl beneath his breath. Even he seemed humbled here.

We stopped maybe twenty feet from the Great Mother.

And nobody said a thing.

No words. No breath.

Until she roared.

The sound hit like a tidal wave.

It ripped through the air so violently that I felt it in my teeth. Errax staggered beneath me—not in fear, but from the sheer blast of force.

Bella cried out behind me, Talonor flinching as molten air clapped over his wings. Hunter didn't scream. He just bent low and gritted his jaw, one hand on his sword hilt.

Gods, I felt it too.

That low, gut-full panic that said, this was a really stupid idea.

The Great Mother's wings flared open—each one felt like half a mountain in itself—and then Errax answered.

She didn't roar back.

Not yet.

She barked.

A sharp, sudden yowl—a challenge or a greeting, I didn't know. The sound cracked down the basin like thunder, and the wild dragons jerked in response, hissing from across the crater as if their queen had been insulted.

And that's when Cornelius appeared.

Perched on a slick stone just behind us, silent and small and impossibly still. Rain beaded on his shell where mist touched it, but he didn't blink or flinch. His eyes glowed ember-bright, reflecting quiet wisdom and sharpened memory.

And he was listening.

Simply and fully, like the cosmos had been painted on the back of his golden gaze.

He didn't speak.

He didn't need to. Cornelius was a sort of historian—I thought—watching, reading, remembering.

Because what came next wasn't for us.

It was for them.

The dragons spoke.

Not with words.

With sound. Movement. Like magic laced through roar and breath and low, guttural screeches that made the rock beneath us whisper in fear.

The Great Mother Dragon lifted her head and called out again, deeper this time, like bedrock fracturing.

Errax responded—cracking her tail, baring fangs.

Then Krakos spoke, his fire glinting along his jaws as he let loose a high, spiraling scream that tore at the stars themselves.

Talonor, confused but ready, let loose a thunderous rumble that rolled across the crater like a boulder pounding down a windwashed cliff.

And the nest... erupted.

Wild dragons shrieked—some in alarm, others in a sort of song, still more in low, throaty clicks that reminded me too much of the Sythers. Their wings shuffled, tails coiling and snapping as the ground trembled with an eager, ravenous rhythm.

It wasn't random.

It was language.

I'd never seen anything like it.

Roars layered in pitch, each answer timed, each note a phrase that passed between dragons too ancient to concern themselves with the chaos of men.

I clutched tightly to the saddle.

The voices grew louder, rising now to match each other in pitch, tempo, volume.

And gods, the fire building behind it—

"Uh…" Bella's voice cracked behind me. "Am I the only one getting a very bad feeling?"

"No," Hunter said beside her, voice dangerously calm. His hand clasped his sword's grip.

"Don't," I whispered. "Just… don't yet."

Errax was dead still beneath me. Not panicked. Not tense. Resolved.

She was letting it happen.

The chaos.

The shaking.

The power rising from the pit of the Harrowhorns like fire climbing through ancient veins.

And still the dragons screamed, each voice bellowing through the others until the air itself vibrated—until a thousand invisible wires tied between us all began to snap one by one.

"Cornelius?" I shouted over the sound. "Are you following this?"

He didn't turn. Just watched the dragons with twin lava eyes blazing.

"I don't speak dragon," he called back calmly.

"What?" Bella gasped.

"I guide creatures of fate," Cornelius said, not even blinking. "I do not interpret the fury of gods wrapped in wings."

Bella shook her head. "Well that's fucking reassuring."

"I'd be ready to fly if I were you, as fast as those wings will carry you," Cornelius offered, still just watching.

The air thinned.

Everything smelled of dragonfire.

And then the voices stopped.

The entire nest—

Every. Single. Dragon.

Silent.

No breathing.

No tail flick.

No wing shift.

I wasn't even sure my own lungs had remembered how to work. The quiet that came was so pure and holy I almost teared up with the weight of it.

And then…

Errax moved.

One step forward.

Not a stomp.

Not a bow.

Just a single step.

Deliberate.

She stood tall.

Then roared.

It echoed across the basin with reverence, not rage.

A declaration.

A demand.

The Great Mother Dragon lifted her head and roared one final time—and it wasn't rage, either.

It was music.

It was mourning.

It was the voice of a creature who had seen kingdoms drown, gods fall, and skies torn open at the seam, and all the while, kept her fire caged between ivory teeth just waiting to be unleashed.

Errax didn't bow.

She didn't yield.

She simply growled low—soft, but sure—and stepped forward again.

Another roar.

Light sparked along her scales.

And the nest exploded into noise.

Wild dragons screamed in response—shrill shrieks and low, churning war rumbles. Dozens stood, rearing tall with wings spread in reply. Others took to the air—agitated, or maybe celebrating, or maybe choosing sides. Chaos rippled through the crater like blood swirling through a bowl.

My fingers clenched around the saddle as Errax bared her teeth and held her ground.

And the Great Mother…

She inhaled.

Her jaws opened.

The fire within flared—

"Hold!" Hunter shouted, yanking Talonor's reins hard. A torrent of freezing wind spiraled upward from his dragon's scales, wings bent to shield Bella.

Krakos bristled, muscles surging, claws punching cracks into the stone.

"Move!" Bella shrieked. "Ash, move!"

I couldn't.

I didn't.

The Great Mother's mouth opened wider—

And flames spiraled out.

But—

They didn't strike.

She let out a slow rumbling breath of scant dragonfire upon Errax and me. It washed over us like mist, yet warm and somehow soothing. I felt the mild burn on my fingers and through my hair. It reminded me of summer sea waves washing over my face and blowing back my hair as I swam deeper into the waves.

The dragonfire shimmered like a pinpricked midnight sky.

A flicker.

A strange, weightless swirl of pale violet and blue that curled toward Errax… only to fade just before touching us.

Gone.

Set to die before impact.

A test.

A sign.

Something else.

The Great Mother's eyes shifted—caught the light of her own fire in them.

And that's when I saw it.

They changed.

Just slightly.

A flicker.

Recognition. Approval. Maybe even something worse.

Acceptance.

And then she stepped back.

One ancient limb after another grinding in slow deference.

Errax lowered her head—not a collapse. Not submission. An answer. Their silent pact sealed in a breath neither one needed to take.

"What the hell's happening?" Bella half-hissed.

I turned my head slowly.

Paused.

Met her eyes.

And smirked.

"She's joining us," I said.

The wild dragons all around lifted their heads in a slow, building cacophony.

And they roared.

The heavens split.

And I knew.

The tide had just turned.

The sun crept over the eastern peaks like a shy child, painting the broken bones of Storm's End in hesitant strokes of gold and amber. Smoke still curled from the ruins - lazy wisps that spoke of battles fought and lost. Of hope scattered like ash across bloodied stone.

I guided Errax down toward the courtyard, her wings spread wide and graceful despite our exhaustion. The flight back had been long, but something burned bright in my chest that had nothing to do with Eden's absent warmth. Something closer to triumph.

Hunter and Bella landed beside me, Talonor touching down with a soft thud against the cracked flagstones. Even Krakos seemed different now - his crimson eyes blazing not just with rage, but with purpose.

"They're back!" A shout went up from the walls. Boots scraped stone as survivors rushed to gather.

Darren emerged from the command tent first, his silver armor gleaming dully in the newborn light. Carina was right behind him, her hand already on her sword hilt as she strode forward.

"Where in the Infernal Depths have you been?" Darren's voice carried across the yard, sharp with concern rather than anger. "I was beginnin' to think you weren't coming back..."

I swung down from Errax's saddle, my boots striking the ground with newfound certainty. A smile tugged at my lips as I felt it—the shift in the air, the darkening of the sky that had nothing to do with clouds.

"We went recruiting," I said simply.

Carina's eyes narrowed. "Recruiting? In the dead of night? What kind of—"

Her words died as the first shadow fell across the courtyard.

Then another.

And another.

Wild dragons descended from the clouds like living storm fronts—dozens of them, their wings blocking out the sun as they circled lower. Moss-scaled titans with glowing eyes. Obsidian beasts rippling with ancient power. Each one a nightmare made flesh, yet moving with deadly purpose.

The survivors stumbled back, weapons half-drawn. The air filled with their shouts and screams at the sight of the beasts. After the decimation they received by the queen's forces, their remaining forces were no match against the hundreds of encroaching dragons. But I just stood there, arms crossed, watching their faces transform from fear to awe.

"By the gods," Darren breathed.

Beside me, Bella tried and failed to suppress her grin. Hunter stood straighter, his hand relaxed on his sword pommel, pride evident in his stance.

The wild dragons landed in a wide circle around us, claws scraping stone, wings folding with precision that belied their savage nature. At their center, Errax stood tall, her blue scales shimmering like she'd been crowned by the dawn itself.

I turned to Darren and Carina, my voice carrying clearly across the sudden hush.

"Get your surviving riders ready. The winds of war have shifted in our favor."

Darren stepped forward, his eyes wide with disbelief as he scanned the ring of wild dragons. Their massive forms loomed over the broken walls of Storm's End like ancient guardians awakened from stone sleep.

"How?" he breathed. "These creatures have been our enemies since the first riders dared the skies. What changed?"

I glanced at Errax, feeling that warm pulse of connection between us grow stronger. "My dragon spoke with their Great Mother Dragon. They've agreed to join our fight against the queen."

"Great Mother Dragon?" Darren said with eyebrows raised and fingers spread wide. "Here? In the Harrowhorns?"

I nodded with a smirk that was impossible to hide. "Right under your noses."

"Just like that?" Carina's voice was sharp with suspicion. "Errax asked and they just said yes?"

"Nothing is just like that," I said. "But they hate her as much as we do. Maybe more. She's killed many of them and they know the blight she spreads upon our world. They want vengeance."

The wild dragons shifted restlessly, their scales catching the growing light. Several of them bore old scars that looked suspiciously like the work of Syther blades.

"And the Terradyne?" Carina pressed. "What of them? They refused to help. We gladly welcome the dragons, but will that be enough to lay siege upon all of Emberveil?"

I drew a deep breath. "Cornelius?"

For a moment, nothing happened. Then, like mist taking shape, he appeared beside me. His ancient shell gleamed with morning dew, and his golden eyes studied the gathered wild dragons with something close to approval.

"What do you think?" I asked him quietly. "Will the Terradyne join us now?"

Instead of answering, Cornelius lowered his head and closed his eyes. The silence that followed was heavy.

A murmur ran through the gathered survivors. I felt my heart skip as something shifted behind me—the scrape of stone against stone.

One of the fallen blocks in the courtyard began to move.

Not crack or crumble—movement. Like flesh instead of rock. Ancient runes flickered across its surface as it rose, pulsing with pale green light.

Then came the sound—a deep, thunderous trudging from the tree line. The remaining walls of Storm's End trembled.

The Terradyne tree leader emerged from the forest.

He towered above us all, his bark-clad form radiating power that made even the wild dragons stir uneasily. Roots writhed at his feet like living ropes, and his moss-draped shoulders seemed to catch starlight that hadn't yet faded from the dawn sky.

One massive step. Another.

The earth shook with each movement.

He stopped at the edge of the gathering and spoke. A single phrase in that grinding, ancient tongue that sounded like mountains speaking to the sky.

I turned to Cornelius, holding my breath.

Cornelius' eyes opened slowly, and when he spoke, his voice carried the weight of centuries.

"The Terradyne," he said, "march to war."

The words hit like thunder. That same thunder rushed through my veins from my tippy toes to my scalp—surging, brimming, electrifying every pore and muscle in my body.

Around us, more stone began to move. More earth stirred. The Terradyne rose from the ground itself—dozens of them, each unique, each terrible and beautiful in their own way.

"They say the wild dragons' choice has shown them truth," Cornelius continued. "That if such ancient enemies can unite against the queen's evil, then perhaps prophecy speaks true after all."

My hands trembled at my sides. "They're really joining us?"

"They are." Cornelius's eyes met mine. "But they want you to understand something, Ashlyn Moonriver."

"What?"

"This is not just about vengeance anymore. This is about balance. About returning fire and water and earth to their proper places in the world. The Terradyne remember when magic flowed pure; before the queen corrupted it. They want that world again."

I looked around at our gathered forces—wild dragons perched like storm clouds given form, Terradyne rising like mountains come to life, the surviving Stormscales standing straighter now, hope kindling in their eyes.

"Then they'll have it," I said firmly. "We all will."

The Terradyne leader's glowing eyes fixed on me, and I felt the weight of ages in that stare. He inclined his head slowly; not a bow, but an acknowledgment.

A promise.

Above us, the wild dragons roared as one—a sound that shook the very foundations of the mountain. The Terradyne responded with a deep, resonant hum that vibrated through the stones beneath our feet.

And in that moment, as dawn broke fully over the ruined fortress, I knew.

We were no longer just survivors.

We were an army.

And the queen's reign was about to end.

CHAPTER 39

The cell stank of old blood and old fear.

I blinked slowly against the thick torchlight that poured down in flickering licks of orange over soot-blackened stone and rusted iron. My arms were bound behind the legs of the chair, the ropes digging deep into raw, split skin. My ankles had long since numbed, seared by hours of pressure, but my back ached with every breath. My torso burned, carved by more than a few lashes. I didn't wince anymore. You learn not to feed them the show.

My mouth was gagged—thick leather, cinched tight.

My magic... severed from me somehow like half my heart was cut out and tossed away like a cancer. I felt a deep void within me. Half the man I used to be, in more ways that one. I felt as helpless as a newborn babe at the mercy of merciless adults.

I rolled my head back against the chair, breathing slow through bruised ribs.

One ring of mages. Eight total. All in velvet robes that dragged with too much ceremony for a place that reeked of filth and mold. They stood in a loose circle around me now, their hands lifted with fingers twitching in flickers of pale green and red. Magic murmurs muttered low from cracked, wine-stained mouths. Their eyes glowed faintly with spell light as they chanted in unison—slow, drawn-out syllables meant to keep the suppressing circle strong.

A fire crackled in the torch near the cell bars. The staff—my staff—lay just beyond my reach, its polished gold length stretched across the black stone outside the cell. My magic. My fire. My legacy.

Faint, flickering flames curled from the bearded mouth of the phoenix head at its crown, as if mocking my helplessness.

The queen keeps it close.

Tempting cruelty.

Reminding me: 'You are still mine.'

I let my head sink forward again. Sweat beaded beneath my hairline, chased down over scraped temple and broken cheek-bone. My jaw clenched beneath the leather gag. There were no words in me anyway. Only fire. Only fury.

She did this.

Mortriana.

My stepmother.

Queen of Allovan. Destroyer. Tyrant. Widow crowned in blood.

And this—this was her mercy.

I exhaled hard through flared nostrils.

No magic. Not since they stripped me of it—somehow. She had secrets still. After all this time, all these years, she hid more secrets from me than I could have dreamed of.

She'd used the staff. The bond. Had poisoned it decades ago, embedded a splinter of her power into its core when she first gifted it to me, when I was just some frightened, sharp-eyed boy they paraded around as an obedient heir to violence.

And I'd carried her leash with pride, not knowing it wrapped tighter each time I used it.

Gods, I'd been such a fool.

I shifted slightly, the wood groaning beneath me as the mages' chant echoed louder.

I tried again—just a flicker of fire beneath my ribs, just a pulse of warmth to light the shadows coiled in my belly.

Nothing.

Only ice.

Only silence where the inferno used to live.

I slammed my heel once against the floor in frustration. The flicker of magic in the nearest mage's hand brightened. Coward.

But I didn't look at them.

I couldn't.

Because every time I closed my eyes—

Her face rose to meet me.

Ash.

Ashlyn Moonriver.

Gods damn her.

That sharp tongue, that firelit glare, the way her freckles had multiplied in the sun. The way her eyes—not a remarkable shade, never bright or glowing—could pin me through my armor like I'd been stripped to the bone.

The first time I saw her I thought, interesting. Pretty little wild thing.

The second time I saw her I knew she'd unravel me.

And she did, piece by motherfucking piece.

A girl from nowhere. With a spine bound in iron and scars wrapped around her wrists and ankles like trophies of a triumphant escape from a miserable life. She'd put her own scars on me. Binding me in ways I never imagined. I was hers, and she'd been mine... until...

Everything about her screamed mistake for me. But I couldn't help myself. The way she looked at me under a starlit sky before a dragon ride. The fire in those eyes. The passion in them when I took her. The feeling of her cool skin against my fiery touch. The way her breasts bounced gently as I made love to her. Everything.

Every fucking thing about her had hooked me. Even our curse only made me want her more. The gods did everything they could to keep us apart, perhaps for every right reason.

And I—the idiot prince raised in steel and strategy—I fell for her anyway.

And now I was here.

Gagged.

Bleeding.

Magic torn from my veins.

Because I was weak.

Because I always put her above myself.

Above war. Above crown. Above every god damned command the queen had ever given me.

I used to burn villages on whispers of rebellion.

Now?

Now I burned for her.

I used to call soldiers by their rank.

Now I call her name in my sleep.

Fire and water.

Impossible. Wrong.

And yet, when we nearly killed each other with our first time naked together, half my soul begged to die that way—clutched in her grip, seared by her love.

I looked up again.

The mages hadn't moved.

But the spell circle between them glowed faintly stronger. They were feeding it—keeping the seal tight on my elemental source. I could feel the invisible restraints now. Like chains slipped between my marrow. Like dragon nets pulled tighter one heartbeat at a time.

Ash would slaughter them.

Fuck, she'd salt the earth they stood on.

If she knew I was here.

If she knew what the queen was whispering into the ears of

her courtiers, what she was building in the depths below the throne, she'd tear Emberveil stone from stone to reach me.

If I asked—she would fly into the heart of Calcaedus itself and ride the damn volcano into the sky.

And maybe that was the problem.

Because I'd go further.

If she was caged—if she was the one bound in shadowed iron and left to rot in a worm-eaten dungeon—I would have set the world ablaze already.

I would burn kingdoms on the off chance she might see the smoke and know I was coming.

She's the strongest woman I've ever known.

And somehow—gods be fucking damned—I was hers.

I always had been.

Ever since she looked me in the eye like I was just another man wearing too much armor and not enough honesty.

I hated how much that unmade me.

How much she saw through me.

Loved it.

Feared it.

Craved it.

Through fire, through ruin, through blood-soaked skies—I was hers.

And now?

She was the only thing in the world worth surviving for.

The queen could promise glory. Could promise thrones and armies, immortality sewn from misery. But she'd never understand what Ashlyn Moonriver meant to a man like me.

And that is why she'll lose.

That's why I'll survive this.

Not for vengeance.

Not for the crown.

But for her.

The feisty, impossible, wild-born miracle who made me

believe I was more than a weapon, more than the queen's sharpened son.

The only woman who looked through my fire and saw a man still worth loving.

I will not die here.

My fire's not gone.

It's just waiting for her.

Lightning laced itself through my spine. No flash in the sky, not even a rumble. Just the sharp, white-hot pain of every nerve ending inside me catching fire.

The mages were pushing harder now—all eight of them, hands raised like puppets offering prayers to pain. Their trance thickened, spell markings glowing across the floor in that dull red-green bruised light. They didn't speak anymore. They chanted with their bodies. The air was thick with suppression magic, poisoned incense, and misery.

Gods, I could feel them slicing through my connection to fire like string between flicked fingers.

I groaned low behind the leather gag, my body arching slightly before I forced it still again.

If I moved, they'd know they were winning.

So I let it hurt.

Let the agony crawl marrow-deep as the queen's leashed casters dug into me with their magic. Their spell was layered thick and sure enough to hold a lesser man until death.

But I wasn't lesser.

I was Cade Phoenixfire.

Or—I had been.

Now, I wasn't sure who the fuck I was anymore.

Except hers.

I so badly wanted to fight.

But with the suppression spell locked into the floor and laced through my veins like freezing venom, there wasn't much left to do but rage silently inside myself.

I squeezed my eyes shut against the burn building behind them, and cursed in my bones.

Ash.

Gods, Ash.

Don't come.

I felt it in the pit of me—that maddening, hideous buzz of anguish. The one her body would ignite the second she stepped foot into Emberveil. She wouldn't hesitate. She'd burn through the stables, through the Syther guards, through the fire-cursed battlements built by cowards and men too tired to remember what real strength looked like.

She'd come for me.

And they'd try to kill her.

And they might win.

And it would destroy me.

More than this cell.

More than whatever dark spell these songless bastards could conjure up.

I groaned again, something ugly and feral behind my teeth, and tugged hard against my bindings.

Nothing.

Only the grind of rope against torn skin.

Odiun, please—

That was the first prayer that crawled its way into my head, involuntary as breath.

I never prayed.

Not really.

War raised men who carried gods in steel and blood, not quiet songs and folded hands.

But tonight, I didn't care.

Please don't let her come. Not yet. Let her be safe. Let her run. Let her—

Live.

Because if I die here, I'll die loving her.

But if she dies here?

It won't matter whether I live or not.

I don't know how long I held onto that thought—clung to her face, her voice, the feeling of her slipping her fingers through the back of my hair when the world was just quiet enough to hope.

I saw her with smudged ash on her cheeks, blood on her jaw that wasn't hers, looking up at me like I was more than just the queen's weapon.

I saw her standing next to Errax, hand on her saddle, whispering something only the wind and dragons understood.

Ashlyn, with her angry eyes and sad heart, her jokes that never quite folded the pain inside them. I could feel her even as the torment reached a fever pitch—her presence sitting in my chest like an ember that could never fully die.

And right then, I hoped.

Not hope that she'd come.

But hope enough that she'd live.

That she'd get far enough away. That Krakos would carry her high out of reach. That Errax would fly like her life depended on it—and that Ash would tear holes in the sky, not in herself.

I wanted her to drink wine again. To laugh too loud. To paint. To claw her own name into history with proud, ink-stained hands.

I wanted her to be—

Free.

Not ruined by saving me.

Not destroyed trying to fix what I never deserved in the first place.

I slumped forward, my head heavy against the bone of my shoulder as pain rushed through my nerves again—more than magic should've allowed.

The circle was cracking.

Or maybe I was.

The floor wavered beneath me, red-green symbols splitting like old skin around scar tissue. Everything blurred.

My body trembled. My heartbeat pounded loud and ugly in my ears. My thoughts weren't words anymore, just flashes of images:

Blood spilling on the old stones of Emberveil.

Ash screaming behind Syther blades.

Her lips stretched in a sob I couldn't reach in time.

Everything—everything screamed inside me.

If I could give her one thing, just one...

Let her live.

Please, gods—if you're still here, if Odiun still fucking listens, take her pain from her. Let her be free of this war.

Let her be the girl who swims barefoot again, who draws charcoal dragons and dreams up peace in a world on fire.

Let her be Ash again.

If you need something to take?

Take me.

I'll burn as long as you want.

Just let her go.

Let her—

Darkness.

It swept in soft and unshakable.

My body wilted entirely, muscles no longer screaming but just quiet.

Dead quiet.

And through the end of it, in the cold and the silence and the red-black burial mask of pain closing over my eyes—

I thought of her.

Sitting by firelight. Freckles dancing over her nose. Hair half-tucked into a braid, mouth holding the edge of a grin that tasted like wine and danger.

My Ash.

Not a weapon. Not a prophecy.

Mine.

I let that dream carry me as I slumped into unconsciousness, whispering her name silently against the gag.

Ash.

Let the queen do what she wants.

I'll die loving her.

But gods help me...

If she dies?

Then so. Will. All. Of. Them.

And I'll burn this entire mountain to reach her.

But then... the darkness finally swallowed me.

CHAPTER 40

The sky roared around us.

Not with wind, but wings.

Hundreds of them. Great, wide, leathery limbs slicing the heavens as wild dragons filled the sky like a living storm—dark and endless and carrying the scent of vengeance on every pass. Beneath each massive scaled chest dangled freight unlike any the skies had ever seen.

The Terradyne.

Stone-skinned giants lifted from the depths of the mountain —trees with roots coiled in anger, boulders carved into fists, moss-shrouded watchers older than war itself. Each one suspended like ancient gods held aloft by fury and breath. Their arms hung steady, unmoving as they flew, but their eyes—those elemental eyes like glowing resin and shattered granite—burned straight ahead.

Toward Emberveil.

Toward the queen.

Awaiting her reckoning.

Errax's wings carved a clean path near the front of the formation. The dome of the sky stretched wide above her and folded beneath in rolling valleys where the clouds split like parting silk before us. My thighs gripped her just behind her shoulders, hands steady on the forward rigging, but I didn't dare steer.

I didn't need to.

She knew where we were going.

The dagger-shaped towers of the sprawling city of Emberveil loomed now on the horizon. Their obsidian points were laced with sharp clouds that hadn't moved for hours. Smoke poured in curling columns from narrow slits in the mountain walls, black veins leading deeper into the mountains and the volcano of Calcaedus like it was bleeding from the inside.

And I was about to cut it open the rest of the way.

I leaned forward, pressing one hand to the warm scales at Errax's side. "You ready, girl? There's no turning back now."

She pulsed beneath me, the answer riding her breath like a growl.

Just ahead, Krakos surged beside us, his black hide gleaming, his crimson eyes narrowed. His body moved smoother than it had in days, his grief and rage forged into purpose. His rider… gone. But not forgotten. Never forgotten.

Hunter and Bella rode just behind him on Talonor, whose gray wings cut the clouds like a sword kissed by starlight. Hunter's hair was tied back, his jaw set. I hadn't seen him blink since we left the summit. Bella's brow was furrowed so tight it might never come undone, her hand tight around the grip attached to Hunter's saddle strap, but her gaze never left mine.

They had followed me here.

Across a thousand miles.

Across grief. Blood. Fire.

And gods help me—I'd die for both of them.

Bella—my sister in trauma. Who had grown up with her body chained and her strength spit on. Who now soared through the high winds like the warrior she had always been. I remembered running through Faewood with her, barefoot and full of bruises.

Stealing bread from Garris. Hiding under the floorboards. Crying over lost girls. Laughing over shared blankets.

And Hunter—Commander. Brother in arms. The only one who had ever truly stood beside Cade when his soul began to fray at his edges. Loyal beyond logic. Carved by principle. Who'd sworn to protect both of us at the cost of his own peace. And now flew into hell on a grey dragon with only his blade and a prophecy he was still trying to defy.

We were the ones left. And we had come to end this.

Below us, dragon after dragon carried their Terradyne cargo like sacred offerings through avalanche-thick mist. From here, it was like the world wore wings. Every gust bent beneath us. The air didn't fight our entry—it fled.

Emberveil was that close.

"She'll be ready," I said out loud, though no one could hear me.

Cade had always said Mortriana Vissex never left doors unlocked unless she wanted you to open them.

This army—even this moment—it was what she wanted.

Not because she feared us.

But because she was waiting for me.

Because Cade was her trap.

And I was the one thing she hadn't caged yet.

"She wants me in that throne hall," I muttered, more to myself. "Wants to see if prophecy breaks when it's cornered..."

I smiled then, slow and bitter.

Let her try.

The sky thinned around us as we dipped beneath the last pass. The scent hit first—smoke and burnt sulfur, sharp like brimstone, like something old and foul had been smoldering just beneath the surface of the mountain for centuries and the queen was simply fanning it to life.

Emberveil bloomed across the ridge of Calcaedus like a cancer. It was built to be a beacon of hope, but over time, and through generations of greed-lust it had fallen from the once mighty city sung about from ages past.

The towers stretched unnaturally high. Twisted spines of black iron and charred stone reached toward the heavens like claws. Walls laced with lava-glass flickered red like hearts still bleeding. Arrow slits glinted with soldiers' eyes. And the gates—

The gates were open.

Not all the way. Not enough to invite.

But enough to say, come. Let's finish this.

"She's taunting us," Hunter's voice cracked hot behind me, carried on wind.

"She knows we're coming," I called back. "And she doesn't care."

"Or she cares too much," Bella offered, spitting hair from her mouth. "She's playing the long game. Cade's her bait."

I didn't answer.

Because I already knew.

Because the moment I closed my eyes, that dread wrapped around me like a chain cooling at my throat. Cade was in there. Beneath those towers. Broken. Bound. Or worse.

And I had waited long enough.

Errax roared, her jaw dropping wide as a trumpet of defiance tore through the sky.

The wild dragons echoed her call, their voices ripping into the wind like bursting flame—one after another, wings spread wide as they screamed their fury into the open air. Krakos answered next, his cry a blade scraping against grief. Then Talonor, then the rest.

Above us, thunder cracked—not made by storm, but by the war cries of dragons.

Behind us, the Terradyne began to shift.

Writhing.

Breathing.

Awake.

Wet with cloud-slick and wind, their arms unfurled, fingers like tree-branches and broken boulders cracking from ancient roots.

Carried by dragons. Delivered by legend.

They came.

"How does this end?" Bella shouted beside me, eyes sharp, voice barely rising above the dragon song.

I looked forward.

At the gates.

At the mountain.

At the queen's crown.

"No more war after this," I whispered. "No more slavery. No more oppression and cruelty. No… more… queen…"

Errax dove.

And we followed her down.

The plains opened beneath us, wild and vast—painted in streaks of shadow and dying sunlight. Beyond them lay the silver spread of Great Skymirror Lake, shimmering like a mirror polished by giants, wide enough to swallow whole cities in its reflection. For a breath, I forgot. Forgot the fire, the pain, the pulse of fear that never truly quieted under my skin. I forgot everything... except the way dusk caught the wind in Errax's wings.

She flew with purpose now, low and sleek, carving through the currents like a viper mid-strike.

But I saw it first.

The bridge.

The Veilreach.

It rose from the eastern banks like a ribbon of black stone strung across the sacred lake. Wide as five wagons, it curved elegantly toward Emberveil's obsidian limbs, connecting death to dominion with every carved step along its spined edge. Lantern posts lined the edges—none lit, none warm. Just hollow iron frames left to peer back at the faces of the dead that crossed it.

Suspended over the oldest still-water in Allovan—

And directly before it…

Blazebreak Keep.

"They've fortified," Hunter called from his saddle, his breath ragged above Talonor's shoulders. "Gatehouse is manned."

I saw it too.

Dragon riders stationed on the platform before the miles-long bridge, crouched beneath crimson and coal-black banners snapping hard in the rising wind. Their dragons were sleek, brutish things—short-snouted, armored in flame-dark indigo scales that shimmered blood-red as the sun fell. Defensive formation. Dozens of hard-trained riders. Two airborne scouts circling wide.

One broke formation.

And took off toward the castle.

"There!" Bella shouted, pointing. "She's been warned!"

The scout climbed fast, then tipped north, wings flaring as it raced toward Emberveil—toward the queen.

"She'll be ready for us before we're even off these plains," I muttered, heat flaring under my armor. "She wanted to be."

Hunter pulled alongside me, Krakos close behind. "Do we engage now? Break formation, wipe the gate clean before they reinforce?"

I hesitated.

It wouldn't take much. With Krakos and Errax at the front and the wild dragons flanking, we could break the gatehouse in minutes. We could burn the Blazebreak Keep asunder, but that wasn't our target.

"She wants our attention," I said. "She wants us to fight our way to her. To drag out the battle and weaken us before we get to her."

"What are you proposing? Split up our forces?" Bella arched a brow, her hair wind-whipped and smoke-scented.

"No," I said, grinning faintly. "I'm proposing we force her hand before she forces ours."

"How?"

"We fly. Fly past the riders of Blazebreak Gate. We fly with all our speed straight at her."

"But we'll be flanked," Hunter shouted in the rushing winds.

"No. We'll let her think that," I said, hoping for once I'd have the upper hand against the bitch. "We have a surprise behind they would never expect."

Bella raised a curious eyebrow. "Oh…"

"Errax." I leaned down to my dragon's neck. "Tell her to trail behind, and kill all that follow us…"

Errax screamed a high-pitched roar that trailed off with a broken grumble. The wild dragons roared by the dozens, their roars trailing back like a shimmering wave of horn blowers.

"Good girl," I snarled. "Good girl…"

The lake spread wider now beneath us, the water gleaming with molten gold as the sun bled toward the edge of the world. Emberveil's towers darkened in silhouette—tall, grasping things ribbed with crimson iron. They looked like bones torn from the ground and held mid-prayer.

"Odiun," I whispered under my breath, barely audible above the scream of wind. "If you ever heard anything… hear this."

I closed my eyes.

"I've lied. I've stolen. I've let people scrape pieces off me until I wasn't sure what I had left. But I have never begged. Not once."

My heart thudded deep in my chest.

"But I'm begging now."

The wind twisted tighter around me.

"Please…" I whispered. "Let him be alive."

The pain surfaced sharp behind my ribs, but I didn't hold it back.

"Let me reach him," I said hoarsely. "Let Cade be alive long enough for me to get to him. Because she will not win. Not with him rotting in her chambers. Not with his fire shackled, and his heart breaking alone in that mountain."

Tears stung the corners of my eyes.

"He's more than a prince. More than your Cinderyn mage warrior. He's mine. And I am not letting him die to build her god damned throne."

The sky ached with orange as the sun bowed at the edge of the lake. Twilight crept in.

We were almost there.

Hunter raised his sword in silent salute.

Bella wordlessly reached across the gap between us and gripped my arm.

The wind howled louder.

The bridge loomed near.

And the queen's trap shuddered in its final, desperate pull.

"I'm coming," I whispered. "Cade, you hold on just a little longer. I'm coming."

And this fire?

This fire was for both of us.

We dropped.

And the dark mouth of the waved walls of Emberveil waited below.

The wind howled over the Great Skymirror Lake as a thousand wings churned the clouds above it. Below, the water reflected the coming storm—not of nature, but war. Dragons filled the sky like gods returning to reclaim the realm. Stormscales in shining silver and black, wild dragons with glowing eyes and fire-battered wings, and above them all—Errax leading the front with me fixed firmly to her back.

The army was unlike anything the world had seen.

And I was at its head.

Not because I wanted to be.

But because I had to be.

The city loomed ahead—Emberveil, towering out of the mountainside like a jagged scar. Its spires were obsidian fangs stretching toward a sky caught halfway between dusk and fire-light. The bridge—the Veilreach—glinted with ancient runes that pulsed faintly red, the queen's magic seething through them like poison.

I eyed it with no affection.

There was no room for fear in my blood anymore. Only fury.

Ash.

That was my name. Funny how a name could predict a life.

Hunter soared beside me on Talonor, his coppery armor bathed in the golden mist that rose from the lake's edge. He looked carved from resolve—every line of his body tense, every breath measured. Behind him, Bella rode tighter still, her short sword tucked tight across her back, her ocean-blue eyes trained on the battlefield ahead.

They didn't need to say a word.

They were ready.

Just like me.

This was no longer about saving a prince. Or even saving ourselves.

This was for everything.

For every child buried at Storm's End.

For every Stormscale rider who bled for someone else's war.

For every whispered memory of rebellion crushed by fire.

And most of all—for the future of Allovan. For the future of our world!

In my mind, I whispered what I didn't have breath to say aloud.

Here we go.

The edge of the city came into view—a chain of outer walls stacked like jagged rings atop the lower ledge of Calcaedus. Banners whipped in the wind—red and gold, blazoned with the queen's house crest: a curled crimson dragon before a crown of black iron burning.

Not subtle.

From deep within Emberveil, I heard the horns.

Low. A deep thunder that cracked through the sky like the groan of dying gods.

Horns echoed from the twisted spires of Raven's Bane Castle, carried on the wind and fire-wall air.

At once, the city's outer defenses sprang to life. Dragons crackled into formation across the balconies and towers like vultures cheeked on fury. Red-armored soldiers appeared like ants along the high ramparts. Above them, the queen's Syther legion hissed as they marched into place—clang of armor, scrape of discordant blades echoing out over the battlefield to come.

The air thickened.

From behind the dragon riders of Blazebreak Keep flew to join their comrades from the castle. They surely thought they had an upper hand attacking from the rear since our army flew past. I felt the dark smirk cross my face as I gazed back at them.

The city stirred like a sleeping monster finally acknowledging the knocking at its gates.

Behind me, the Terradyne moved into position—massive limbs shifting with purpose as the wild dragons carried them forward. Their roots trailed time. Their eyes glowed like ancient lanterns, unblinking and full of what only old stone could understand: patience, pain... and vengeance.

I guided Errax forward, the wind snapping my braid back from my cheek. Her scales shimmered silver-blue as the sun's light hit her from behind, painting her like a fallen star.

And then—

The mountain behind the city gave a sound I'll never forget.

Crack.

Boom!

Calcaedus groaned.

A pulse of vibration rolled down through the base of the city and into the lakebed far below, rattling the clouds themselves into sudden, unnatural spirals. The very wall of the volcano's summit trembled—and then it ruptured.

Like a god breathing deep and deciding, for the first time in an age, to exhale.

From the top of Mount Calcaedus, a bellowing plume of black smoke, cinders, and glowing fire belched skyward in a spiraling inferno. A volcanic scream filled the air as the summit tore itself open, spitting molten anger into the stratosphere, casting ash across the bright blue skies and dimming the sun itself.

The eruption was fierce and furious. Wicked.

Behind us, Stormscale dragons reared midair, wings flaring back in alarm.

Cheers turned to cries.

Bella gasped beside me. "Is that—?"

"The gods…" Hunter whispered, pulling Talonor up short.

But I—

I didn't flinch.

Because I know fire. I was raised in it.

And I am not afraid of the mountain's breath.

No. My fire is older.

Stronger.

Mine is the will to decide what burns and what lives. I am an Aqualorian. I am the essence of water. And I fear no blaze. The fire should fear me!

I bent forward in my saddle. "Errax."

My dragon responded instantly, wings sharpening as we dove clean through the rolling wave of smoke.

It didn't blind me.

It woke me.

The queen thinks she commands fire.

She forgot—I survived hers.

I raised my hand.

A golden shimmer lit inside my chest.

Eden.

She stirred.

Then surged.

And in one pulse of power, a burst of incandescent light exploded in my palm, solidifying into the shape of a golden blade as bright as sunrise.

The wind caught the hem of my coat.

And I stood straight in my saddle, blade raised to the darkened smoke-sky above me—

And pointed it directly at Raven's Bane Castle.

My voice echoed down the mountainside like a rolling scream of divine reckoning.

"Bring it down!"

The dragons roared.

The Terradyne bellowed.

And the armies of fire met the dawn of war.

The horns wailed again, overlapping and deafening, a death dirge that shook the very marrow of the world as the skies above Emberveil split wide.

And from that chasm of flame and smoke—

They came.

The queen's dragons.

Hundreds. Thousands.

Dark-winged beasts with scales like charred bone and smoke-glint obsidian. Their eyes shimmered violet, corrupted by the Cinderyn's fire, glowing like coals in a dying forge. Each one swooped from high towers, from caverns in Calcaedus's jagged flanks, bursting from beneath the volcanic ridge like curses loosed all at once.

Their riders glinted crimson and black, armor threaded with molten veins, helms shaped like screaming serpents. Spears hung burning from their hips, and glyphs shone like blood along their gauntlets.

The Blaze Queen wasn't just ready.

She'd been waiting.

The full might of Emberveil rose like a living storm to meet us.

A sea of wings filled the air, and the light dimmed—half by volcanic ash and half by sheer scale as the enemy moved in formation. They circled above their city, hunger churning in the wind, then dove.

I watched them come with my jaw clenched, wind screaming past my ears, the pulse of Eden's magic flaring bright in my hand as my golden sword hummed louder, its glow pushing back against the arrival of so much darkness.

They want to protect their queen. I hope they kissed her goodbye.

"Hunter, left flank!" I shouted through the storm as the first wave of Emberveil riders broke forward, cutting toward our front line in a downward V that threatened to tear our formation apart.

Hunter, Bella and Talonor veered instantly, wings snapping open wide as they led the first strike of Stormscales into place. Lightning flared around them—Hunter's shout practically lost to the roar of twisting dragons and unleashing magic.

My breath came fast and sharp.

Errax and I pierced straight into the thick of the bellowing smoke.

Among darting, shrieking dragons, all spines and scales and leathery whip-like tails, our army met hers.

Not with hesitation.

But with vengeance.

The first collision hit like thunder.

Steel clanged against talon.

Fire met fire midair with explosive consequence—a burst of gold against red, Eden versus dragonfire.

A scream tore through the sky—one of ours.

A Stormscale rider spun from the clouds in a downward spiral, his dragon trailing smoke and flame as it plummeted toward the lake below.

I bit down on the scream building in my throat.

Focus, Ash. This is war. You knew it would cost.

Bella's voice rang out over the clamor—"Above! On your flank!"

I spun Errax up, the world tilting into wild vertigo as a black-winged enemy swooped toward me, breath flaring red.

The rider raised a burning axe to strike.

I lifted my gold sword high and summoned Eden through my core.

"Now!" I cried, slashing wide.

The weapon responded—light screamed from the blade like starlight. The enemy's blow collapsed beneath me as their dragon recoiled, howling, and I guided Errax forward in one smooth motion, flipping our position so we slashed beneath their exposed belly.

Gold tore through scale.

The dragon shrieked.

It toppled in a flail of wings and screams, its rider roaring as they tumbled toward the smoldering cliffs below.

Errax circled and rose again, slick with blood and sweat, her body thrumming from the impact.

I panted hard.

Another roar, this one deep and ancient, silenced the field around me.

The Terradyne had joined the sky.

Carried aloft by wild dragons, they leaned from their mounts and hurled great chunks of stone, slamming into enemy towers. One boulder cracked a parapet clean in two. Another burst into blossom-light—roots exploding from it mid-air, wrapping around a dragon's neck mid-flight and dragging it down, hard.

The ground forces had reached the foot of the Veilreach—the Stormscales in gleaming silver charges and carved leather, enemies clashing on obsidian stone bridges beneath the rising glow of the volcano.

And there—in the center of it all—

Raven's Bane Castle, high on the cliff.

Unmoving.

Watching.

A black crown on a burning mountain.

My heart screamed.

I yanked Errax toward it, eyes locked to where I felt him—deep inside those walls.

Cade.

Still alive. He had to be.

Some part of me knew. Felt him like a second skin, like fire I'd touched too long to forget. He was hurt, god yes. Maybe dying.

But not gone.

Not yet.

"Hang on," I whispered low, voice breaking as wind and ash scoured my cheeks. My eyes stung, but not from smoke.

"Hang on, Cade. I'm coming."

A screech tore past me—Krakos, thundering through fire-plumes, his mouth rippling flame into another enemy dragon's face. He spun midair, danced over wings too slow to match him, and brushed past me in a burn of heated wind. No dragon matched the might of Cade's beast. It was like watching an eagle hunt sparrows.

And for one breath, I could almost pretend Cade was there.

Almost.

But then I remembered.

He was the reason I was here.

And I could not fail.

I dove.

Errax folded her wings tight and we sliced into the next formation of enemy beasts, Eden crackling down my blade as golden lightning streamed from our path. Wild dragons joined us, riding our wake into battle, their eyes on me.

On me.

I was the key.

They knew.

I was the Gold-Marked.

Slave-born.

Sea-found.

Made of bruises and scars and small feral dreams.

Chained to the floor once by men who thought me less than real.

But I wasn't that girl anymore.

I'm a woman wrought of suffering and pain. I'm a survivor. And I'm going to burn this whole city to the ground if that's what it takes.

Wielder of Eden.

Breaker of thrones.

And this?

This battlefield curled around my scream like flame around bone.

A red-winged dragon shot fast from my blind. Errax tilted hard.

I met the rider's blade with mine—connected steel—and twisted, breaking his elbow clean before I kicked him backward from his saddle.

He fell.

And I didn't look back.

As one, the dragons behind me roared.

The Terradyne bellowed in kind.

The wind cracked with flame and fury.

Chaos engulfed the city's edge.

Enemies flew. Friends fell. Screams ripped the skies open at the seams.

And in its heart, the castle stood waiting.

Horns blared again—one long note stretched across the city.

They knew we were coming.

I narrowed my eyes.

Clenched my fists around my magical sword's hilt.

And I pointed once more toward Raven's Bane Castle.

"For Allovan!"

CHAPTER 42

The sky was ablaze with war and flame.

And for once, it wasn't just a metaphor.

Above the Veilreach Bridge, dragons spun in screeching arcs, clouds torn apart by wingbeats and smoke. The Emberveil riders came fast, sun-glint flashes of red and black armor slicing through misted air like daggers hurled from on high. Their dragons were sleek and brutal—scaled in iron grays and gore-streaked blacks, eyes burning with murder. Their formation didn't falter as they dove.

The Stormscale ranks rose to meet them in a roar of wings and flame.

I saw Carina first—unflinching, deadly, her silver-streaked braid snapping behind her head like a tail of her own as she guided her dragon into a collision path with two enemy fliers. Scorching dragonfire seared the air, followed by the shriek of tearing scale and the thunderclap of bodies slamming in midair. A burst of blood and flame painted the sky between towers.

"Incoming!" Hunter shouted behind me.

Errax banked hard to the right, and I dropped low over her

neck as a bolt of fire spat past us, flashing sunfire orange as it tore open a column of air just feet away.

To the left of us, a Stormscale dragon was struck—its rider clipped mid-dive. I saw the moment the harness failed. The man twisted once, then fell, disappearing below the clouds with a scream.

"No, no, no…" Bella hissed behind me.

Below us, Emberveil waited—its towers claw-like, walls crawling with archers and firecasters. Between the spiraling spires, narrow bridges ran like veins connecting the queen's castle to her inner sanctum—a spiderweb designed to trap and punish.

And every single stretch of it opened its jaws wide for us now.

Because the battle had begun.

"Darren's pushing forward!" Bella shouted, pointing to the west flank. "And the riders of Blazebreak Keep are incoming fast!"

I smirked. *Let them come…*

And sure enough, the general of the Stormscales led the charge above the second wall of Emberveil. Darron's dragon dove hard through a cluster of enemy riders, carving a path wide enough for a flight of wild dragons to follow. Arrows rained upward from archer galleries below, scattering like burned paper against scaled hide.

I looked to Errax.

"Now."

She roared.

A liquid, thrumming sound that made the air quake.

Below, one of the Terradyne dropped.

A wild dragon struck by a fiery bolt had flipped midair, spasming uncontrollably, its wings shuttering as it twisted. The massive body of the Terradyne it carried hurtled limp from its grip—down, down, past the defensive line and into Lake Skymirror with a thunderous, earth-shaking splash.

"Shit," Hunter cursed as his dragon veered past us. "We're losing them!"

Another blast came from the left—dark magic, fire-stained. Errax dipped, using her tail to clip a rogue Emberveil dragon in the jaw. It spiraled away, missing one wing. But not before its rider loosed a second volley.

The spell struck a wild dragon dead-on. She shrieked, tangled midair, and her claws released the boulder-sized Terradyne she'd been hauling.

The elemental fell straight into the upper walkways of Emberveil—smashing through blackstone like a hammer through glass.

The Ancient bellowed—not in pain, but fury—its body rising tall amidst shattered towers as its fists pounded the parapet below. Cries went up across the city, panicked and sharp as alarms rang.

A breach.

And below us, war poured in.

"Go now!" I shouted into the wind. "They're cracking—we fly!"

Errax didn't wait.

She dove, wings tucking in tight as we nosed through chaos. Fire and smoke blurred around us, dragons clashing midair, bodies falling, screaming, below. My lungs burned with the closeness of it all—the heat, the acrid tang of scorched stone, the smell of things that had bled and would not again.

Across from us, Krakos joined the charge—raging, beautiful, his muscles tighter than iron as he tore through a trio of enemy dragons like paper. One claw sweep ripped a lesser rider and mount in half. Bella whooped once behind me, even through the tears in her voice, "That's it, boy!"

But Emberveil did not die easy.

She screeched in kind, erupting with spells from her towers. Enchanted ballistas roared to life across the upper walls, launching spears of enchanted bone into the sky. One found a target.

A wild dragon bellowed as the bolt skewered clean through its belly. Its rider screamed—no, not screamed… wept—reaching for the reins as the beast pitched sideways.

They tumbled.

Then silence.

Then impact.

The ground shook again.

"They're trying to drop more of the Terradyne before they land!" Bella shouted.

"Protect the carriers!" Hunter yelled. "Errax, flank right!"

I steered with knees and thought, the connection between her mind and mine swirling hot with urgency. She veered wide as another volley loosed—then folded her wings again and dove.

We passed too close to the outer wall—flame licked my boot. Any closer and—

"Hold steady!" I barked, wiping soot from my eyes.

A Terradyne landed behind the queen's western watchtower, its body cracking the dome like an egg. From the crater, it stood —taller than most roofs—and raised two enormous arms. Then it sank both fists deep into the wall.

Blackstone shattered.

The queen's forces screamed.

And Emberveil… blinked.

I felt it.

A whisper.

A tremor in the queen's long-dormant heartbeat.

Fear.

The mountain shifted beneath us. Not from nature.

From fury.

"This is it," I whispered, voice cracking.

That was when I saw her.

On the jutting balcony of Raven's Bane.

Standing tall as hellfire wrapped her silver hair in violent curls. Eyes black, twisted with magic and shadow.

Mortriana.

The queen.

She lifted one arm toward the sky like she meant to draw all of creation toward her grasp.

And her mouth opened.

But I couldn't hear what she said.

Because the battle screamed louder still.

Emberveil had opened its jaws.

And we were the flames climbing down its throat.

The sky was chaos.

The sun had all but vanished behind smoke and wings—black silhouettes streaked with flame, the dragons of Emberveil and Stormscale locked in a churning riot of color and cries. Lightning split the clouds. Not natural. Magical. Summoned by firecasters chanting along the queen's balconies, their hands outstretched in mimicry of gods.

But even gods would bow to this war.

A Stormscale dragon screamed above me, its flank split from shoulder to hip. It spun downward in a dying spiral, tail lashing wildly, crashing through one of Emberveil's tower bridges with a sickening crunch of stone and bone.

I choked on ash.

"Keep moving!" I shouted, heel digging into Errax's side as she carved another low arc around Raven's Bane Castle.

To my left, Krakos tore through a pair of Emberveil riders with a mastery so brutal it bordered on poetry. His black scales gleamed beneath the flame of another fallen tower. A smaller red dragon dove to block his path. Krakos met it mid-air, jaws locking fast around its throat, and in a single savage motion, snapped its neck with a crunch that echoed across the sky like thunder cracking stone.

"Another down!" Bella's voice rang through the wind behind

me. Hunter swooped his dragon in parallel, his blade slick and red as it flashed in the sunless morning.

But it wasn't enough. We weren't punching through—we were bleeding just as fast.

"The dragons of the Blazebreak Gate are nearly on us!" Hunter shouted to me. "We can't fight every direction! We need to focus our forces!"

I nodded once, eyes peeling toward the incoming battalion of dragon riders, and then toward the heart of the fortress. Raven's Bane. The tallest spire glowed menacingly now, coiled in strands of unnatural lightning. I only saw the long tendrils of the queen's flowing dress as she disappeared into the dark hall of Raven's Bane Castle.

"She's hiding in her throne hall!" I shouted through smoke. "We have to get there!"

"If she dies, they all fall!" Bella added. "The Sythers, the riders —they'll have nothing to rally behind!"

Errax bucked upward with a sharp shriek, wings flaring as we veered wide. Below us, a great cathedral trembled—a Terradyne had landed near its side, collapsing an entire bridge with the weight of its knotted arms. From its stomach, fire bloomed.

From behind a tremendous roar shook the dusk. My gaze shot south. Just as the dragon riders of the Blazebreak swept into our ranks, a huge set of wings descended from the thick, shadowy clouds.

"The Great Mother Dragon!" Bella shrieked with sheer optimism in her voice. She glared my way with a clever snicker. "You knew…"

I just smirked back as I whipped the reins. *Errax! Forward!* The rush of gravity bit deep in my chest as my dragon descended, angry winds whipping past my ears.

The sky behind boomed in blazing amber light as the Great Mother Dragon unleashed a hellstorm on the riders of the front keep of the city. The battle may be scattered, but we sure as Infernal Depths had some raw power at our flank.

Hunter rose beside me now, his face streaked with soot, a gash torn down one arm. "Ash! I might know where he is!"

My heart slammed in my chest. "Cade? Where?"

"She'd keep him close to use as bait," Hunter shouted in our sharp descent, Bella clutching his stomach tightly from behind. "He's going to be in the cells of Emberveil, but our best way in is from that balcony. Every door will be sealed tight with lock and magic. Those would take time to break down, time we don't have!"

Hope flared. Painfully bright.

"You're sure?"

He met my eyes. Hard. "No. But it's our best chance."

"Then go!" I said. "We follow your lead!"

Hunter spun Talonor into another brutal dive. Krakos followed like a ghost of vengeance, his body shearing grim lines through the smoke. Bella clung tightly behind Hunter, her braid snapping like a war-banner.

"Errax," I whispered. "You know what to do."

She growled.

We dropped.

Toward the cathedral and the chaos below.

Down, down—the mountain opened beneath us, carved in spires and cruelty, each layer of Emberveil stacked like a rotten tooth. Flamecasters shrieked spells from every corner. One of them lit a bridge on fire as we passed beneath.

A dragon's charred carcass tumbled past us in flames.

We ignored it.

Hunter plunged in, Krakos hot behind.

Then us.

The darkness swallowed everything. The chaos of war erupted at the front of the city.

CHAPTER 43

They poured from the heart of the city like a flood of knives.

The Sythers.

Dozens at first. Then hundreds. Their hunched, pale bodies crashed over the shattered parapets and leapt over burnt barricades like feral waves, twisting corkscrew limbs ending in blades slick from slaughter.

"I see them!" Hunter shouted above the wind.

"They're charging at the dragonless Stormscales on the ground!" Bella's voice cracked.

I knew I needed to get to Cade. I *knew* it. I *felt* it with every fiber of my body. But…

I couldn't.

Instead, I told Errax to dip—right at the horde of Sythers.

"Ash!" Bella screamed behind me, darting to my side. "You can't! We have to go!"

"They're slaughtering the Stormscales!" I shouted, tears streaming—whether from smoke or rage, I didn't care. "They'll all die if I don't—"

"They're baiting you—," I heard Bella's words as I flew down with lightning in my arteries. "Don't let them keep him from you again."

I looked back. Hunter was already sending Talonor after me, dragging his blade along the saddle strap like it was habit. Errax's wings fanned wide under me. Darren and Carina followed.

The queen knew what she was doing.

Send the Sythers out now. In numbers. In madness.

Banking on my fury.

Banking on my grief.

But it was working.

"I can kill them," I whispered, teeth bared. "I can wipe them all into the dirt."

"You can't kill them all," Bella shouted. "We have to get to Cade and the queen! You stubborn daughter of a..." Her final words were drowned out by Errax's unleashed dragonfire, but I got the point. I knew she was right. She always was. She should've been the one to get the Gilded Radiance. Not me. But the fire in my chest raged too savagely to quench. I hated the Sythers. I hated them for all they've done. Haley's face burned into my mind. The dragon trinkets she'd made and would never make again. Hate bellowed in me like the forge back in Bramblebash.

No more. No more children slaughtered without futures at the hands of those monsters.

That struck something deep.

And for a moment, the warmth of Eden faltered.

But only for a moment.

Because the Sythers shrieked.

They came screaming up the plaza in a wall of bent limbs and teeth, blades held high—dozens of spears with hooked ends. Their leader bellowed—a high-pitched, guttural howl that sounded like bone whistling through stone—and he pointed straight at me.

"Darren! Get your Stormscales ready for an attack!" Hunter yelled. "Ash, we have to—"

A horrendous boom shook the stone ground.

The ground beneath my boots cracked.

Everyone froze.

Another tremble—this one harder. Debris slid across the battlements.

I spun.

A terrible noise rose from the city's edge—like something massive crawling free from the bones of the world.

"I know that sound…" Bella muttered in the dead air.

And then they came.

The Terradyne.

Dozens. Over thirty of them at least, bursting down from the higher cliffs with fury given form—great arms of stone and bark slamming through Emberveil's upper tier like doom wielding fists. Moss-draped titans with antlered crowns. Others armored in glowing root-plates and gritted stone tusks.

They bellowed as they crashed into the Sythers with hurricane strength.

The impact shook the air.

A dozen Sythers were obliterated instantly.

I shrieked uncontrollably at the sight; fists lifted to the air as Errax corrected her flight back up.

Their ranks collapsed like snapped reeds beneath a river's rise. Bodies flew in all directions—some hurled over walls, some pounded into the ash-streaked tiles until nothing remained but pulped shadows. Their blades screamed against Terradyne hides, but it was like swords slicing glaciers. Stone met steel.

And steel lost.

One Terradyne—taller than the rest, his bark armor striped in glimmering turquoise moss—grabbed a Syther with two massive hands and crushed it with a sound like thunder snapping bone.

The wild dragons overhead shrieked in triumph, wheeling to

shield the elemental giants as they advanced. Fire and soot burst skyward. Emberveil brightened in flame.

Eden's power rose in my chest.

The rhythm beat with the Terradyne.

With every stomp. With every war cry.

And for the first time in too long—

I felt true hope.

"They're doing it," I whispered. "We have the queen on the run."

"Which is exactly why we have to go now," Hunter said, voice unshakeable. "This is our window. Before she drowns Cade in her magic trying to stop us."

"Ash," Bella's grip found my shoulder again. "Let them fight. This is what you rallied them for. You did this—now it's time to finish it."

I nodded.

My throat sealed with emotion, but my legs moved.

Errax was already back on trajectory at the queen's palace, her breath steady, green-gold fire dancing along the seams of her jaw. "Take me to him," I whispered, pressing my forehead to her neck for just a heartbeat.

"Let's bring him home."

Krakos rose to fly beside me, eyes glowing sunset red. He turned his enormous head toward the high peak—Raven's Bane Castle. Ash and Bella caught up too.

Krakos roared.

The sound sent birds fleeing from ruptured towers. Dragons twisting midair. Stone splitting deeper.

The whole city heard him.

The queen heard him.

We soared past the crumbling spires where enemy dragons peeled back from the Terradyne's assault below. The plaza disappeared, swallowed in fire and fury. The edge of the caldera curved steep, studded with roots of obsidian and rivers of old lava carved dry.

We followed the wind's curve.

And there—there it stood.

Raven's Bane.

The highest spire. Tower of the queen.

Carved into Calcaedus's black heart like a chill dagger left to bleed the world.

Its crowning arches clawed the ash-white clouds.

A staircase of fire ran down from its doors, lit with blood-red torches. Glyphs pulsed across each, old and dangerous. The rune seal shined like a heartbeat.

"Fly low!" I shouted.

Errax complied.

We skimmed hard along the edge of the ridgeline. Krakos behind us, Talonor ahead. We dodged flying beasts in formation. Even with a battalion of Sythers dead, and many of her dragon riders killed, they still outnumbered us and swarmed to protect their mistress.

"Ballistas! Strike them before they angle!" Bella shouted.

I leaned down, Eden flaring in my palm, and conjured a golden blaze through my free hand. The cord stretched tight, and as I let go, the radiant spear soared in blinding light—

It hit the first turret square in its firemouth.

Explosion.

Flame and shrapnel roared into the sky.

"Nice shot!" Hunter called.

We banked again.

The castle gates loomed now.

The sky screamed as another of Emberveil's dragon riders crashed into us.

Spines of black flame streaked from their dragons' mouths, clashing mid-air with bolts of gold from Eden and hellish orange spirals of flame from Talonor and Krakos. Steel sang against steel as Hunter parried a strike mid-dive, his blade sparking against the hooked glaive of an enemy clad in molten-red plate.

Errax shrieked beneath me, ducking left as a dragon with blade-studded wings swiped low overhead. I nearly lost grip of her reins as we spun and dove, skimming so close to Raven's Bane Castle's outer rampart that my boot scraped stone and showered sparks behind us.

"We're not going to hold this long!" Bella cried into the wind, her arms locked around Hunter's waist as Talonor veered into a rising spiral.

"We don't need long!" I shouted back, Eden flaring hot in my palm. A wingless Emberveil dragon shrieked toward us—a malformed brute thick with deep scars in its shoulders. I didn't flinch.

I lifted my hand and hurled.

The golden bolt smacked into its snout like judgment, erupting in blinding light. The rider screamed wordlessly as the beast flailed, slamming into a tower and disintegrating in fire and stone.

But for every dragon that fell, three more took its place.

We were circling, boxed in above the queen's high castle. The spires had narrowed around us like teeth closing on prey, and I felt every beat of Errax's wings shudder under the strain of battle, her exhaustion coiling beneath her strength.

"She's sending everything she has!" Hunter shouted. "Her full airforce is converging!"

"She wants to drown us before we get close!" Bella hissed, eyes sculpted sharp with rage and worry.

And for a moment... I wasn't sure we were going to break through.

Then—

They came.

The wild dragons.

A mass of unbridled fury in the shape of dragons. They

erupted from the clouds like flame-touched blades—death given wings. Their mouths opened in endless shrieks as they dove, slicing downward into the Emberveil ranks with merciless precision.

I watched one—a great beast with spined silver horns—catch an Emberveil flier mid-bank and tear both rider and mount in two. Another snapped a rider's head off with a whip of its tail. The skies above Raven's Bane turned into a starstorm of scales and teeth.

One by one, the Emberveil riders broke formation.

And then, She arrived.

The scream that split the heavens caused all to shudder and shiver.

No, this sound made the others silence. For a single beat, the battle paused in the air, all wings halting like startled birds, every neck craning.

The shriek came again—deafening. And the mountain answered.

The mouth of Raven's Bane Castle belched smoke so thick it clotted the lungs of the wind. Flame spiraled wide out of the gate, and with it… came something worse than fire.

Brigodon.

The queen's dragon.

The first time I saw him, he'd looked like death sculpted from obsidian and blood. But now—now he descended like a mountain torn loose from the volcano and dipped in nightmares.

He was vast.

Colossal. Far bigger than Krakos. Even larger than the Great Mother Dragon, and still in his brutal prime.

Brigodon's eyes burned violet, not with fury—but with loyalty. His blackened scales shone like stars across a void, each webbed wing larger than two siege towers laid end to end. Horns curled along his head—twisting upward like the broken spires of dying gods.

He was alone. No queen on his back, but that didn't make him any less deadly.

The sight of the monumental beast of legend made my blood go cold.

"She sent him alone," I said. "No rider."

"She doesn't need to ride him," Hunter growled. "He is her will made flesh."

We hovered still, midair, as Brigodon rose into the skies above Raven's Bane, and the wild dragons paused.

Even Krakos stopped flapping, hovering as if unsure whether to strike or flee.

Then Brigodon roared.

It wasn't just sound—it was movement.

A wave rippled through the air, bending magic itself. Columns cracked. The pressure of it hit me like a hammer to the chest, even shielded by Eden. Errax bucked beneath me, crouching low midair like he wasn't just bigger—like he was older.

Then he moved.

Brigodon sailed past us with long, lazy flaps of wings the size of small villages. He didn't dive. He didn't scream again.

He stalked.

One slow circle over the battle, his gaze raking across every wild dragon, every Terradyne, every rider—

Until his eyes locked onto me.

Oh gods.

A chill unfurled down my spine. My stomach dropped as if someone had just whispered a word of power I wasn't supposed to know.

Brigodon had recognized me.

We'd fought before. The time I luckily defeated the queen. It was only a battle, but he remembered. He absolutely fucking remembered...

"What... what is he—" Bella stammered.

"He's after me," I said, narrowing my gaze back at the monster.

"Don't engage alone," Hunter ordered. "Ash—I swear—he'll tear you—"

"He's not attacking," I said.

And it was true.

Brigodon hovered above the battlefield like he was savoring the moment before the kill.

No aggression.

Just focus.

On me.

"He won't let you near the queen," Bella said, grim. "He's her final shield."

"No," I murmured. "He's more than that."

We watched as Brigodon wheeled up toward Calcaedus's summit. His mouth split, and violet fire lit the sky.

Dragons shrieked and scattered.

Three wild dragons were caught mid-turn. One disintegrated in a second, nothing left of it but raining bone. Another dropped, torn in half by the edge of flame.

Errax recoiled sharply.

I called upon Eden, the golden sword of magic raging with power in my hand.

"Ash—please," Bella said. "Don't be reckless. Wait—think! This is what the queen wants!"

I stared into the firestorm.

And saw Cade, chained again in my mind. Wounded. Waiting. Dying.

And somewhere behind this monster, the throne room where she expected to end me.

My soul tightened around Eden.

Lit with gold flame.

And I made my decision.

"I don't care what she wants."

"We fly," I said.

Straight through him.

Straight into hell.

Errax shrieked in reply.

And we flew up.

"No!" Many shouts came from below. Bella, Carina, Darren. But my mind was made up. I couldn't let Cade die. And if that fucking dragon was going to stand in the way of us, then that monster was going to feel every ounce of rage inside me.

The final assault against Raven's Bane had begun.

More shouts from below trying to stop me, and frantic dragon wings flapped to catch up to me, but Errax was swift in her pursuit.

If this is when I die, then let it be so. I'm not going to cower anymore. I'm going to fight. It's what I am. I readied all my magic, knowing it most likely wasn't enough. But I couldn't stop myself. The love I'd felt was too powerful to let slip away.

I can't lose him. I just can't…

A shadow slipped across the sun.

Not a cloud. Not smoke.

Something older.

Wider.

A hush washed through the warring sky as Brigodon banked higher above the battlefield. Violet fire laced through his teeth as he opened his colossal wings and screamed again, and this time…

This time the air split.

Everything—every breath, every spell, every dragon's flap—fractured with the sound.

But then—

Another roar answered.

Deeper.

Older.

Sadder.

And furious.

Across the battleground skies, a new shape rose from the clouds over the caldera — a dragon not summoned, not ridden, but roused.

The Great Mother.

The elder of the wild dragons.

For one suspended moment, everything froze.

As if even war needed to acknowledge what had arrived.

She broke through the haze like a dying star falling in reverse. Her wings stretched twice across the skyline, torn but regal, rippling with wind-worn triumph. Moss and scars adorned her, centuries of war tattooed in silver lashes of time across her gray-violet hide.

And yet she flew, fierce fire already curling around the base of her throat.

Her eyes locked on Brigodon.

Not with challenge.

With judgment.

This wasn't two dragons fighting for territory.

This was old rage. This was memory demanding its debt.

Brigodon spat flame, violet and vile, down toward the Great Mother Dragon before she'd reached him.

She dove under it neatly and rose again—tail curling like a whip as she climbed to meet him head-on.

And then—

They collided.

The sound was gods being ripped apart.

Brigodon slammed into her shoulder with a crash that made the clouds shudder. Talon met talon—a flurry of black and stone-colored blur as claws raked across scale. The Great Mother Dragon shrieked, her jaws snapping around Brigodon's throat once—drawing blood, actual blood that spilled through the air like rubies scattered from his veins.

But Brigodon wasn't done. He twisted mid-fall, coiling tightly, and slammed his horns into her chest. She bellowed, wings beating with gale-force winds as she pushed upward again.

My heart pounded in my chest as I watched helplessly, but brimming with hope.

"By the gods," Bella gasped from Talonor. "They'll tear the sky down."

"They already are," Hunter said grimly, guiding his dragon higher, keeping pace with us as we rose after them.

Below them, war faltered.

Even the queen's own kept their distance now. Fliers scattered. Firecasters pulled back from rooftops as debris from the aerial struggle rained down like burning hail.

We had to dodge a falling fragment of a half-melted tower—an old obsidian brace hurled downward from the sweep of the Great Mother's tail.

Krakos screamed a challenge from below, black wings catching the falling light as he cast his fury up toward Brigodon.

"I can take him," Hunter shouted. "Krakos and I—we can flank behind the Great Mother and—"

"Wait," Bella said, tugging at Hunter's shoulder. "Those two are the closest thing to living gods of this world. This is their fight."

Carina's voice sliced in from the opposite flank as she and Darren soared in on speckled gray dragons, both wide-eyed and wild.

"We can't just watch!" she cried out. "We owe her everything! She brought the wild dragons!"

Darren's jaw was clenched so tightly I thought his teeth would crack. "She's the reason half of us are still in the sky!"

"I know," I said softly.

The Great Mother Dragon roared as they fought. She sliced and clawed in a violent burst of ferocity unlike anything I'd ever seen. She was slower than the evil queen's dragon, but she had an instinct that surely was teaching every single dragon below lessons in savagery.

She attacked relentlessly, biting, bursting incinerating fire upon the great dragon. Indeed it was like two gods battling.

But Brigodon had already begun to overpower her.

He twisted hard while locked against her side, latching claws around her wing's joint, and ripped.

The Mother's scream cleaved the air.

Her wing bent, not fully broken—but shredded enough that her flight wavered.

Brigodon took the opening.

He rolled atop her midair—world-rending size pressing her down from the sky.

Krakos bellowed a warning.

Errax dove with them.

So did Talonor. So did Darren. So did Carina.

But we were too far.

Brigodon opened his jaws.

A blast of violet flame.

Straight across her face, into her eye, into her scaled jaw. It burst through the thick scales, muscle and even bone. It was the most terribly violent thing I'd ever seen.

Half of her head vanished in fire.

The Great Mother Dragon screamed—and then her wings crumpled.

She spiraled downward, blood and fire trailing from her ruined body.

No roar this time. No final shriek.

Just wind wailing around her once-mighty form.

"No... no no no—" I felt the panic rising before I could stop it.

She hit the side of the one of Emberveil's great spires.

The tower spike twisted through her midsection like a blade through cloth, catching her broken body on obsidian steel as stone and fire poured downward in a rain of ruin.

She convulsed once—great tail writhing.
Then stilled.
Krakos dove beside her.
But it was too late.
Silence hit harder than any roar.
Then—
The wild dragons howled.
I'd never heard sound like it.
It wasn't battle.
It wasn't a war cry.
It was grief.
Agony given breath.
They screamed. Roared. Their screeches bent sharp and bright through the ash-choked sky like mourning set to music. Some spiraled. Some backed from the fight entirely. One lost control of its flight completely and crashed hard into the side of Emberveil's south tower, breaking apart bone and wing.
The loss shattered them.
Their highest matriarch.
Gone.
Errax trembled under me.
I felt her breath quiver.
The Mother was like a lost mother to her. Her source. Her link to ancient blood.
Now she was skewered on the queen's city.
Brigodon circled slowly overhead—wings casting long shadows over the carnage he'd caused. He didn't roar.
Because he didn't revel.
He simply resumed his post above, mourning nothing.
He was waiting.
The queen would be watching.
She knew I'd see this.
She wanted me to mourn before I fought.

Carina was already pulling back, her face pale, staring down at the wreck of the tower, her expression unreadable.

Bella looked to me.

Tears in her eyes. Not just for the death. For what it would do.

"What now?" she asked.

I gritted my teeth. Ready to die if necessary.

I stared at Brigodon overhead, then down at the wild dragons breaking formation, some shrieking, some spiraling away.

I closed my eyes.

Errax pressed her head higher, looking up at the sky like a widow deciding whether to climb to her husband's pyre.

"No more waiting," I said.

Eden flared golden up the length of my arm.

"Ash! Wait!" Darren roared. He flew up to my side on his dragon. His hardened features grizzled like stone.

"I can kill it," I said through clenched teeth.

He sighed, exhaling through his nostrils as a sort of plea. "No. You cannot. You cannot fall now. Don't you see? None of us can stop the queen. You are the only chance we have at tomorrow. I can't send you to your death at the maw of that beast."

"I can't not try..."

His dragon drew closer so its wings nearly beat against Errax's. "You mustn't. I will hold the demon dragon back while you go." His daughter Carina flew beside him, her serious glare hitting me like shattered glass. I could tell from the look in her eyes she meant the same as her father.

I swallowed hard.

"Go," the leader of the Stormscales said to me. "Kill the queen. Save the future we have one last fucking shot at."

"I can't leave you..." a tear streamed down my cheek I quickly swiped away, choking down more.

"You think the Stormscales are afraid of any dragons?" Darren said with a dark grin. "We were bred for this. This is our moment. This is our one chance at redemption too. This is our chance for revenge. But if you don't make it, then this is all for nothing…"

"I—" I muttered.

"Go," Carina said with a stern nod. "Before I knock your stubborn ass out and fly you up to the fucking ugly castle myself."

Errax grumbled beneath me, waiting for my answer.

I hesitated. I didn't know what to do. But then the words in my head from back on the beach in Bramblebash returned to me. *It is time. You must free me. You've awoken to your true self, and so you must awaken me…*

I gripped the reins and tightened my seat on the saddle. "Fight hard. Hold their forces back. I've got an ancient dragon to awaken."

Errax took me forward, straight towards Raven's Bane Castle. Behind, I heard Darren barking commands, and I felt Hunter and Bella fly after me.

I spun to tell them to turn back, but by the fiery stare Bella gave me, I understood. They were with me until the end.

CHAPTER 44

$\mathcal{E}$mberveil's skies were chaos unfurled—dragons locked in spirals like blades in a grinder, wings torn to ribbons mid-air, fire screaming through veins of smoke so thick the sun couldn't find us anymore. There were too many sounds to count —shrieks of dragons, the whistle of death-marched spears, the cracking groan of ancient stone collapsing under fire. But one sound haunted me over all the rest.

The Great Mother Dragon's death moan.

Her massive broken skull still smoldered above the high temple spire, her great body impaled like a sacrifice the queen had waited centuries to offer. Her wings hung limp around the arches, three wild dragons still shrieking in a blood-wrung circle around her body, like children unable to accept that home would not rise again.

My gut heaved with grief.

No time.

No time for mourning.

It was a monumental loss to our forces. But I had to make it up to the keep. I had to make it to Raven's Bane. I had to face the

"

queen. It was the only way left. Straight at the evil heart of the wicked city.

"Ash—!" Hunter's voice ripped through the air. "Look down!"

I spun Errax in a sharp arc and caught the sight just as the smoke split.

The Terradyne.

Gods.

The stone-born warriors of the mountain were still standing —but some… weren't.

One—the twisted, moss-crowned giant that had towered above Storm's End—was now facedown in a pool of fire, unmoving. Limbs broken. Roots severed. His twin had a spear through his chest. Fire flared as branches still burned on his back. The Sythers had learned how to kill them.

Shock rushed through me like a frozen tide.

"No…" I breathed.

All around the upper ridgelines, Emberveil's crimson-crafted spears tore into our allies with renewed hunger. At least a dozen tree-bound Terradyne now shrieked as Sythers doused them in red-blight pitch and lit them alight with laughing torches. Roots curled on themselves. Limbs flailed. Smoke vented in geysers from holes where bark had been hammered off their shoulders.

"This can't—" Bella's words stopped with a gasp.

Outside the ruins near the queen's back wall, I spotted two rock-bodied Terradyne squadmates—crack-shouldered, giant-limbed. Both were flailing blindly. One tumbled after being struck in the eyes with a molten-red bolt. Sythers crept behind the tumbling behemoth and shoved him toward the waterfall edge lining the back half of the Ember gate, a sheer drop almost a thousand feet down Calcaedus' ridge.

I didn't even have time to scream.

He tumbled.

Toppled.

Gone.

Another followed.

Then another.

And I—

My hands gripped the rigging as Errax reeled skyward—but I didn't tell her to.

She felt it.

The war was shifting.

We were bleeding too fast.

"Damn it!" Hunter swung by on Talonor, the two of them flushed with iron and sweat. "We're losing ground—she's pulling everything she has!"

"We can't fall back," he shouted. "Keep your focus. It's time, Ash!"

Raven's Bane Castle loomed above us like a carved threat of shadow and glass-blood. Tapestries licked by fire flapped from its studs. Smoke poured from its uppermost spires, and somewhere behind its arched, blackened windows, I knew—

She watched.

The queen.

With her cursed half-smile.

Every second I lingered...

Cade suffered more.

Brigodon let out a thunderous roar that cracked the sky. Darren, Carina and their men flew valiantly upward as the monstrous queen's dragon began a slow descent at them; flames licking out of its massive maw.

"Get to her," Hunter said suddenly, straightening in the saddle. "Now."

Bella turned beside him, eyes wide, soft—but her mouth was set sharp. "Ash," she said, her voice soft with something thick and heavy in it. "It's time."

My jaw clenched and I narrowed my eyes at my target.

Errax. Fly. Fly like this is your last flight. Because it very well may be...

I swallowed.

The sky howled.

I turned to Bella up on Talonor's back with Hunter, nearly flying straight.

She grinned, because of course she did.

"Bring us her crown," she said.

Then I faced forward.

Errax surged.

"Fly," I whispered. "Fly!"

And together—we tore through thick smoke toward the queen's gate.

Time to break a throne.

The wind was still screaming behind us, even up here, even with the balcony doors just ahead.

Errax's claws clanged against black stone as she landed, her wings folding slow and stiff. Blood slicked her neck and thighs, some of it drying, some not. She was trembling, not from exhaustion, but from restraint—like every inch of her was begging to follow me through that doors at the far end of the jutting black balcony to the keep.

But she wouldn't fit.

Not this time.

Not in this part of the fight.

Not for what came next.

Krakos touched down second, his great shadow darkening the entrance as he landed with clawed footing so precise I felt the slab we stood on vibrate—not crack, not groan. Just flex. Talonor landed last, his gray hide flecked with ash and splinters of bone from the upper air. I caught Bella's hand as she swung down and gave her a look.

This would be it.

She nodded once, no words.

Hunter dismounted with practiced grace, his blade already half out of the sheath in the same breath. "This is the high tier," he said, scanning the double doors of black iron. "Top of Raven's Bane. There's nowhere else to run now."

And no one left to hide from.

The doors stood nearly three times my height—sleek obsidian carved with serpentine grooves that shimmered faintly in golden swirls. No guards stood watch. No fire burned around the arch. Just stone. Cold. Quiet. Waiting.

Bella stepped up beside me and poked one of the handles with the tip of her dagger. It creaked on the hinges as the immense doors moved slightly. She let out a soft, sarcastic chuckle. "This is absolutely not a trap."

Hunter gave a humorless half-smile. "Doors like this don't open unless she means them to."

Still, I placed one hand on the iron just beneath the carving of the queen's burning crown, and with one solid push, the left door creaked wide on ancient hinges.

A hiss of warm air met us like breath.

And then the silence swallowed everything.

Inside, the corridor was nothing like I imagined.

It wasn't a grand hall. There were no banners hanging from the rafters. No throne visible yet. No gold walls.

It was just black stone.

Spider-veined with red. Slick.

The dragons hissed on the balcony, unable to fit through the tall, yet narrow doors. I waved for them to stay, and that it would be alright. At least I told myself that.

The floor gleamed like polished onyx under the flame of a single torch far ahead, half-collapsed in its wall-mount. A faint glow lit the corridor beyond, flickering and low—too low for how deep the torch must've burned down—but no other light followed.

Nothing about it made sense.

Hunter stepped forward beside me, his blade now fully

unsheathed. "No guards. No footsteps. She's either that confident—"

"Or already waiting just past the dark," Bella finished grimly.

Fear coiled at my stomach's edge, twisting sharp.

This was it.

Every memory, every horrible scream, every burn over my back, all the wandering and wondering if I would live longer than tomorrow—it all spiraled into the mouth of this hallway now.

I drew Eden's blade, the golden fire carving a slow pulse through the stone at my side.

"Let's finish this."

We stepped inside.

The air grew colder with every footfall. Not like when the wind shifted or the weather turned, but like heat itself had been drained from earlier parts of the castle to feed the place ahead. My boots tapped like whispers against slick stone. Shadows swam slowly just beyond the reach of the torchlight.

But then—something scuttled across the floor.

Right at the edge of my boots.

And I screamed.

A full, high, startled sound, like I didn't have dragons behind me or god-killing magic in my palm.

I nearly dropped my sword.

"By the lakes—" Bella blurted, already sweeping her dagger left. "What is it?"

"Something moved!" I squeaked, half-dancing to the side. A tiny squeak came as it continued scuttling across the floor. My heart thumped hard and I clutched my sword.

Hunter froze.

His eyes tracked the motion.

Then—

He blinked.

"It's a mouse."

What followed was a beat too long of silence.

I stared at it.

It paused just near the curve of a floor stone, small brown body frozen mid-scamper, eyes wide with that eerie rodent glisten.

"Of course," I breathed through gritted teeth. "A mouse. In the murder hall of darkness. Of course…"

Bella snorted. Looped her arm through mine.

"You could torch half the continent," she said cheerily, "but that fear of mice? That's forever, babe."

I shuddered dramatically. "It looked bigger in the shadows."

The torch at the end of the hall flickered again—brighter this time.

Hunter frowned.

"The fire… it's changing."

The flame pulsed then went perfectly still.

And then—

Wind.

It didn't come from behind, from the outside winds. It came from within the keep.

A vicious blast of cold air surged inward with taloned force. I heard the doors slam open, heard Bella inhale sharply, felt Hunter lurch as the wind picked him up along with her and flung both—

Backward.

The doors screamed on their hinges—

And I turned just in time to see them slam shut.

Locked.

Trapped.

I ran.

"Oh gods—"

"Bella!"

"Hunter!"

My voice rang off cold stone. I threw myself at the black doors. Pounded once.

They didn't move.

No creak.

No glimmer of light.

Nothing.

"No!" I shouted. "Open, open—you don't get to—!"

But the silence that followed was deep.

Larger than silence.

It was a hush sewn by choice.

By her.

The queen.

I spun back to the single torch still lit at the far end.

Suddenly—it didn't seem so distant.

Just waiting.

Alone.

Like me.

I swallowed.

And took my first breath alone in the queen's castle. For the last time.

The air in the corridor thickened with every step I took.

A heaviness settled inside my lungs, like I was trying to breathe through tar. The golden glow from Eden's blade pulsed faintly in my hand, casting slow arcs of light that made the shadows on the walls twitch and stretch like living things.

Wind no longer howled through the stone—silence had curled around the hall like a prayer unanswered. There were no echoes of battle, no cries of dragons, no clang of sword on sword anymore. Just the sound of my footfalls, and the frantic drumming of my heartbeat, and the queasy, sharp-tongued voice in my head whispering: This is wrong.

Somewhere behind me, beyond those sealed black doors, Bella and Hunter were shouting for me. I could still hear them faintly, fists beating against wood that would not break. Words smothered before they ever reached my ears.

I was alone.

Of course I was.

I staggered forward another step, raising Eden's blade before me, golden light washing out across the black floor like syrup poured over ice. It lit the stone beneath me, reflected up the walls, but it didn't bite the shadows back entirely. The deeper I stepped, the closer the dark seemed to lean forward again, eager to reclaim what I tried to illuminate.

Then—

"Warm thinking, child. But dim your fire—it won't reach far where ancient wrongs have rooted deep."

I spun.

"Cornelius?" I whispered.

There he was.

His translucent, half-faded shape hovered just over my right shoulder. Only half there—ghostly, like mist curling from a hot stone, but clear enough that I could see his shell marked by cracks of time deepened since I'd last truly looked. His head bobbed slowly.

"Don't ask how I slipped in," he murmured gently, "I'm not even sure I did."

"What is this place?" I breathed, my voice cracking. "It—it doesn't feel real."

"No," his voice was low, like a hush etched into truth. "It's not."

"A spell?"

"A crucible."

I blinked at him. "Meaning what?"

"Meaning, it will press every edge of your fear against every muscle of your will. And the queen designed it just for you. We are in the palace, yet also not..." Cornelius took a step closer to me—almost floating above the ground, his clawed feet not even brushing the stone. He turned to the walls, to the floor, gaze sweeping with quiet dread.

"I have a bad feeling about what you're about to see," he said.

There was sorrow in his voice. Shame, even.

I clenched my jaw. "How do I fight it?"

His head slowly wagged. "You'll have to dig deep. Deeper than your training. You're going to have to become the prophesized Gold-Marked you were meant to be."

"What?"

He turned fully to me now, eyes glowing faint in the gloom. "Your true test begins, Ash."

My chest tightened.

"But…" he continued, voice softer, "your Gilded Radiance is not just a trinket of power. It's your soul speaking in light. It will do more than blind shadows—it will show you truth if you let it."

I breathed hard, nodded once. Swallowed thickly.

"Use your magic," he said, "and pray it saves you. I have shown you all I have to show you. The rest of the journey is yours… May Odiun, and all the forgotten gods watch over you… I pray to see you again child… Good luck, and remember who you are…"

Then he vanished.

No smoke. No spell.

Just gone, like the last warmth pulled from the air with him.

I stood in the golden dim of my blade, the only light. Gripping the hilt tighter. Pressing forward.

The corridor opened into a hollowed chamber—round and echoless.

And I saw him.

A figure beneath the single flame mounted far away across the dome.

He stood centered—tall, unmoving.

My breath caught.

Cade.

The shape was unmistakable. Broad shoulders. Jaw like carved stone. Hair blacker than the void around it, tousled, with strands fallen across a brow I'd memorized in grief. He wore no armor now—just charred storm-leathers etched with veins of red. His arms were bare to the elbows, and veins glowed faint beneath his skin, laced with flickering embers as though his blood itself burned.

A fog of violet smoke curled around his feet, coiling like something alive.

"Cade!" I shouted, hope rupturing out of me so fast it startled even me.

But he didn't move.

He didn't raise his head or speak my name.

He just stood there in the center of the room, surrounded by that awful hum. That dark vibration under the floor, shaking so subtly it might've only been my heartbeat—but wasn't.

The staff slid free from his right hand with a long, scraping sound.

The golden phoenix head sparkled for only half a breath—then dulled.

In his left hand, the tip of a blackened sword trailed against the floor with a scree that vibrated my teeth. Its edge pulsed—no longer the stained blade I'd seen him wield before, but one imbued with something wrong. Infernal. Its runes didn't glow—they bled.

"No," I whispered.

It hit me, full force.

That wasn't my Cade.

Not really.

But it was.

Every inch of me screamed both things at once.

He lifted his head.

And the moment I saw his eyes, I stopped breathing.

They were still blue. Still cold fire. But stained.

Black bled out from his pupils in spider-weaving rings. Shadow curled beneath them like he hadn't slept in moons. His skin—tan and glorious days ago—had gone ash-grey across the jaw like rot tickling at perfect symmetry.

But worst was his expression.

Not blank.

Pained.

Resolved.

"Ash," he said.

My name in his voice was a blade in the ribs.

"Ash, you need to stop." He stepped forward once, and the runes on the floor beneath his boot shimmered faint red.

My grip tightened on Eden's hilt. "What—what have they done to you?"

He exhaled, head tilting as if he expected me not to understand. "I asked them to do it."

The words scraped across my chest.

"No." I shook my head. "No you didn't."

"I did." He took another step. That horrible fog seemed to breathe with him. "To save you."

"This isn't saving me—"

"I feared it would come to this," he continued, hands clenched now. "You shouldn't have kept going. You shouldn't have insisted."

"Insisted?" I snapped. "Cade, I fought through fire and death for you. I burned half the gods-forsaken sky for you! For this!"

"Yes," he said, voice trembling now. "You did fight to get to this point... You're strong, Ash. Stonger than you know. Stronger than the queen knows..."

"I don't want your god damned pride," I sobbed. "I want you."

His shoulders twitched, visibly. Hurt flickered. Then he looked down.

"You can't get to her. The queen—I can't let you harm her."

I blinked. "What?"

"I..." He raised his head again. The shadow grew heavier across his face. "She's... changed something in me. I can't explain it. But now I know—if she dies... everything breaks. She's part of the binding holding magic in its place. Holding peace."

I took a step back, horror twisting my gut. "You're lying."

"I'm not. I'm protecting Allovan."

"Lies—You're wrong. You know it deep down inside, Cade. Find yourself. You're still in there… Please…"

"If she dies," he said, quieter now, "We all die. All of us."

"No," I whispered.

He lifted the blackened sword.

"If you mean to harm her…"

His voice cracked.

"You'll have to kill me first."

For a long, still moment, I stopped breathing.

He stood before me, sword drawn.

Glowing.

Wrong.

But still him.

Still Cade.

And I loved him.

And he might be the end of me.

I took a trembling step toward him.

His eyes flickered, the blue swallowed further by streaks of inky black. He didn't lower the sword.

The sound of his armor echoed off the stone as he stepped forward, slow and deliberate. Every thud of his metal boots against the floor matched the rhythm of my heartbeat—steady, sure, and drenched in dread.

His cloak trailed behind him, dragging through the violet mist like it belonged to another era—a relic from a prince shaped in fire now barely holding his form together. That cloak had been splayed behind him the first time I ever saw him on Krakos's back—regal, terrifying, beautiful.

But he wasn't beautiful now. Not to me.

He felt like a nightmare I couldn't shake.

"Cade," I said, voice small—but not yet broken. "Please. Wake up from this. This isn't you. We can still beat her. We can still win…"

His steps faltered—just for a heartbeat.

Then they resumed. Clink. Clank. The staff in his right hand hissed with flame. Not warm fire. Not even Cade's fire.

It was cold. Serrated. The kind that didn't comfort, the kind that crawled down throats and left skin blistered from within.

"There is no fight to be had against her," he said, his voice softer now, but strange—split, almost. His tongue twisted his vowels, made them wrong. That was his mouth. His cadence. But not his voice. Not entirely. "The queen... my stepmother...she is balance. Rhythm. The tether Allovan clings to."

"No," I breathed, my grip tightening on Eden. "She's the flame devouring everything."

"She contains it." His chin dropped slightly, and I could see the sweat shining faint on his brow despite the cold shadows. "Without her, the old barriers fall. The veil between gods and men splits. You don't understand what she's doing, Ash. What she's holding back."

I stared into him, searching for something—anything real inside his stained eyes.

"You know what she's doing," I whispered, daring a step closer. "She's killing. Enslaving. She's bled this world dry and sells power like it's coin. She destroyed your father. Your kingdom. My family." I swallowed. "Me and you."

His mouth twitched. Pain flickered. But it was gone too quickly. "There is no me and you, Ash. Not anymore. I don't know if there ever was..."

My knees nearly buckled. A deep breaking tore my heart into shards, splintering out into the rest of my body, erupting tears down my cheeks.

He nodded once. Slow. Almost sad. "I... I only needed you alive long enough. I needed your power."

The words fell like ash. "You... you're lying... she's controlling you somehow..."

And everything inside me caved.

I shook my head slowly, my braids sticking to the damp along my jaw. I wiped the tears back as a deep fire burned hot in my core. "No…"

"Yes," he said, too calm. Too straight-faced. "When she told me what you were—I had to get close. You were the sword I needed to unsheathe, the key to an older door neither of us knew how to open."

"Stop," I breathed, but my voice trembled like a child's hands.

"You were born of prophecy," he said, stepping into the golden shine of Eden at last. The light cast long wavering shadows across the side of his face. His mouth. His torn armor. "And I was taught to obey prophecy. You only ever had one purpose, Ashlyn Mist. You are to be destroyed, and then the world can finally know peace. You're the missing piece, the final piece to the puzzle that will heal our world. You thought what we had was love, but it was just lust. I've always desired most what I couldn't have… and in the end, you were easier to get than I'd hoped. There was never anything special between us. It was all just an illusion."

Every part of me screamed in denial. I could barely hold Eden upright.

"I don't believe you," I whispered.

"You don't have to believe me," he replied. "Only understand."

The volcano shuddered beneath us.

A deep, groaning quake hiccupped through the walls, sending great cracks through the floor of the throne hall. Bits of stone crumbled from the vaulted ceiling, scattering between us in small thumps like the chamber was trying to cough itself apart.

Dust slit through the air.

"Cade," I choked, trying to breathe through the stone tightening in my chest. "Please. Please fight whatever she's done to you. You have to remember me. Remember the bond between us. Its stronger than her dark spell over you. We are connected more than anything I've ever felt before. You showed me what it truly meant to be alive. That wasn't wrong. That wasn't a lie. I still feel it. Don't you? Deep down? Don't you still love me?"

He stood still.

Silent.

I took another step forward.

"I love you," I said, louder now. "Even when you tried to push me away. Even when you said no, even when you a miserable, unsufferable asshole, I still—still love you."

His eye twitched.

His jaw tensed.

For a fleeting second, the runes near his feet dimmed.

My heartbeat lifted.

"Cade—"

"I never loved you. You're nothing but a slave orphan. Did you really think you could be with a prince? You're a fool. Just an ignorant child swept up in something you don't understand. Your feelings are misguided. I could never love someone… like you…"

Something twisted in me.

He spoke it cold.

Flat.

And hollow.

It didn't sound like him. Not even wrapped in the queen's magic. It sounded like a line memorized from a script written in someone else's ashes.

I took a step back. It felt like walking off a cliff.

"The queen needs your magic. You're the final one. And when she has it, then all will be the way it was meant… The Cinderyn will rule for another ten thousand years. The queen will protect us, and punish those who rebel with the fury of her fire."

I wanted to scream.

I wanted to believe he was lying.

But he'd buried the words so deep in detachment, they didn't even echo anymore. No more hesitation. No more pain.

Just duty.

Just betrayal.

"Then why did you bleed for me?" I said, voice escaping raw and wild. "Why hold me when I broke? Why catch me from the sky and beg me not to die, Cade—why kiss me like I was a world you couldn't reach fast enough?"

"I was a crown prince," he replied. "Even if I had feelings for you, we could never be. Even with the curse lifted, it was all just *one, big, lie.*"

A sound left my throat I didn't recognize.

It wasn't a sob.

It wasn't fury.

It was loss cracking its way out. Pure, dumb, broken loss.

The volcano roared again. Louder. Bolder.

Like the mountain grieved with me.

From behind a long crack in the wall, molten light slipped through, orange-gold licking the base of the throne room floor, and Cade's shadow flickered against it. For the barest breath, I thought it looked like a boy.

Not a man.

Like someone younger. Someone who hadn't turned yet.

But then he moved.

And the cold light made him monstrous again.

He gripped the blackened blade tighter.

And I knew what was coming.

"I'm sorry, Ash," he said. "I wish it didn't have to end this way."

Like someone reading a final line before a curtain fell.

"I can't let you past."

"Cade," I said one last time. "Please…"

He said nothing.

He stepped forward and lifted the sword to strike.

"You'll have to kill me," he said again. "Or I'll kill you."

And in that moment—the earth cracked beneath both of us.

I raised Eden.

And everything I loved became a battlefield.

Then the fight began.
And it would end one of us.
Or maybe, both.
And already—I didn't know which I feared more.
Not anymore.

CHAPTER 46

*S*teel met magic in the space between our hearts.

Cade's sword came down like thunder.

I cried out as Eden flared to life in my palm, gold-light screeching against the black blade he swung. The clash split the air between us, sending a shimmer of heat racing through the onyx floor. I staggered back a half-step, barely blocking his second strike as he hammered forward, relentless.

He didn't pause.

Didn't hesitate.

Didn't pull his swings.

Cade Phoenixfire—my love, my betrayer—was trying to kill me.

I was astonished my magic could withstand his blows. Any normal man standing against those strikes would be cleaved in two, but my magical sword hummed with power.

His blade whirled like a storm-god's pulse, brutal and reactive —everything I'd trained for between tears and kisses now twisted into a razor meant to end me.

"Cade… please—"

But he didn't hear me.

Or maybe he wouldn't.

I ducked beneath his third blow and rolled backward across cracked obsidian. Eden's flame arced out from my hand mid-spin, a half-slash that forced him back for one precious heartbeat.

His boots skidded on the molten-slick stone, but only just.

He straightened, breathing sharp, dark eyes near lost to the void as fire curled around his limbs like living chains. Violet sparks danced along his collarbone, his jaw clenched tight hard enough to crack a tree root. His glare was unreadable—but there was hurt beneath it. I could feel it pulse beneath every strike.

Why are you doing this? I thought, knowing the answer.

The queen had taken him. Bent the hollow places in his heart into weapons. Somehow she had changed him. This wasn't the man I loved. But he was in there still. I had to believe that.

"...I can't let you through," he said through clenched teeth, voice rough but quiet. "The cost will be too high, Ashlyn."

"Cade," I begged, stepping back, lowering Eden slightly, "you don't have to do this. You're not well. Please, I can—Cornelius can help—"

"I need to save this world from you!" he roared, and flame erupted from his shoulders like wings snapping open.

The burst of magical fire rolled out from behind him in a concussive shockwave, slamming into the walls of the queen's sanctum with a shriek of heat and light. The oil sconces along the back wall exploded in a rush of smoke.

I raised my radiating sword just before the fire swallowed me whole. Her light scattered the flames in a protective shell—but even still, my arms shook from the force of it.

His magic was so... powerful... it was like the queen's when I fought her.

"I am bound to Mortriana," he said hoarsely, stepping closer as the smoke between us faded. "If she dies... everything ends. That is the price of failure."

Tears spilled. I hardly noticed them.

"That's a lie! She's controlling you! You have to fight whatever is inside you!" I shouted. "Look around you, Cade! This is your father's palace—twisted into a graveyard! How many more have to suffer before you believe she's the reason for all this chaos and war?"

His mouth clenched.

A flicker of something—of him—shivered in his ruined eyes.

Then it hardened again.

"I loved you," he said. Voice soft. "But that's over. There's nothing left between us, Ash. You're nothing to me now…"

It hit like a spear between my ribs.

"And now I have to be the one to end your rebellion." His hand tightened on the twisted black sword. "I've made peace with that…"

My breath caught in a sob. "By the gods—Cade—"

"I'm sorry," he murmured, voice breaking on the end. "But it has to be this way… there was never meant to be a happy ending between us."

He raised the sword again.

"No!" I screamed, and swung my sword, lit by the godlike Gilded Radiance in me to block just as he lunged forward.

Our blades collided—gold fire against blackened infernal metal—and the heavens above us cracked.

This time we didn't just clash.

We broke.

Eden's light split across the chamber in a harsh arc, throwing molten reflections against the stained window arches. Sparks rained from the point of impact, and I felt every jolt through my bones.

"You have to stop—" I cried, parrying another hit, harder this time, pushing him back a few steps. "This isn't you. The Cade I knew wouldn't let the queen turn him into her monster! He's stronger than her. He's better than what she trained him to be."

He came again, a blur of flame and muscle, striking with the desperation of someone who'd already written his own eulogy. I barely deflected his sword from slicing my side, turning his blade into the wall with a scream of steel on stone.

"I'm not hers! I don't belong to anyone!" he shouted—biting those words like they hurt more than any wound. "I'm doing this for Allovan!"

"You're doing this because you're being controlled!" I snapped, my sword's grip singing in my hands. "But I'm not. Not anymore."

He roared and struck again, black fire curling along the length of his sword like a dragon lashing through rot. I danced back, pivoted, brought my own blade down across his next stroke— and finally, for just a heartbeat, he faltered.

His knee buckled.

I could've landed a heavy blow onto his neck.

I didn't.

"Cade," I said softly, desperately.

His head lifted. Shadows writhed behind his eyes.

And behind me, Cornelius finally spoke.

His voice was low and grave, like thunder cracking in winter.

"Ash."

My breath hitched.

"Ash, you're going to have to kill Cade."

"No…"

"There's no other option. He can't hear you. He can't listen. The queen has twisted him. His soul is corrupted. That soul—the part of him that's left… she's holding it in her jaws now. I'm sorry, child."

My legs quivered.

But Cornelius pressed on, bloomed louder in my mind, unrelenting.

"If you don't stop him—if you don't kill him—he will kill you. And if you die, then everything ends. The fire she's kindled will consume Allovan and scorch your history into nothing. The

Terradyne. The Whisps. The Aqualorian remnants. All of it—ashes."

"You must live. Even if he does not."

Tears streaked my face. "I can't," I whispered, even as I lifted my blade. It glowed fiercer. Eden responded—not cold. Not harsh. But resolute.

"You loved him," Cornelius said gently.

"I still do, Cornelius… I always will…" I rasped.

He paused. "Then—that's what'll make your blade true. Do it. Finish it so you can get to the queen. We're running out of time!"

Eden's sword in my hands crackled white-gold. The magic swelled until it hummed in my wrist and split the floor in silver veins. Light poured around my feet like sunrise breaking in reverse.

I stared down Cade from the shadow of his doubt and raised the blade again, heart in shreds, arms shaking.

"I don't want to hurt you," I said through tears—but my voice didn't waver. "I swear I don't. Don't make me… please… I love you… I can't lose you. I've lost everything. Please…"

My voice cracked.

He inhaled.

And fire wrapped around him like a crown.

He stepped forward slowly, his eyes glinting in the flames like he'd already decided how the world ended.

"One of us has to die, Ash. There's no other way. I'm sorry…"

And then he charged.

Our love, our hate, our grief—all collision.

Our magic collided.

Gold lightning burst from Eden, met by spiraling violet flame from Cade's blade and staff as he drove them straight against me, our hands locked in opposite flight, our weapons screaming for each other's blood. The boom rocked the entire chamber—pillars cracked, walls wept flakes of ash, and embers rained down like a funeral storm.

He shoved with more strength than I'd ever seen in him. Worn, wrathful, unyielding.

My knees scraped stone; sparks split down the side of my boot.

Another blow, and I grunted with effort, sweat streaking down my back beneath my torn armor. Cade moved like a man with nothing left to lose.

No, not a man.

A weapon.

His sword arced wide and I parried, but too late—his blade sliced clean across my shoulder, crimson blooming instantly into my sleeve. I cried out as my sword flared gold-hot in response. My own magic lashed out in raw defense—Eden didn't like me hurt.

The light brightened, its wail ringing off the walls as I spun low and sent a searing wave of power across the cracked floor— but Cade jumped it, rolled beneath, fire already curling along his phoenix-head staff.

His mouth opened, and he roared a word long and old, and fire exploded from his call—straight toward me.

I threw Eden across my chest like a shield and screamed as the impact rocked me off my feet, heat clanging through every nerve. I hit the stone hard, coughing smoke from my lungs. Eden blinked in my palm and dimmed, just for a second.

I barely had time to rise before Cade was on me again. His sword whirled down toward my head—

Clang!

I caught it mid-swing. One-handed.

Eden locked against his blade, and I pushed up with every-thing in me, sobbing as blood streamed from the slash on my shoulder.

"Damn it!" I cried. "Stop this! I don't want to fight you! The queen is the enemy, not me. Wake up from this!"

"You can't win, Ash!" Cade shouted, fire wrapping around his limbs again. It spilled from his mouth, his eyes, the cracks in his armor—his very veins carried it now. A moving pyre. "You don't understand the depth of her power. She will not fall! And I— I won't let you die proving otherwise!"

He lunged again, and this time I ducked, spun, and drove my magical sword into the meat of his armor. I felt the resistance— then it gave, sliding into the joint at his side. He grunted loud and broke away, staggering, one hand clutching his ribs.

"Cade—!" I tried again. "Stop this! I don't want to hurt you!" I barely saw him through my tear-soaked eyes.

"You keep saying that," he spat, staggering upright. "But you're damn good at trying!"

Then his eyes went black.

I'd never seen them like that—not even against the queen.

No blue.

No ember.

As if the last of him had finally sunk into the queen's rot.

The fire ignited in a spiral around his body, too bright to be natural, too vicious to aim. It screamed in tongues I didn't under- stand, burning the very carvings from the walls.

Then he rose and ran at me.

I barely had time to raise my sword before our blades met again—and again—and again. Sparks flew with each clash as blue-fire and gold-light tore grooves into the stone around us. The floor cracked under our feet. The room became white-hot with rage and colliding magic.

He caught me hard with the hilt of his sword to the gut, and I yelped as I dropped to one knee—

And that's when he struck.

He tore my sword from my hand with his flame-bound grip and slammed me back against the floor.

I cried out as the heat around us swirled tighter, violet fire crawling along the stones toward my legs. Cade straddled my hips, his blade lowered—blackened now, its edge pulsing not with power, but with intent.

The blade hovered at my throat.

I couldn't breathe.

His eyes burned under the ruin of his brow—rage, hurt, betrayal—

And something else.

"Go on," I hissed, trying and failing to keep my tears at bay. "Prove to me you never loved me. Because I don't believe you."

His jaw trembled.

But he didn't push the blade farther.

He didn't move it—

Just... hovered.

His hand shook.

"You love me. I know you do. I know it more than anything in this miserable, fucked up world. I love you Cade, forever..." I whispered.

"Shut up—"

"You had the chance to kill me," I snapped, "and you didn't. Why didn't you, Cade?"

He didn't answer.

But his breathing grew uneven.

And I saw it.

The way his eyes flicked—not to me, but behind him.

Where Cornelius's golden shell shimmered ghost-like against the shadows. Half-visible. Half-real. Still and silent.

He hadn't noticed it before.

It startled him now.

I used it.

My magic ignited—Gilded Radiance erupted from my chest—bright gold, alive, thrumming like a river suddenly unchained.

The floor cracked.

The room flashed white.

Cade was thrown backward with a furious roar—he hit

Cornelius's shell and stumbled, crashing over the shell and onto his back.

I was already moving.

I grabbed my dagger, rolled over the broken marble tiles, and flung myself on top of him.

My knees pinned his shoulders.

Gold magic wrapped around his limbs like bands of light bursting from my palms.

I held the dagger to his throat, my whole body trembling against his chest.

And he stared up at me.

Still possessed.

Still stained.

But his eyes…

His eyes flickered.

"Do it," he rasped, almost a whisper.

I choked.

Tears slid down my jaw, splattered onto his cheeks, his hands—

He didn't move.

He didn't even flinch.

This man—this weapon, this warrior—lay under me now, eyes open, throat bare, and begged me to put him out of his misery.

I cried harder.

"Cade," I whispered. "You couldn't kill me. Even when you could."

His jaw clenched, but his gaze finally broke—it drifted, like he couldn't bear to hold mine.

"You're still in there," I said. "You're still fighting."

"I'm tired, Ash," he whispered. "Tired of losing. Tired of being a pawn. If this is how I die, so be it. Give me a warrior's death. Everything inside me is black. I'm a plague in this world."

My hands shook.

I could end this.

I had to.

If I didn't—if the queen made him fight me again—I might not have the upper hand a second time.

My tears dripped faster, freckling his chest.

"I can't," I said through a sob.

"Do it," he whispered, closing his eyes. "Be stronger than me. Because if you don't kill me, Ash, then I'll kill you."

I raised the dagger.

"Kill him, Ash," Cornelius begged. "The queen's magic is too powerful over him. There's no way to break it. It's too deep in him. I'm sorry, but do it while you can!"

"There has to be another way," I sobbed.

"Ash, it's him, or the world…" Cornelius said beside me, half-translucent and with a somber tone. "Love isn't strong enough to break the sickness in him. You have to get to the queen, and he'll never let you while he draws breath…"

Something inside me stirred. It was like crippling pain of the heart so intense I didn't think I could live anymore. I couldn't live without him. He was my everything.

Then I kissed him.

I couldn't help it.

It just happened.

My lips crashed over his—warm and desperate and aching with everything I couldn't say.

The world spun—and for once, I welcomed the fall of it.

Fire cracked around us—but I didn't care. The burn couldn't hurt more than what I was about to do.

I pulled back.

Cade's eyes were closed.

I raised the dagger to strike.

Then—

His hand shot up.

And caught my wrist.

I gasped, too stunned to react.

He pushed up suddenly, twisting me partially off him—but not away.

Instead of shoving the dagger down—

He leaned in.

And kissed me.

Again.

Softer this time.

And trembling.

"Cade—" I whispered, terrified and breathless.

His eyes filled with tears.

"My name," he said softly.

His voice cracked.

"You said my name."

Light flickered around his chest—faint gold mixing with red, violet bleeding into fire.

"No one's said it like that in so long."

His jaw trembled.

And then he gasped—once, hard. A sob caught in his throat—and I felt it.

I felt the weight of whatever held him—

Shatter.

"Ash… is that you?" he asked, voice breaking.

His hand let go of the dagger.

The look in his eyes was clear.

Real.

"Cade?" I whispered.

He nodded once. "You… you saved me. Ash. You pulled me free again."

My heart screamed in my chest.

He reached up and cupped my jaw, voice wrecked. "I owe you... everything."

Tears spilled down both our faces.

I let the dagger fall.

He curled both arms around me.

And for one perfect moment, we were whole again.

Then I slapped his chest.

"Stop making me save you all the time, you miserable ass!" I said, gasping through tear-giggling sobs.

He barked a laugh and pulled me upright with him. "No promises…" His smile and returning color to his skin warmed me to the core.

His strength was back—and this time, it was his.

He stood, his normal fiery light flickering along his arms again.

"Ready to end this? Together?" I asked.

He smirked—that familiar cocky grin that still made my stomach flip.

"Let's finish this once and for all."

CHAPTER 47

The heavy doors groaned open with the snarl of stone over stone, grinding on ancient hinges created in the old days.

Cade pressed his shoulder forward, bracing until the blackness peeled back in twin arcs—revealing Bella and Hunter on the other side, both frozen mid-step, mid-breath, as if the seconds had thickened into ice while they waited.

"Ash—!" Bella gasped, her dagger already drawn, her eyes wild and wet. "Ash, is he—?"

But then her eyes cut past me.

To him.

Cade stood at my side.

Tall. Whole.

His face bloodied, but his eyes—those sapphire eyes I'd sworn once to never believe again—were clear. Haunted, yes, and trembling beneath, but clear. Lit from within with something bright and still his.

"By Odiun," Hunter breathed, stepping forward but not before dragging one shaking hand across his sweat-slicked jaw. His voice cracked. "You're alive."

Cade gave a ghost of a smile and nodded solemnly. "Barely."

Bella's lips parted as if to say something, but she dropped her dagger and strode forward, flinging both arms around Cade and hugging him without hesitation, her cheek pressed against his blood-flecked shoulder. "Don't you ever do that again, Phoenix-fire. Or I'll kill you myself!"

"I'll try not to," he said softly, gently returning her embrace.

Hunter took a cautious step around me, eyes scanning every inch of Cade like he didn't quite trust the moment.

"You back?" he asked warily.

Cade turned to him and extended a hand. "The queen had me. But… Yes, I'm back."

Hunter hesitated. Then, slowly, he grabbed it.

They clasped wrists like old warriors at first—but then, without a word, Hunter tugged him into a bone-crushing hug, thumping his back hard.

"You stupid bastard," he muttered.

Cade grimaced. "You have no idea."

I nearly broke then. Not from fear. From the impossible weight of love and loss pressed together in relief.

But the moment was brittle, brief.

The floor rumbled under our boots again—a low, guttural growl from deep within the mountain.

The war hadn't waited.

And it wasn't going to.

Cade pulled away and turned down the corridor that stretched deeper through the queen's inner fortress. "Come on," he said. "We don't have long."

We followed.

The hallway bent unnaturally—like something had shifted in the architecture itself, twisted the paths that once served as a king's anchor into roots grown sick with darkness.

Cade led the way, the swirling fire of his staff guiding each step. Where once I'd thought I might fear that flame, now it was the only light I trusted not to falter.

Behind us, Bella and Hunter moved in near-sync, keeping a careful eye over their shoulders. The tremors had grown stronger. Dust trickled from the elaborate archways above. Carved reliefs depicting Queen Mortriana's bloody triumphs were fracturing at the edges, splitting down the middle like declarations finally being undone from stone. Each Gold-Marked slain seemed to be immortalized for her to feign over like a morbid trophy collection.

We emerged onto a wide platform at the edge of the final courtyard.

The last threshold before the bridge.

Even now, battle raged in sound and light behind us—outside the castle walls, high in the air, and deep below in the choked streets of Emberveil. Dragons still screamed their fury into the fading heavens, and the Terradyne rumbled their grief in roars that split the low hills with earth-breaking resolve.

Brigodon's still out there, murdering countless. I have to hurry. This has to all end...

Somewhere on those fields, my people were dying. And every passing second meant more of them falling.

We turned as one toward the great doorway at the northmost end—a set of scorched iron gates so crudely forged, they looked as old as the volcano they led into. They marked the threshold to the final passage the ruling line kept hidden since the building of the castle: a bridge forged in lost fire, built across a chasm of blackened air stretching between Raven's Bane and Mount Calcaedus—

Straight into the volcano's heart.

The final gate had already been drawn open.

Smoke wafted out like a warning. Like breath exhaled from a mouth that dreamed in flame.

The bridge gleamed faintly within—broad and wicked. Black

stone lined with runes that pulsed embers at our approach. That was my destiny ahead, and there was no turning back.

It stretched across the abyss like a question no one ever wanted the answer to.

"That's it," Cade said, his voice tight.

He didn't need to say what waited on the far side.

We all knew.

"She's waiting for me to bring your dead body to her," he added, glancing at me. "That was to be the last step in her halting the old prophecy. With your death, the final Gold-Marked fallen, she'd slay the great slumbering dragon and take its essence. Living for eternity in its stead."

"Bet she's not expecting all of us," Bella said, voice strained. "We have a chance. Surprise and the Prince of Emberveil beside the Gold-Marked."

"Not to mention you, Bella. You've proved to be quite tough and hard to kill yourself," Cade answered.

"He's right," I said, nudging her arm. "I couldn't have ever gotten this far without you… without all of you…"

"Let's go," Cade said, grabbing me by the hand. "For Vâllathór. The slumbering dragon encased in lava. Locked away before mortal history began. He must rise."

"Here we come, Mortriana," I whispered. "Kill the bitch, waken the god-like dragon. Can't be that hard…"

"She's not going to let go of her power," Cade said. "Prepare for the worst."

I nodded, squeezing his hand, taking a deep breath, feeling Eden radiating deep in my core. *Here we go, Ash. You can do this.*

I looked down at the bridge.

A thousand feet across.

Only one path.

No turning back.

I turned to Bella. Then to Hunter. Then to Cade.

Three people who knew me inside out.

Three people who had bled, burned, and fought beside me every step of the way.

"I never thought I would live long enough to get here," I said with a smile that came heavy and lopsided from grief. "We have to find a way. But if I die… I just wanted to say…"

"Die?" Hunter smirked. "You plan on dying, Gold-Marked?"

Bella's eyes shimmered, and she reached for my hand. "No. But if we do, we do it together."

I took her hand without hesitation. She gripped Hunter's. And there we stood, hand in hand. All four of us in a line, staring into the abyss.

Cade squeezed my hand. "You brought me back," he murmured. "Let me walk through the fire with you."

Hunter and Cade pulled the outer parts of our row together, placing their calloused palms over our joined hands, his expression fierce and soft at once.

"May Odiun guide our blades," Hunter said. "More than ever…"

"May he hold our names in his halls," Cade added quietly.

I closed my eyes.

And spoke what I'd been holding all these years. A final prayer stained in cracked salt and stubborn love.

I quoted a passage from the prophet Solemn I had memorized.

"Great loss plagues all who go to war with the fire wielders… but not anymore…" I narrowed my eyes, deep hatred bellowing within me like dragonfire in my lungs. "Not anymore… Not ever again…"

Bella whispered Amen with a trembling breath.

Cade kissed my temple.

Hunter squeezed once before stepping back toward the bridge.

Then we looked forward.

Together.

And began the walk toward the end.

The chasm growled below.

And the last battle waited in ash ahead.

The bridge moaned beneath our boots.

The sulfur air clung to our skin like poison-washed silk. Our footfalls rang hollow over the black stone bridge—each step punched down into silence, swallowed by the sheer drop yawning open beneath either side.

Beneath the bridge, the deep throat of Mount Calcaedus breathed like the lung of some forgotten god—venting heat and ash between cracks in the mountain's crust, far below the bridge's edges. Molten rock glittered faintly in the darkness—a cruel starlight cast by fire instead of sky. The scrape of dragon claws across distant cliffs echoed now and then, like muttered warnings too far below to heed.

We said nothing.

Still, as the end drew nearer, Cade's fingers tangled with mine. Our pace slowed just slightly as we approached the far platform—where the bridge connected to the volcano itself, carved into obsidian and lead, etched with runes older than Allovan. Glowing symbols flickered and crawled along the stone face like humming orange veins beneath black skin.

Here, on the edge of history, we paused.

Not because we lacked the will to go forward—

But because we owed the past that much.

"We say something," Bella whispered. "Before we step inside. We... we have to."

Her voice cracked. Not with fear.

With reverence.

Hunter turned toward her slowly. "What do you want to say?"

Bella opened her mouth. Then her voice broke. "I—I don't know. I just—Odiun help me, I don't know if I'll see any of your faces again. And I can't—I can't go through that door without knowing I said something."

Cade nodded once. "Then say something now. Say it to all of us."

So she did.

"I love you." She looked at me. "Ash, you made me brave when all I wanted was to disappear."

She turned to Hunter. "You protected me long before I remembered how to protect myself."

Then to Cade. "And you? You gave me my first hope that monsters could still find their way back."

Hunter exhaled, hard.

He hooked an arm around her shoulders and pulled her tight, just long enough to show it mattered.

Then—he looked to me.

No smile this time.

Just truth.

"I always thought I'd die in some bleeding quarry outside Bramblebash, nameless and sore. But you changed that. You changed all of it."

My lips quivered as she stared deep into me. I knew that look. She was my only family in this world, and she meant more to me than all the riches, freedom, and dragons in this world. "I love you too."

We hugged and began to enter the volcano, but Cade grabbed me by the shoulder and spun me to face him.

My eyes met his. Dark lashes streaked with ash, cuts on his cheek not yet fully healed. Fire lived behind his veins again. Real fire. Honest fire.

He reached out. Pressed his palm to my chest.

"I was darkness once," he said slowly, voice low enough the mountain might've leaned closer to hear. "You lit something no one else saw. If this ends in fire—at least I die human."

My heart slammed against my ribs.

I leaned in. Touched my forehead to his.

"Then let's go burn her kingdom down," I whispered.

We turned to the door.

The archway loomed—half-forged from ancient scales, half-carved into the living rock of the mountain itself. At its center burned a glyph like a closed phoenix eye—sealed until I approached.

The moment Eden's magic brushed the edge of the seal, it pulsed golden—and split.

The doors opened.

And hell breathed us in.

The chamber was vast beyond imagining—too wide to measure by paces, too deep to see the bottom. Lava glowed in rivers like veins beneath the cracked floor, pooling far below in a molten lake ringed by black iron teeth jutting from the mountain's bedrock. Chains hung unused from the high domed ceiling, some broken, others draped down into fire—and even they glowed faint from residual power.

Steam slipped from vents lining the chamber walls. The air rippled with magical heat and something else—

Old power.

Primordial.

Older than Odiun.

Before us, far across the great hollowed ring of stone, rested the queen.

And behind her...

The dragon.

Vâllathór.

The air nearly left my lungs at once.

Her enormous head broke through the far rock wall like a massive statue. Her head, filled with hundreds of horns of all sizes was as large as Brigodon! Her breath alone shifted the air. Her scales were a canopy of blackened silver, each marked with thick grooves and scar tissue, lined with ridges that caught the red light like glinting bones beneath a dying sun. Horns twisted from her spine like sunken ships, broken in some places, burned blunt in others. Her claws—each as long as ships—curled loose across the stone, unmoving.

And yet—

She was alive.

Her thick eyelids were closed, but her huge dark nostrils stirred as she breathed slowly. The already smoke-filled interior of the volcano wreaked of dragonfire from those nostrils.

I shook.

"You okay?" Bella asked hoarsely. "You ready for this?"

I nodded.

But I wasn't.

I was crumbling in awe.

"Fifty times Krakos," Cade whispered beside me. "My father used to tell us…"

He trailed off.

I looked at him sharply. "What?"

He hesitated.

Then said, "It's forbidden for anyone except the king, or queen, to enter this chamber."

"Then how do you know what's in here?"

He exhaled. "Because when I was a boy, my father told me stories—before she killed him. He said the queen changed after what he told her was in here. That she believed she could reshape the bones of gods."

I swallowed.

The queen stood alone beside a black marble altar—waist-high, polished to a mirror shine. Upon it, a pyre burned. Not natural fire—green-edged flames awakened with soul-ink etched into the base. Scarlet ribbons of smoke rose in coils like whispers turned visible.

She hadn't turned toward us.

She didn't need to.

I felt her the moment we stepped through the door.

Her power unfurled like a cloak across the cavern's breadth, long and full of rot. She didn't speak, but her smile reached my skin before her voice did.

She waited until we approached the edge of the ring. Then—

"Ashlyn Moonriver," she hissed. "I'm somewhat surprised to see you here, alive. Yet also not. Cade always has been… weak…"

My blade lit, gold humming up my wrist like a second pulse.

I stepped forward, Hunter and Bella flanking left, Cade to my right.

But I didn't answer her.

Not yet.

I studied her instead.

She wore no crown.

Only a long cape stitched with dragon scale and shadow, sleeveless robes of void-colored silks that grazed her ankles. Her arms were bare up to the shoulder—a choice. Her hair poured silver down her back like poured mercury. Her lips, crimson. Her mouth was already outlined with smoke. Her expression?

Expectation.

"I'm glad you're here," she murmured. "All of you."

We stopped twenty paces away.

"I'd normally ask you to surrender and give up this madness," I said evenly, "but you've wrought too much wrong. There is a reckoning here for you, you evil bitch."

She tilted her head, amused.

"Even now, humor?" she asked. "Can you not sense the gravity of this moment in time? I am ascending. I am the reckoning, orphan. After I consume your essence and then that of Vâllathór, the world will be mine…"

Orphan—I flinched despite myself.

"Don't," Cade growled. "Ash beat you once. She'll defeat you again."

"Mm," the queen purred. "Still so sensitive, my prince. Still clinging to that flesh like it's yours now."

"You don't own him anymore." I said behind gritted teeth.

Mortriana's smile sharpened.

"Yes. I felt it—when the bond shattered. I won't lie. It hurt."

She placed a hand over her chest with mocking care. "Doing it in this very room though—oh, Cade. Romantic. The orphan pulls you from the darkness just in time to beg at my altar." She looked at me again, deeper now. "Will you kneel with him, little worthless, unloved girl? Or must you burn again first?"

"I'm going to wipe that smug look right off your ugly face," I said flatly.

Hunter sneered. "I can't wait to see that."

Cade raised his staff, its runes gleaming now with molten light.

Bella took my hand for the briefest second, then released it. "She burns," she whispered. "Right here. Right now."

The queen's eyes darkened.

I rallied Eden and lifted my golden-flamed sword. I felt the rune on my neck sizzle alive in golden light.

That same golden light bathed the chamber.

And in the distance, the sleeping dragon stirred.

Stretching.

The final breath before war.

Mortriana turned back to her altar.

And for the first time—

She drew her own blade.

Curved, long, crimson like blood.

Elegant.

Notched with spells.

"Well," she said, her voice suddenly dripping with promise. "Shall we then?"

I didn't answer.

And the volcano trembled with prophecy.

The final battle had begun.

CHAPTER 48

The queen stood like wrath given form.

Her eyes—those infinite black voids—met mine with ice-edged satisfaction.

"The prophecy's time has come," she said in a voice far too quiet for the cavern but which echoed anyway—rattling between our ribs like sermon made of steel. "And my ascension to eternity is nearly complete."

I stepped forward onto the cracked stone, Eden flaring in my palm with a thrum of golden defiance. My armor spun to life in a rush of light—brilliant and gilded, plates fusing across my arms, chest, and thighs in a perfect shimmer of forged grace. The moment the helm of magic crowned across my brow, golden wings of flame curled up behind my ears, and Eden's sword solidified, humming in my grip like the world begging to be rewritten.

"No," I said. My voice echoed alongside hers, the golden light of my magic burning the air like a sunrise over a world scorched by shadows. "The time of your reign ends tonight. A new world is coming—one without war. Without fire-forged chains. Without death masquerading as order."

Cade flanked me, stepping forward toward the queen and the massive slumbering dragon, flame already winding down his arms like coiled vipers. As he lifted his hand, a seal of fire cracked alive beneath his feet, spreading diagonally into the floor like a sun breaking through storm clouds.

"We stand together," he said, his own voice tinged now not with desperation, but fury—measured and glowing at its core. "And with her magic and my fire, tonight you die, stepmother."

The queen tilted her head backward and laughed—a laugh that rose until it wasn't a sound anymore but a cry like towers falling. It clanged in the air like striking chains. Like final bells tolling.

"Do you know," she said, half-mocking, half-reverent, "how many of her kind I've killed?" Her eyes scanned me like a miser counting coins. "How many Gold-Marked miracles from long-dead prophecies I've watched bleed out on my feet?"

A cruel smile slid across her flame-edged lips.

"Dozens. Each easier than the last." She turned to me fully then—a magical staff of black smoke and flame flowing up from her hand. "And you… You are nothing more than a little girl from a gutter town. A slave girl with salt water in her eyes and sand in her tongue. You are nothing, Ash Mist. No one will remember you when your corpse hardens on this sacred altar of mine."

Her voice dropped into something softer. Almost gentle. More terrifying because of it.

"But they will remember me. They will kneel at the fires of my name."

She extended one hand behind her toward the altar, where smoke curled up toward the towering slumbering form of Vâllathór. The dragon still did not stir—but even asleep, her breath opened chasms in the stone with each exhale.

"Once I consume your Gilded Radiance, child," Mortriana continued, almost lovingly, "and siphon the final breath from this ancient beast's spirit… the new world will be forged. And I will rule it. I will hold every spark of will in my palm and crush rebellion with the fist of flame."

I stepped forward, Eden's light burning brighter, snarling now in my hand.

"That's not how this ends," I said evenly.

Something in my voice turned sharp—holy.

"This world will rise again without you in it. I'll release the dragon's soul from your chains. And when you're dead and lost, and your name scattered to smoke like the cities you torched, no soul will build altars to remember you."

I raised my blade.

"They will remember me. And they will remember that I quenched the bitter fires of a forgotten queen."

The queen tilted her head again, her smile warping.

"Then so be it."

She raised her staff and sword.

And began to chant.

Low at first—like dripping oil hissing into fire.

The symbols on the altar flared to violet, then red, then blinding orange. The slumbering dragon stirred—just slightly, but the motion rolled through the chamber like a sleeping earthquake.

A *crack* split the air as the seal above the dragon fractured.

Then—

Boom!

The volcano answered.

A violent, skin-rippling explosion slammed through the cavern from deep beneath the floor. Cracks spiraled out from the obsidian walls like dark lightning. Fissures roared up toward the ceiling, rocks dislodging like falling teeth from ancient jaws.

The whole mountain shook.

Hunter lunged forward, barely keeping his feet on solid ground. "We need to kill her now! At this rate the whole place is gonna drop on our heads!"

I felt it—every rumble, every curse of the mountain as magic twisted too far, unmade too long. Time was shattering.

The golden power of my magic responded with a surge of light. It poured through my veins like molten mercy, encasing my legs, my chest, my mind. Power flared from my spine like wings unchained. My blade extended itself with radiant fire, and every rune inscribed down its center gleamed white-gold with promise.

"She fears you," Cade said, fire dancing across his back like a cloak forged in old gods' breath. "She wouldn't have summoned this fury if she didn't."

The queen's eyes narrowed.

"She should," I said through clenched teeth.

Cade stepped forward, lifting both hands over his shoulders—the fire wreathing him collapsed inward over his skin like twin serpents ready to strike. His staff became a sword of flame, runes along the pommel glowing like stars folding in time.

Hunter readied his blade—but Cade reached out, catching his arm before he could take another step.

"No," Cade said, voice deep and resolute. "This is a fight only magic can decide."

Hunter frowned. "Like hell. We came this far together. We finish it together!"

Bella stepped beside him, matching him breath for breath.

But Cade shook his head. "She'll rip you apart before you raise a blade."

Then I nodded to them—gently but firm. "Stay back. Wait. For me. Protect Bella. I can't..."

"Never!" Bella shouted with fists balled. "We fight together!"

Gods, she's so fearless. But this isn't a fight she can win.

Hunter swayed with his sword ready, eager to attack, and Bella held her sword out too, and I smiled. "We finish this together!"

I felt an enormous pit in my stomach, like a ball of iron digesting down all my gut. I knew what I needed to do...

With a burst of magic from my fingertips, a ball of golden energy rushed at them, forcing them back.

They shouted in protest, being forced to the room's rear. They fought to break free, but I couldn't let Bella get harmed. I couldn't live with myself.

My spell hung all around them as they were forced against the wall. Bella's gaze screamed she wanted to help. But she would do better there, rather than dead in a pool of her own blood.

Her demeanor shifted as the thoughts stormed through her head. "End this, Ash." She mouthed the words so I could see.

Hunter, seething in fury, fighting to break free of my spell, wasn't as accepting of his position.

"I'm sorry," I mouthed back. But then Cade and I turned back to face the queen...

Hunter suddenly shouted, "Make it hurt. Make her pay!"

Cade shifted beside me.

And the queen cleared her throat. "A new age is upon this world! We are moments away from the most glorious transformation this world has known since the creation of our kind by Odiun! But first... little traitors, little snakes, like you need to be dealt with..."

She slammed the head of her staff into the cracked stone altar.

A tidal wave of fire burst outward—

The firestorm tore through the chamber, a wall of infernal wind and raw destruction, but together Cade and I didn't run.

We met it.

Eden glowed with a brilliance that drowned the queen's spell cast in radiant gold, its energy surging from my blade and forming a swirling disc of protection before us. Cade's flame slipped beneath mine like a molten phoenix tail, weaving around the golden light and reinforcing it with Cinderyn fire.

The flames hit us like a god's slap—forceful enough to rend any normal armor-clad soldier asunder.

But we were ready. Together, we were strong.

We held the line.

When Mortriana's spell wave crashed against us, our combined power turned it, split it left and right like parting a rotted sea. The queen snarled from her fire-bound altar, her voice rising now, rattling through the volcanic chamber.

"You dare defy destiny?" she shrieked, fury dripping from her tongue. "You are nothing! Mere worthless orphans who time will gladly forget, and know that I will enjoy tasting your blood!"

Eden's power pulsed down my arms, steady and firm, her voice whispering inside me just loud enough to feel like roots cracking through old earth.

My lips twisted toward a grin.

I lifted the sword as the wave disintegrated around us, the chamber clearing just enough for Cade and I to see the queen clearly. She'd stepped from the altar, her cape crackling with volatile flame that trailed across the floor like ripping banners. Her staff hummed with a sickly reddish glow—the rubies burning deep like blood boiling inside sealed skin.

With a wild cry, she slammed the staff's end into the earth and shouted a spell—not a whisper anymore, but a rage, full-bodied and ancient.

The glowing fire around the room ignited again, this time in deep violet. The floor cracked wider beneath our boots, the walls shivering as something moved from beneath Mortriana's feet.

A spell that tasted wrong shot through the air.

From the lava fissure beside her, the fire trembled—then twisted up into shape.

Not mist. Not magic.

A beast.

The fire took the shape of an enormous serpent—an asp, its colossal jaws lined with erupting coals and smoldering embers.

Its eyes were twin pits of burning hunger, dark and swirling like storms about to break. As it rose, it towered over us—far taller than the queen herself, far larger than Krakos even, its glistening coils shimmering with heat that rippled through the air, sending waves of smoke trailing like breath across every scale-shaped ripple. We stood frozen, adrenaline coursing through us as the creature hissed, molten lava bubbling at its being, transforming black stone into liquid fire with every movement.

Its tongue flicked out, tasting the air with a sinister hunger, and then it lunged. The ground shook with a tremor that echoed through the heart of the cavern, threatening to swallow us whole.

"Cade!" I shouted, adrenaline sharpening my senses. Desperation clawed at my throat; we had to act quickly.

Cade didn't even flinch. With a fierce intensity, he raised his sword, its edge glowing with the heat of a thousand suns, and stepped forward, muscles coiling like a spring ready to unleash a storm. We weren't just going to stand our ground; we were going to fight back.

Without waiting for the asp's strike, I pulled on Eden's power, feeling it respond with a pulse that blazed through my veins.

It unleashed its attack. The asp's colossal jaws snapped shut with a reverberating crack, barely missing Cade as he rolled to the side, dodging the fire that erupted from its mouth. I fired a bolt of Eden's energy forward, golden light searing through the darkness like lightning. It slammed into the asp's side, the impact sending shockwaves through its serpentine body. The blast was powerful enough to knock the asp off balance, but it quickly composed itself, eyes narrowing dangerously.

"Watch it!" Cade shouted, dodging debris that fell from the ceiling as the mighty beast recoiled, clearly enraged by my initial assault. "Keep going!"

With a fierce roar, the asp twisted its massive body, launching itself at me with the speed of a great storm, its coiled form a blur of molten fury. I barely had time to react as it struck, but I summoned the power of Eden into my blade and swung with all my might. The sword met scale with a dazzling explosion of energy, cascading sparks in every direction as I felt the shock reverberate through my arms.

The creature let out a guttural howl, its fury shaking the very walls of the chamber. It reared back, scales gleaming with molten light, and struck again—this time with both jaws wide open, aimed directly for my heart.

"Cade!" I screamed, spinning back in time to see him leap into action. He spun his flaming sword, a blazing arc of fire trailing behind him, and swung it with the precision of a seasoned warrior. Cade's strike connected with the snake's neck, just as it barreled toward me. Flames erupted where our powers met, a dazzling display of our combined magic that sent the serpent crashing against the stone, scales flaking away like burnt parchment.

"Don't let up!" Cade yelled, breathless but fierce. The asp writhed on the ground, rattling across the cavern floor, and I could see its molten blood pooling beneath it, fuming with the promise of more fury.

I pressed forward, Eden flaring brighter in my palm, sensing the rhythm of the battle thrumming in my chest. "What's the plan?" I shouted over the creature's growls, realizing we needed to end this quickly before the queen could reassert herself.

"Distract it!" Cade replied. He knelt, gathering fire into a swirling maelstrom that danced around him in dangerous flickers. "I'll harness the energy I can draw from its heat. We need to find a weak point!"

I nodded, understanding instantly. With a fierce cry, I lunged at the asp, aiming for its eyes—the single points of vulnerability in its otherwise scaled exterior. Eden's blade glinted in the dim light, and I slashed at the right eye, the golden energy exploding on contact, causing the creature to rear back and hiss in raw pain.

It recoiled, scales vibrating furiously, and I danced back out of reach just in time to avoid its sweeping tail. The cavern trembled with its fury as I felt the energy shift, Cade channeling the heat around him.

"Now!" Cade shouted, his voice rising above the chaos—raw determination in every syllable.

I charged again, moving like a comet in flight, my focus clear. With every ounce of magic I had, I thrust Eden deep into the serpent's jagged scales—a direct stab aimed straight at its heart.

The asp convulsed, and for a moment, everything paused. Time felt like a brittle glass, ready to shatter under the weight of fate. Victory or demise hung precariously in the balance. A hatred seethed in the mighty serpent as it regrouped. And before our eyes, we watched as it pulsed in deep fiery waves. Its body transformed before us. With each breath its massive body grew in size. Its massive head doubled, its fangs sharpened longer, and its powerful body grew.

"Uh... Cade?" I staggered back as it towered over us.

It recoiled, then twisted in a full circle and snapped again, this time toward Cade. He raised his flame-spun sword and shouted a summoning phrase in the old tongue of Cinderyn flame, crimson runes along the floor spinning like dials around him.

From the fire at his feet, a shape burst upward—

A bird of fire.

A phoenix.

Not just a summoned familiar—but a soul-shaped flame with wings as wide as a dragon and talons formed of compressed molten steel. It screamed once—a cry like mourning and fury braided together—then launched into the air with blazing speed.

It collided with the asp midair.

The sound was deafening—fire on fire, curse on curse. Sparks exploded across the ceiling, flame wrapping and slashing as the two magical beasts tumbled over the sacrificial altar in an aerial brawl.

The queen snarled, clearly angered by Cade's surprise beast.

He arced his blade toward the queen, and the phoenix screeched, twisting under the asp's body and slashing upward a second time. The asp hissed in return—a guttural, bubbling sound that made my teeth ache.

"It's my turn." I seethed in hatred at the queen.

I charged in beneath their battle. The moment opened just wide enough to attack. My feet rushed as quickly as I'd ever run, moving at full sprint to reach the queen up-close.

I slashed at her right as the magic coiled around her staff faltered.

She caught my strike with the shaft. Eden's gold clanged loud against the blood-red blade, and the impact sent a pulse of energy exploding over the cracked dais.

We both flew backward.

I hit hard, rolling as heat streaked across my chest.

She rose slower.

But alive.

Burning.

I could hear the strain in her breath now, and there—it was faint—but… yes.

A tremble.

Cade landed beside me in a crouch. His armor glowed molten at the edges, sweat racing down his temple.

"We're getting to her," I gasped.

"She's cornered herself," he growled. "Show no mercy—Don't let her get composed."

The queen's laughter cut clean through our moment.

Mortriana straightened slowly. Her staff trembled in her hands, the rubies bleeding a thin mist of shadow now in place of fiery gleam.

"Do you fools truly think," she said, shaking with some unholy fervor, "that two orphans—two afterthoughts—can burn down all I've built?"

She raised her hands.

"I killed King Phoenixfire," she said, looking at Cade. "Your father. The strongest Cinderyn of our time. You remember the smell of his skin melting, don't you? No one ever expected me to shatter the crown. And no one would believe you if you told them. But none of that matters now. None will ever oppose my rule again!" She grinned with eerily sharp teeth as the two beasts battled above us.

She looked at me, fire snapping in her irises.

"I am Queen of Blaze! The fire that knows no end! And I will not fall to a bastard and his slut!"

Rage ignited behind my eyes.

I stalked forward, Eden flaming hotter than before.

Eden. Not anger. Clarity.

My soul sang.

I raised my blade skyward, golden light threading across the chamber like a brand new dawn.

"You are less than us," I shouted. "You've shown who you really are, Queen of Ruin!"

But instead of raising her staff—

Mortriana laughed one more time.

Not a cruel laugh.

A mad one.

And she screamed something in an ancient tongue, loud and cracked.

The altar behind her pulsed.

And her body...

Began to change.

It started at her hands. Her black and crimson gauntlets peeled off as if melting. Her pale skin hardened, then darkened— scabbing black like charring paper.

Her nails grew—curved, yellowed.

Her face twisted.

Her silver hair turned shadow-grey, fell past her face in snarled, tangled cords.

Black cracks split across her mouth, traveling up her cheekbones like dark lightning. Fangs erupted from her gums, sharpening and lengthening all at once. Her armor crumbled off her torso, revealing flesh—no, bone—no, stone wrapped in skin—beneath.

Smoke burst from her shoulders as horns tore through the top of her skull. Two jagged, twisted obsidian horns with crimson glowing cracks down each side sprouted upward like thorns made from dragon claws.

"What the hell is happening?!" I gasped in horror, nearly stumbling backward.

Cade's hand caught my elbow—even he sounded afraid.

"No," he whispered. "No, no—she... she's gone too far."

"What is that!?" I shouted, turning toward him.

Cade didn't look away from her. "She's been taken by the tainted magic of the Cinderyn. It's not just old power—it's corruption. Warped beyond reason. In ancient times, some of our kind dove so deep into cruelty, into death, they lost themselves... became monsters..."

He inhaled sharply and finished like it hurt to say it.

"They turned into demons..."

Oh gods.

The queen—Mortriana—finished changing.

Power coiled around her now like sulfur winds.

And worst of all—

She smiled.

Teeth like jagged glass, black gums twitching between every breath.

She towered now. Fifteen feet tall. Bone-crusted claws curling where hands once were. Her voice came next, but it wasn't her voice anymore.

Not the cruel queen I knew.

This one was cracked.

Broken like a rift in the sky.

"The hour is late, and for you, there will be no dawn," she said in a voice like burned bone. "Your prophecy..." she hissed, stepping forward, molten rock melting beneath her feet with every step. "...was wrong."

Cade tightened beside me. His sword flared again. "Ash—"

"I know."

She was something else now.

Not a tyrant.

A force.

We couldn't back away.

And we wouldn't.

Because this was it.

The end.

The last war.

"I'll keep her on her flank," Cade whispered, drawing flame across the edge of the blade until it sparked sun-hot.

"You'll have to use Eden for more than light."

"I know what to do," I said, and I raised my blade again.

Behind us, the walls quaked again. Both the phoenix and asp exploded into it with a force that could topple smaller mountains.

Above us, lava cracked in the ceiling.

Before us, a demon queen burned down the last of her skin, and roared at the heavens.

We ran in together.

And the final battle began.

CHAPTER 49

The moment her scream ended, the room fractured wide open.

Not in stone. Not in sound.

In magic.

From the blackened altar where Mortriana stood—now a shape of flame and twisted, bone-crowned fury—her hands snapped upward, and the world shattered around them.

A low pulse hit first, like the quake of a mortal heartbeat too large to fit inside flesh. One long, cratered thrum that split the air in half. Then the fire went quiet. Dead quiet. Even my magical sword dimmed in my palm like her light had been strangled.

I opened my mouth to speak—to scream maybe—

And the shadows came.

They didn't crawl. They didn't swirl at my edges like uncertain smoke.

They ate the room.

The flame disappeared. The altar, the collapsed walls, the dragon—everything vanished into a wave of ink thick as grief and rich with rot. Magic rose around us like old blood forced through new veins. Velvet black, with veins of twisted scarlet streaking through it. It didn't pull us under—it pulled us out.

I felt Cade's magic flicker beside me, then collapse entirely.

He gasped.

I reached out, scrambling through the suffocating dark—

My fingers found his.

His hand caught mine.

And he squeezed.

Hard.

A lifeline.

A promise.

We spun through the abyss together.

Through darkness.

Through silence.

Through the final storm of her making.

Reality slipped.

I couldn't tell which way was up anymore. Couldn't feel my body with any certainty. Only the warmth of Cade's fingers around mine, our palms pressed together—trembling, clinging like the last two stars in an endless sky of uncreation.

Then the queen's voice arrived.

Not whispered.

Not shouted.

It simply was.

All around us, winding through the mist like fire laid gentle across a lover's spine.

"Oh, children," she cooed, her voice sliding between centuries of sorrow and elegance. "It's beautiful, isn't it?"

Cade tensed beside me.

I felt him, even in the weightlessness, even as the void drowned our senses—his breath catching, his grip trembling but still refusing to let me go.

The queen's voice swelled again, higher now—milk-sweet and

acid-sharp. "This is what lies beyond the lies you were told. This —this blessed quiet—is the last breath before gods truly wake."

I pulled closer to Cade with what little strength I had. My legs didn't work. My magic didn't spark. Eden was silent, buried too deep beneath whatever black-spelled curtain she'd drawn over us. But I had his hand. If nothing else, I had that.

"Tales will be sung of this moment," the queen's voice went on, tinged now with gentle pity. "I've waited so long for the end of worthless idols and zealots. Why fight when you face an unstoppable god?"

"Shut up," I breathed. My voice cracked but still rose. "Just shut the fuck up! You're no god. You're a devil. Look at you. How can you be so blind and stupid?"

Her laughter curled tighter through the dark—soundless and thick.

"Ashlyn," she sighed, almost tender. "Such fire left in you. Even now, blind in the void. You think there's meaning left here. You think the sweat of your fight, the tears of your friends, your love—it was all going to build something? I have become more than a woman. More than a queen. I am everything!"

"You don't know anything about us!" I roared into the black.

The spinning slowed—just long enough for my lungs to suck in a real breath.

Silence.

Almost.

Then:

"I know Cade," she said, venom laced beneath silk. "Better than you could even dream."

I felt him shift against me. Heard his breath hitch.

"You sweet little idiot," the queen sighed, amused. "Do you know how he came to me? Do you know what quiet sobs he choked on in my cathedral as he begged me to teach him to be anything but what his blood made him?"

My chest cracked open.

"Cade," I whispered.

But he said nothing.

The queen pressed on, her voice laced with honey and horror.

"He was weak. Unmade by every choice not his own. Born a prince, but never a king. A boy shattered from the moment his father died and left him in my palace with his shaking hands and that pathetic little blaze in his eyes…"

"Stop it—"

"Oh, Ash," the queen crooned, "he just wanted something he couldn't have. He's always wanted what he couldn't reach. That's what you were, you know. Not love. Not destiny. Just another thing just out of reach."

"You're wrong," I hissed. My grip on Cade tightened so hard my knuckles burned through the numbness. "He's kind. He's warm. He stronger than you could ever know!"

The queen laughed again, a hollow sound that cracked with crescendo.

"Then why has he failed me so? Time and time again his weakness shone through like charcoal where there should be diamonds?" she asked.

My heart seized.

But Cade's hand didn't let go.

"You don't get it," I whispered. My voice steadied, stone against flame. "You couldn't understand someone like him if you shattered him a thousand times. Because underneath every oath, every spell, every chain you wrapped him in—you still couldn't kill the man who caught me when I fell."

There was a pause.

A breath.

Then—her voice, icy-cold. "He loves poorly. Like someone who never knew how."

I screamed it now. "Because no one ever showed him!"

Cade moved beside me.

And I realized—

He was crying.

He was silent.

But I could feel the tears sliding down his face.

Still he held my hand in the void, tighter than ever.

The queen's next words came sharp.

A blade's edge.

"But I made him strong. I forged that pulp-hearted thing into something that could kill without flinching. And now I become far more than this."

She didn't raise her voice. She didn't need to.

"From this moment on," she said, "I won't need him. Or you. Or anyone."

"And the first thing I'll do as god incarnate…"—

White light shattered the dark around us.

And suddenly time caught fire.

The queen appeared before us—not just her voice anymore.

She stepped from the black mist like a ghost given body, her demon-form fully unleashed. Horns spiraled from her crown. Her robes were ash and deep cloth, fire swirling around her hips in circular waves. The blade in her right hand gleamed cold and curved—etched in so many runes it bled shadow where it cut the air.

We both froze—stuck motionless, like statues with souls.

Cade, holding me like we could weather it, gave me a troubled look, like something terrible was about to happen.

I tried to squeeze his hand, but no muscles worked. I tried to call Eden. I screamed within for her! Nothing… I could tell Cade was trying the same. Desperately reaching for his magic, but none came…

And the queen raised her dagger to his throat.

"Cade—!" I screamed.

But I couldn't move.

I didn't have Eden.

I didn't even have magic.

The queen snarled a wicked, sharp-toothed smile.

"Such a pity," she whispered. "You wasted your last words crying instead of saying goodbye."

"No—!"

The blade flashed.

A line of silver caught the red-lit dark.

And then—

A choking sound.

Cade spasmed.

Blood flooded his collarbone.

And he fell.

Back.

Weightless.

Like everything that had ever mattered was dropping into silence.

I screamed so loudly my voice split. My body pitched forward after him, and I caught nothing—nothing but the echo of his name as it tore from my throat.

"Cade!"

I screamed his name again, and there was nothing.

No answer. No fire left in his throat, no cough of defiance from the chest of the man who once breathed blaze into the sky like a war hymn.

Just a body in my arms.

Cade lay slack, his jaw tilted toward the heavens, blood pooling so fast it coated my knees. His throat was a ragged crimson tear, his chest heaved once—shallow—

"Cade—no, no—" I sobbed, using both hands to press the heel of his own cape against the gaping wound. "You're okay. You're okay, just stay with me, stay with me!" Hot blood poured through my fingers like I was trying to plug the wound. "Don't you dare leave me, you beautiful stubborn bastard—don't you dare—! You can't! You can't leave me now! Please… oh god, please…"

His mouth moved.

Shuttering with effort.

No sound formed, no voice slid out—but he shaped the words anyway.

I love you, Ash.

Then his head lolled sideways, his cheek slackening into my shoulder.

And he stopped breathing.

"No!"

I shoved my hands harder against his skin, sobbing so loud it didn't sound human anymore. "You're not gone! Cade, don't you fucking dare! Don't you do this to me!" I gasped. "You said we'd burn her together—you said you'd stay by my side! I can't do this alone. I can't... I couldn't save you when it mattered... I'm so sorry. My love... I'm so, so sorry..."

But there was no fire left in him. No laugh. No snark. No warm glint behind those glacier-blue eyes.

Only silence.

A deadly silence that screamed inside my chest louder than any spell ever could.

Above me, the queen laughed.

Her voice rolled like thunder across the void carved in pain.

"Oh," she sighed, mock-gentle. "Did you think love could save a kingdom? That that little ache in your chest would keep him standing?" She smiled, dark and glistening. "Pathetic."

I didn't look at her. I couldn't.

I stared down at Cade's face, my thumb brushing the blood slicked along his jaw. A sob punched out of me, but behind it a crack appeared—deep inside my center.

Little.

And glowing.

At first, I almost didn't notice it.

But my hands—

My hands trembled.

And then—

The light came.

One pulse. Gold and soaked in tears and fury and fire.

Then again.

Stronger. Brighter.

It flickered once more—and this time it didn't dim. It surged up my arms like a tide, flooding golden warmth across my chest, down my spine, through my skin.

Eden had returned.

But it wasn't just Eden.

It was something else—

Something ancient.

Something vast.

I looked up—slowly. My eyes blurred with tears, blood on my lips—

And every inch of me on fire again. But not in pain.

Alive.

Lit.

Lit with a light so golden it seared the edges of the room, lit like a sun had stolen my spine and finally remembered what I was for.

The queen stumbled back, just a single step. Her grin faltered.

Hatred shifted into something smaller. Colder.

Confusion.

"No," she whispered. "I'm subduing your magic. I've mastered it. Every time… I mastered it…"

I rose from Cade's body like vengeance clawing out of a grave.

My golden light poured upward with me. The swirl of it caught in the folds of my armor, my hair, the cracks in my skin. Eden burned so bright in my palm I thought it would melt my bones—but I didn't care.

I was finally holding all of me.

I looked at Mortriana.

And I wasn't crying anymore.

"You have no power over me," she spat, rage replacing confusion—her voice cracking with disbelief. "You shouldn't have your magic now!" Her hands flew forward, attempting some magic to subdue me again, then shook her hands in frustration.

I took a step toward her and she flinched again.

Good.

"I feel them," I said, my voice steady and wide like the ocean in a storm. "The ones you killed. The others."

The chamber pulsed.

"The Gold-Marked you slaughtered."

Behind me, there was a whisper—a sound like voices on the water's edge.

Then another.

And another.

Until the air behind me shimmered.

And I saw them.

Ghosts.

Ten.

Twenty.

Hundreds.

Gold light shaped in faces, in figures clothed in fire and grief.

So many women and men—

Their techniques etched into their postures, their names no longer erased.

They stood behind me, solid in light and ready in wrath.

"They're with me now," I said.

My voice broke halfway through—but not from weakness.

From power.

Power surged up through my chest and into my throat like I'd been drinking starlight too long and finally let myself overflow.

"And they're all saying the same thing."

I stepped forward as flame coiled up my arms, dripping light from my fingertips like jewels.

"To end you. To wake the dragon."

I crouched down like the wind flexing through trees.

And ran.

Ran like I had Cade's blood in my heart and hell in my lungs and an ancient choir screaming inside every beat of my heart.

The queen flung a burst of shadow-magic toward me—the kind that shredded through dragons.

I ran through it.

No flinch.

No scream.

Golden light shattered the shadow like it was glass.

And in one breath, I was in front of her.

Too fast.

Too bright.

I reached for her throat.

And grabbed it.

She gasped—hands scrabbling uselessly against my arms.

Her spikes of flame backlashed but Eden burned them before they touched me.

"You killed the only man I ever truly loved," I seethed, each word a wave crashing in my throat. "You took away the one thing that mattered most in this world. And maybe once... that was enough to die for."

I squeezed her throat slightly and felt something in her panic. Not pain.

Fear.

"But look around," I whispered, golden light bleeding from my pores. "This world is worth more than one man now."

She groaned, clawing at her staff.

"I've got friends who would die for me."

The ghosts behind me echoed louder—one stepped forward, face ageless, armor glowing. Then another. Hunter and Bella appeared in the sea of faces, and my heart fluttered and the blood in my arms pounded.

"And I've got enough magic left to kill the evil inside you until even your hate can't survive." I seethed. Magic roared up my arms and my magical sword burst from my hand.

"You little witch—" she rasped.

She brought her staff up and slammed its head into my abdomen.

The spell cracked like thunder.

Pain.

Gods.

Agonizing.

A white explosion erupted across my ribs—shaking every inch of my magic loose. I screamed, stumbling backward.

My magic—

It bled.

Pulled out of me like a thread yanked from my soul.

"No—no—no!" I gasped as my knees hit stone, every inch of me splintering in pain. "I—I can't—!"

"My final spell," the queen whispered, her tone triumphant. "Torn from a scroll stitched in the leather of your ancestors."

Flames curled around her broken crown as she loomed.

"It was always the Gold-Marked who could end me. So I found a way to end them first. Steal their power, before they can use it."

My body collapsed. Tendrils of golden magic flowed from my stomach into the head of her terrible staff, soaking it up and out of me. I felt empty, like my life leaving my body, and I wondered what had just happened. How did I get so close, only to lose like this?

The ghosts behind me flickered.

Faded.

My voice gone.

Magic gone.

Strength gone.

Cade's name a broken ember in my throat.

She stepped forward.

I can't let it end now. I'm so close. Cade gave his life for this, to give me the chance… I can't die. Not now, not after everything we've been through.

"Ash!" Bella screamed in the distance behind me.

I tried to break free, but I had no strength left in my arms. They felt weighted like anvils, impossible to pick up as my magic fizzled away… *not like this…*

And raised her shoulder, hefting her huge curved blood-red sword. Her devilish eyes were hungry, hungry for my power. For the last of the Gilded Radiance ever, for…

Then—

A *snap*.

Bone.

The queen shrieked.

Cornelius had lunged past me like thunder trapped in a turtle's shell—

And bit her right through the ankle.

I heard the sharp break of bone snapping in two.

Blood poured. Black and putrid, like sulfur and smoke.

She toppled—screaming.

"You—bit—me?" she shrieked, all elegance turned to mad fury. "You little bastard!"

But I was already rising.

The second her spell broke contact from me, Eden surged.

Not like before.

Different.

Alive.

My breath came ragged, gasping—but full. The faces and ghostly bodies behind me surged back.

Cornelius stood beside me; mouth bloodied. I heard him shout one word as he passed:

"Fight!"

And so I did.

I leapt at her with everything I had.

The queen staggered back, even in her rage, her throat snapping curses as her staff swung wildly—but I caught her by the shoulders and slammed her roughly to the ground.

She rolled.

Screamed. Kicked.

Everything felt like fire and muscle and wind, and I straddled her chest and shoved my hands over her jaw.

"What are you doing?" she shrieked, her voice cracking in genuine horror for the first time.

"I just remembered something," I croaked, pressing harder.

"You're—no—" Her flames roared out of her body and staff and sword and mouth as she fought.

I summoned Eden and pressed my power down upon her. But it wasn't all Eden. There was something else in there fighting in me. Something ancient. Something in my blood. Something I'd never known was in me until that very instant.

I used that newfound power to pull on her. Not physically. I pulled hard on something within her.

Water.

We're made of it. Mostly.

The queen's eyes bulged.

"No! What?" She gasped in pain as her chest heaved upward from my tug.

"I may not be able to beat your magic with mine," I rasped. "But there's something else in you that I crave. Something very important to you, to all of us. And it just so happens... I'm fucking Aqualorian. So that water in you belongs to me now!"

I drew the water out of her with my hands pressed tight against her jaw.

Her skin shriveled.

Her lips cracked.

Moisture rose from her eyes, nostrils, ears—blood followed, rich red joining the swirling stream.

I pulled until my whole body shook.

Until her limbs thrashed weakly. "No, no, no," she moaned. But I showed her no sympathy. She took the only thing I truly loved, and I had no pity sucking every drop of water from her blood, leaving nothing but her wretched demon body.

Until the orb of water bloomed in my palm—pure, gauzy blue mixed with red, the size of a grapefruit.

She gasped.

Her voice failing.

"You… can't… I'm… the world needs…"

"No," I whispered, my magic now a roar behind my eyes.

"The world needs mercy," I said. "It needs something you never had the strength to give. It needs love! Compassion! Empathy! Things you never had a shred of!"

Her chest rose one last time.

Then fell.

Her mouth opened to say something—

But her body cracked like burnt paper.

Crumbled.

Blackened.

Ash. Nothing more.

The orb in my hand remained—a shimmering thing of terrible purity.

Behind me, the ghost-army exhaled.

Then vanished, one by one, into the golden air.

CHAPTER 50

The volcano hissed.

Like breath caught in the lungs of something far too old for breathing.

Around me, the world trembled. The last spasms of a mountain too full of death. Lava churned in faraway veins, veins I could hear instead of see—deep, pulsing channels that thumped in time with the dying queen's magic as it bled out from the walls.

The heat hadn't faded with her death.

But the madness had.

The swirling fire that once coiled in the arches of this hell—that danced around her like a monster—was gone. Snuffed like a candle.

I stood at the center of everything she'd tried to build. The dragon still slumbered, breathing softly as the monstrous asp summoned by the queen faded. It fizzled like a swarm of wasps dispersing into the wind. The terrifying snake faded into nothingness. A spell broken like glass. And with that, the phoenix faded as well.

The queen was dead, and all her spells, too, died.

The last rune flared on the altar—then broke, its red spell-mark snapping like a heartbeat broken from rhythm.

And behind me, the body of Cade Phoenixfire lay still in blood gone cold.

It took everything I had not to run to him.

But I couldn't yet.

Because Cornelius was right.

I hadn't saved anything until the dragon woke. That was the key. That was the whole mission. Kill the queen, awaken the slumbering dragon. Save Allovan.

I could still hear Vâllathór's voice in my head all the way back on the beach of Bramblebash the day the rune on my neck sparked alive for the first time…

"You did it!" Cornelius cried behind me, and despite everything—despite the war and the screams and the blood and soot still in my mouth—I spun when I heard it.

Because never in my life had that little tortoise's voice sounded so loud or so alive.

"You did it!" he repeated again, this time stamping both feet against the broken stone beneath him. His shell glowed slightly in the volcanic light, the lines across its surface dimming and pulsing like a heart still kicking. "By the roots of the old gods and the blood of the drowned courts, Ash—Ash! You did it!"

His little eyes were alight—burning bright and orange and gold in a way I'd never seen before, their edges catching the reflection of the fire that licked at the very edges of the altar now. He turned in a tight circle and looked up at me with something so close to pride I nearly forget what came next.

"What do I do now?" I asked, stepping toward the pyre.

He jerked his head to look behind me—toward the great maw of the chamber where Vâllathór, the sleeping dragon, still rested like a great beast, almost part of the mountain itself.

"Now?" he said. "Now you do what no one has done in the Ember Age."

I looked up.

And there she was.

The dragon.

Vâllathór.

Coiled still at the edge of the old world, who hadn't moved during the battle even once, not even when the queen shed her skin and became the decrepit demon of lore.

She had slumbered for centuries.

Gods, she was beautiful in the most terrifying way possible.

Her massive head protruded into the mountain chamber, her body hidden within Calcaedus's heart like a cathedral of scale and bone.

I felt her dormant power in my chest—the old magic. Wild. Untamed.

A lullaby made from everything I never understood about this world.

And suddenly, it all felt too much.

Too big.

"I'm not ready for this," I whispered. "I can't..." I sobbed thinking of Cade. His lifeless body on the ground as I heard Bella whimper back at the cave's entrance.

Behind me, Cornelius was quiet.

Then—

"Finish it," he said. "Fulfill the prophecy. Fulfill your destiny, child."

I took one shuddered breath—inhaled the ash, the smoke, the lingering echo of Cade's last gasp—

And I turned to the pyre.

It still burned.

Not like the fire she controlled. Not like the queen's madness incarnate across the altar. This fire...

This fire was not angry.

It was tired.

It burned low but deeply—colored like the inside of a thundercloud, reds shot through with molten gold, licking softly against the edges of the pyre like it waited for a new story to live in.

I stepped to the edge and lifted my hand.

The orb shimmered in my palm—still warm. The orb of liquid that was the last essence of the queen's body, mind and soul. Still thrumming with faint flickers of light and breath and spell.

The queen's life force.

The water of her. The blood she never let rest. Her essence, stripped and spiraling through my fingers.

"I... don't know what this will do," I said aloud, though I didn't expect anyone to answer.

"Prophecy will catch you," Cornelius replied quietly. "Trust yourself, Ash." His tone was soft, comforting, powerful.

It took everything not to turn again.

Because it wasn't reassurance.

It wasn't comfort.

It was truth.

I felt my feet inch closer.

Beneath me, the floor cracked one more long line—spider-webbing outward beneath the dais. The volcano shifted again, and the world groaned with it—louder now, like even Calcaedus was waiting for me to falter.

I stared into the fire.

I thought of Cade.

My blaze-born prince.

The boy who refused to let me rot in the chains they gave me. Who cut his crown in half just to kneel beside me.

Who died for me.

And I couldn't save him.

My fingers trembled harder. My lip quivered. My chest heaved in sorrow.

But I stepped to the final stair of the altar.

The heat licked up my arms.

And still I thought of him as I stared into the flames.

"An old part of the prophecy," Cornelius said from behind me. "They used to whisper it in the Halls of Glowing Stone, long before the Cinderyn and Aqualorians feuded."

The fire danced.

I gazed down.

At the moment that would end it all.

"At the heart of the volcano," Cornelius spoke, "where the dragon slumbers—fire must turn to water."

His voice grew slower. Sadder.

"Madness must turn to sanity."

I stared forward. My breath felt like stone.

"And violence," he whispered, "must turn… to love."

My throat closed.

The thumping in my chest thrummed. My knees wobbled and my hands shook. But I choked my tears down.

I didn't cry. *Do it for him, Ash. Do it for him.*

Instead, I looked through the gold flame—down, down, until I saw the gods themselves. It was like staring into life itself, and death.

So ancient.

So terrible.

So waiting.

I lowered my hand.

The orb pulsed one last time.

I clutched it.

And I let it fall.

Down into the fire.

Down to where madness ended.

And the new world began.

Behind me, boots slapped against stone, quick and uneven—desperate and half-mad with the urgency of survival.

"Ash!" Bella's voice cracked. "Ash—what did you just—"

They reached me as the last hiss of the queen's extinguished flame peeled across the cavern like the exhale of a dying god.

Bella ran up beside me first. Hunter was just behind her.

Both fell silent.

The orb—the queen's life, torn clean from her magic—had vanished beneath the smoldering soot of the black pyre. In its place, foul vapor spilled upward in snaking tendrils, curling along the charred altar edges like what was left of her tried to cling to the world. The air reeked of dying magic now. Not the acrid twist of fire or brimstone, but something older. Something foul, like a spell's last scream leaking into ruin.

We crouched there on the edge in silence, not daring to breathe too hard. Even when the fire fully died. Even when its red was swallowed by soot and smoke.

"Ash…" Hunter muttered, breathless. "What did you just do?"

My voice hardly lived in my chest. I tried to speak and only managed half a sound.

Bella swallowed hard beside me and wrapped one arm around my shoulders, her other hand reaching out to grasp mine tight. "You disappeared into darkness. But… was that from her? Was that part of the queen?"

"Her life," I managed, throat scraping from ash and grief. "I took what was her… and I dropped it into the fire."

"It just… vanished," Bella whispered, peering over the blackened rim of the altar into the boiling pit that had once looked like the mouth of the old gods.

I didn't answer.

There was nothing to say just yet.

Because in the absence of the fire's scream, something worse was dawning.

A feeling.

A subtle shift like air being sucked backward through stone.

Like gravity giving up.

Bella's arm tightened across my back.

And then the ground beneath the altar groaned.

The puddle of smoldering mire went still.

Then... it moved.

Bubbling.

Boiling.

Veins of black split through the surface again—but they didn't burn. They didn't rise in smoke. They shimmered. The ripples morphed into waves. The pit lingered, alive and churning, as if the queen's essence had not drowned... but been re-shaped.

And it wasn't flame anymore.

The bubbling slowed.

Thick black swirls settled across the once-hoarse basin, like jelly turned to water. The smoke gave way to steam, and color began to creep back into the world—not chaotic, not burning.

Blue.

A pale blue glow unfolded at the center.

Not fire.

Water.

Still and cold as the dawn before snow.

Bella saw it first.

"What..." She stepped with me to the edge of the altar, voice gone glass-soft. "What is that?"

"I... I don't know," I admitted, blinking heated tears from my lashes. "But I think it's working."

Hunter wrapped his palm around my shoulder. Silent. Strong. Present in the way only he could be as something he didn't understand slipped out from under gods-deep prophecy. His eyes stared down into the glow, lost but unmovable.

The altar had filled.

No heat radiated from below anymore. Only a calm pool, cutting stark and cold against the scorched stone, steam whispering upward in rivulets laced now with scents of pine and morning snow instead of brimstone.

It was... beautiful.

And then—

Bella inhaled sharply and clutched my arm.

"Ash. Your hands."

I looked down.

My arms were still extended toward the pool, hovering softly above the surface.

My hands had gone inside.

When had I—

I didn't remember moving them. But my fingers disappeared past the wrists, submerged in the water.

And it didn't burn.

It didn't scald.

But it wasn't gentle either.

It felt like standing at the edge of memory. Like something was searching through me, back through time, through scars, through night after night of curled silence next to the moonlit wall in Bramblebash—the cellar where I used to count breaths so I wouldn't cry and wake Bella.

And deeper still.

To my first name.

My true name.

Ashlyn.

"Are you okay?" Hunter asked roughly, moving closer—but Bella stretched one arm out, catching him.

"Look," she breathed.

The water rippled again.

From somewhere inside the pool, light flared.

Not white.

Not gold.

Not violet.

But an ancient blue that shimmered like glacier ice, threaded with golden veins that pulsed once—twice—

Then the pool calmed entirely.

Bella's grip on my arm trembled.

"I don't know what we did," she whispered. "But gods, I think it mattered."

That's when the sound came.

Not from the altar.

But from behind it.

From beneath the stone carved around something older than Emberveil.

A wind.

A breath.

No—not a breeze. Not a gale.

A wind carried on heat, wider than the mouth of the mountain, deeper than the veins of the world.

It hit us all at once.

A single, explosive exhale.

Searing, massive, tender, and terrifying all at once.

The cavern roared as it came. Dust flared upward in every direction. Loose cloth snapped backwards, hair whipped forward, and heat blasted over our faces with a moisture-rich sting that tasted like ash and ocean and bone.

Bella yelped and shielded her eyes.

Hunter swore and staggered a step.

But I didn't move.

I couldn't.

Because I knew what that wind had come from.

We all did.

And we didn't speak—

Because she was no longer asleep.

The dragon had awoken.

Vâllathór.

Born before ruin. Slumbering longer than stone remembered to whisper.

She rose.

Gods help me, she rose.

Soot rained down from the ceiling as groans echoed across

the chamber like cathedral bells finding grief instead of worship. I turned. Slowly.

Just in time to see the dragon's eyes slowly open like a mourning veil. Her head rose as it cast an unnatural shadow down on us. The rock wall behind her crumbled and broke as she raised her head, her long, horned neck breaking through the thick rock wall like a scythe cutting through hay. The mountain felt as if it was crumbling down all around us, but somehow it only broke where the great dragon broke free.

One colossal wing flared outward, knocking full swaths of ancient rock from their foundation without even touching them. A single beat of motion—slow, stretching—bowled the air into a cyclone.

She lifted her head above us.

And there were her eyes.

Golden.

Radiant.

Like suns flooded with memory.

I fell to my knees without deciding to.

So did Bella. So did Hunter. I'd given everything I had, and I had nothing left to give. I gave in. I gave everything I had to her majesty. She was the most beautiful and frightening thing I'd ever seen.

The moment Vâllathór's enormous body stood fully upright, the last of the queen's madness truly died.

Because no curse could stand under that gaze.

I didn't weep.

But something inside me cracked.

Not grief.

Not pain.

Humility.

The dragon's chest moved once then twice, flame rising in curls down her spine, smoke twisting upward from the corners of her huge scaly mouth like incense finally freed. Her scales glimmered with dew-vapors as her neck turned slowly—painfully slow—as if even waking was a resurrection.

Then—

Her head dipped.

Low.

Not in threat.

But acknowledgment.

To me.

"We did it," I whispered.

No one echoed me.

They didn't have to.

The air told us everything—and it said: A new age begins now.

Vâllathór… had returned to the world.

And I had not died.

And neither had hope.

Not yet.

Not today.

CHAPTER 51

Vâllathór's eyes were godlike in a way I found difficult to look away from. They were like staring into the heavens, into divinity, into oblivion.

Each golden iris peeled wide from a film of ancient sleep, the whites of her eyes streaked with veins of sorrowed magic that shimmered beneath the volcanic gloom. Vâllathór's head rose in measured, arresting motion—up from where it had been curled across the scorched stone like a resting mountain wrapped in time.

I stood frozen at the altar's edge, staring up.

And up.

The breath in my chest forgot how to move.

Her eyes—gods.

No creature, no person, no force I've ever stood before had met me like that.

Bella's hand squeezed mine once. A grounding pulse that made my blood start flowing again. She was locked beside me with her mouth slightly open, as if something holy had drawn it ajar. Hunter was wordless on my other side, one hand still resting on the hilt of his blade, but even his war-trained body stilled completely as the weight of the dragon's wake curled around us.

Vâllathór's neck stretched, massive and lined with plate-wide ridges of silver-flecked horn. Ancient flame steamed from the vents along her body as she moved. Her wings—gods, her wings hadn't even spread yet, and already I could feel them uncoiling in the air like a truth the world had forgotten to tell.

She eyed us all in a silence made from centuries.

Then slowly, she drew in a breath.

And the entire cavern shifted with it.

The altar dampened. The fire at the chamber's edge dimmed. Even the lava rich in the veins far below hissed a note lower. It was as if the volcano itself had waited for her to draw breath again before it would continue to believe in heat.

Cornelius stood two steps ahead of me, eyes wide.

He stared up at her.

At the thing he'd spoken of in quiet riddles and riddled dreams.

And for the first time since I'd known him… I saw tears glistening under his golden eyes.

Big, bright welts welling slowly and tracking silently down the patterned creases along his leathery cheeks, sliding to the cracked edge of his moss-green shell. His tree-trunk feet stayed planted, but his body trembled just slightly, as if the moment had peeled him open and there was nothing left to keep that awe from leaking out.

He'd waited a thousand years for this.

Guided me from the darkness toward a myth.

A myth that now… blinked at him like she remembered him, too.

My voice nearly failed at first.

But I had to say something.

She had to know.

I stepped forward.

"Great dragon," I said, my voice quiet, tentative, frayed. "You're free."

The chamber echoed the word. *Free.*

I lifted my chin, shoving back the grief clawing through my chest.

"Queen Vissex the Cinderyn is dead," I continued. "She was the one who wanted to drain your life away. But she's gone. You're free again."

The dragon's breath stirred again, curling smoke against the domed ceiling.

"And…" I swallowed. My eyes burned. "Allovan is free from the queen's terrible chaotic rule. At great cost however, and not without loss…"

My fingers trembled around my golden sword's hilt, though it remained dim in my hand now. At peace.

"This world was cracked," I said. "We broke it. We let power destroy meaning, and we let fear decide leadership. But I didn't fight this war because I wanted a throne. Or a name carved in quiet places."

My throat tightened even more.

"I fought… for peace. I fought for my friends. I fought for a man I loved—"

I broke.

"I fought for a chance at something kinder."

Eyes still on the beast, I slowly raised my flame-woven hand and placed it over my heart. The action sparked faint rings of light across the marble floor, like Eden was nodding beside me.

"So," I whispered.

"If any part of you can still choose—"

My gaze rose toward the massive dragon again, catching the flicker of her golden, unknowable eyes.

"Let this world see peace again," I said. "Please."

Vâllathór blinked—or what passed for a blink—and in that

second, I knew that she was more than a dragon. She held a power within her that dwarfed my own.

No sound echoed in return.

But the warmth in the air shifted.

Like some invisible mist had drawn in closer to us.

She hadn't spoken.

But I didn't think she needed to.

Because behind us, the cavern crumbled—

And the dragons arrived.

Krakos fell first through the fractured dome above, his wings bloody at the edges, his massive black body still alight with fires not fully cooled. He moved with care, even in his urgency—even in his pain. He landed half on his side, one shoulder catching the cracked slope of a crumbled pillar, his neck already craning downward as he let out a low, heart-punching whimper.

Not for himself.

But for the body before him.

Cade.

Krakos inched closer.

He bowed his head once.

Touched Cade's shoulder with a breath that steamed like sorrow.

"Shit," Bella whispered, soft and pained and close beside me. "I'm not ready for this…"

Talonor and Errax followed through the broken arch soon after—wings thunderclapping as they dropped in past the breach, smoke trailing the bruises of battle across their flanks. Talonor ground his claws to regain balance mid-landing. Errax hit the stone hard then tipped her jaw to scan for me.

But Krakos didn't rise.

He remained beside his rider—they were bound by blood and bonded in heart.

I turned.

Saw him again.

Cade.

Laid still as stone.

Black leather soaked in drying red.

His lips open just slightly, parted from his last breath like he was still trying to speak my name.

I stepped back toward him.

The pull was magnetic.

Painful.

I couldn't not go.

I broke from the others.

I ran across the broke floor toward his dead body. Lava sizzled up gasps with each of my steps, steam licking my boots—but I didn't care. I fell to my knees beside him again.

Laid across his chest.

My scream broke with tears. "I'm sorry," I sobbed. "I'm so sorry, Cade. I didn't save you—I tried, I—"

My breath hitched like it had never learned how to be steady.

"I can't do it. I can't walk out of this place without you. Not after everything—not after all we've done." My hands curled against his chest armor, nails clawing at the scorched fastenings. "I thought we made it... I thought we could..."

I let myself cry now.

Not for legend.

Not for war.

But for the man.

The one who hurt me and held me and taught me that love could ache and still be right.

"You said we'd burn it all down together," I whispered, lips pressed to the crook of his neck. "You don't get to leave me here. You don't get to finish this without me."

My hand cupped one cold cheek, cradling it. "I love you," I croaked. "You idiot. You stubborn, perfect, infuriating man—I love you... forever..."

My forehead sank to his.

"Goodbye," I whispered.

"Goodbye."

I didn't hear her move, but Vâllathór came close.

The weight of her was impossible to ignore—every breath a chorus, every step a quake waiting for permission. The massive dragon shifted her body forward, trailing smoke from her long neck as she leaned, leaned, leaned down, colossal golden eyes fixed on the broken man in my arms.

And on me.

Tears soaked Cade's collar now as I pressed my forehead to his, running my hands frantically across his skin like if I just warmed him fast enough, he'd come back.

But the truth sat heavy between us.

He was still.

Lips parted.

Eyes closed.

Breathless.

"No," I whispered again. I couldn't say anything else. Nothing helpful came anymore. Just that word—the slow erosion of my chest. "I don't want to do this all without you..." I heaved tears and choked on gasped breaths.

Vâllathór's shadow dipped lower.

With that same reverent deliberation, she lowered her head, the halo of her breath ruffling what hair still clung to Cade's forehead. Her gold eyes blinked, then narrowed with something that looked close to... understanding. Maybe even sorrow.

Then she spoke.

Not like a human. Not in a tongue I'd ever heard in my mostly awful life.

Her voice was ancient. Deep.

Cracked like stone, and dripping with the echo of things forgotten.

A slow roll of syllables echoed across the inner hollow of her throat as she exhaled—something between a dragonsong and thunder made soft for the grieving. The sound poured down on us.

I didn't move.

Cornelius stepped forward then—so close to me I felt his breath on my neck.

He blinked up, slowly. "I... I don't know the words," he muttered through his breath. "I can't... gods, I've studied her voices for so long..." He trailed off. "I don't understand this one."

I wiped my nose uselessly on my wrist, still hunched over Cade's chest.

"I do," I heard Errax say inside my head.

I jolted.

Her voice was calm. Sad.

But steady.

"The Elder Mother speaks only once with this tongue. It is given only in death. It... is the Last Gift."

I held my breath.

"She says," Errax continued slowly, her voice shaking in my thoughts, "... she has one sacred gift left in her long life. And that she may give it—just once."

My gaze darted frantically from Cade's face to Vâllathór's.

"To be used not on the greatest warrior, or the cruelest enemy. Not even to reward devotion. Only... to be placed upon one deserving."

The hollow between my ribs cracked open wider.

"Only someone who stood on the brink," Errax said, "and chose sacrifice without hope of return. She deems Cade Phoenix-fire deserving."

I couldn't breathe.

The tears started again, heavier now, as Vâllathór slowly began to open her jaw.

Her great silvered tongue curled back beneath ridges of scarred flesh. And from beneath it—

A light surfaced.

Small.

Smooth.

Round.

She curled it forward on her tongue with a sound like breath over glass, then let it drop.

A pearl.

Glowing with internal light.

Not gold. Not red.

White.

A soft, flickering white like moon on milk.

It descended, not fast—graceful as snowfall.

The pearl hovered just above Cade's body.

I didn't move.

I didn't dare breathe.

It pulsed once with light.

Then fell—

And landed upon the ragged wound carved through his throat.

The moment it made contact, light erupted.

It wasn't harsh. Not like war-magic. This was soft, glowing, tender.

It soaked through him.

Down through armor, bone, blood.

The pearl vanished into his skin in a final blink of shimmer—

And the light around it fell still.

For a horrible, endless moment… nothing changed.

Time paused.

And then—

He breathed.

It started with a twitch at his throat.

Then his chest rose—just barely.

I choked on my own gasp and sat upright, eyes locked to his features.

Another breath.

Then his fingers twitched.

"Cade?" I whispered, too afraid to hope. "Cade—?"

He coughed.

Sharp. Wet.

Then groaned under it.

"Oh my gods—" My voice broke and I fell over him again, wrapping both arms around him and smoothing back his hair in a frantic wave of sobs. "You're alive—you're—you're—"

He coughed again, bone-deep and desperate, then rasped, "Stop squeezing me… to death."

A laugh tore out of me like something sick and beautiful all at once, cracking loud through quiet like hope finding its legs. I kissed his cheek, then his jaw, then his brow.

Then, unable to hold it back—

I kissed his mouth.

And to my infinite joy, he kissed me back.

Fingers weakly curling into my tunic.

Tears spilled between both our faces as I cradled his jaw with shaking hands.

"My gods," I whispered. "You idiot, you beautiful cursed idiot—you came back. You fucking came back."

His voice rasped, dry as cracked earth. "You're not getting rid of me that easy."

"You broke my heart—"

He smiled with half a wince. "Hi gorgeous."

I tried to smile but my lips quivered too hard. "I didn't get to say goodbye."

This time, his expression crumpled.

"I heard you," he whispered.

I gasped.

He swallowed. "That you loved me."

I sobbed again and cradled him close.

Behind me, someone sniffled.

Bella.

Then another sound.

Hunter.

I turned just as both of them came forward, openly crying now as they sank beside Cade and collapsed half-laughing, half-sobbing across my shoulders.

"Asshole! Will you stop trying to die all the time?" Bella covered her mouth with one hand. "I'm not grieving you again!"

Hunter gasped, pointing at Cade with wide, wet eyes. "You—do you know what you put us through! Do you always have to be so fucking dramatic?"

Krakos let out a whimper so deep it shook dust from the broken wall.

Cade lifted a hand weakly toward his dragon.

His dragon nuzzled it.

"By Odiun's ghost," Cade muttered as all of us fell around him like warm ruin. "How am I alive?" He'd been so lost in me and his dragon, he apparently just saw the enormous Elder Dragon hovering above us all. "But the gods…" His mouth gaped.

"It's over, Cade. We won. Your step mother is dead. And Vâllathór brought you back. She had the gift to give one time of life, and she gifted it to you… to us!"

He smiled.

Then coughed again.

"Which means I think I may officially… have lost count… of how many times… you've saved me now."

I laughed through teeth and snot and tears.

"That better be the last fucking time," I snarled, kissing his forehead hard as my voice cracked, "or I'll kill you myself. I'm not joking this time."

"Oh stars," Bella wheezed, fanning her face. "This guilt cry is never going to stop. You hitch one sob and I'm back down again!"

Hunter didn't say anything.

But he took Cade's hand.

And held it.

And that gesture...

Gods, it undid me all over again.

We wept together.

War-shattered and miracle-bound.

The cavern held us like the bone of something better, something older.

Cornelius stepped beside us, tears still trailing his cheeks, eyes red-rimmed and gleaming with golden peace.

"The gift," he said softly, voice thick. "Thank you, great dragon. I hope I prove it worthy."

The great dragon tipped her head toward us one last time.

Then lowered it gently—slowly—until her muzzle nearly brushed the stone.

A bow.

A benediction.

Then—

Furling her wings inward, she stepped back into the shadows of Calcaedus.

Her enormous body disappeared into the heart of the volcano, leaving only crumbling stone in her wake.

We lay together in a heap.

Tears flooding dark soil.

And for the first time in my memory—

There was no fire.

Only light.

Only breath.

Only the unbearable beauty of having been broken.

And still...

Still loved back.

CHAPTER 52

We left the volcano and stood back out on the obsidian balcony of Raven's Bane Castle.

The sky cracked open like it remembered how to breathe.

Vâllathór roared from within.

No, it wasn't a roar. Not like Krakos's scream, or even Brigodon's bellow, who'd flown off after the queen's death. This was something bigger. Ancient. Older than wind and louder than the silence of gods who'd watched with their mouths closed for centuries. The sound didn't carry across the air—it carved it.

We stood at the edge of the altar platform in stunned silence, bodies still trembling from the war, ashes still webbed through blood, magic clinging to our skin like oil in light. The dragon—the Elder Mother Dragon, the dreamer of myth, the sleeper of stone—emerged from the upper crest of the Calcaedus.

The volcano let her rise.

Stone peeled like eggshell as Vâllathór unfurled her wings. Each enormous panel of silver-black webbing cracked the air, their edges brushed with the glow of gold magic passed down by names no longer known. Her chest inflated, flame moving visibly beneath her armored ribs, thunderous and slow, and with a slam of force that staggered even Krakos…

She burst into the sky.

Smoke and lava churned behind her, ember and mist spiraling around her long tail like veil ribbons as her body cut upward through Calcaedus's ceiling. The gap of her power flaring blew open the remnants of the volcano's broken dome—we raised our arms against the wind but none of us looked away. Not even as wind lashed our cheeks, or ash peppered our armor, or molten cracks spat sparks inches from our boots.

Because she was flying.

Alive.

Awake.

Free.

Vâllathór blazed through what remained of the upper caldera, wings pumping like the breath of flame reborn. The air hissed as she ascended, heat trailing beneath her like the tail of a comet birthed in vengeance and miracle alike. Then—

She broke through.

Sunlight, whole-sky-wide and glorious, seared down through the hole she tore in the heavens, and for the first time since our arrival on Emberveil's cliffs, the light was warm.

She soared out over Allovan on wings that once held empires at bay. And the world watched.

We moved to our dragons. Bella grabbed my arm—shaking, streaked in blood—and tugged me with a wild light in her eyes. Hunter followed her silently, wrist bloodied from a split in his gauntlet but jaw set, his blade still drawn, as if the war might reach once more toward us even now, at the edge of awe.

Cade staggered beside me, his whole body supported by Krakos's shoulder, the great dragon cradling him with one claw as if re-learning how to greet a fallen rider. Cade didn't speak. Didn't smile.

He just stared at the hole Vållathór made through the volcano's peak.

We glared down at the war torn remnants of Emberveil, still smoldering, alive with thousands staring up in awe at the great dragon.

The world lay beneath us.

And every soul in it had stopped moving.

Far below, carved into the bleeding ruin of the battlefields, the city had fallen silent. Fires still smoked from shattered towers. Dragons banked slowly across the city's drag-scarred hollows, gliding now instead of diving. Not fighting.

Watching.

Every Syther body upon the wall had turned away. Even those not dead—those twisted and writhing behind what remained of Emberveil's upper barracks—were stopped mid-motion, blades wavering in confused fingers as if the blood in their veins had suddenly gone ice.

They looked up.

I saw it—in every twisted, sick body—the moment they realized. That their queen was gone. That the fire she'd chained them to was no longer theirs.

They ran.

Sprinted from the walls like plague-flames whipped by wind, retreating into the caves to the south, into the smoke-blackened ravines where the mountain's tears still bled. Screeching as they went, falling over each other in mindless escape.

Elsewhere—in the upper guardwalk, then the eastern bridge, then the crowns of the tower spires—Emberveil's dragon riders slowly sheathed their blades. Their dragons curled wings around themselves like dogs losing the scent of their mistress.

And they knelt.

They didn't fight anymore.

They didn't speak.

They just... knelt.

One by one.

A thousand dragons spread across the crumbled city.

A thousand riders bowing low.

Cloaks fell to the ground.

Armor rang as it hit the stone.

From the cliff of the volcano, a chorus of wind passed around us.

And every flame guttered.

No one had to announce it.

They knew.

Everyone who could feel the size of Vâllathór spiraling above understood in their bones what had happened.

The queen was dead.

And something better had been born in her place.

"Look," came Hunter's voice beside me—barely above a whisper.

The Terradyne stood in rows across the fallen walls of Emberveil.

Still.

Stunned.

Their old, knowing eyes—if such things could be called eyes—watched the sky as if it had offered them a hymn.

I didn't speak.

I couldn't.

Because Vâllathór at last circled above—all wings and tail and quiet—and the clouds parted.

And that's when they roared.

Not the dragons.

The Stormscales.

They began to shout.

A deep, chest-grown bellow that shot up like thunder through the broken teeth of Emberveil's fortress city. It bled from the lower levels of the caldera outward.

Victory.

A tide of it.

The roar rolled and rolled, growing.

The dragon riders of Stormscale raised their fists, their blades, their lives to the sky.

And the wild dragons arched their backs and swooped down and around in tight spirals like sky-writing birds.

And for one staggering heartbeat—

We were all just part of something that had survived.

Next to me, Cade sank to one knee, and I dropped too.

We watched Vâllathór spiral wide across the golden light— and at her widest arc, she shrieked once.

Not in threat.

But in celebration.

Then with one final swoop, she burst higher into the heavens and disappeared into the clouds.

Gone.

Free.

And we were left behind—not smaller.

But chosen.

I turned to Cade.

And in that holy hush that followed her exit—

I kissed him.

The descent back toward Emberveil felt nothing like the first time we'd faced it.

Where once flame, grief, and ash hung thick enough to choke the soul, now—wind swept clean paths across the sky. Our dragons flew without formation, no military order in their wings, no fury in their beat—only freedom. Krakos flew ahead beside Talonor, their arcs wide as if measuring the contours of victory for the first time.

Errax carried me lower, my heart still stuttering in my chest as we neared the castle steps.

Below us, the world waited.

Stormscales lined the base of Raven's Bane. Shoulder to shoulder. Blade to blade.

They had formed in rows—not out of necessity—but reverence.

Survivors.

Soot-coated, bone-tired, scarred, still bleeding in places, several with arms in makeshift slings, others missing bits they'd once counted on.

But they stood together.

When Krakos smacked down onto the flagstones—his claws clawing into the ground like a war-born king coming home—an instant cheer broke like thunder.

I landed next, and Errax crouched down gently, lowering her neck so I could slide from the saddle.

The moment my feet hit stone, the world tilted around me— too bright, too real.

Then Carina was running across the courtyard.

Her wild blond braid had long unraveled. Her face was streaked with soot and tears. Ash glimmered along her jaw like cracked marble. A split ran across one of her pauldrons, the edges smoking faintly. Her breastplate was broken at the hip; her belt barely clung to her waist.

And her eyes were torn open in pain.

But I didn't see that right away.

I only saw her, alive.

I ran toward her, and we collided, arms thrown around each other like we'd both held our arms open and empty for far, far too long.

"We won!" I gasped against her lion-strong shoulder. "We won, Carina—we beat her—"

She didn't say it.

She didn't move.

Just sobbed. Shuddered.

I pulled back slightly, cupping her face, blinking fast as she curled inward.

Carina didn't weep like a soldier.

She wept like a daughter who'd just lost her entire sky.

Something inside me sank.

"No," I breathed. "What... Carina, what—where's your father? Where's Darren?"

She didn't answer with words.

She simply turned.

A slow pivot of shoulders toward the eastern drawbridge, where the column of Stormscales had parted.

One dragon approached in silence, the crowd parting like a sea already drowned in grief.

The dragon walked.

Not soared.

Its claws landed heavy upon the blood-streaked stones of the bridge, armor pitted and dented along its flanks. Its neck bowed slightly, a priest readying for mass.

And draped gently across its back, lay a broken body.

Darren Iconnas.

Wrapped in the tattered flag of the Stormscales. His greatsword laid across his chest. His armor soaked through, punctured in blood-soaked places. His face rested in full view, peaceful as still water.

One breath from death's reach, and already the silence honored him like a cathedral would its last saint.

I didn't shout.

I didn't scream.

I covered my mouth as my legs nearly buckled.

"Oh, gods..." I whispered, tears flooding hot behind my eyes as my throat choked. "No. Oh gods, no—"

Carina pressed her face into my shoulder and broke.

Truly sobbed now.

Ragged.

Wrong.

Enormous.

I wrapped both arms around her tight enough to starve the grief, but it didn't work.

Nothing would've right then.

"I'm so sorry," I whispered into her hair. "I'm so, so sorry, Carina. He was—he was—"

I couldn't even finish the sentence.

He'd been more than a general to the Stormscales. More than a warrior or a tactician.

He'd been the spark behind the rebellion. The one who begged for change without asking for forgiveness. Too proud to rest. Too angry to forget. The soul of it all, even when coated in blood.

And now... he was gone.

Carina shook in my arms.

I heard Hunter behind us sigh deep enough to empty the mountain and the sea.

Cade was already stepping forward—to the dragon's side.

Still pale, still gasping from his own resurrection—but whole. Alive. Firelight dancing across the back of his wild black hair.

He walked the last few paces to Darren's body. Laid a hand across the man's shoulder.

He didn't say anything at first.

Then I saw him bow his head.

A man giving grace to one who once tried to kill him.

"General Iconnas," Cade said aloud.

A hush swept through the courtyard.

Cade's voice was raspy but clear. "We once fought across opposite walls. Spoke in threats. Drew lines in fire. Each believing the other had spared too little, or too much."

His eyes were soft now.

"But I'd be proud to have fought beside you."

I covered my tears, my chest burning.

Cade brushed his hand once down the man's shattered vambrace. "You led with fury when peace wouldn't listen. You died an honorable death—and there aren't many who get that right."

Cade lifted his face to the sky.

"And we will carry your legacy forward."

Carina's sob eased just slightly.

She pulled back, her face streaked with the kind of grief that looked like molten glass—not shattered, but reshaped in heat.

She didn't speak.

Not at first.

Then she turned to me.

"You're still here," she whispered, touching the corner of my jaw like she couldn't believe it. "We won."

It was disbelief, blooming slow across her smudged face, like a flower afraid to open in winter.

I nodded, fresh tears spilling anyway. "We did."

She laughed—half scream, half wonder, raw and soaked with grief and joy alike.

Then I stepped back.

Not to leave her.

But to take the next step required.

To call it what it was.

To name the miracle.

My golden magical sword of the Gilded Radiance erupted from my hand and I slowly turned toward the crowd.

My voice shook.

But it didn't falter.

I raised the blade over my head—glowing still with the light of every girl who'd burned before me.

"The queen is dead!"

Silence.

Then a beat.

Then a swell of noise so loud it cracked.

Stormscales cheered.

Shouted.

Dropped their weapons, their pain, and let beast-shouts of victory fly from their bloodied lungs.

"The queen is dead!"

They echoed it.

The soldiers who'd bled from one city to the next. Who'd buried brothers in smoke and fathers in frost—

"The queen is dead!"

Bella's voice joined mine as I shouted again, breathless, sword held high.

"Allovan is ours again!" I cried. "May one thousand years of peace reign!"

The courtyard shook with cheers.

"Let slavery forever rot in the past!"

Roars. Claps. Screams that cracked from lungs in triumph.

"And may hope burn brighter than flame—"

I raised the blade higher.

"—because we are still alive!"

The whole fortress roared beneath me.

The dragons shrieked above.

And the people of Emberveil stood in awe and deep contemplation.

I turned slowly, dizzy with adrenaline. Looked to Bella.

She was grinning.

That cocky, stupid little smirk that looked far too sure of itself even in a war.

I mouthed the words.

Oh my gods. We actually did it.

She raised one brow.

Winked.

"I never had a doubt."

Then Cade's fingers found mine again, and I clenched his hand tighter than anything.

We stood together, broken in blood, a blade still slick in my palm—
But free.
Really, truly free.
And for the first time since I was a child—
I found peace.

<h1 style="text-align:center">CHAPTER 53</h1>

That night in Cade's bedroom, we were getting ready to sleep after our victory. As we stood at the foot of the bed, Cade kissed me deeply, his hands moving to undress me. I returned the kiss with equal fervor, helping him remove his clothes as well. There was an electric charge in the air, a sense of anticipation and excitement that had nothing to do with the war we had just won.

In the sanctity of Cade's chamber, the victory that had been won on the battlefield felt like a mere whisper compared to the urgent need that consumed us both. The air thickened with the scent of triumph and the unspoken promise of release from the relentless tension of war. As we stood beside the grand bed, our clothes fell away in a frenzy of hands and lips, each piece discarded like shackles finally broken.

Cade's gaze drank in the sight of my naked form, a reverence in his eyes that made me feel like a goddess.

He reached for me, his hands skimming my curves with a delicate roughness that sent shivers cascading up and down my skin, through my core.

I responded in kind, my fingers mapping the contours of his

battle-hardened body, every ridge and scar a testament to our shared ordeal.

With a swift motion, Cade lifted me and laid me upon the bed, his body following mine, his hardened cock grazing the soft valley between my thighs. The contact elicited a moan from my lips, the heat of his arousal against my wetness making me desperate for more. Cade's hand found my center, his thumb circling my clit with maddening precision that had me arching off the bed, my body aching for fulfillment. But with a newfound assertiveness, I placed my hand over his, stilling his movements.

"Not this way," I said, my voice a sultry whisper that betrayed my need. "I want to take control this time."

Cade's eyes darkened with desire at my words, a silent acknowledgment of my demand. He rolled onto his back, his cock standing proud and ready, the evidence of his own desire clear for me to see. I straddled him, my knees pressing into the soft fabric of the bed, my hands resting on his chest for balance. With my eyes locked on his, I positioned myself above him, the head of his cock nudging against my slick entrance.

Slowly, I sank onto him, the feeling of his girth stretching me open, sending a jolt of pleasure through my body. Cade's sharp intake of breath mirrored my own as I took him fully inside me, the sensation of being filled so completely making me feel powerful and in control. I began to move, my hips undulating in a hypnotic rhythm, each roll driving Cade deeper within me.

The sight of me above him, my breasts bouncing with every movement, my hair cascading down my back in wild waves, was almost too much for him to bear. He reached up, cupping my breasts in his hands, his thumbs brushing over my hardened nipples, eliciting moans of pleasure from my lips. The sensation of his hands on my body, coupled with the feeling of him inside me, sent waves of ecstasy coursing through my veins.

His musk poured into my nostrils like a drug I was completely lost to.

I drank his aroma. I devoured his animalistic urge to take me, because I was the alpha now. I had tamed the dark prince, and he would be mine forever now.

I leaned forward, my hands braced against the headboard, my body rocking back and forth, my clit grinding against the base of his cock with each movement. Cade's hands slid down to my hips, gripping me tightly as he thrust upward to meet me, the rhythm of our lovemaking growing more fervent with each passing moment.

Another moan left my lips and I stared down at his chest as I sank my nails in. He winced and I didn't apologize. He bit his lip as his gorgeous face stared up at me, drinking me in as he took me.

No pain. No boundaries. It was pure. It was dirty. And he was *all mine.*

The sound of our bodies coming together, the slick sound of my wetness enveloping him, filled the room, mingling with our ragged breaths and murmured words of love and encouragement. I felt the tension building within me, a coil wound tight with anticipation, each thrust bringing me closer to the brink.

Cade could sense my approaching climax, my inner walls tightening around him, and it drove him wild. He sat up, wrapping his arms around me, our bodies pressed tightly together as we moved as one. My legs wrapped around his waist, my arms around his neck, our lips crashing together in a passionate kiss that seemed to shatter the heavens.

The new angle had Cade's cock rubbing against me in just the right spot, sending shockwaves of pleasure radiating through my body. I broke the kiss, throwing my head back, my cries of pleasure echoing off the stone walls of the chamber. Cade's lips found the sensitive skin of my neck, kissing and nipping as I rode him harder, the world narrowing down to the sensation of our bodies joined in ecstasy.

With a final, desperate thrust, I felt myself tumble over the edge, my orgasm crashing over me like a wave, my body convulsing around Cade's cock as I cried out his name. The sensation of my tightening around him was too much for Cade to handle, and with a low growl, he found his own release, his body shuddering beneath me as he filled me with his warmth.

We collapsed onto the bed, a tangle of limbs and heavy breaths, our hearts beating in sync as we basked in the afterglow of our shared climax. I lay atop Cade, his arms holding me close, our bodies still intimately connected. The room was filled with the scent of our lovemaking, a sweet perfume that spoke of victory, of passion, and of a love that had been forged in the fires of war and had emerged stronger than ever.

In that moment, as we lay in each other's arms, the weight of the world we had fought so hard to save seemed far away. All that mattered was the here and now, the feeling of Cade's heart beating beneath my cheek, and the knowledge that we had faced the darkness together and emerged into the light. It was a perfect moment, one that would be etched into our memories for all eternity, a testament to the unbreakable bond we shared.

As sleep finally began to claim us, I whispered three simple words into the quiet of the room, my voice soft but filled with conviction. "I love you."

Cade's response was a gentle squeeze of his arms around me, a silent vow that he would always be there to protect me, to cherish me, and to love me for as long as the stars shone in the night sky.

"Can you believe it?" I muttered, lost in the depths of his eyes and in the pure bliss of his smile.

"There's no fucking way we won, right? This is all a dream? We died didn't we?" he half-laughed.

"Well... you did. I know that much for certain," I said as he slid his fingernails up my arm, sending the hairs there stiffening. "What was death like? Do you remember any of it?"

He mounted me unexpectedly, and with a completely serious

tone that startled me, he said, "It wasn't as bad as not being able to take you whenever and wherever I wanted."

Our laughter mingled with the dying embers of the fireplace, a symphony of joy and contentment.

"You can have me whenever you want, King Cade Phoenixfire…" I raised an eyebrow and gave him a seductive shrug. I even played with my hair for good measure.

"King…" he sighed. "I don't like the sound of that at all…"

"Well you've got a whole kingdom and continent that's going to be calling you that, so you better get used to it." I twisted his nipple for an exclamation point.

"Ow," he smirked past the pain. "Well… If that's what I'm meant to be… then I suppose they're going to expect you to be my queen…"

My heart swelled with a love so profound it threatened to burst from my chest. Cade's proposal, though unconventional in its timing, felt right in every possible way. I was his, and he was mine—a truth that had been seared into our very souls through the crucible of war.

"Yes," I said, my voice trembling with emotion. "Yes, Cade Phoenixfire, I will marry you… but I don't think I can be a queen."

"Give it time, it'll grow on you…" he said and I wrapped my arms around him, tearing up into his neck. "I can't believe this. It's like a dream. Actually, it's more than a dream. I never, ever would have imagined this to be my life. Thank you, Cade. I'm so happy. I could scream from the mountaintops." I couldn't contain myself and shouted out up into the room, the ecstasy of my newfound life building like a steamy release. "You've changed everything about my life. I can't thank you enough."

"Ash, you were the one who changed my life. So I must thank you… will you help me rebuild this kingdom to be what Allovan needs it to be? It would be the greatest honor of my life…"

"Yes… Of course I will."

Cade's eyes lit up with a fire that had nothing to do with his elemental affinity. He pulled me close, his lips finding mine in a kiss that was both a promise and a celebration. It was a kiss that spoke of a future filled with hope, of a love that had been hard-won and was all the more precious for it.

As our kiss deepened, the embers of desire that had been banked by our shared climax were fanned back to life. I felt Cade's arousal growing once again, a testament to the insatiable hunger that existed between us. I pressed my body against his, reveling in the feel of his hardened length against my bare skin.

Cade groaned into the kiss, his hands roaming over my body with a reverence that made me feel like the most cherished woman in all of Allovan. He broke the kiss, his breathing heavy as he looked into my eyes.

"Are you sure you're up for more?" he asked, a playful smirk tugging at the corners of his mouth. "I don't want to wear you out on our first night as future king and queen."

I returned his smirk with one of my own, my hand sliding down his chest to grip his cock firmly. "I think I can handle you, Prince of Blaze."

With a growl of approval, Cade flipped me over onto my back, his body pinning mine to the bed. He entered me in one smooth stroke, the sensation of our bodies joining together once again sending a jolt of pleasure coursing through us both.

This time, our lovemaking was slower, more deliberate. Cade moved within me with a measured pace, each thrust designed to stoke the flames of our passion without rushing toward the inevitable conclusion. I pushed my hips and ass back, pulling him deeper inside me, my nails raking into his muscular behind as I matched his rhythm.

Our bodies moved together in perfect harmony, a dance as old as time and as new as the love we shared. Cade's lips found the sensitive skin of my neck, his teeth grazing my pulse point as he whispered words of love and adoration. My heart soared with each utterance, my body alight with a pleasure that was as much emotional as it was physical.

As we climbed higher and higher toward the peak of our passion, the world outside the castle walls ceased to exist. There were no armies to command, no kingdoms to rule—there was only Cade and me, two souls entwined in the most intimate of embraces.

I felt the familiar tension building within me once again, the coil of anticipation winding tighter with each passing moment. Cade's pace quickened, his hips driving against mine with an urgency that spoke of his own impending release. A sharp smack of his hand on my rear tripled my arousal and I bit down into the sheets to contain my coming explosion.

It was a celebration of everything that symbolized what we'd been through. We fucked to celebrate the first time we locked eyes and couldn't kiss. We fucked to celebrate overcoming the curse that threatened our very lives with the deepest temptation I've ever experienced. We fucked to show the world that together —we were invincible.

With a cry of ecstasy, I tumbled over the edge, my orgasm washing over me in waves of sheer bliss. Cade followed me over the brink, his body shuddering as he reached his own climax, his seed spilling deep within me.

We lay together in the aftermath, our bodies slick with sweat and our hearts beating as one. Cade rolled off of me, pulling me close so that my head rested on his chest. I listened to the steady rhythm of his heartbeat, a contented sigh escaping my lips.

"I never want this night to end," I murmured, my fingers tracing idle patterns on his chest.

Cade pressed a gentle kiss to the top of my head, his arms tightening around me. "It doesn't have to, my love. From this day forward, every night will be ours to share."

I lifted my head to look into his eyes, my own eyes shining

with unshed tears of happiness. "I can't wait to see what the future holds for us."

Cade's gaze was filled with a determination that left no room for doubt. "Together, we will rebuild Allovan. We will bring peace and prosperity to our people. And we will do it as partners, as equals, as husband and wife."

My heart swelled with love and pride. I knew that the road ahead would be filled with challenges, but with Cade by my side, I also knew that we could overcome anything.

As we drifted off to sleep, our bodies entwined and our spirits at peace, I realized that I had found my true home in Cade's arms. And though the battles we had faced were now in the past, I knew that the greatest adventure of my life was only just beginning.

CHAPTER 54

Five days later.

The sky over Emberveil was the color of seafoam kissed by sunshine—endless and bright, unmarred by ash or smoke for the first time in a generation.

A breeze rolled gently over the rebuilt courtyard of the Raven's Bane Castle, curling through petals scattered across the sunlit stone in soft, dreamlike flurries. Flower garlands looped between marble arches now revived with gold trim and fresh paint. Terraces once blackened by war bore lush tapestries of emerald and opal, and blossoms in brilliant reds and oceanic blues cascaded from every column and railing. Clusters of roses peeked through slits in the stair railings, drifting petals down to the aisle like a blessing offered by the sky itself.

Emberveil had not just survived the fire.

It bloomed beneath it.

Below the white banners fluttering above the spires, citizens had gathered—hundreds of them. With thousands more below in the city. Peasants, nobles, artisans, soldiers… all standing side by side in the courtyard terraces and ringing the outer balconies. Garments in every color shimmered in the daylight, from the black-and-silver armor of Stormscales to the elegant sky-blue cloaks of the outer river lords. Riders stood behind their dragons atop the castle's cliffs as silent sentinels, every massive head bowed. Even the Terradyne stood on the eastern wall—immense, slow-moving shapes of living stone, their slow moving bodies like statues representing the past.

At the heart of it, a long aisle stretched down white-carpeted flagstone steps, flanked by raised platforms where the wedding party waited.

At the end of the aisle—

Cade Phoenixfire.

Clad in ceremonial black and crimson—the old colors of the royal house, but reborn in softer silk and undyed velvet—he stood tall, hands clasped neatly in front of him, his wavy black hair drawn back into a simple braid, one pale strand having recently grown white where a wound had healed. He held his phoenix-forged staff—now a decorative piece for the occasion—at his side, its jeweled avian head gleaming in the sun.

And dressed in her finest blue and silver robes, Bella stood just to the left of the pathway, her place of honor undisputed, sobbing softly into a folded handkerchief before the ceremony had even begun.

Hunter stood across from her with an exasperated smile, one gloved hand resting casually on his sword hilt as if he might elbow Cade out of nervy stillness at any moment.

Then the music began—harp strings threading over drums.

And applause echoed.

Because I had arrived. The sight of all of them nearly locked my knees tight.

My breath caught as I stood at the edge of the garden hall and stepped forward.

The moment the crowd saw me—just the first hint of pale lace trailing my step, the hush held, like the city was afraid to breathe.

I walked slowly, the silk of my train sliding like language over the stone.

And for once—

Gods.

For once, I felt beautiful.

I don't mean that in the way flowers are beautiful. Or even in the way battle-worn women find beauty in scars.

I meant I felt—

Unshakably radiant.

Like I wasn't a former slave, or orphan, or threat.

I felt... like a queen.

The gown was unlike anything I'd ever imagined wearing. It had been designed in secret by three seamstresses who had all sworn they'd rather die than let a wedding dress this fine go unfinished if brigands attacked.

And it showed.

The fabric was a blend of moonlit silk from the Sun Sea Isles, threaded with lace so fine it shimmered independently in the breeze. The sleeves draped in pointed arcs down my arms, embroidered with tiny crystals shaped like teardrops from the South Cape Sea, which lived on the shores of Bramblebash. The bodice hugged my waist in a cascade of layered silk feathers, edged in deep blue thread that shimmered with magic-infused light every time I moved. The back... gods, the back—low enough to bare all my bare skin. I intentionally called Eden enough to have the rune glowing on my neck—now no longer a curse, but a badge I wore with pride.

The train trailed behind me like liquid starlight, dozens of feet of gossamer silk draped with the softest pearl-petals from the trees of Emberveil's outskirts, swaying with the breeze like I had commanded the sky to dance for me.

A crown—floral, not golden—rested atop my head. A circlet of blue lilies, radiant white lilacs, and tiny glints of deep blue grape hyacinths together like generations finally kissing. The veil that drifted behind fluttered faintly with magic, drawn through with runes of protection, of peace, of love.

And around my neck hung a single tear-shaped stone—blue as memory.

A piece of my heritage. It symbolized my place as an Aqualorian. I was Aquafae. And damn proud of it.

Cade had it made for me days after the battle ended.

I walked forward.

And I felt the crowd bow.

I felt the warmth of their belief in me, and my heart—my whole body—felt so… full.

"Miss Ashlyn…"

A voice cracked just beside the aisle.

I turned, startled.

A woman knelt at the end of the front bench, her hands clasped tightly over her lap. Her dark curls were streaked with grey now, and her veil was slipped partially aside in her scramble to speak.

Her eyes were bright.

Wet.

"Rose!" Her name erupted from my lips as I threw my arms around her. "When did you get here? I've been asking about you for days!"

"Gettin' me up on a dragon's back isn't at the top of the list of things I want these old bones doin'… But I'm here now miss. And by Odiun, I've never seen anyone so stunning in all my life." Her smile lit my heart.

The city seemed to shimmer around me.

My own tears hit before I knew they'd formed. She wiped my tears away gently. "Don't! You'll ruin your makeup and I don't need that on my conscience." She winked and I choked down my tears.

I gripped her hands in both of mine.

"I missed you," I choked.

Rose stroked my cheek with one trembling palm. "You found a way. I knew you would. I just knew it." She winked.

I nodded, unable to speak.

She pulled me to her chest, and for a moment, I felt like a girl who'd lost her whole family and had just found the last star still shining.

We embraced without shame.

The entire aisle watched.

But no one spoke.

Not even Bella, who now had both hands pressed to her chest and was mascaraing all over her sleeve without the decency to stop.

When I rose again, I kissed Rose's knuckles once and nodded silently.

Then I turned forward once more.

And I walked.

Down that long white aisle.

Each step felt like a prayer I hadn't known how to offer before. The sun warmed my dress, the breeze caught the corners of my veil, and my heart—that wild, battered, lion-hearted thing —beat with something I'd not dared admit I wanted:

Joy.

I reached the altar.

Cade turned toward me.

Gods.

He was beautiful.

His mouth parted slightly when I neared. No words. Just awe smeared across battle-forged features.

When I took my final step and stood in front of him, I thought my heart had already reached its limit.

Until I saw Cornelius.

The little bastard stood at the base of the altar, right by Cade's side, upright and polished, his moss clean, his eyes in full shine.

He grinned at me. And I had to choke down the tears again.

I tried to wave the tears away with my fluttering hands as waves of chuckles mixed with deep sobs rolled through the crowds.

Bella took my hand as I stepped beside her.

Hunter dipped his head. "You're late," he teased under his breath.

I rolled my eyes at him. "Then hold the aisle next time."

Cade handed his staff to Hunter, folding his hands before himself as he beamed at me.

The priest towards the altar cleared his throat, arms raised solemnly.

The crowd quieted.

The priest opened his mouth.

And then stopped.

His hands dropped.

"I—I..." he stammered.

Then let out a huff and stepped aside, scratching the back of his neck awkwardly. "Apologies. But this... this isn't my wedding to speak over."

And with that... he vanished into the crowd behind the altar like a man who just realized he was a stand-in for something far greater.

I blinked, turning sharply. "What—?"

The altar shifted.

Light caught the edge of the high platform behind us. Cade couldn't contain his smirk.

"What did you do?" I whispered with a raised eyebrow.

And a man stepped out from behind the stone arch.

He wore flowing white robes trimmed with streaks of pale aqua-blue, his silver beard trailing nearly to his waist, his hair long, swept back, shimmered with the slightest lavender tint, like a reflection of the sea at moonlight.

He radiated calm.

His presence was... grounding. And yet electric.

Like the press of imminent rain against the shore not with warning—

But with love.

My breath caught.

Still, I didn't know why yet.

"Who…?" I whispered.

Cade turned to me, his soft smile was wide and edged with the tears he wasn't bothering to hide anymore.

"You don't recognize your own father?" he said. My chest broke wide open.

Every breath I'd ever taken, every heartbeat I'd dragged through fire and dirt and memory—it all paused, frozen beneath the weight of those words.

My *father?*

I whipped my head back toward the man now standing at the altar, the sunlight slanting through the banners behind him, halos of gold and blue kissing the shoulders of his sea-washed robes. His beard shimmered faintly at the tips, like it had braided saltwater into every strand. The aquamarine streaks across the hem of his sleeves curled like river eddies. His eyes—gods, his eyes— deep icy blue and endless.

And kind.

Oh gods… they were kind.

He was watching me the way I'd always imagined a father might look at a daughter who had survived when the world did everything it could to stop her.

Like she was a miracle who had found her way home.

"I…" My voice fractured. "I don't—"

He stepped forward, one hand raised—not in ceremony, not even in reverence.

In apology.

"Ash," he said, and it wasn't just my name—it was an invocation. A promise.

My knees nearly gave out.

Cade's hand found mine in an instant, anchoring me with all the weight of his presence, but I barely felt it.

The man before me breathed in, long and trembling.

"I am Orion Moonriver," he said.

And suddenly the world tilted sideways.

Every half-dreamed fever vision I'd ever had of my parents.

Every time someone whispered that I looked like I came from the sea.

Every unanswered prayer, every scream I'd ever swallowed in the dark…

"I thought you were dead," he said, and his voice cracked on the word dead like he'd been carrying its weight for years. He put his strong hands out for me to take, and I took them. Like a warm blanket on a snowy night I felt safe. Safe from everything the world could throw at me.

"Father…" I muttered through quivering lips and a shaky breath.

"I see you daughter. I'm here…"

I broke. Completely. I fell into his arms and sobbed, thinking of all the hell I'd endured. Every minute of terrible life in chains had ended, and when the chains truly broke, my entire life formed into something I didn't recognize. "This doesn't feel real…"

"It's real," he said with tears seeping out of the corners of his wise eyes. "By all the gods I've found you. I thought I lost you. And here you are, the most beautiful bride this world has ever seen."

The sobs swept through the crowds as Cade cleared his throat gently. "May I, King Moonriver? May I take your daughter's hand in marriage?"

My father released me and bowed his head. "You, King Phoenixfire, may. And may our houses see a peace that reins for centuries."

Cade nodded and took my hands.

Bella shoved her way in and blotted my tears away. "There... Now you can..."

"How?" I muttered.

"They told me you were gone. An infant taken by the land. But I—I felt it. When the flames over Emberveil broke days ago..."

He blinked, tears now fully streaking down his cheeks.

"When they told me the queen had fallen." A swallowed breath. "When they told me it was by an Aqualorian girl. A girl with our power in her blood and a magical blade of the Gilded Radiance in her hand..."

His voice dropped.

"I knew it was you."

I gasped.

Tears spilled so fast I couldn't stop them. My fingers clutched Cade's like I might come apart piece by piece if I didn't hold on.

"Damn it, Ash," Bella murmured. "You're ruining your makeup and mine."

My father.

Alive.

Standing before me.

"You—" I tried to speak but my mouth refused to form the shape of it. "You're real?"

He stepped closer then, unspeakably gentle, his robes whispering as they moved.

He reached for me.

And I didn't back away.

I let him cup the side of my face in both hands, his palms warm, trembling.

"You have her eyes," he murmured.

I sobbed then.

Not softly.

Completely, helplessly.

My entire body shook as I flung my arms around him.

I didn't ask if it was okay.

He didn't flinch.

He pulled me into him like I had never left, arms wrapping around me tighter than anything I'd ever known. His hand cradled the back of my head, fingers sifting through my hair, and I held him like a memory finally forgiven.

"I'm so sorry," he said. He was shaking now, too. "I'm sorry you were alone. I'm sorry I wasn't there. I should've moved the gods themselves trying to find you, Ash… But I thought—" His voice broke entirely. "I thought the lands took you."

"They didn't," I wept against him. "I'm strong. Stronger than anyone knew…"

He kissed the crown of my head.

We held each other until the sky remembered to move again.

When I finally pulled away, Cade was smiling through his own tears, one hand still resting lightly at the small of my back.

My father looked at him. Then at me.

Orion cleared his throat and whispered softly, "I would like to marry you now."

I don't know if I nodded, but Bella pinched my arm to get me to stop crying.

But the utter weight of that moment—the splintered, impossible joy of a life once missing, now returned in full to bind me to the one I loved… I breathed through the tears as the crowd sniffled and sobbed.

"Ready?" I asked Cade.

He smiled and nodded; glowing.

My father extended his hand to us both.

"Then, my daughter," he said, "let us begin."

Cade glanced my way once more, brushing a tear from my cheek with his thumb—soft, steady, his lips parting with affection that shook me clear to the mark still branded beneath my dress.

"You ready?" he mouthed.

I more than nodded.

I squeezed his hand back like my answer could rewrite history.

"Yes," I whispered.

Orion Moonriver placed Cade and my hands together. He then stepped behind the altar, hands raised gently as the wind curled soft through his silver-blue robes. The sun caught the edge of the sapphire sigils embroidered at his cuffs, and when he lifted his head, his voice rang out across the square like water flowing down granite—strong, grounded, and clear.

"Today," he said, glancing between us, "a kingdom is born anew, not from conquest, not from chains—but from love."

The crowd held its breath.

Orion turned to Cade first, expression flickering with pride. He was still crying, though he smiled through it like all the broken years had finally twisted back into something good.

"Cade Phoenixfire," Orion said, voice steady as tides. "Prince of Blaze and Embers. Rider of Krakos. Survivor of the tyrant Mortriana Vissex. You have stood at the edge of war and chosen peace. Will you now take this woman not just as your queen, but as your partner—one hand to steady you through light and shadow, through joy and ruin?"

Cade's eyes never left mine.

"I will," he said, his voice hoarse from emotion. "There's never been a choice more certain than this." He inhaled, a breath catching somewhere deep in his chest. "I choose her forever."

Several gasps sounded through the crowd. One loud sniff came from Cornelius.

Orion smiled and turned to me.

"Ashlyn Moonriver," he said softly, the name clinging to the wind like a psalm from the sea. "Gold-Marked of legend. Daughter of the sea and the Gilded Radiance. Breaker of Chains and Herald of the Prophecy. Do you accept this man as your husband, your king, your equal in heart and duty—through the seasons of this realm and every one that lies beyond it?"

I wiped a tear from my cheek with the back of my hand, then nodded once, fiercely.

"I do," I said, breath shivering. "I choose him. Even if the skies fall—I choose him."

Cade's hand gripped mine tighter, smile trembling, a breath like hope breaking inside him.

Bella openly sobbed at my side. Hunter just muttered, "By Odiun, finally."

The crowd chuckled—quiet and warm—rippling with something deeper than joy.

Something sacred.

Orion nodded, then placed his hands between us, palms up.

"Then place your hands together," he said, "and let the waters bear witness."

We obeyed, palms pressed. His hand closed over ours—a warmth surged where our skin met.

The rune on my neck flared softly.

The flame glowed softly on Cade's shoulders.

Two colors. Two magic-born fires.

For a breathless moment, they glowed together.

Then became one.

With a reverent bow of his head, Orion stepped back, gesturing toward the twin crowns resting atop velvet-cloaked pedestals.

One fashioned of shimmering black encrusted with crimson rubies and glittering diamonds, circled with veins of amber and ivory. Cade's.

The other gleamed in river-gold, its center gem the very color of the Eden crystal I wore—a piece of who I was before this world had a name for me. It was light, delicate, intricate and the most elegant, yet powerful, thing I'd ever seen.

Orion lifted Cade's crown first, cradling it with both hands as he spoke.

"By the will of Odiun and all the forgotten gods. By the light of a brighter tomorrow. By the sovereign will of this people, and by the command of this old king—" he placed the crown gently upon Cade's head "—I name you, Cade Phoenixfire, High King of Emberveil and the realm of Allovan."

The courtyard filled with cheers—but not wild ones. Not yet. Not until we both were crowned.

Orion turned to me.

I didn't move.

I couldn't.

He lifted the queen's circlet, stepping gently forward.

"By the miracle of survival," he said, "and the power of her own making, I name this child not lost, but returned."

He placed the crown upon my brow.

A shimmer rolled through me—too soft to be magic, too deep to be just emotion.

"My daughter," he whispered, steadying it, "Queen Ashlyn Moonriver. Destroyer of Mortriana Vissex. Freer of Vâllathór the Elder Mother Dragon. And now queen sovereign of the realm we will name together in peace."

The assembled crowd erupted.

Not in one voice.

In many. Thousands. Tens of thousands of shouts and hollers. I even heard the low howls of the Terradyne.

From the dragons above, roars rumbled like thunder made loyal.

Stormscales pounded shield to stone.

The Terradyne bowed their heads, thrumming at my heart-strings.

Even the air felt like it paused to soak the moment deeper.

Cade turned then—his eyes still locked on mine—and reached for both my hands.

"I would say something clever," he breathed, stepping closer, "but my brain stopped working the moment you walked toward me in that dress."

I laughed—wet and blistered by joy—and kissed him.

Full. Unapologetically.

The cheers rose higher still—arcing like fireworks over the towers of Emberveil and lighting up the entire kingdom beyond.

We held each other through it, laughing into our kiss, breathless and astonished and foolishly, miraculously, alive.

When we finally pulled apart, Cade raised one hand for quiet.

And despite the roaring crowd, it came.

He glanced over them. At the gates. The ruins. The city below.

Then he turned to face all assembled.

"Citizens of Emberveil," he proclaimed.

The name rang with memory.

He paused.

Then shook his head gently.

"No," he corrected. "Today marks the end of Emberveil."

Gasps shot through the crowd. Soft murmurs.

He let them settle.

"What was built in fire and ruled by terror deserves no throne today."

A tension rippled then.

One he quickly broke with the next words:

"But we will not tear it down in vengeance. We will build it forward in truth."

He looked to me.

Then toward the spires where the banners hung.

"From this sun-forward day," Cade said, voice clear and swelling with purpose, "this realm shall be called... Dragondawn Empire."

A pause. A collective hush.

Then—another eruption of thunderous joy.

Hunter turned to Bella. "Was that on the name list?"

Bella shrugged, eyes wide. "I thought we were going with 'New Ashlands.'"

I laughed, shaking my head, flushed and overwhelmed.

Then turned to the crowd again.

"And so begins a new age," he said. He raised our joined hands. "The Ember Age is over. Today begins anew. From this day the world will live in the Age of Radiance. May hope and love shine upon us forevermore."

"May it sing down the rivers. May it fly with dragons," I said in as strong a voice as I could muster. "May hope ring from every corner of the world."

The cheers reached their crescendo—and Cade spun me for one last kiss.

When our lips met, the sound of a thousand voices called our names.

And somewhere behind us, Cornelius raised one stumpy foot with a proud little cheer and said, "Finally."

Bella threw her arms around me not two minutes later and sob-laughed into my hair. Hunter hugged us both. Krakos bellowed from the terrace. Errax exhaled smoke in lazy ribbons.

Hunter then pulled Bella in close, hugging her with far too much enthusiasm. I smiled wide.

And above everything—

I was loved.

I was whole.

I was crowned and held, kissed and chosen.

I thanked Odiun for blessing me with the golden rune on my neck that blazed to life that day on the beach, the first time I saw Cade. The symbol of the Gilded Radiance I was blessed with, changed my life forever.

And I—

Ashlyn Moonriver—

Had survived every fire the world gave me.

And found joy anyway.

Like stars in water—

Reflected into something new.

And finally, truly free.

CHAPTER 55

One week later.

The wind whipped through my hair, loosening strands from the crown braided into the back, the fabric of my deep sapphire cloak billowing out behind me like a banner in flight. The roar of Errax's wings cut through the air in rhythmic pulses of thunder—steady, strong, light with purpose.

The skies had never felt wider.

Beneath us, the world unspooled in splashes of late morning gold—sun kissing meadow and forest, olive fields stretching to the horizon, hills cresting like playthings in the lap of gods. And there, to the south, the glistening stretch of the South Cape Sea lapped against the broken shoreline of Bramblebash.

The place where it began. The place where I began.

Errax dipped low, her sleek blue scales catching the sun, casting prisms on the clouds that trailed behind us. Behind and slightly above, Talonor followed, carrying Bella on his back. I glanced back toward her, and her grin—sun-flushed and reckless—was answer enough to the lift in my chest.

She lifted one hand and whooped. "I still can't believe this is your idea of a royal decree!"

"Come on," I shouted over the wind, laughing. "You didn't think we were going to let someone else deliver it, did you?"

Both dragons banked in tandem now, swerving down through a pocket of mist curling off the sea, righted themselves just in time to burst forth into golden light—and there, ahead, nestled on the sandy beaches, was Bramblebash.

The village looked new.

But not in that polished, overwashed way of rebuilt cities. No —this was something purer. Realer.

Warm strips of wood timber framed fresh homes patched with colorful panels and ivy-covered stone. Smoke carried from two forges side by side now—the second clearly half-finished. Children darted along the boardwalks built beside the new tide pools, chasing each other beneath knotted nets hung between posts. Ropes, sails, and fishing poles rested beside freshly harvested barrels of clams and kelp. Workers sang quietly as they hauled beams along the outer edge of a new community building.

It didn't look exactly like the Bramblebash I was forced to grow up in, and yet in a weird, sick sense, I felt like I was back home. Back home to a place I hated.

It looked like after I'd killed the queen, the town had remembered its old kindness and began rebuilding in that light.

Still—I remembered.

So did the ghost of every bruise I had once hidden in the hollows of my ribs. The familiar sting of steel around my wrists and ankles caused the hairs on the back of my neck to straighten.

We landed side by side on the sand.

Errax's claws touched down with the ease of grace earned, her wings folding back with the practiced swiftness of a dragon born to command winds. Beside us, Talonor hissed as he tucked his wings, crouching low enough for Bella to vault off him with one smooth motion.

She shook out her hair and turned to me. "You good?"

I nodded. Not because I was.

But because I had to be.

I stepped onto the shore. Bramblebash sand clung to the soles of my boots—the ones stitched with leather from the very forests I'd once been denied entry to. My cloak trailed faintly behind me, and when I straightened my regal circlet on my brow, I saw the people coming out into the main square.

Dozens of them. Men with fishing nets draped on their backs. Women with trowels and hammers, sweaty from rebuilding. A few children paused halfway through a game, jaws slack as they watched the dragons tuck their wings. A baker with flour on her apron lifted a hand as the sun hit my cloak and gasped.

They didn't recognize me.

How could they?

I was a girl transformed—a woman cloaked in command and dressed in the silks of royal war-peace, the Gold-Marked runes on my neck visible through the sheer drape of my sleeves. Power hummed behind my lips now. My cheekbones looked carved from light. My eyes—once 'unremarkable brown' and overlooked a thousand times too often—now burned.

I looked like a queen.

But inside…

That little girl from the cellar still watched.

I stepped forward.

Slow. Purposeful. A rhythm more divine than regal.

The crowd parted around me like surf around shore rocks.

Some bowed before I reached the square.

Others just held their breath.

I saw recognition blooming in some of the older faces.

Then whispers:

"Is it her?"

"She looks like…"

"Couldn't be. She vanished years ago."

"But that mark—"

"She came from the sea, remember? It couldn't be her."

The armory loomed just ahead.

A squat stone building with an old wooden sign still swinging on rusted hinges. Still stained with soot at the edges. Still carrying the scent of charred iron and sweat in its punched-out timber bones.

I climbed the stone steps without hesitation. Bella stayed beside me this time, one step behind and to the left—my advisor and my sword, if need be.

I didn't knock.

I raised my fist and slammed it once against the heavy oak.

The door creaked half-open.

And then the man I once feared more than death peered through.

Garris.

Older, yes—but not by much.

Still heavy-jowled, with eyes too small for a head too wide. His greasy hair had gone more grey than black, but his fingers were the same—pink and thick like squab sausages, already twitchy at my arrival.

He took one look at me and straightened, wiping his apron needlessly on his side, palms tightening by habit.

"Oh," he said, voice trying and failing to land on reverent. "Your Majesty. I—I wasn't expecting…"

He blinked in disbelief, clearly shaken by the Queen of Dragondawn at his doorstep. Beads of sweat poured down his slick brow.

"What do I owe this honor?"

Still the syrupy voice. Still the illusion of servility coiled around presumed power like he hadn't once laughed while I choked on blood in the corner of his floor.

I said nothing.

Let it sit for a breath.

Then stepped closer.

His nostrils flared. His eyes flicked to Bella. Wariness now, sitting just beneath his tongue.

Good.

I tilted my head, raven braid slipping over my shoulder.

"You don't recognize me?" I asked.

He blinked. Swallowed.

A spark played through his features, lighting recognition just faintly—

"No," he said. Too quickly. I don't think he knew exactly who I was, but there was something going on in his skeevy, sinister brain. Somehow he knew something was askew. He was shyster enough to know when someone was trying to play him.

I smiled—cold.

"Oh..." I stepped up into the doorway. He shifted back without realizing.

"I think you do," I said softly.

Stillness.

My voice licked the air like flame tasting for kindling.

I strode through the forge, my old home, like I owned the place. I walked with my back to him, and then I spun, playing with the cuffed chains hanging on the wall. They clanked as they hung. "You do know me, and I know you."

"I'm sorry, my queen... I..."

"I'm home," I hissed. The words seethed through my clenched teeth.

His mouth flattened, seemingly putting the pieces together. And then he lied. "I don't understand."

I throttled forward, stopping inches from his fat face.

"For years, you beat me. You caged me. You sent me to sleep on wet floors and worse..." the hatred had built in me to a point I didn't know if I could control it.

"I—" Garris's voice caught. His fat lips worked once, then twice. No words.

"You treated me like a rodent. Like a dog." My voice, lower now. "And I was four."

Silence.

He stuttered then—half-step back. Half-spin of his hand like he might reach for something behind the door. "I didn't know—I —I swear, I'm not like that now. That was war time, and things were different then, and—look at you! You turned out wonderful. You're the queen now—Queen Ashlyn Moonfrost—no, Moon-flower..." He gulped and wiped his brow sweat away with his sleeve.

"Moonriver," I snapped, advancing one final step.

He hit the wall.

I loomed.

And let every inch of magic seethe beneath my ribs as the mark on my exposed neck began to glow, Eden's pulse rising at my anger. I was full of purpose, full of rage, full of a thirst for revenge.

Full of fire I controlled.

And I leaned close enough for him to taste the truth in my words when I said, "I wanted to do this in person. I wanted this moment to come from my mouth to your ears. From my power to your sniveling, coward-coddled mind. Right to your miserable, fat, ugly face."

His lower lip trembled.

"I hereby outlaw slavery. In all forms. In every hamlet, city, and gate of Allovan."

The magic surged behind that statement—Eden's mark flaring once, causing a jarring flinch on his face.

"It is punishable by death and deemed a betrayal of this crown's most sacred vow."

For a heartbeat, all he did was blink at me.

Then collapsed to his knees and tugged at my tunic.

And pissed himself.

A quiet fell over the armory like the breath after a drawn

blade fails to land—their lives had splintered at this door once, but now, we were the only ones left holding the sword.

Garris collapsed onto all fours, sweat clinging to the creases below his eyes despite the sea breeze curling through the doorway. His mouth opened again, but no defense came. Just the wheezing sound of a man realizing his time had finally run out.

"I—please. I didn't... I didn't know..."

His hands rose, shaking fingers curled into near-prayer. "Your Majesty, I—if I could undo what I did—if I had known who you would become, how important you..."

"Known what?" I cut him off, the words clean and sharp as any blade I'd ever drawn. I stepped closer. Magic split the air in a wild shimmer along my fingertips—filling the room in terrifying golden magic, its flames licking at his flesh. At that moment, I felt like a god. A goddess of vengeance, a goddess of retribution, and all I wanted to do was burn out every last ounce of life in his retched, vile body.

"That I wasn't trash? That I wasn't yours to break and sell? That I might someday claw my way out of the life you shoved me into?"

He flinched, the flames of my magic teasing burning him away to nothing.

"I'm not interested in the person you pretend to be now," I whispered. "Only the one who thought my pain was more profitable than the truth of my spirit. I was a child. A fucking child!" I kicked him hard in the ribs, hearing the crack. He began to cry.

Then I straightened. The breeze caught the hem of my cloak, flaring it just enough for one of my daggers to flash in the light. I pulled the flames back into myself, forcing myself to calm. I didn't want him to die, even though he deserved it. By Odiun, he deserved it. But his sentence wasn't death, it was something better...

He whimpered and cried crocodile tears.

"I outlaw slavery in all forms—from this day until time forgets this kingdom," I said, voice ringing out so that even those loitering in the square could hear. "Every chain is to be shattered, every ledger burned. And that's not enough."

Garris's eyes widened.

I leaned closer.

"All former slaveholders are to pay a debt to those they enslaved. A living repayment, in labor, in food, in restoration—not for a month. Not for a year. For as long as their victims deem them owed."

At that, something stung in Garris's narrowed eyes. A spark. A flicker of hate.

He didn't say anything.

But I saw it.

The way his jaw clenched. The way his lip curled like he might say something monstrous—might think I wouldn't still burn him to holy ash if he dared.

I stepped forward again, Eden's mark blazing gold on my bare neck.

Magic surged between us, hot and immediate, spiraling lightly just past his shoulder and searing into the wooden beam behind him with a sharp hiss of steam and smoke.

He screamed, scrambled back, and fell into the old fire pit behind the counter. His hand landed hard on the coals.

He yelped in agony, tears springing from his eyes.

"I'm sorry!" he sobbed. "I didn't mean anything—gods, please, have mercy!"

His sobs rattled the walls.

"Mercy," I echoed hollowly.

I knelt beside him—calm, patient, like the child I once was now fully grown and gazing down at the monster under the bed.

"Would you have given mercy to me at four?" I asked.

He didn't answer.

"I didn't think so."

Then I stood.

I turned sharply and strode back toward the open door.

Bella remained just outside, her frame relaxed, one elbow on the doorframe, eyes looking upward as if listening to church bells far away.

She didn't move.

Didn't speak.

Until I stepped past her.

That's when she spat on him, it landing on his face and dribbling down his cheek.

Not a gesture.

A commitment. A closing rite for what this town had once allowed.

Let no one say we didn't return to the hearth of our past.

Let no one say we didn't look it in the eye.

We walked back into the sun.

The crowd now watched in hush, Bramblebash's people stunned into stillness by more than just the dragons behind us.

They saw who I was now.

Who I had always been.

Ashlyn Moonriver.

Gold-Marked daughter of Eden.

Queen of a kingdom reforged with its own fury.

I didn't need their applause.

But still, a little girl stepped forward from where she'd clutched her mother's hand at the edge of the crowd. Her hair was wild. Her dress dusty. But her eyes—big, brown, and fierce.

She walked up to me without fear and reached for my hand.

I knelt without thinking.

"I want to be like you," she whispered. "When I grow up."

I tried not to cry.

But something in her voice—fragile and vast all at once—split me straight through.

I smiled.

"You already are," I said.

And in that moment, that tiny flame of hope blooming behind her lashes was worth every battle I'd ever fought.

"You can be whatever you want to be in this new world, child. Dream big."

Then I stood.

Bella was beside me again with her usual smirk half-suppressed. "You gonna announce the sun rising next, or are we allowed to make a dramatic exit now?"

I tilted a brow. "You didn't enjoy that?"

"It was the most satisfying thing I've ever seen," she said. "But I'll be damned if standing next to a literal queen isn't making me start to sweat."

"Queen," I echoed, the word ugly on my tongue now that everything felt whole. I turned to her sharply as Errax lowered her body beside us.

"Don't call me that," I said.

Bella snorted. "Why not?"

"Because we're both free now," I said. "No more titles. No more chains tied to names. Just us."

She grinned, gave me that sideways look I'd come to love.

Talonor shifted nearby, the wind catching his wings in a way that scattered white sand around our boots like snowflakes from heaven.

"So," Bella said, already swinging her leg over his broad back. "What now?"

I looked toward the horizon, where the sky bled pink and lavender into the sea like someone had painted the end of the world in soft pastels.

And I grinned.

"Whatever the hell we want."

Eden stirred in my chest.

And something distant and golden laughed inside me—like maybe even the gods were finally satisfied.

We mounted.

Errax stretched her wings.

I gripped the reins gently and leaned forward.

"Let's go."

With a rush, we surged skyward.

The dragons launched from the sand and broke the sound from the people's lips. Wings spread wide. Roars split across the valley. Bramblebash watched—silent, awed.

We rose with the wind, arcing high above the cliffs, the sun casting long golden shapes across the ocean now gleaming like it was holding the fire of my childhood in its currents.

And then, together—Bella beside me, hair tugged free in laughter, Talonor twining in tight loops behind Errax's tail—

We sliced into the light.

We flew toward sunfall.

Toward the rest of our story.

Free.

Ungoverned.

Infinite.

And smiling like only survivors can—mouths full of light, hearts beating like we'd stolen time itself.

I had everything. Not like I'd ever imagined or dreamed. I had *everything*.

And looking into Bella's eyes as she whipped the reins on Talonor, I smiled wide and knew this was only just the beginning.

THE END.

Sign up and join the Reader's Group, and get the
Free Short Story Prequel-*PhoenixFire*
ZanderWolfe.com

Joining the Reader's Group will get you the first info on
upcoming projects!

If you enjoyed this book and you want to help me the author out,
please leave a review on Amazon and/or Goodreads. The number
of reviews a book has, has a huge impact on an independent
author's success.

AUTHOR NOTES

So here we are—at the end of the beginning of what might become a sprawling world, with Allovan at its heart. *Queen of Chaos and Ruin* marks the end of the arc in Ash and Cade's story, and I couldn't be more excited for this release and the future of my romantasy journey.

Ash is the epitome of the rags-to-riches arc, with all the traits I love in a protagonist: fearless, smart, sexy, quirky, and absolutely badass. Her loyalty to Bella, her addiction to Cade, her thirst to save him—those were the things that made her the character I *had* to write. I hope that all came through loud and clear for you.

Bringing her father back at the end was a surprise even for me —it hit hard and brought tears to my eyes while writing it.

As for Cade… well, he's that powerful, dangerous bad boy I think so many of us love to read. Dark, brooding, gorgeous—and so deadly. Torn between his love for Ash and his loyalty to bloodlines and empire, he had to run the emotional gauntlet before finally surrendering to what they both deserved. Ash healed so many broken pieces of him—and yeah, he's one lucky bastard getting to marry her in the end.

Side characters like Bella, Hunter, Cornelius, Rosa, Darren and eventually Carina were all critical to helping Ash and Cade become who they needed to be to stop Mortriana. And what comes next? That's not set in stone yet. I'm leaning toward Carina's story—or maybe Bella's. Got a suggestion? Hit me up via email at my website and tell me who you want more of!

The prophecy is fulfilled. The queen is dead. Mortriana was a bitch-ass demon who nearly ruled as an eternal, immortal fire queen. Thank the gods Ash came through. That final battle was intense! Cade being brought back to life really got my emotions worked as I wrote it.

The other scene I was most looking forward to writing? The waterfall. When the curse breaks. When they finally, fully give in to everything they've been denying. That passion, that release, that love. I poured everything into that scene—and it might be my favorite... besides the ending, of course.

Getting this duology out into the world feels surreal. For a year and a half, I've been building toward these dragon battles and slow-burn romance scenes, and now readers get to soar through the skies with me. This world is still new and just beginning. I hope to keep writing stories that bring deep emotion, tension, steamy chaos, and unforgettable characters you'll fall in love with—or lust after. Or both.

This is the end—for now. Time to head back to writing more stories and dreaming of dragon-filled skies.

Stay wild,

Zander

ABOUT THE AUTHOR

Zander Wolfe writes the kind of fantasy he always wanted to read—filled with dangerous magic, forbidden love, and women who refuse to be tamed.

He's a firm believer that the best stories are the ones that make you *feel* something long after the last page.

He's from the Midwest, which means he grew up with a love for bonfires, thunderstorms, and people who wave at each other while driving for no good reason. When he's not writing, he's probably at the gym, hiking some quiet trail, painting late into the night, or getting lost in a romance novel he told himself he bought "for research."

Zander drinks too much coffee, listens to fantasy soundtracks like they're gospel, and has a soft spot for sad movies and complicated characters. He writes because he believes fantasy should be just as raw and emotional as it is epic—and because sometimes, the heroine deserves everything she wants.